Sunrise

A novel inspired by the true story of the famed

Johnston-Felton-Hay mansion in historic Macon, Georgia.

Other Novels By Jacquelyn Cook

Magnolias

The River Between

The Wind Along The River

River of Fire

Beyond the Searching River

Sunrise

Jacquelyn Cook

Smyrna, Georgia

BelleBooks, Inc.

ISBN 978-0-9768760-9-0

Sunrise

Sunrise is based on factual accounts of the lives of Anne Tracy Johnston and William Butler Johnston, also the lives of their family, friends and historical peers. Locations and settings in Macon, Georgia and elsewhere are portrayed as accurately as possible. However, **Sunrise** is ultimately a work of fiction as imagined and invented by the author, and thus is subject to all disclaimers applied to such fiction works.

Published by: BelleBooks, Inc. • PO Box 67 • Smyrna, GA 30081

We at BelleBooks enjoy hearing from readers. You can contact us at the address above or at BelleBooks@BelleBooks.com

Visit our website – www.BelleBooks.com

First Edition February 2008

10 9 8 7 6 5 4 3 2 1

Cover design: Martha Crockett
Interior design: Martha Crockett
Cover Photos: © Deborah Smith and Feng Yu, Fotolia.com

CREDITS
Poems of Sidney Lanier
Sidney Lanier, edited by Mary Day Lanier
©1981 University of Georgia Press
Used by Permission

Dedication

for

Ann and George Felton

who wanted to preserve the

devotion of a great family

and for

My family

without whose devotion

I could not have written this book

"An excellent job of characterization. My family has really come alive for me. I shall treasure this book always."

—Lisa Felton, Great-Great-Granddaughter of Anne Tracy and William Butler Johnston

A Johnston and Felton Family Tree

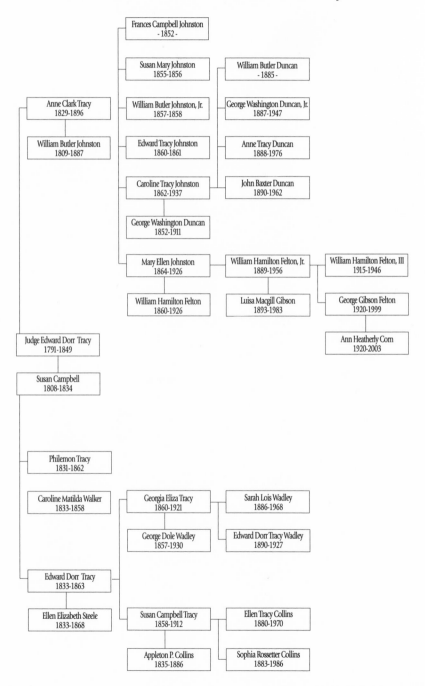

Chapter I

Macon, Georgia 1849

The ginkgo tree, shimmering like gold against the October sky, drew Anne Tracy to the crest of the hill. In her fluttering crepe, she felt at one with the tree, stripped of purpose, as it soon would be when its fan-shaped leaves deserted all at once. Her father had brought the sapling from the Orient, promising to take her there. But Papa was dead. He had left her an heiress at twenty, yes, but for what good when she had no place in life.

I wish I could have stayed at his bedside, but that was Aunt Carry's privilege as his wife. There's no room for me now.

Anne felt as formless as the shadows, awkward in her black garments. She had such enthusiasm for life that, even before Papa's passing, the Aunts had whispered she would shame them by breaking the strict code of mourning. But this spot was home, and she forced back her anger and uncertainty, trying to absorb the peace of the scene she so loved before they sent her away.

Beneath the brow of the hill, landscaped boulevards terraced down to the Ocmulgee River. In the quietness, a steamboat drifted. Anne's face warmed with a rising glow, and she parted her lips to drink in the beauty. She wished she could paint. The paddle wheeler hovered, etched against forest of pine emblazoned with dogwood, maple, hickory—crimson and amber with autumn's palette.

A locomotive whistled. The steamer's stacks responded with

1

a blast of sound and sooty smoke. The race to the cotton ware-house was on!

Anne smiled. She liked the vibrancy of Macon, Georgia, and she knew, much as she longed to see the countries she had studied, preparing to tour with Papa, it was here she wanted to live. Macon had sprung full grown amid the wilderness upon the signing of the Creek Indian Treaty twenty-odd years ago. On the fall line between the foothills of the Appalachians and the sub-tropical Coastal Plain, the town was delightful with year-around flowers. But the warmth went deeper, overflowing into people of graciousness and hospitality.

Anne was proud that her father, Edward Dorr Tracy, had been Macon's second mayor, and she painfully swallowed her shyness to speak to workmen and gentlefolk alike. Yet, she knew that her social prominence and the mores of 1849 left her with little say in the course her life could take.

Matrimony's all women can hope for. Haven't the Aunts warned me often enough I'm passing marriageable age? Anne thought. But she could not overcome being stiff with her few suitors. She never flirted over a fan like a proper Southern belle. She knew her voice held too little of her Georgia mother Susan Campbell's gentility, too much of her Connecticut-born father's correctness.

But most young men seem shallow. Silly. It irks me to hide my intelligence. I want to discuss Shelley, Keats, and, oh, especially Byron.

She had had her coming out at sixteen. She adored dancing the old cotillion sets at balls, but she dreaded the Sunday after-noon at-homes, knowing any girl who did not have forty callers was a failure. Papa carefully supervised her suitors, warning, "We must be careful since you're no beauty." What humiliation she had endured when he rejected some as fortune hunters.

What guide will I have now?

She deplored her plainness. Straight, dark brows made her face severe, but her despair was her heavy brown hair. With only a hint of auburn and no curl at all, it resisted the curling iron even though she left it in the fireplace until it was hot enough to singe. *Did I inherit nothing from my beautiful mother?*

The thought pained. She lowered her lashes, and the tableau appeared, vivid as always. Her mother had sat swathed in quilts with the baby, Little Edward, nursing at her breast. Anne, five, and Philemon, three, listened as she taught their Bible lesson through fevered lips. When her sisters had entered the darkened room, Susan had exhorted the weeping women to live every day to be prepared for death, and then she uttered words Anne would never forget.

"Carry, I want you to take my children. I do *not* want them to go to the North. Don't let my family be parted. Queeny, take care of my children's principles, implant in their breast, faith as you have got, my dear Christian sister. Eddy, I believe you will yet marry . . ."

Philemon had pressed his wet nose against Anne's arm. She clutched him against her, sensing more than understanding, vowing no one would take her brother from her. Crooning, Anne had swayed in the darkness and squeezed her eyes tight.

Now the sound of laughter made her open her eyes and blink in the sunlight. A dozen neighborhood boys, pounding along on bare feet, ran around the corner of the Tracys' house. Schoolbooks and shoes thrown aside, they had picked up bows and arrows and were whooping, playing Indians. Pattering behind them, seven-year-old Sidney Lanier made a sweeter tune, a whistling Anne thought as lovely as a robin singing in the rain.

"Why Sidney, honey . . ." she said, stopping the child whose grandparents lived behind the Tracy house in a cottage on High Street, ". . . How did you make that beautiful music?" Her voice was a warm lilt she could never manage with adults as she knelt beside the winsome little boy.

Delighted by her attention, Sidney held up a river reed, cork-stoppered at the end, with six finger holes and a mouthpiece. "I made myself a flute. Papa doesn't like for me to play the violin."

To Anne's amazement, Sidney produced a cardinal's simple "pretty-pretty" and then a trill like a mockingbird. She knew that his mother, Mary Jane, had begun teaching him piano when he was only five. Sidney had learned the guitar, organ, and violin, his favorite; then a window sash fell, taking off a half-inch of a middle finger. Anne shook her head in wonderment. Undaunted by the loss, Sidney had turned to the flute.

The handsome child fanned back long lashes from gray-blue eyes and looked up at her as if he read her thoughts. "Miss Anne, I just have to make music!"

Anne smiled. "God has given you a great talent." Tenderness swelled, and she brushed back the brown curl that fell over Sidney's face. A twinge in her breasts made her realize it was not just a home of her own she wanted. It was children. She hungered for a family devoted as hers had been. She could make room in her heart for a great many.

She kissed Sidney's forehead and let him run after his playmates. Guilty thoughts plagued her. She had never lacked anything. Plump, bustling Aunt Carry had fulfilled her mother's deathbed request and kept the three children together. Anne never released her grip on Phil, but her stepmother would not let her touch baby Edward. After the proper year of mourning, Aunt Carry had married their father. She gave them two half sisters and a half brother. But slender, quiet Susan was a loss Anne never forgot, a void that would not be filled.

Anne sighed as she picked up the mourning bonnet she had tossed beneath the ginkgo. She could be more thankful for her Campbell aunts if they did not always try to curb her high spirits and curiosity to learn about life. They fluttered round her like a flock of hens. They taught her, protected her, but sometimes with so many she felt pecked.

It was time to go to yet another set, who lived in Alabama. Anne clapped on the offending hat with its knee-length swath of chiffon, but even as she tied the ribbons beneath her determined chin, she vowed she would come back. Only Macon felt like home.

Turning, she saw a man motioning to her as he cut across the parkway of Mulberry Street. She wondered why he was moving on such a wave of energy. The boulevard ended at the bottom of the hill, and his flat-heeled boots ploughed the spongy dirt as he climbed the steep ascent of Georgia Avenue to reach her. He looked as if the red dust never settled on *his* clothes. His cosmopolitan long jacket with a stylishly shaped-in waist was a city style that set him apart from the others on the street, proclaiming him a dynamic businessman. But his high top hat threatened to tumble. She giggled. It wouldn't dare!

What is his name? He's been to the house working with Papa. Oh, yes. William B. Johnston. He owned an iron-front jewelry store in one of the two downtown blocks of Mulberry, Macon's main thoroughfare.

Anne adjusted the heavy veil over her face as Mr. Johnston neared, but it was the inner cloak she slid over her eyes that shut him out.

"Miss Tracy!" Mr. Johnston said too loudly in his eagerness. He swept off his hat and smoothed brown hair precisely combed over his ears. "I'm so glad I caught you. I've been on a lengthy buying trip to New York. I've only just now heard of Judge Tracy's passing."

Anne nodded formally. She knew the mellow tones of his pleasing voice came from a Virginia-born father and a childhood spent on a Georgia plantation, but she noticed his speech had gained a rapid pace since his serving as a watchmaker's apprentice in New York City.

"I wanted to extend my condolences," he said. Then he withdrew a step.

Above his trim beard, his cheeks reddened. Anne wondered if he feared he had overstepped their social barrier, but Macon usually allowed none of the snobbish planter-aristocracy practiced in the older cities of the neighboring Piedmont. Here, merchants and industrialists built houses beside the white-columned mansions of the landed gentry.

She tensed all the more at the stiffness between them, but she tried to put him at ease, responding in gracious tones, "How kind of you, Mr. Johnston. I know my father counted you as a friend."

"Oh, I wouldn't put myself forward to say he thought that much of me," he blustered. "But I had planned to speak with him—about . . ."

His pomposity fell away. Face open, hurting, he gazed at her with a heat that made her shiver. Then he stammered, "I-I hope you'll let me be *your* friend. If there's anything—anything at all you need . . ."

"There's—nothing . . ." *What does this man want? I don't understand the hungry way he's looking at me.* She felt herself standing away, viewing the scene, remembering how neighborhood children used to come to play—not with her—but with the dolls Papa had bought. *Does Mr. Johnston see me as money? Did he plan to borrow from Papa?*

She had heard the man opened his jewelry store with only two hundred dollars capital. But, no. She recalled Brother Phil had talked about Mr. Johnston's peculiar ways: he had bought *Central Railroad* stock at thirty cents on the dollar, but because he believed in odd numbers, when his holdings rose to $99,900, he would buy no more.

Anne hid her hands behind her, twisting them. The unusual little man confused her. He had spoken with an air of importance when he discussed railroads with Papa, insisting they would link Macon with the world. Now he was stuttering like a schoolboy. She felt uneasy, and yet as she watched with averted eyes, she recognized painful withdrawal behind the quiver of his pointed brown beard. *A kindred spirit?* But he was twenty years older than she, old enough to be her father.

Silence suspended between them like glass. She swallowed, knowing *she* must break it.

"You're very kind, sir, but I'm being sent to spend my mourning period with my Campbell kin in Montgomery. I'm about to leave." Dismissal sounded clearly in her voice, but his fuzzy whiskers trembled again, and she relented. Gesturing, she said, "I'm having one last moment with the view I love most."

Mr. Johnston followed the direction of her gaze, and a smile played over his straight, firm lips. She guessed it amused him that she turned from the boulevards, laid out by city fathers claiming the pattern of the Hanging Gardens of Babylon, and looked instead across the river at the east bank where the Old Ocmulgee Fields were once farmed by Creek Indians. Beyond were the ceremonial mounds of other Indians with origins lost in antiquity.

Their mystery had always fascinated her, but she could think of nothing intelligent to say.

I've been trained to act with poise, she thought. *Why is it so hard for me to talk with a man? Especially Mr. Johnston. He seems better than anyone else, remote, lifted high on a pedestal like God.* Struggling, she said inanely, "I like to recall Hernando De Soto discovering this place three hundred years ago." She smiled. "His priests baptized two Indian converts right here in the Ocmulgee."

"Yes," he said, but he appeared unable to say more.

Anne ducked her head and forged ahead with the conversation. "I've read the diary of De Soto's march through Georgia, and I've always been glad the Indians were wily enough to know the Spaniards were seeking gold. I believe they purposely sent them in the wrong direction."

"It's refreshing to talk with a young lady who's taken advantage of her education. I haven't had the opportunity for classical study, as you've had, but I always figured the Indians knew of the treasure in our mountains. Did you know I've been buying gold from our Dahlonega miners and selling it to the U.S. Mint at Philadelphia?"

"Oh? Really? It's good De Soto never found it." She frowned. *So, is making money all that matters to him?* "I'm sorry, but it's time for me to go."

"May I write to you?"

"Would that be proper?" she asked.

Narrow shoulders drooping, Mr. Johnston took his watch from his waistcoat. Swinging the heavy chain that connected it to the opposite pocket, he looked at her for a long moment. Then, he snapped open the case and consulted the watch as if it could answer her question.

"Perhaps not at this time," he said without lifting his head.

~:~

Alabama's like Georgia, Anne thought as she trudged along a clay road on her Aunt Frances Campbell Rowland's plantation. *Same cotton fields. Same pine trees. Why am I so homesick? I'm not a child. Why does it hurt so not to have a papa any more?*

Anne hated November's gray skies as much as she detested wearing black, but her muscles and nerves screamed to get out of the house bursting with three talkative sisters. She felt sorry for long-suffering Uncle Isaac Rowland who provided a home for his wife's spinster sisters, Eliza and Flora. *And now another old maid. Me.* Aunt Eliza was loving, but Flora was a complainer, talking of nothing but illness and death.

Anne tried to be helpful, but life on a cotton farm was so different that she could not find what she should do. She missed the afternoon calls of Maconites, the evening musicales and theatricals, her chattering circle of friends.

She kicked at a pile of leaves. The Council of Aunts decreed she should stay here, hidden away for prescribed grieving, but she was young, in vibrant health, eager for activity. She chafed at the mourning etiquette fashioned by Queen Victoria's reign. She would never get over missing Papa. She pictured him, hands folded in prayer.

You haven't tried to pray, she told herself. *Well, God couldn't be interested in my silly problems.*

When she returned to the house for the noon meal, Uncle Isaac handed her a letter. She blinked in surprise. It was from Mr. Johnston. Around the table, all eyes were upon her.

"Probably business," she said, shoving the letter in her pocket.

Through the fried chicken Anne was indifferent. Next the salt-cured ham claimed her attention. Hunger quieted, she began to wonder. As the vegetables were passed, she fingered the letter. By the time the apple dumplings were served, she did not take time to add whipped cream.

Excusing herself, Anne went into the library. She took down a book and placed the letter inside the pages so that she could read it unnoticed if anyone entered.

Macon, Georgia
November 23, 1849

Dear Miss Anne,

How are you? Fine I hope. I thought you might like news of home.

I saw your brothers at a political meeting. Philemon is becoming quite a handsome young man—if a bit impetuous. He spoke heatedly about the South's equal rights to all this land acquired in the War with Mexico. Young Edward Junior remained sedate. It is he, I think, who will be more like Judge Tracy.

Yes, Anne thought, *Lit looks like Papa.*

She felt warmed by the friendly letter. She read Mr. Johnston's discussion of the Missouri Compromise with growing pleasure. Mr. Johnston excited her more than any suitor she had known. He, like Papa, recognized that a girl could have a mind.

The library desk provided an ample supply of paper. Anne dipped a pen in the crystal inkwell and then sat so long thinking of a beginning that she dropped a spreading blot.

Montgomery, Alabama
November 29, 1849

Dear Mr. Johnston,

How nice of you to send me news of home. All of the friends my age seem too busy to write . . .

She read it over, tore it up, embarrassed.

It was ridiculous to be afraid of him at this distance, but the agony of a polite reply hung over her for several weeks before she tried again.

Montgomery, Alabama
December 15, 1849

Dear Mr. Johnston,

How nice of you to send news from Macon. I miss being in town. I like business and bustle and people about. I'm not suited to quiet plantation life.

But I'm much happier now that the weather is warm and sunny. My uncle gave me a little horse that gallops like the wind. I love to ride. Do you?

Sincerely,

Anne Clark Tracy

Mr. Johnston's answer was immediate:

. . . I'm not suited to country living either. Perhaps it was best, after all, that my father left his entire plantation to my eldest brother. Business has treated me well.

Do I detect bitterness, Anne wondered, *or merely bragging?*

Christmas came, and the entire Campbell clan gathered on the plantation. Anne became her joyous self again, seeing Phil and Lit. When the time came for them to leave, she clung to them, feeling part of herself gone.

Aunt Frances, jolly and plump, began teaching Anne to sew, but still she felt restless. She decided to write Mr. Johnston again.

. . . A rainy New Year. I hate rain. At least this house has a lovely library. I'm reading Greek mythology and poetry. I especially like George Gordon Lord Byron.

He replied:

. . . Fire broke out February 19, on Cotton Avenue. It destroyed all of the buildings. The loss was over $100,000.00. Fortunately, I represent Hartford Fire Insurance Company, and most of the businesses had insured with me.

Letters from Anne's family only included personal news, and she was pleased that Mr. Johnston kept her abreast of Macon happenings.

One hot autumn day, a year after she had left Macon, she received a thick envelope.

> Macon, Georgia
> October 17, 1850

Dear Miss Anne,

Your letters show a sharp and witty personality and your well-developed literary interests, giving evidence of your fine education at the Episcopal Institute of Montpelier, reveal you as the only sort of woman with whom I could spend my life. When you return to Macon, will you allow me to court you?

I must tell you that when I opened my jewelry store in 1832, I also sold swords and dueling pistols. My fortunes increased greatly because the Macon volunteers bought from me when they marched off to fight the Creek War of 1836 and again four years ago when our brave lads joined in fighting the Mexican War.

I was part of the group that built the *Central Rail Road* from Macon to Savannah. It is the longest railroad in the world owned by one company. I am also a director of the *Macon and Western Railroad* that connects us with Atlanta. These railroads make Macon the Queen Inland City of the South, and my real estate investments turn tidy profits.

Now, you may have heard that my bank floundered in the Depression of 1837, but thanks to my lawyer friend Christopher Memminger, that problem is straightened out and I have netted $50,000.

At any rate, I am now secure in my fortune. I am turning the jewelry store over to my brother, Edmund. I am retiring from active business to manage my investments.

I expect to take a year off to make a Grand Tour of Europe. Would you do me the honor of accompanying me as my wife?

> Sincerely yours,
> William Butler Johnston

Shocked, Anne flung down the letter and ran out to tramp the falling leaves. She had shared her interests on blank, impersonal paper, and they had become friends. *But how could I ever talk in person with the man?*

She was afraid to cry. She might not be able to stop.

Face it, you ninny, she scolded herself. *You've read too much of Byron. You want to experience love, but you're never going to find it.*

⌣⁞⌣

The silent winter was over at last, and Anne returned to Macon, having agreed to be courted, nothing more. Her anticipation mingled with dread.

But when Phil met her at the depot and they drove through town, she wanted to leap from the buggy, shouting, "I'm home," running, arms outstretched, hugging all she met, stopping only to sniff the glorious gardens. Spring never crept in here, crocus by crocus. It burst forth in a symphony of color and scent, and she drank in camellias and daffodils, flowering crabs, tea olives. Above it all in the treetops, swags of wisteria shed their heady fragrance.

"Romance is in the air," she cried.

Phil laughed. "There's a cotillion tonight. I'll be glad to escort you if you don't mind going with a mere sibling."

"I'd be proud to go with a brother who's grown so dashing while I've been shut away," Anne said, hugging him warmly, loving the man as much as the boy she had mothered.

They arrived at the Tracy house, and Anne could see Aunt Carry's round form silhouetted against the sunlight from the open end of the dogtrot porch.

As soon as Anne could fulfill a proper greeting, she bubbled out a request to attend the ball.

Aunt Carry mopped her face with her ever-present handkerchief. "Let's wait. Don't you think you should?"

"Wait?" Anne's breath seemed to stop, but then her eyes narrowed. " Haven't you been saying I'm about to pass marriageable age? How can I wait?" She saw she had struck the right nerve and lowered her lashes lest a twinkle escape.

Aunt Carry blustered, and then agreed. Anne pressed further.

"I'm sure it's time I advanced from black crepe to lavender taffeta."

"Well . . . Maybe, but only if you promise to keep mourning bands on your forearms."

At that moment, Anne's friends began arriving. Some showed wedding rings while others boasted of upcoming nuptials and extended invitations to bridal showers and teas. The remaining few whispered of still deciding between gallant suitors.

Is everyone attached to someone special? Anne wondered. *Except me?*

❦

That evening as they paused at the door to the ballroom of Macon's grand new hotel, the Lanier House, her fingers dug into Philemon's arm. Her lavender seemed insipid. All of the others looked like belles as they waltzed, bright skirts billowing, gazing adoringly at their escorts. Anne's legs quivered for flight. The remembrance that Phil danced even though he walked with a limp made her stiffen and step across the threshold.

A dozen young men came forward.

She felt her face glow with the wonder of it. *I'm like a new girl in town.* Her dance card soon filled, and she whirled into the throng.

After the fourth set as she stood hot, breathless, waiting for her partner to bring her some lemonade, she noticed a change in the youthful chatter of the crowd.

Mr. Johnston stood in the entrance. The way parted. Heads nodded deferentially.

Anne rued her prominent cheekbones, and she splayed her fingers to keep them from showing like flaming flags as Mr. Johnston made his way across the room toward her.

He bowed stiffly, kissing her hand. "Why didn't you let me know you'd come home?"

"I . . ." Her throat felt so dry she could hardly speak. "I only just arrived."

13

The orchestra struck up a Strauss waltz, and he offered his arm.

"It's—taken," she strangled out, reaching gratefully for her partner's proffered punch cup. "Lemuel Jones . . ."

Anne scrunched down to the boy's height as he glared at the elegantly tailored gentleman. Freckles popped out and red hair bristled, but Lemuel stumbled over his own big feet, sloshing lemonade. Defeated, he backed away, mumbling.

Tight-lipped, they danced with Mr. Johnston's unanswered proposal clanking against their silence.

Aware of his eyes probing her, she could not hear the music. She perspired, willing the evening over.

"May I call on you tomorrow afternoon?" he asked, and then hurried to add as Phil claimed her, "May I escort you to the next cotillion?"

"Yes." It was a small sound.

❧

The next afternoon, Mr. Johnston arrived with two horses.

"Oh, I'm not dressed properly," Anne apologized. "How thoughtless. I should've . . ."

"Nonsense. It'll only take a moment to change. It was thoughtful 'cause I told you I love to ride."

But she frowned, dreading to leave him unguarded. There was no escaping Aunt Carry who was seated on the porch, looking smug.

Anne hurried into her gray wool riding habit. When she returned, she feared she had not been fast enough. She did not like the intimate look of the conversation.

"Have fun, you two," Aunt Carry said just a shade too heartily.

As they cantered out the Vineville Road, Mr. Johnston spoke little. Anne relaxed, enjoying the freedom of outdoors.

❧

Anne was dressed for the cotillion and tensely waiting

when Aunt Carry tapped at her door and told her that her escort had arrived. She went out, exclaiming in surprise. It was not Mr. Johnston but Edward, Junior, who made a flourishing bow and presented a nosegay.

"Mr. Johnston sent word he is detained on urgent business. He asked me to take you," he said in a voice that was already a deep, arresting rumble even though he was not quite eighteen. "He'll meet you there."

Anne made a grand curtsy. "Thank you, Sir Knight."

She smiled at Little Edward, thinking he was the handsomest young man she had ever seen. The family characteristics—long nose, heavy brows, and thick, dark auburn hair—rested best on Lit. *We really should quit calling him by his baby nickname,* she thought as they started for the dance.

When they entered the ballroom and Lit spoke in his manly tones, a bevy of belles turned, wafting fans and fluttering eyelashes. Lit deserted her.

Anne stood in a corner, trying not to tap her foot in anger. *Phil wouldn't have left me hanging. But Aunt Carry took the baby away from me. Lit and I aren't as closely tuned.*

Her dance card remained unfilled. She leaned toward the music. Lines were forming for the cotillion. She wet her lips and teeth to make them shine. She laughed gaily at a pretended sight. Emptiness hurt her chest. She hated standing alone, missing the energetic figures, the changing of partners, the marching through arched arms. Surely somewhere in that swirling throng was a man handsome as her brothers who could sweep her away into an ecstasy of romance.

She glanced around. Eyes were watching her over fans. She knew she was smiling too broadly, waving her hands too much. Heads nodded close. Whispers passed. She had not wanted it known Mr. Johnston was courting her. Her throat trembled. *It must have become obvious.*

He came late, pleading business, but at least she was claimed for a waltz.

﹏

When Mr. Johnston left her at home, she was surrounded by the Aunts. Anne stood in the middle of the parlor, feeling like a June bug, foot tied, dangling on a string.

"Mr. Johnston declared his intentions," said Aunt Carry. "But you haven't replied."

It was an accusation, and Anne stammered, "No. I . . ."

"We care about you, dear. God cares." Aunt Queeny put into Anne's silence.

No, Anne thought. *You're all just afraid I'll shame you.* Aunt Carry's next words were confirmation.

"Surely, girl, you've sense enough not to refuse a rich man like Mr. Johnston. A lady must marry or have no place in society."

"Anne, dear," Aunt Eddy ventured, chins wobbling, "You don't want to end up an old maid in someone else's home."

Anne had never considered sweet little Eddy's sad life, but she recalled irritating Flora. *With my temper I'd wind up like Flora.* She jerked, shifted her foot. "I'd hoped for love," she said, chin high.

"Love!" Carry snorted. "Security's more like it. As Mr. Tracy gave me."

"Love will come after you adjust to marriage," said Queeny.

"Papa left me property—even a business. Couldn't I run it?"

Eddy smothered a scream and fell back, swooning.

Queeny spoke firmly. "You know that ladies in your social station don't work! You've money enough to take care of you, but with Mr. Johnston, you'd live in luxury,"

"What matters," asserted Carry, "is that propriety demands you be engaged soon. If you're not married while you're still twenty-one, people will talk."

What am I to do? Anne wondered. *Papa realized I have a mind and feelings. He would have made a proper match for me. But Papa's dead. My life's before me. There may be no one to love me, but I must find some way to make my life count.*

Chapter II

Summer settled over Georgia like a murmur of contentment. In the humid midday, Macon society retreated behind their shutters. All but the young.

Anne reveled in being able to walk to her friends' homes again. The girls spent the lazy afternoons migrating through the houses on College Street and Georgia Avenue, new Greek Revival mansions with towering columns lifting porches two—even three stories high. Alone with those she trusted, Anne let herself be funny and gay.

Later in the afternoons, ladies in hats and white gloves visited one another for tea, tiny sandwiches, and cakes.

After sunset, everyone emerged, seeking entertainment. Anne liked the Shakespeare readings, but she especially enjoyed the musicales. One evening she invited Mr. Johnston to join the group gathering in the rotunda of the Raines' house for a fluting. Little Sidney was to play with the men.

Anne felt awakened by the plaintive, soaring notes, amazed at the child performing on a real gold instrument. She smiled at Sidney, thinking his legs were stretching like a new colt's.

Mr. Johnston looked down at her, and she glimpsed tenderness in his gaze. She tensed. *He's sitting too close.* Unwanted warmth steamed over her.

Afterwards when he was walking her home, he said, "Today was my last in the jewelry store. I'm true to my word—I've retired.

Now I can claim all your afternoons. Would you like to go horse-back riding tomorrow?"

Anne felt the pressure of his simple words in the depths of her stomach; she was not ready to give up girlhood pleasures. *Aunt Carry wouldn't let me go out without a chaperone with anyone else. But she knows his intentions. I do, too, and he's pushing me too fast. Why do I feel so torn? I long for adventure, but, oh, I don't want to leave home.*

Mr. Johnston stopped, waiting for an answer. Twisting her hands, she replied, "That would be lovely. Four o'clock?"

∿:∿

The afternoon seemed airless as Anne guided her horse through the pine forest skirting the muddy Ocmulgee. Mr. Johnston kept cutting his eyes at her, and she wished her corset strings were not laced too tight for breathing.

He reined at the riverbank beside a canoe. "I had this put here for us," he said. "I thought canoeing would be cooler."

Anne nodded, unable to speak. *The decision is upon me. How can I escape?*

He paddled upstream. There was no sound save for the shallow water bubbling over stones. They were totally alone. He brought out a tiny box.

Anne's hands shook as she opened it. "It's beautiful," she said as the diamond flashed. A mockingbird's trill reminded her of Sidney and her longings for a home filled with children. Most of her friends would soon be married in a flurry of June weddings. But acceptance choked her. *Oh, I can't, I can't. But he's a nice man. I hate to hurt him, but I don't love him.*

"I'm still in mourning for Papa." She pointed to the black bands on her forearms. More was called for, but she ducked her head. "I don't wear rings." She showed him her fingers then hid them behind her. *My hands are too big,* she thought miserably. *Surely he's noticed that.*

Without reply he pocketed the box, but his face drew down with such sorrow and self-doubt that she ached for him.

Have I ended his intentions? Anne wondered.

⌣⋮⌣

In a week, Mr. Johnston called again. They were invited to join a group for picnicking. As the carriage clattered across the river bridge and into the Old Ocmulgee Fields, Anne felt exhilarated. She liked exercise, and these carefree friends were fun.

Mr. Johnston looked grim, but he said, "You're lovely in that white dress, Miss Anne."

"Thank you. The Aunts decided I should take another step out of mourning."

They want me to capture you, Anne fumed, suddenly cross. The muslin was itchy. She thought it far too elaborate for her lanky figure as well as for this stage of bereavement. It had rows of lace ruching from her shoulders to her toes.

The carriages stopped at Fort Hawkins, an old Indian trading post dating back to Thomas Jefferson's order. Lit and the younger set shouted in a mock battle, storming the hewed-log fort. Anne fought a mischievous yen to join them. But she noticed Phil already ahead on the path through the fort gardens; he had a girl on each arm. She resigned herself to acting her age.

The laughing group ambled along the woodland trail. Coming out in a clearing, they stood silenced, awed each time they saw the ancient, flattened pyramids rising from the level plane of the Macon plateau.

Then the chattering resumed as they climbed the spur at the side of a fifty-foot mound, thought to have held a temple for some prehistoric tribe. Anne walked apart from Mr. Johnston, independent, unaided.

The top was broad, flat. Mr. Johnston drew her apart. "Over here. Let's look at the view."

Anne stared down at the mansions of Macon, the church spires, Wesleyan Female College crowning College Hill. Homesickness flooded through her. *But I have no home. The dogtrot house is Aunt Carry's now.* Anne shared a bedroom with half-sisters Caroline Matilda, eleven, and nine-year-old Harriet. The baby of the family, Campbell Tracy, was the pampered man of the house since Lit and Phil had moved to their own quarters. *I wish I could just do that.* But that was unheard of. Only as a wife could she have a home, exert a say in civic, even church affairs.

Mr. Johnston waited beside her, perfectly still. At last he said, "I have business in New York City in August. I'm booking passage from there to England. Then France. Italy." He handed her a long velvet box.

With shaking fingers she lifted out dangling earrings.

"They're fine Etruscan gold," he said.

"Beautiful." *I have such love in my heart to give. Why doesn't someone want it?*

"Will you marry me?" His beard trembled with emotion.

She lifted the shutters from her eyes and gazed into his vulnerable face. She thought she could trust him to take care of her like Papa would have. *There's something behind his closed, inward look,* she told herself, *a secret I might one day discover. It's time to become an adult.* She drew a tremulous breath. "Yes."

⌣∴⌣

Anne hovered in the doorway of Christ Episcopal Church and peered at her Campbell kin, who were prominent from Georgia's governor's mansion to the nation's capital. They had converged for her wedding. It was August 2, 1851.

She admired the beautiful old church, built in the form of a Roman Cross and surmounted by a dome. The setting could not have been more perfect with a myriad of candles glowing in the sparkling glass chandelier. Family cocooned her. Expectantly, they waited for her to make an entrance.

The organ flurry began. *How can I take the first step?* Anne agonized. *I wish Papa were here.* But Philemon stood beside her. Now it was she clinging to Phil's hand, leaning upon him. She flashed him a look of panic.

Phil crossed his eyes and stuck out his tongue. "You and Mr. Johnston act as if you're about to be shot," he hissed.

Anne giggled. She stepped out, trying to smile but glad of the tulle veil covering her face. She had chosen a simple satin dress with a tight bodice, short sleeves, and a train that flowed sedately. She clutched her white prayer book in one kid-gloved hand and squeezed the other into the crook of Phil's arm.

They reached the altar, and she did not die. Dazed, she blinked at the Reverend Shanklin. Beside him Mr. Johnston looked slim and dignified in white tie and tailcoat. Her eyes blurred in the candles' flame.

The ceremony began—was over.

Then everyone crowded around, kissing her cold cheek, shaking Mr. Johnston's hand with respectful bows. He acknowledged the introductions to her endless family with reserve. Anne gritted her teeth on hearing Aunt Carry behind her, calling him "the rich Mr. Johnston." A strange sensation made her prickle as she realized she was married. *Already the ones I love seem to be standing away.*

Philemon Tracy hovered on the fringes of the group, holding up a toast but choking with concern. *Why did she marry him?* Phil wondered. *I don't need my glasses to see she doesn't love him. Not the money. Papa left her well enough fixed. She's led such a sheltered life. How will she face it if she has to step out alone?*

He wanted to snatch her back from that man. Anne looked across at him. He grinned.

I'm going to miss Phil, Anne thought.

It seemed the receiving line would never end. Then she had to cut the wedding cake. Anne tried to smile as her new husband saluted her with a slender glass of syllabub. They were led to a feast of turkey, chicken, and Virginia-baked ham. Tables swayed beneath embossed cakes, salads, and every delicacy the Aunts could envision. She could scarcely swallow.

Mr. Johnston had taken out his watch, and she willed her eyes to stay wide and dry.

"It's time for the train," her husband said. "First Savannah, next a small surprise, then New York City." He beamed at her. "Then at long last our honeymoon voyage to Europe."

Phil pushed his way through the well-wishers. He draped his

arm across her shoulders and whispered close to her ear, "Look at it this way, Annie. You can gratify your long-indulged curiosity about that region at the North. You can see a live Yankee in the Yankee country."

Anne laughed shakily. *Sassy, irreverent Phil. How can I do without him?*

The Aunts gathered round, kissing her good-bye in a swirl of lavender-scented silk. She wished for her mother. The Aunts had told her nothing. Today she was an innocent bride. Tonight she was expected to be a wife. Her groom, exactly twice her age, was a small, dark shadow in the background, and she suddenly lost the courage to begin the journey.

Chapter III

William Butler Johnston felt an urgency to spirit Anne through the Macon depot and secure her aboard the train. He had seen her face. He knew she did not love him, and he feared, even now, she might change her mind and flee.

The whole wedding party followed, embarrassing him by filling the station with raucous merriment.

Well, William thought, *I'm proud for them to see that the President of the Central respected me enough to provide his private car.*

But when they reached the train, he gasped. Mischief-makers, probably led by Edward and Philemon, had draped President Cuyler's car with bunting. Worse, they had smeared "Just Married" everywhere.

"I'm sorry," Anne whispered as they climbed onto the car's end platform.

William managed a laugh. "It'll wash." But the chuckle sounded false to his own ears. Then Anne's two smallest siblings, Campbell and Harriet, scrambled up after them, clinging to her, crying. With anguish William saw tears wetting Anne's cheeks.

Two long blasts from the whistle, the signal to release brakes and proceed, made the children shriek. William handed the youngsters down to Carry Tracy. For the first time he put his arm around Anne, steadying her as the train, the very ground, shook.

How can I still the shaking of my heart? William wondered as the bell clanged, drowning out farewells. With hissing steam and creaking brakes, the locomotive moved out.

William drew his bride inside the car. He paused. He must be careful, understand her innocence. But emotion pounded his senses. How long he had been in love with her from afar! *She's even more beautiful than she was when she blossomed at seventeen*, he thought, watching her moving about the car murmuring compliments on the mahogany furnishings. Memory of how painfully he had waited, planning to ask Judge Tracy for her hand, holding back, fearing rejection, made him even more unsure of himself. His relatives were country folk. Hers were socially prominent. Does she think me a social climber? Will she be ashamed of me? Will she know how acutely I feel the lack of going to college?

Then Anne turned. The smile she gave him was tremulous, but it filled him with exultation. Her father might not have arranged the marriage, but she, herself, had consented to be his. He would woo her, dreaming he could one day make her love him.

Crossing the distance between them, he took her hands and led her to a table prepared with the finest food money could buy. The train settled into a soft chugging as it rolled through the dark forest of the red-hilled Piedmont; then it plunged into the flat, sandy coastal plain, speeding over zigzagging rails at forty miles an hour, pressing across two hundred miles of Georgia toward the sea, taking them into new territory.

When they reached Savannah and took a buggy down the cobble-stoned street to the waterfront, William was relieved that Anne's reticence of the previous night was overcome by delight. He smiled tenderly as she clapped her hands like a child.

"Oh, Mr. Johnston, my first steamship! The smokestacks are like a river boat, but look at those towering masts."

Hope sprang that he might make her happy.

"Oh, please, let's stay on deck to watch," Anne begged as they drifted with the tide into the Atlantic Ocean. She exclaimed again as the sails billowed over her head.

Then the waves began to toss. He laughed as she clapped

one hand to her stomach, the other to her mouth, and rolled her marvelous brown eyes at him.

"Don't worry. It's a calm summer's day. Just keep your gaze fastened on the coastline and your mind on the surprise I have for you. We're going to stop at Washington City. I've made an appointment with Secretary of State Daniel Webster. I expect he'll write us a letter of introduction to the Diplomatic and Consular Agents of the United States in Europe."

Anne threw up her hands excitedly. "You mean I will meet the man who affected the Missouri Compromise and the Compromise of 1850?"

"The same." He smiled at her awe, thinking his own wealth and prominence might begin to impress her. "Others worked, of course, but it was largely he who averted war between the North and South."

"Do you s'pose he knows about the meeting in Macon this summer denouncing his Compromise of 1850? Phil and Lit attended, and—you know hot-tongued Brother Phil. He asserted rather loudly that a state has a right to secede from the Union. I think so, too. All my kinfolk support Southern Rights . . ."

He watched her eyes grow wide with fear as a new thought struck her.

"Oh, Mr. Johnston! You have business dealings at the North. If the nation separates, which side would you choose?"

The boat rocked, sending her sliding across the deck to retch at the rail, and he did not have to answer.

William wore his newest outfit, tailored by the most expensive establishment in New York City, to check into the Astor House. Proudly, he escorted Anne across the lobby. It was one of New York's finest hotels. They made slow progress because everyone bowed and called him "Mr. Johnston."

She's impressed, he thought gleefully.

Anne looked pleased with their room. "I'm glad you like it," he said. "I'll take you round the town later, but right now I must leave you and go to the City Bank of New York. You see I'm their representative, and I must attend to work for a few weeks."

"But I thought you were retired," Anne protested. "I read in *The New York Times* about the Great Exhibition being held in London. I thought this stop was overnight. I'm eager to sail."

"I'm sorry. I'm free from daily job, yes. But I sit on several boards. And I have to superintend my real estate and other investments." He took a roll of bills from his money clip. "Here. Go shopping. Buy some bright pretty clothes."

Anne put her hands behind her. "I don't need a single thing. My seamstress at home made traveling suits for easy walking. Not black. Brown and gray. My trunk's overflowing."

"I'll hire a guide to show you the city." He saw fear flash in her eyes before she lowered them and shook her head.

"Is that done here? The Aunts would be scandalized if I went out without a chaperone. People here respect *you*, but there's sentiment against us Southerners. When you left me with the baggage, a man rudely laughed at my drawl and asked, 'What part of the South are y'all from, honey?'" She took out a book. "I always carry something by George Gordon Lord Byron. I'll wait for you."

He was surprised that her usual curiosity did not make her defiant enough to go out. *I've disappointed her again.*

When William returned to their suite each evening, she was never ready for him to be romantic. It was clear she merely tolerated his groping attempts at lovemaking. He was overwhelmed with grief when he awakened in the night to hear her crying.

The steamer *Pacific* loomed over them, bells clanging, whistles signaling. William knew he looked silly, but he could not stop grinning. *I feel like the Christmas I was eight when I got all those firecrackers and Roman candles.*

There were no actual fireworks as they walked up the gangplank. *But there should be. We're embarking on the Grand Tour of Europe!* He had planned every detail. He patted the pocket that held his cherished itinerary.

Anne's excitement completed his happiness. He had gained ground with her in Washington only to lose it in New York. She had been so unhappy during their stay at the Astor House that he had feared she might write Philemon to come and take her home, but now she sparkled. William wished he could keep her like this, cheeks rosy from the crisp autumn air.

They stayed on deck, looking down on the New York dock where a band was playing Irish airs. Clapping time, Anne eavesdropped unabashedly as a group of Irishmen laughed and hugged a fellow who was boarding, obviously returning home. William's gaze turned to the sailors handling the ropes, but his eyes kept pulling back to Anne's radiant face.

The steamer's whistle blasted. It was high noon, November 8, 1851, as the *Pacific* sailed into New York harbor.

"Oh, Mr. Johnston," Anne said, voice suddenly husky with tears, "I just realized *we* are leaving our native shores, taking our last looks at our Fatherland!"

Filled with emotion, he could not speak. She looked as young and innocent as she had when he had fallen in love with her. He had bided his time, saved his money. Now he wanted to crown her with jewels, gown her in the finest silks.

But she had not accepted his gifts, his money—him.

He leaned as close as he dared and drew a deep breath of her cleanness. *If only I could make her love me.* He grasped for hope. On shipboard there would be multi-coursed dining, the dancing that she loved, moonlight strolls on deck, quiet nights in their handsome stateroom . . .

The ship's bell signaled. He smiled and offered his arm. "Shall we go below for lunch?"

William surveyed himself in the mirror. This handsome swallow-tailed coat should help him meet the challenge of the evening. Hungry, mouth watering at the prospect of an elegant dinner, he started across to Anne's dressing room. The ship swayed. Planting his feet apart, he tapped at her door, opened it at her invitation.

"Why Miss Anne," he said dismayed, "You're only half-dressed. It's time for the evening meal."

"I'm dizzy," she wailed. "I can't get to my clothes. The floor's constantly tilting."

"But slightly. The weather's considered smooth," he said. "You'll get your sea legs. Here let me help you."

With his arm around her, she took a few steps. Just as she straightened with confidence, the floor dipped. Anne retched, hanging her face over the porcelain washbowl.

"I'm sorry. You'll have to eat alone." She fell across the bed. "Byron said, 'the waves sound beneath me like a steed that knows its rider.' I can't agree. I didn't know I'd be a poor sailor. Just let me stay on my bed in my suffering."

Fantasies dashed, he left her.

ᨀ∴ᨀ

The next day was no better. Anne could not acclimate herself to the rhythm of the waves. Even the gentlest motion dizzied her. Days passed, and she clung to her bunk, retching with every roll.

"You must take some nourishment," William said at last. "You're getting weak."

"I can't! I can't! Don't let me spoil your fun. I've never gotten sick in my life. When I did, I made a big mess of it." Tears made trails down her pale cheeks. "I'm relinquishing anticipations of the Old World. I wish we could turn back for home."

Disappointment was a bitter taste in William's mouth.

Then they struck a heavy cross-sea. For twenty-four hours, the ship struggled, and all were seasick, but none as severely as Anne. Feeling hurt that Anne did not want him to see her ill, he gave up trying to help and engaged a lady passenger to stay at her side as a nurse.

Eleven-and-half days after sailing from New York, they heard the welcome cry, "Land in sight!"

"I did live to reach solid ground," Anne said, with a forced smile. When they docked at Liverpool and she tried to stand, she fainted. William lifted her tenderly in his arms and carried her off the ship.

ᴄ:ᴎ

In the Waterloo Hotel, Anne lay on a fainting couch, looking forlornly out the window. "What a curious combination of sun, rain, and mist," she wailed. "What can be seen here through a November fog? But how will I ever re-cross that angry sea to the bright skies of our sunny land?"

Without a word, William handed her a comic almanac that read, "November is the month to commit suicide."

She began to laugh. With a bit more determination, she said, "I've been a terrible bore. You've been so patient and sweet."

ᴄ:ᴎ

After a week, William coaxed Anne to take a carriage ride around the city, but she was disappointed in Liverpool.

"It's devoted entirely to mercantile pursuits. I want to see beautiful architecture. Art. Hear wonderful music."

"I'm afraid I've had little time to acquire a taste for those things," he said tartly. "But, then, you must realize how important the port of Liverpool is to the South. It is here our cotton comes on the way to the great looms at Lancashire."

"I s'pose." Her darkly smudged eyes swam with misery. "I wish I could see our cotton fields," she said, sighing. At that moment she glimpsed a team of draft horses dragging a sled laden with cotton bales. Leaning out the carriage window, she exclaimed, "Can you believe the size of those horses? They're like small elephants!"

Relief washed over him as her interest kindled and she drew her journal from her reticule and added a note about the horses. She wrote detailed accounts of the buildings and monuments they were passing.

"Look at that splendid bronze monument to Lord Nelson. I read that the four figures represent his greatest victories."

Proud of the knowledge she displayed, he placed a warm hand over hers, the first loving touch he had dared since they left New York. She did not pull away. His mind reeled. He had feared he would have to settle for a platonic relationship. His breathing became erratic, and he struggled to keep his voice light.

"I'll be finished here soon. On December first we can leave for London."

"Oh, I hate fog. Mists at home were warm and fuzzy. This air feels like a wet dishrag hitting you in the face. Please. Let's skip London and go to France. We can tour England in the summer and see the gardens. I've never known anything could be as cold as England. I know I shouldn't let damp, gray weather make me melancholy, but I'm starved for sunshine."

He looked at her, pale, so thin her clothes were hanging from bony arms. His itinerary had seemed near to Sacred Writ, but he pushed it down in his pocket and grimaced. "Paris it is!"

Radiant, she looked up at him with luminous eyes and parted lips in the unguarded expression that so captured his heart. If only he could get the words out of his mouth to tell her. He knew he must keep her laughing. Grasping at what he saw from the carriage window he spoke sardonically, "Have you noticed the irregular want of beauty in the ladies here?"

Surprised, she peered out, snickered, indicated another homely miss. By the time they reached the Waterloo Hotel, they were giggling uncontrollably.

William gave a few swift orders as they passed through the lobby. Anne was shivering as he propelled her to their rooms.

Heart pounding, he closed the draperies, shutting out November. He stoked up the fire, while she exchanged her damp clothes for a wine-velvet wrapper. He pulled a settee close to the grate and made her a nest in a down comforter. Trying to think of something to say, he knelt and massaged her cold feet. Flames began to leap up red and gold.

"Umm," Anne murmured. "That feels good. You've made the room so warm and cozy." She arched her back, preened. Courage fired with desire, he was about to lift her and make a place for himself beside her when a knock sounded.

A waiter entered pushing a table laid with damask, china, and flowers. The rich smell of red meat escaped the candle-warmed silver servers.

Anne stiffened, drew back.

"Do you think I should leave off milk toast and chicken soup and eat solid food?"

"Yes. It's time."

He cut her the most tender bites of English roast beef. She ate with increasing enjoyment, laughing again about the ugly women they had seen. Then he tucked her into the comforter and fed her spoonfuls of plum pudding. He leaned closer, brushed his lips against her hair, her cheek, whispered, "Kiss me."

Anne raised her lips, met his gently.

"You're so lovely."

"Me? Plain me? "

"Yes."

It was all he could say, but he kissed her again, thoroughly this time. For the first time she responded with pleasure. With rising confidence, he took her in his arms.

⌣∴⌣

December 1, 1851 fell on a Monday. They left Liverpool by train at nine in the morning. All day they rode over frost-obscured ground. When they entered London by gaslight, William looked worriedly at Anne. Her whole body drooped with weariness and her face showed little excitement at the great city he had especially wanted to visit.

Checking into a private boarding house, they found there were few other visitors. The clerk told them, "Ye can't see nothing to advantage in this deserted season."

"Oh, please, Mr. Johnston," Anne begged, "let's do go on to Paris."

He sighed. "As soon as this heavy fog lifts, I'll go out and make arrangements."

But on Tuesday afternoon when William entered a pub to ask directions, he discovered that momentous events had transpired in France on that Monday. He accepted the invitation to join two men at a table.

A wizened fellow took a long drink from his mug and began explaining. "Aye, Paris has been waiting, knowing something was about to 'appen," he said. "But What? When?"

31

William leaned forward. The man did not move the upper part of his face when speaking, making the sound of the words different. William strained to understand.

"The day began as usual," a bearded man broke in. "Prince-President Louis-Napoleon gave a grand reception at the Elysée Palace. Those Frenchie aristocrats were dancing and drinking. They ditn't even notice that 'e stepped into a private room from time to time to consult his man preparing orders . . . What was that chap's name?"

"Duke Morny," said the first man. He laughed, "I reckon he fooled them by announcing he was off to the Opera-Comique. Everyone danced on, saying if a coup d'état came, it would not be tonight. But, oh, these French! We 'ave it on good authority that six conspirators were awaiting 'im and six army brigades moved out after midnight.

"Paris awoke on the second of December to read placards signed by President Louis Napoleon. The coup d'état was swift. You don't want to travel in France now."

William listened as others in the pub added details. Then he hurried back to the boarding house to explain to Anne. "This man is the nephew of Napoleon Bonaparte," he said, feeling proud that, for once, he had knowledge to impart to her. They told me how Louis Napoleon endured exile, then prison. He escaped, became president, and now he's voted himself into a presidential term extended to ten years. The situation is too unsettled for me to take you to France."

"I'm not afraid."

"My dear, I'm glad you're feeling yourself again, but they say that always in Parisian uprisings, the most dangerous moments come on the third day."

"Well, then, we must simply make the best of it and see London. I'm stronger at last. Fog or no fog, it is impossible to remain within doors with such a world around us!"

Anne scolded herself that she must conquer her homesickness. *Being married without love is worse than I expected, but I've no*

one to blame but myself. This man won't put up with poor health and cross temper much longer.

But when she peeped out at the grayness, she had to force her usually positive outlook. She donned all six of her flannel petticoats and her brown wool suit that was short enough not to drag in the street. Winding on an extra shawl, she wondered how she would walk, but she told Mr. Johnston, "I'm ready to launch a tour of London."

They hired a carriage and drove to St. Paul's cathedral. Worshipers had left, and Anne scurried about making notes. Next they drove through Hyde Park.

When they passed the Crystal Palace, she cried out, "Please, let's stop. All that glass! It's such a fairy looking structure! Look. Trees are growing inside."

He made a face. "I'm sorry to tell you. The Great Exhibition closed in October."

While we languished in New York, she thought with fire in her eyes. "It would have been nice to have seen Queen Victoria and Prince Albert open the world's fair, but let's look anyway."

She determined not to complain, but as they walked through the aisles, deserted except for a handful of people, anger turned to sighs.

"I'm sorry I had so much business."

So, he read my feelings. Anne turned her face from him. A few stalls remained stocked. The French booth hung with tapestries so rich that she had to finger them.

"Look how beautiful. You say you don't know how to appreciate art. Let me teach you. Oh, if only we can get to Paris. If you can see the Louvre . . ."

"Patience, Miss Anne," Mr. Johnston said, laughing.

She pouted her lips. "I prayed once for patience. Later I discovered what a lot of suffering Job got before he learned it. Do you really think we can't go to France?"

Their guide intervened. "Best stay in the sane rule of Queen Victoria. It's dangerous to travel in France, mum. Mrs. Robert Browning sent word to friends that along the boulevards they've replaced 'Liberty! Equality! Fraternity! with Infantry! Cavalry! Artillery!'"

"Well," said Anne, "if I must endure cold and fog, I must."
But the rain had begun again when they went out. Her hair matted in strings down her neck, and wet petticoats wrapped round her legs, weighing her down.

❧

December 10, 1851

Dear Aunt Carry,

The fog is so thick today that I can't see the street below my window. I've decided on that as the rule for staying in to write the family—I'll write the Montgomery folks next—Otherwise I brave the cold and damp.

I really am drawn to the antiquities. Westminster Abbey was awe-inspiring, but Mr. Johnston spent the time talking to a stranger about banking and investments. Odd how he's so standoffish with folks at home and makes instant friends here.

Anne paused, remembering how she had begged him to join her at Poets' Corner by Chaucer's tomb. He had asked, "Who?"

No wonder he didn't know that Byron, in his own lifetime, was considered second only to Shakespeare. Mr. Johnston's a pragmatic man. How can I expect him to be romantic? She realized she would never know the wonder of love Lord Byron described. No gleam had come in Mr. Johnston's eye until they visited the tower that housed the Crown Jewels. Again he embarrassed her, asking how much money they were worth. Pen poised, Anne wondered if she dared ask Aunt Carry if it were permissible for a wife to tell her husband gentle people never talked of money.

❧

Gray skies cleared just when Anne felt she could bear them no longer. They strolled through the Zoological Gardens. She flexed her shoulders in the sunshine, but the beautiful trees turned her heart toward Macon. She sank to a bench, trying to swallow her tears. Her new husband was watching her curiously, and she spoke in a false lilt.

"One nice thing about your itinerary. I've had letters from the Aunts. But none from that lazy Lit and Phil."

"Does your family mean so much to you?"

"Of course! Doesn't yours?"

"Well, yes—but I don't need them around me all the time like you do."

Anne panicked. During their engagement, they had talked of nothing but their Grand Tour. She *had* to know.

"You *do* mean to live in Macon?" she blurted. *I need family. I'm used to having them there when I want them.* She suddenly felt terribly alone.

"Ummm." He tugged at his beard. "I want to build a grand mansion. The Yankees rather laugh at the simplicity of our houses. You must admit they would hardly make a display on Fifth Avenue."

"I hated their brownstone!" she snapped. "I think the South's white-columned Greek Revival infinitely more beautiful."

"But you must admit they're simple and unadorned."

The trees were casting long shadows now, and as they sat, not knowing what to say, Anne shivered, persisting. "I'm a subtropical flower. I'm afraid I lack the fortitude to live at the North."

He made no reply, and she glanced at him from under the brim of her bonnet. He had withdrawn behind that introverted shield, and she could not tell what he was thinking. Should she risk an unwomanly assertiveness?

"Besides, I disagree with their political insistence on an all powerful Federal government," she dared to say. "And . . ." her voice softened. ". . . I love our servants. I miss Adeline as much as the family . . . I wish you had let me bring her."

"But you know I heard that rumor that British abolitionists were meeting American boats at Liverpool, absconding with slaves."

Sadly she nodded.

He took his gold watch from his pocket and snapped open the case. "I fear what lies ahead of us," he said with a great heaviness. "In spite of Mr. Webster, our nation is reaching a turning point." Consulting the timepiece, he moved briskly. "I must get you out of this night air."

She sank into misery. *I'll never feel one with him.* They had become friends in their letters, but now she found he was all pride. His only interests were business and making money. Family and faith meant all to her. She had been raised in orthodox religion where spiritual values were too real to be bought and sold or compromised.

She straightened her spine. *I got myself into this marriage, and I'll make the best of it.* But as mist settled over Regents Park, she reflected it would take one wiser than Daniel Webster to help her and Mr. Johnston compromise.

Anne doggedly followed Mr. Johnston's precious itinerary. They visited the tunnel beneath the Thames by descending one hundred winding steps. As they strolled the thoroughfares under the river, she exclaimed, "I can hardly believe the brilliantly lighted stalls."

Suddenly something caught Mr. Johnston's eye. "Look. Some trinkets made in France."

Anne stopped before the display of tiny, cone-shaped vases. Some of them were gilt with portrait medallions while others were porcelain or silver. All were unique.

The clerk became alert, "If the missus plans to travel in Europe, she's got to have a tussie-mussie," he said. "The streets give off owt but a glorious scent, and m'lady will need the tussie," he demonstrated with the minute bouquet of flowers, "placed in the mussie, the moist moss, to keep her nosegay fresh."

"They're all so lovely, I could never choose," Anne said, about to move on. Then she lifted a vase of ruby glass entwined with silver filigree and cupped it in her palm. "Oh, I do like this one with a pin. I can fasten it to my lapel when I get tired of holding it."

Quickly the man tied together sprigs of rosemary, lavender, lamb's ears, and love-in-a-mist. He placed the nosegay in the ruby vase and beamed. So did Mr. Johnston, who stopped her when she reached in her reticule and paid for it himself.

Anne sniffed the fragrance from her tussie mussie as they toiled back up the hundred steps, thinking that it did improve the dank odor.

"I'm famished," she exclaimed. "At last my appetite has returned."

⌣⋮⌣

"I wrote everyone that the tunnel is London's most curious sight," Anne said as she stood in Madame Tussaud's wax museum. "I was wrong. This is it. History comes alive here."

Figures of kings, queens, and generals were grouped in handsomely furnished settings. Anne's excitement mounted when she entered the rooms devoted to relics of Napoleon. "Look! The carriage he used in exile in Saint Helena. The cloak he wore at Marengo." Her voice hushed as she stood before Napoleon's wax figure lying in full uniform on the camp bed on which he had died.

At closing time she still lingered, gazing at portraits of Marie-Louise and Josephine and exquisite specimens of Sèvres porcelain.

"Perhaps I do need to get away from family, Mr. Johnston," she whispered. "England is just like visiting more cousins." She laughed. "The exotic is calling me. I can hardly wait to see France!"

"We will take our chances. I'll attend to our passports tomorrow."

Chapter IV

"Another boat!" Anne exclaimed, chagrined. She glared at the English Channel, feeling foolish. Yearning to see Paris and the art that had illumined her studies at boarding school, she had forgotten one small problem: getting from England to France.

She shrugged, laughed at herself, and strode into the ladies cabin. Others with serious, resigned faces were trying to get fixed to be nauseous.

But the crossing was smooth. Only Anne was seasick.

They landed at Boulogne at last. Anne followed Mr. Johnston through customs on unsteady feet, plucking at his sleeve, apologizing.

"Nonsense, my dear. I'm sorry you must suffer."

When they reached the Hotel de Boins, she sank into bed, still queasy, wanting no supper.

At daybreak, sunshine awakened her. "Glorious," she shouted, stretching her hands toward it as she leaped from bed. She flung on her clothes, singing. The train for Paris left early.

Anne shivered as they walked to the station. The morning was bright but cold. She was disappointed upon seeing the train, thinking the French cars looked similar to the English; then they stepped aboard, and she sighed in delight. These had foot stoves filled with hot water. She snuggled down, warm.

⋌⁚⁃

Paris! Anne took out her journal, noting they arrived at six o'clock, December 17, 1851. She could scarcely stop looking long enough to breathe as they boarded an omnibus and rode down the Rue de Rivoli. They turned under an arch and stopped in the court of the Hotel Meurice. Its grandeur astounded her, and she looked at her husband with new eyes, realizing he accepted nothing but the best.

The next morning when they went through the lobby, Mr. Johnston insisted their rooms be exchanged for some even larger. Her growing respect faltered as she wondered which embarrassed her more, his demands or his statement that money was no object.

Both were forgotten as they walked down La Rue de La Paix and entered the Boulevards.

"Look! Look!" Anne exclaimed. "All of Paris is art. The buildings, the food, those flowers on the corner. Have you ever seen such colors?" Her voice had risen to an octave she reserved for playing with children, but she felt as excited as a child awaiting Santa Claus. She pressed her nose against shop windows, hurrying from one to the other. "I love this. And this," she said. "You see! It is safe. The streets seem in perfect order."

"I don't wonder. There are soldiers everywhere," he replied, surprising her by slipping his arm about her waist.

Jerking her head around, she drew against him. In her excitement, she had not realized there were armed guards. Glad of her husband's nearness, she thought the bay rum he used in grooming his beard smelled familiar, dear. His solid bulk felt warm, comforting.

"Oh, those walls," she whispered, noticing some damaged buildings for the first time. "Marks of bullets."

"And over there. Cannon holes. But they're old," he said, patting her. "Probably from the Revolution of 1848. See? Some of these places have been repaired."

Suddenly Anne's knees buckled. She leaned heavily on his arm. Smiling, he led her toward one of the chairs grouped along the boulevard. They sat down and ordered coffee.

Anne peered over the rim of her cup. "All of the seats face

out as if Parisians spend their time watching people." She counted passers-by. Half wore uniforms. Leaning close to Mr. Johnston, she gave a nervous laugh. "I rather feel as though I've dragged you to the brink of a crater."

"A little fear becomes you. Roses are blooming in your cheeks." He ducked his head shyly after giving the compliment.

Anne's hands flew to her face. Wonderingly, she watched him as he tugged at his beard. *I've always felt so ordinary, and this man insists on perfection. What can he see in me? It must be the aura of Paris.*

They sat gazing into each other's eyes until their coffee got cold. He closed his hand over hers. Anne breathed deeply, sensing that in the rarified atmosphere, they were absorbing each other's presence for the first time. They had no need to struggle with speech as they shared a lovely silence.

At last he spoke. "Are you recovered from the crossing enough to go out tonight? The celebrated magician Houdini is appearing at the Palais National."

"Yes!"

⌣:∾

Anne stood in the lobby of the Meurice, dizzy with excitement at beginning a real tour of Paris. Mr. Johnston presented their valet de place.

Anne caught her breath as the handsome young Frenchman bowed and kissed her hand. He told her his name was Isadore. Speaking low in his throat, he added a romantic timbre that sent a tingle through her.

"I shall conduct you to the Tuileries, the famous royal palace of Bourbon Kings," Isadore said, smoothing already sleek black hair. "It is across the Rue de Rivoli from your hotel."

When they entered the Court of the Tuileries, Anne shrank back. Rows of troops were being reviewed.

Isadore spoke in his soft voice, concealing his mouth behind his hand. "Much of the ancient magnificence has been destroyed, Madame. The circular structure begun by Catharine de Medici, it has been altered by later rulers of France into this square." He gestured toward the south wing. "The palace connects by that gallery with the Louvre, which contains celebrated collections of pictures and museums too numerous to-to see today. Instead, I shall take you into rooms that were occupied by Louis XVI in 1789, when his family was forced in by the revolutionary mob."

Anne was disappointed that little furniture remained, but she craned her neck to admire the gilded ceilings and silk and damask wall hangings in the now empty throne room. These were the types of things she had been eager to see.

"The mob destroyed the ornaments and burned the throne," Isadore lamented rolling his hands outward, and then clasping them together again, "but that Gobelin tapestry is from the time of Louis XIV."

"Oh," Anne exclaimed. "The coloring and finish is so exquisite it's almost impossible to realize it's not a painting. Isadore, I'm delighted to tread the palace of the kings of France—even though this has since been the home of Emperor Napoleon."

Anne dared to speak a few words of the French her father had taught her to Isadore who was so fluent in English. Then she laughed at her own attempts.

The suave Frenchman looked at her admiringly. "But no. You do well. However, I will secure you an-an instructor to aid you, if you like."

"Wonderful! And, Mr. Johnston, you must join me." She realized she had been leaving him out.

"There's no need to try. I could never learn it," he replied with a firmness that ended the subject.

"Since Madame enjoys the tapestry," said Isadore with a deep bow, "I shall take you next to the Gobelin establishment."

Inside the government-owned factory, they were allowed to watch the looms. Anne marveled at the workman seated behind the warp. Working on the wrong side, he occasionally referred to the painting placed at his back to adjust the color of the silk and wool thread.

"He might take years to finish a single piece," Isadore explained.

"It's very like the fabric of our lives, Mr. Johnston," Anne said.

"We see the knots on the wrong side, the slowness. God sees the final picture."

But her husband paid no attention to her mood. He entered the carpet room—where threads were cut on the right side—asking the cost of the far-famed Gobelin carpet.

"Ah, monsieur, sixty to 150,000 francs."

Anne was pleased that they attended high mass à La Madelaine. Then they procured a carriage and joined the favorite Sunday afternoon promenade down the Champs Elysées. Anne sat forward, staring in amazement. She had never seen so many beautiful, dark-haired women. They wore ruffled gowns in startlingly bright colors and hats with enormous plumes. But what surprised her most was the way they twirled and dipped their parasols *No Southern belle ever handled one quite so flirtatiously.*

"Have you ever seen such an enormous throng of chattering people?" Anne said over her shoulder. "Why, you can scarcely tell it's Sunday. Oh, my, they're actually buying and selling!"

Anne turned to see that Mr. Johnston was not looking where she indicated but at her. Cocking her head to one side, she put her hands on her hips. "What?"

"You! How you sparkle! Are you so very happy?"

"Oh, yes! Especially since tomorrow will be devoted to the palace of the Louvre. I can hardly wait."

Creases showed between his brows. "I thought I'd let Isadore take you. I . . . know nothing of art. I don't have your classical education."

"Oh, please! It won't be the same unless I can share it with you. Say you'll go for a little while."

William felt apprehensive as he followed Anne into a portion of the Louvre that was quite old, having been the royal castle of the monarchy since the 1500s. He glanced uneasily from gilded ceilings to mosaic pavements. Anne, not knowing where to begin but drawn by the grand staircase, led the way upward. She stopped on the landing under an arch as the stairs divided into two branches leading to different paths. Laughing at her own confusion, she chose a long gallery pierced with a skylight.

Mutely, he followed, shaking his head that he could tell no difference when she told him they were standing amidst the choicest specimens of the celebrated collection.

"But, Mr. Johnston," she gasped. "These painters' names and fame are immortal! Look there. Raphael, Correggio. And there. Titian. Van Dyck." Clasping her hands over her heart, she walked about rapturously. "The work of the Old Masters more than un-parallels my utmost imaginings! The colors. Look how this red is repeated here and there. The depth! The eyes. Why, the people are about to step out and speak! Oh, Mr. Johnston, do you see, do you see?"

He swallowed. *Do I? Maybe.* At first it was through her eyes, but when they turned a corner, one painting made him stop. Vivid pink leapt from the canvas. A peach tree made him gasp with its vibrancy.

"Yes. I understand." He reached for her hand, and as her fingers squeezed into his palm, he felt a tingling pass between them, binding them as they gazed.

He looked from her to the canvas, unable to express his feelings. He had never imagined there could be such difference between art and the new photographs. The only paintings he had taken notice of was the work of traveling artists who had come to the plantation with stacks of bodies already completed, needing but to add the heads of the local ladies. He laughed. Anne wrapped him in her smile.

They walked slowly, and she told him about the masters they were viewing, French, Flemish, German, Italian.

"There are so many details in each picture you could stand an hour before one," he said.

"I could stay for a month with Raphael's angelic faces," she replied.

"Suddenly I realize it is your face I must have painted."

"Oh, no!" she gasped, animation draining from her. "I couldn't."

"I insist. I'll have Isadore arrange sittings immediately."

"If you say it's a necessity, but only if you have a portrait, too."

He nodded. Suddenly he was seized with great excitement. *It will be a beginning. I must buy paintings. I will build Anne a gallery of her own!*

Anne fussed with her hair, unhappy with the arrangement of wavy wings on each side of her face. The artist clucked at her, frowning. Clutching the peacock-feather fan he had given her, she tried to sit still. At least as a married woman she could put up the length of her awful hair into a crown of braids. She kept her face impassive, intent on concealing her emotions from the painter. Her back ached. In fantasy, she tried to rekindle the fire she had felt standing with her husband in the Louvre. She was too tired.

The large oil painting was finished before she realized that the man had included the mourning bands she still wore on her wrists. She did not like the picture of her ugly face

He saw too much. He even showed the way I try to veil my eyes. Anyone can look at it and detect the shyness I try so hard to cover up.

But when she viewed her husband's likeness, Anne's eyes widened in surprise. The portraitist revealed a man she had not seen. Moving, speaking, Mr. Johnston impressed with the importance of his money. Silenced by the sitting, stripped of bravado, he showed by his tight face and sloped shoulders and the way he concealed his hand inside his cloak that he hid deep feelings of inferiority.

She began watching him with different eyes. On Christmas Eve, when they attended the French opera, she saw clearly that he did not understand the ballet.

Did I only imagine that we were sharing ecstasy when we viewed great art? Did I flaunt my education? Have I made him imagine himself unworthy of my cultured upbringing even while I felt too unexceptional to be his wife?

❦

"A ball in honor of Prince Louis Napoleon? Of course, I want to go!" Anne almost shouted her delight.

It was the day after Christmas, and they were visiting the American consul, Mr. Goodrich. Just as the diplomat presented them with handsome invitations to the grand affair to be held the following Saturday night commemorating Napoleon's election, another American couple was ushered into the hotel suite. The Hardenburgs were also on their honeymoon.

Anne eyed the petite blonde, who had just the sort of beauty she had always longed for. Her costume, trimmed with gimp and fringe, was far too elaborate for travel; her laugh, an annoying cackle, was much too loud; however, the prospect of another woman to talk with overruled. When the youthful newlyweds requested invitations, Anne smiled at Mr. Johnston who motioned to the consul. Anne and Ruth Hardenburg began an excited conversation about attending together.

"Why don't you join us now?" Mr. Johnston suggested. "I've hired a carriage to take us to Versailles. They tell me it's twelve miles from Paris."

During the two-hour drive, Ruth chattered constantly until they reached Louis XIV's Grand Palace, built in the 1600s at the height of France's power. Anne was amazed at its size and magnificence. Now it was devoted to the glories of France. As the four toured, she took notes of the paintings and statues, lingering especially at Joan of Arc. Suddenly she realized that she wanted to be sharing this with her husband, and she wished they had come alone.

Anne glanced back at the gentlemen, who followed along a corridor of polished-stone walls and floors and said, "Mr. Johnston, we are indeed in marble halls."

Ruth Hardenburg dipped the long, drooping feather of her hat about and said, "What I want to see is the Petit Trianon Louis XV built for the scandalous Madame Du Barry."

Embarrassed, Anne looked at the husbands, who were paying no attention. Mr. Johnston was discussing business with the lanky young man.

I guess I've dragged him to every church and cemetery and museum in Paris, Anne thought. *He's seen all he wants to see.*

But at midday when they went out of the chateau onto the terrace, Anne's excitement overpowered her disappointment. Pausing at the top of the stairs to view the layout of parterres, she was enchanted by the symmetry of the descending terraces and the elegant scrollwork formed by clipped box and yew.

"I'd read that the gardens spread east and west like the sun's rays shining, implying the influence of the 'Sun King,'" Anne said, "but I had no idea of their vastness."

Mr. Hardenburg spoke up as if ready to give up the tour. "The guidebook says it takes two days to walk it."

"Oh, but we must see these wonderful mythological fountains," Anne said in fright that she might have to leave. She pointed. "We're looking down on the goddess Latona and her children."

Anne ran to inspect Apollo's horses coming out of the water. The others stopped to rest beside a quiet reflecting pool. Resignedly, she went back.

Ruth Hardenburg snickered. "I don't care much for frogs and children with pointy tails."

Mr. Johnston was openly eying the curvy, curly haired beauty. Ruth noticed, and she moved deliberately so that her fringe and tassels swung tantalizingly.

Anne touched her own unadorned gray skirt, feeling hurt and surprisingly jealous. *If he preferred that type, why did he marry me?*

"My dear Anne," he said, frowning from one to the other. "Noticing Mrs. Hardenburg's fashionable attire, I fear your wardrobe is too provincial for a State Ball. Perhaps I should take you to one of these Paris seamstresses. I must pick out something for you."

"Yes, do!" exclaimed Ruth, ignoring Anne. "Try a rising young man. Charles Frederick Worth at 7 Rue de La Paix. They say he's designing for Spanish royalty like the Countess de Montijo." She cackled her annoying laugh. "But better not call the famed couturier of Chez Worth a seamstress."

༺⁙༻

William had something special planned, and he plotted how he would get Anne alone without the gossipy Mrs. Hardenburg. He had to admit she was knowledgeable in spite of her adolescence, and she had been helpful buying the Worth gown, but now he wanted rid of her. He planned to drive six miles to St. Cloud very early before the lady in question was up.

Smug that his idea had worked, he guided Anne about the summer palace, seeing only her. Afterwards, they relaxed in the park with its water works and huge trees.

"It's lovely on this hillside looking down upon Paris. I could sit here with you forever," Anne said, sighing.

"I'm pleased you're content, but I had a reason for coming. I must coax you to walk across to Sévres where the manufactory of porcelain had been celebrated for a hundred years."

"Mmmm," she replied drowsily

But once inside, she awoke with a glow of enchantment. "What exquisite specimens! Why these pictures on porcelain are brilliantly colored copies of Old Masters!"

He brushed his hand over his beard to conceal his joy as she stirred his heart. "You must pick a pattern for a set of dishes."

"How can I decide when it's all so lovely?" she asked, lifting a piece of stained glass up to the light.

William immediately chose pure white china, gold edged, each piece to be monogrammed WBJ. "This is for dinners I might host, but please select another."

"Oh, no. Two sets would be too expensive," she demurred. "Just let me look. I want to see how this plain white biscuit is glazed and becomes the finished porcelain."

As they walked through the factory examining each stage, Anne leaned intently toward the artists applying enamel, painting beautiful flowers, figures, and landscapes. Next, the articles were dipped, then placed in clay vessels, shut tight and baked in furnaces.

"Look at that bowl," she marveled as she moved down the line. "I thought it was perfect, but it was retouched and baked again."

"Sometimes pieces are submitted six or seven times to the action of the fire," the guide told them.

William was watching her face as she came upon a pattern with wide borders of bright rose.

"Those are the prettiest dishes I've ever seen!" She exclaimed.

"Give us a banquet service of every size piece."

The guide nodded. "Every dinner and dessert plate will match in pink with gold band, but each center will be painted with a different flower or fruit."

"It's too much," she declared, "but too beautiful to refuse."

Holding hands, they chose pink glasses delicately etched in gold.

As they were leaving, Anne picked up a tiny liqueur painted with minute figures dressed in the slender Empire styles of Napoleon I. She put it down, saying nothing, but behind her back, William ordered this set sent to America, too.

Let that whippersnapper, Hardenburg, top that! William thought, transported that she had let him buy the dress and now the china for their future home. He applied himself to charming attentions as they drove back down into Paris. His emotions were burning at the prospect of showing off his bride in her Worth gown.

⋯∴⋯

The ball was held January 3, 1852, at the Hôtel de Ville. When they arrived with the Hardenburgs at ten, Anne decided there must be a hundred thousand candles blazing in the chandeliers. She stared openly at the sophisticated people, women, with daring décolleté and spreading, shimmering skirts, and men, with ribbons and sashes and bejeweled medals on their uniforms. Everyone glittered and gleamed. *I've never seen such a profusion of diamonds,* she thought.

"You should've let me buy you jewels," Mr. Johnston whispered in her ear.

Anne patted him. "This gown is enough." She could match their mushrooming skirts with the enormous volume of her own. She stroked the dark green moiré, confident because Worth had assured them this watered silk was much in demand. She grinned at the secret of the French women's standout skirts: linen petticoats stiffened with horsehair, which Worth called crinoline.

She smiled up at Mr. Johnston, and whispered, "Thank you, again." He beamed. He had not told her she looked pretty, but the glint in his eyes made her blush. He was gazing at her tonight, not at Ruth. She felt they were alone in the vast crowd.

The orchestra struck up a waltz, and the room became a swirling mass of silks and satins and taffetas sweeping in ever widening circles. Anne caught her breath. "Could we dance? I love that tune by Jacques Offenbach. It's called 'Winter Flowers.'"

He put his arm about her waist and whirled her into the throng. Gone was the embarrassment that had plagued her dancing with him in Macon. She relaxed into his arms, and they were strong, secure. Giddy, she swayed to the lilting three-quarter time through a room fragrant with blossoms and evergreens. They were suddenly young and exceedingly gay.

Then the music changed to a polka. Not knowing how to execute the hop-step-close-step, they sat with the Hardenburgs, watching the lively show.

Then the husbands went outside to smoke cigars, and Anne confided to Ruth, "I'm disappointed the prince president didn't attend. They say he's kindly and good-humored."

"Hump!" snorted Ruth. "They say he's a rogue with women! See that Englishwoman beside that potted tree? She's Mrs. Howard, his *mistress*. These French are a scandal!"

Anne's lashes fanned back in surprise.

Ruth laughed. "You should see your big brown eyes. You're *too* innocent. You've been exclaiming over all these pretty little waltzes by Jacques Offenbach. They're the rage of Paris, but his cancan . . . that's a scandal, even in Paris!"

"We haven't been to the Opera Comique. Let's go see the cancan."

Ruth sucked in her breath. Covering her face with a lace and ivory fan, she whispered, "It's not respectable! They wear no undergarments!"

It was Anne's chance to laugh at Ruth's suddenly prudish

face. She turned and saw her husband's eyes upon her, lighted with pleasure.

"Madame," he said with an elaborate bow, "May I have the honor of this dance?"

She went happily into his arms, and when they left at two in the morning, Anne was humming "Winter Flowers." They were still holding hands.

⌣⋮⋰

The morning after the ball, Anne remained excited by their new closeness. Unable to articulate her feelings, she yearned for the oneness they found in their shared passion for art. She decided to try to recapture it.

"Would you mind forsaking sightseeing with the Hardenburgs? I'd like to return to the Louvre."

"Wonderful, wonderful!" he exclaimed, surprising her.

Day after day they went to stand in the museum. Hand in hand, they gazed, and Anne felt their differences of temperament, of background, of age, vanish. From deep, hidden recesses, their souls rose up to meet.

Leaving the Louvre one bright January afternoon, they stopped at a sidewalk café. They sat discussing the antique statues they had spent hours viewing.

"We must buy something wonderful to display in our home," he said. "Could you bear to leave Paris? I'm eager to see Italy, and I understand there we might make purchases to begin our collection."

Suddenly reserved, she put down her café au lait. Now that they had penetrated one another's shyness, she dreaded risking a disagreement, but she needed to know. "You haven't said where you mean for us to live."

"Why, Macon, of course. If that's what you want. But I'm not really sure what style of architecture. One thing is certain. Since you've introduced me to art, I do know you must have a gallery."

Hugging her arms across her breasts that seemed about to

51

burst with joy, she looked at him incredulously. Then she jumped up and kissed his cheek.

"Oh, Mr. J., you are *wonderful!*"

He lifted his lips to hers, and they forgot they were sitting on the street.

Passing Parisians took no notice.

◡∴◡

President Louis Napoleon, himself, was giving a grand ball at the Tuileries on January 24, 1852. Anne decided that, eager as they were to begin their acquisitions, they must attend the State affair to climax their stay in Paris.

When they arrived in company with the Hardenburgs, they found the Tuileries Palace magnificently lit and decorated. It was completely filled, and the crowd spilled over into the tree-secluded paths of the garden.

They secured a spot on a terrace surrounded by torches where they could watch dancers trying to move in the press of humanity.

As Anne admired the splendid dresses of the ladies, she noticed one woman who stood out from the rest. She had red hair, blue eyes, and delicate skin set aglow by a dress of pale pink satin.

"Who is that beautiful creature," Anne asked. "She's so vivacious, she looks like a sunrise against the dark colors worn by the rest."

"That's Eugénie, the Countess de Montijo I told you about," Ruth replied, knowingly. "Her dress *is* exquisite, tasteful and rich without being overloaded. Gossip is that Napoleon wants to marry her."

"Of course, he would demand the greatest beauty in the realm."

At that moment Louis Napoleon was heralded. He appeared on the balcony overlooking the garden.

"Why, he's such a small man," Anne said, disappointed. "And with that silly, sweeping mustache not handsome at all."

He's not nearly as impressive a man as Mr. J., she thought.

She reached back, needing the reassurance of his strength. He had drifted away. She wanted to follow him, but her bouffant skirt held her locked in the crowd. With unreasoning panic, she peered into the dark shadows of the garden, searching for him.

Rude shoulders jostled her. Strange fingers groped. Anne shrank back. Then a warm hand clasped her waist, drew her close. She sensed it was *his touch.* Warmth flooded through her, stirring emotions deep within her body. Startled, she knew it was he and he alone she wanted. So! Lord Byron was right about falling in love after all.

As she turned in her husband's arms, she felt her face burning. He laughed. He could tell he had rescued her from distress, but he could not know what passion she was feeling.

Suddenly a cheer drew all attention to the balcony. She could see Napoleon's eyes roaming over the ladies, lighting upon Eugénie, devouring her.

Mr. Johnston, too, demanded—and could afford—the best. *Why did he ever ask me to marry him?*

She had realized her romantic dream of Paris, and suddenly she knew the dream was over. They were leaving. She was his teacher, his tour guide, and his advisor on buying a collection. She was painfully in love alone, but she could never expect that her quiet, businessman husband would fall in love with her.

Chapter V

Anne sat on the deck of a steamboat floating down the Rhone. In a mood as bleak as the January day, she eyed hillsides brown with barren vineyards, thinking, *My hopes for romance are as dead as this wine country.* I thought being married to someone I did not love was bad. This is worse. I never knew love could be so painful when it's not returned.

Since they left Paris, Mr. J. had ignored her, sleeping through the train ride to Chalons. Now he was dozing in a deck chair. She supposed she had worn him out with her boundless energy, trying to see all of Paris. She tried to read, but her nerves felt as rough and knobby as the grape vines.

When the indifferent looking little riverboat began passing between hills studded with chateaux and fairy tale villages, she wanted him all the more.

Wake up! Please. She watched him, longing to kiss him, to be caressed, thinking of Byron's line:

*Man's love is of man's life a thing apart;
'Tis woman's whole existence.*

Anne suddenly understood the poet's words. That moment in Paris had changed her from adolescent liking to deep loving. She wanted to breathe in his presence for the rest of her days. She yearned to be loved, not just as a wife to show off in fine gowns or as a traveling companion who could enlighten him on what they were seeing, but desired. *Like Eugénie.*

How can I expect a pragmatic man to respond to my passion for art, for beauty—for him?

He stirred under her gaze, and she said, "You're missing everything. That's not a cloud. It's a snow-topped crest. It must be Mt. Blanc."

"Um-huh," he mumbled.

Mr. J. leaned closer to follow her pointing finger, and the soft fuzziness of his beard tickled her cheek. Anne smiled. Had she ever been this aware of all her senses?

As the boat neared Lyons, Anne shook him to see the rough, gray rocks rising round, forcing themselves into the city, jutting into the gardens that landscaped handsome homes. She pronounced Lyons a singular mixture of nature and art.

That night Anne slept well in the hotel at Lyons and arose eager to continue the journey. Floating down the river caused her no motion sickness, and she felt herself exploding with health.

For the next two days, they lazed on deck. With Mr. J. taking more interest in her, Anne reveled in the view, walled castles, crowning ever more rugged hills that climbed to the distance snow-topped Alps, shining blue and clear in the sun.

When they stopped at Avignon to tour the famous Palace of the Popes, Anne came alive with energy, and Mr. J. rested, caught her zest. Walking, climbing, they missed nothing.

◦⁚◦

How did I ever win this lovely creature? William wondered as he watched Anne fairly dancing, stretching her arms up to the sun, exclaiming over the deep blue Mediterranean. They had reached the seaport of Marseilles.

"Oh, the southern air," Anne cried. "It's balmy even though it's the last day of January!"

William was thrilled that Anne actually took his hand as they strolled narrow streets. Suddenly, she stopped before an inn of crumbly-looking stone.

"This is the most romantic spot I've ever seen," she exclaimed, tugging him into the courtyard. "Just look how it's guarded by slender sentries of cypress and secluded by burgeoning vines. Oh, we must eat here," she begged.

Something was happening. William knew he must seize the moment, but his knees were failing him, and he thankfully sank into a chair. He gazed across the table at her, unable to speak. He had dreamed that if he took her to places such as this, she might come to love him.

Maybe not. Perhaps it was only Paris that changed her. But at least she doesn't pull away anymore when I try to touch her. She doesn't shutter her eyes to me. Now is the time to woo her, to tell her how much I love her.

But William drew up, tight, tense, throat constricted. He could feel his cheeks burning as red as the tiles of the roof. Somehow he managed to toast her with the local wine, sparkling St. Peray. Laughing, Anne agreed that the sea air heightened her appetite. They ordered fish cooked with olive oil.

"Delicious," Anne declared, rolling the light taste on her tongue. "The flavor is like the pecans back home."

Fear flashed through William. She might become homesick again. But he sat back as the waiters returned with violins. Smiling knowingly, they circled them, playing throbbing melodies, singing passionate songs. *Now. This is the time. Speak now, William,* he chided himself.

Anne was smiling up at him with her brown eyes soft. Loving? It seemed their whole relationship hung quivering like the bougainvillea that encircled them in a blaze of pink that would fade, die, and drop away. He pushed back his plate, covered her hand with his, and coughed—then he ducked his chin into his beard.

Miserable, William thought how he could address a board-room full of formidable men in New York City. *Why not one slender girl who is my wife?* But he remembered their wedding, the look on her face.

All he could say was, "I must make arrangements for the diligence for Nice." She did not love him. Could he bear to keep trying? He stammered, "If-if you'd like to wait here . . . listen to the violins. We'll walk down to the sea when I get back."

Anne nodded. She had a dreamy look about her as if she were lost in the music. He knew she understood none of his discomfort.

When William returned, he presented a nosegay of violets and geraniums. He had never seen Anne more delighted. She smiled up at him, touching the bouquet tenderly to her face.

With a lump in his throat, he pulled back her chair and offered his arm. *For whatever reason she married a forty-year-old man, it was not for money,* he thought. *My smallest gifts please her most.*

Anne placed the flowers in the tiny vase of the tussie mussie on her lapel and sniffed it as they strolled along the harbor looking at the vessels. "It's so relaxing here by the rushing, sighing waves."

William put his arm around her, and he was transported when she snuggled sleepily into the hollow of his shoulder. They stopped, watching the stars come out, and he stammered of their beauty. But he could not find the words to tell her of his love.

~:~

Anne wished she could hide the itinerary. She wanted to stay in Marseilles. *What might the music and the moonlight on the water bring out, given time? Here, I might make him fall in love with me.*

But that afternoon, Mr. J. kept consulting his watch and calendar, noting it was February 2, 1852.

Why is he hurrying me? He's a man of so few words. Be satisfied with all you have, she scolded herself. *But it's harder since I've had a taste of love.*

Sighing, she made herself smile as she left the lovely inn to find out what a diligence was.

Anne laughed out loud when she saw it. "That cumbrous looking thing is the most peculiar vehicle I ever expected to see. Much less to ride." It was a strange sort of stagecoach pulled by horses three abreast, and she wondered about its safety. Summoning courage, she joked. "I s'pose if Hannibal crossed the Alps with elephants, we can make it."

They waited as six people got into the interior section. Then a peasant family with a crate of chickens crowded through a door at the back into another division. Anne clenched her teeth when she saw they were to climb into the glass-windowed coupé at the front. Atop all of this at great elevation was a hooded observation seat for driver, luggage, and guard.

By the time all were loaded, Anne felt tired, cross about leaving, and a bit apprehensive. She glared at Mr. Johnston when he snapped open his watch, telling her to write in her journal that it was seven in the evening when they pulled onto the road for Nice.

The night was bright, but they could see little, and Anne was disappointed.

Throughout the long night, they stopped at relays where drivers and horses changed. Four, five, and even six horses were needed in ascending the mountains.

Morning came. Anne awoke and gasped at the views from their high, rocky perch. Turns in the road gave exquisite sea vistas peeping between high Alps. As they wound around the mountainsides, Anne had a sensation that the diligence might tumble over the cliff if she leaned too far toward a window. She clutched Mr. J's hand and shrieked each time the huge vehicle teetered near the edge of terrible steep.

He laughed. "Close your eyes."

"I can't. I must see everything. It's so colorful."

The diligence passed through villages where women wearing bright dresses and large straw hats with tall square tops worked beneath silvery-leafed olive trees. With mounting pleasure, Anne noticed cactus aloes and umbrella pines, and as they progressed, roses and geraniums and orange trees laden with rich bright fruit.

As they climbed and descended with the road overhanging the sea, Anne tensed with the fear of falling. She looked at her husband, dignified, calm. But she sensed that something was driving him. She felt that their relationship was as precipitous as their pathway. They were passing a time when she must tell him how she loved him, but she swayed with the vehicle—away from him. He might think her too young and foolish.

When they had made the crossing and reached a village where the street was so narrow that the people had to step into the doorways for the diligence to squeeze through, all she could say was, "Notice the difference on this side of the mountain. The peasant women's hats have small, pointed crowns."

At least I could let him know what joy I'm finding in all he's showing me. "Oh, Mr. J., everything's in strong contrast to cold, fashionable but delightful Paris. It's difficult to imagine a country more favored by nature than the south of France. When we get to the hotel at Nice, I must write and describe it to Brother Phil!"

Anne entertained a mischievous thought of hiding the aggravating itinerary. She had not wanted to leave lazy, lovely Nice, and as the diligence made its way through the small kingdom of Monaco and on through the Italian Riviera, she declared each area more breathtaking than the last, longing to linger. It was all too beautiful to be cross, but she had to bite her tongue to keep from snapping about the nerve-wracking sound of Mr. Johnston jiggling his watch chain.

Anne hated to be hurried, but at least they stayed awhile in Genoa, walking on streets too perpendicular for carriages, trying not to stare at ladies veiled in white muslin being carried in sedan chairs.

As they viewed marble palaces and lovely villas, Anne began to look more at Mr. J. because he seemed seized by a rising excitement. He was studying the architecture. Here was a marked difference, a style they had never encountered.

"Do you see those slender columns and open woodwork?"

"Yes, Isn't that lovely? Delicate. Airy, and graceful."

"How would you like that in our house?"

Anne nodded, wondrously.

In a gallery they stopped before a painting, smiling agreement. He had it shipped home.

Walking back to their hotel, a former palace, they talked so excitedly about their acquisition that they scarcely noticed it was raining.

But torrents of rain fell for days. Fearing roads might be dangerous or impassable; Mr. J. insisted they continue by steamboat. Anne consented reluctantly.

Rough seas rendered her as sick as she had been on the ocean. When they reached San Marco, she fell into a bed that still seemed to move. She was obliged to stay there all day. Even on the following morning, she arose feeling green. The motion sickness was relived. Why did she continue with this never-before-experienced queasiness?

"Florence! I cannot believe I am standing in the Piazza del Granduca," Anne exclaimed. "I feel as if we, ourselves, have traveled through the Middle Ages into the brilliance of the Renaissance!" She clasped her hands to her heart and then flung them wide. "Who would ever have thought as I studied the rebirth of art and literature that I would actually be in its cradle, gazing at a statue by Michelangelo?"

Sensing stillness in Mr. J., she bit her lip. *Here I go, flaunting my education again. Have I hurt his feelings?* Tensely, she turned.

His whole body seemed aglow from his smile. His beard quivered as he spoke. "This is why—well, one reason—I asked you to marry me. Only a woman of your sensitivity and intelligence could appreciate what I wanted to bestow. This is why I've been rushing . . . . I wanted to give you Florence as a Valentine."

"Florence—as a Valentine?" Tears flowed. "I can never ask for more." She lifted loving fingertips to caress his cheek. Emotions, which had sparked in France, flamed. *How could I not love such a man?*

Bursting with joy, Anne realized they were melding into one mind. No longer worrying, she unashamedly bared her ardor, teaching him how to enjoy each treasure as they moved through the wonder that was Florence. Standing close together, they conveyed feelings in murmurs and half-thoughts as they viewed the Venus de Medici in the Uffizi Palace and Michelangelo's altar in the

Duomo. Gazing at the Baptistery, with Ghiberti's gates of bronze, Anne felt safe to tell her admiring husband that, Michelangelo, born a century after the artist, had declared them as being worthy of the gates of Paradise.

"I wonder if I'll ever feel lifted nearer Heaven?" she whispered. "How can I thank you for bringing me?"

Day by day, their rapture remained. In the Pitti Palace viewing Raphael's "Madonna of the Chair," who held one chubby boy while another stood at her knee, Anne had a rush of memory of her own mother, Little Edward, and Phil. Tears filled her throat.

"You will make just as beautiful a mother," her dear one whispered against her ear.

Anne's tears spilled over. What had he noticed? Was there a change in her? She was crying so easily these days. Until this moment, she had not thought about the sore breasts, the morning sickness. She was afraid to guess. *Oh, could it really be?*

Too emotional for more of the gallery, she asked to go outside.

In the Boboli gardens strolling embowered walks, Anne loved him for being aware of her mood. All was quiet. There were no flowers here, only pungent evergreens, rich-textured shrubs that screened the paths, making private gardens. There was no one to see them walking in each others arms except ancient statues, which were so romantic they made her blush. With the bright greenness of the foliage secluding them, they sat on a sunny bench beside the lake, watching the flash of goldfish at play.

At last Mr. J. broke their silent bliss. "It's time to plan our home. You like the columns of Greek Revival, but they're massive and somewhat forbidding. What would you say—since Italy has awakened our fervor—to our home being an Italian Renaissance Revival palazzo?"

"I would say, Mr. J., that you are too wonderful for words! Yes—with lots of arches, and, oh, we must have a marvelous Etruscan dome."

Excited by her enthusiasm, he quickened. "I see our house as being a turning point. Not only in architecture and taste. In politics as well."

"How so?"

"Well, even though there are more millionaires in the South than the North, the Yankees and English visitors disparage the simplicity of the homes. I mean to build something so architecturally significant that it will symbolize the South's determination to establish a nationality equal to, if not superior to, that of the North."

Anne was astonished at his rising confidence.

With satisfaction, he finished strongly, "I have the means to do it. If this plan suits you, you have only to select the materials, the furnishings, and the art. When we get to Rome, I'll hire Italian artisans to send home to do the work. And oh, yes, we must have some of this white Carrara marble for the mantelpieces."

"With all of the marble quarried right around us in Georgia?"

"Of course, for you it must always be the best!"

For me? His words climaxed all she could wish for.

Leaving the gardens slowly, reluctantly, they paused beneath a rose-covered arbor. He gathered her in his arms with new self-assurance. Responding with all of her being, she lifted her lips. He kissed her as he had never done before, rendering her breathless.

Their excitement remained around them like a haze, and Anne dreaded the day to say farewell to Florence. She asked to return to the Church of Santa Croce. As she gazed at Michelangelo's elaborate tomb and the statues of Painting, Sculpture, and Architecture that sat upon it as his despairing mourners, she whispered, "I feel a mourner, too, to leave here."

They moved past the tombs of Galileo and Machiavelli. "So much of genius in one place," she said. "And, see, there is even a splendid tomb to Dante's memory though 'he sleeps afar' at Ravenna."

Bells began pealing. "I wish I could say I had them created for your particular pleasure," Mr. J. said, lips against her hair.

They hurried into the gardens to experience the fullest vibration. Standing beneath dark cypresses, Anne felt the air was filled with sound.

The chiming ceased, and they waited in a long moment of intense silence before she became aware of the pungency of pink geraniums. Then, softly at first but gently swelling, drifting out from the cloister came the sweet singing of the nuns. Rich, beautiful, the effect was spontaneous and moving.

Anne's eyes starred with tears. "Oh, my dear husband, as long as I live, I will never forget this moment in 'Firenze la Bella!'"

⋋⁚⋌

Anne laughed that the postilion drove the diligence by riding one of the eight horses as they left Siena, but when he added two white, long-horned oxen to ascend the steeps guarding Rome, she watched out the window a bit fearfully.

The odd contraption paused on an elevation in the faint light of the closing day.

Anne gasped at her first glimpse of the city. "The 'Niobe of Nations,'" she exclaimed. "Oh, Mr. J., my feelings are different from any I've had before, the thick rush of associations, the recurrences of days and men long passed."

He signaled the driver. "Let us get out for a better look," he shouted.

Anne stood, gazing down, enchanted. "'Though crownless and childless in her voiceless woe, it is still Rome,'" she quoted. "Oh, I can fancy the shades of heroes around us who have traversed this spot!"

Darkness fell quickly as they crossed the Tiber. At the gate of the city, their passports were examined, but the rifling of baggage, this time, brought an apology.

"Please excuse the delay, Signora," said a black-haired official with snapping eyes. "It seems unforgivable when you have given Italy the gift of your beauty." He kissed her hand and looked her over unabashedly.

Anne's budding ego warmed with the Italian's charm. *Are they even more handsome than the French?* Anne wondered, keeping a smile on her face even though she was tired and the streets looked dark and intimidating without gaslight. Checking in the hotel was slow because everything was filled with crowds come for Carnival.

"Your timing in arriving for special occasions amazes me," she complimented him as she sank gratefully into bed.

Silently she vowed, *I'll never let him know how angry I was at the delays in New York and Liverpool. How could I have thought him careless?*

⌣∴∾

Saturday afternoon, February 21, was cold, and William doubted that Anne would want to go out, but she did not want to miss anything. He felt tired when they left the hotel, but Anne eagerly joined the gaily-dressed people surging into the Corso, the street that became a racecourse during Carnival. William engaged one of the balconies overlooking the street. Seated amidst red and white bunting, they looked down on the most abandoned merrymaking they had ever seen.

I'm glad our tour is nearly over, William thought, leaning back with his eyes closed. *We've been honeymooning for six months. I'm ready to go home. I can't wait to begin our house.*

Anne punched him. "The parade is beginning with people on foot in twelfth-century costumes."

William leaned over the rail as trumpeters and flag bearers passed. Next came oxcarts and carriages filled with men in hooded white gowns, throwing flowers and powdered-sugar candy. Onlookers in the highest windows rained down candy and colorful confetti.

"Look at the group in that balcony," Anne said. "I believe they're trying to whiten each black hat that passes."

William laughed as they let a dusty cloud of sugar candy fall. He agreed, "They haven't missed one yet."

Suddenly the guns from St. Angelo signaled. They turned their attention to French soldiers, who stepped up smartly and cleared the streets.

Then riderless horses, urged on by shouting and by pieces of metal fastened on their backs, ran pell-mell up the street. They stopped at a cloth suspended across the Corso.

65

Laughing, Anne brushed sugar from her dress and gathered up her flowers, declaring, "The horses were the poorest part of the entertainment."

William had had enough. Nervousness had seized him. *When we get home, her family will take her away from me. If I don't declare myself in romantic Italy, I never will. I must plan something special.*

But Anne did not want to miss the fun of watching the uninhibited Italians. They returned to the Corso, filled with revelers determined to improve the few hours left for gaiety before Lent.

At dusk quietness settled. Wax tapers were lit by each person in the vast multitude, illuminating the entire area. The scene was peaceful, inspiring. *Now is the time,* William thought.

But a sudden scrambling made Anne lean over the balcony rail trying to see. "Oh, now the object of each person is to extinguish all the other lights and keep his own burning."

Candles blinked out. In the darkness, moroseness engulfed William. He had let the moment escape him.

Anne felt lost in a sea of ladies veiled in black as she waited for the opening of the Sistine Chapel. The Swiss Guard in their sixteenth-century, orange-and-purple-striped knee-britches entered first. Women were stopped at a railing. Anne strained to see Mr. J., wearing black full dress coat as required, moving with the men penetrating the sanctuary.

The Pope in peaked mitre and flowing robes began the ceremony by sprinkling ashes on the heads of the crimson-gowned cardinals. Anne shuddered at Michelangelo's depiction of writhing masses of humanity, terrified by the Last Judgment. *Discomforting,* she thought.

When she rejoined Mr. J. for a tour of St. Peter's, she said, "I found the Romanists' Ash Wednesday ceremony long and tedious."

"I agree."

But then she saw "The Madonna della Pieta" and clasped her hands over her heart. She gazed at the grieving Mary cradling the crucified Christ on her knees.

"I reaffirm Michelangelo's genius. The marble seems to breathe with Mary's sorrow," Anne whispered. She felt moved with Christ's sacrifice as she looked at the nail prints in His hands and feet. *Eloquent.* She stood until her mind was filled with the Pieta.

She glanced at her husband's rapt expression.

As they left, she could not stop talking of the Pieta. "Did you notice that the folds of Mary's drapery were thin enough in places to be translucent?" she marveled.

"A sculpture in this Carrara marble is something we must have," he exclaimed. "Tomorrow we must begin visiting galleries."

ᘿᘿ

At the galleries William discovered Randolph Rogers, an American sculptor living in Rome, and commissioned him to make them a statue in the pristine Carrara marble. They chose a sketch of "Ruth Gleaning."

As March winds blew in spring, William felt as young and vital as his wife and determined to see all of Rome. Descending into dungeons, creeping through the solemn, awful catacombs, climbing to the roof of St. Peter's, which appeared like a small village with residences for workmen, they spun on an exhausting whirl with never a thought of resting.

The churches and the Christian relics entranced Anne, a piece of the cross; a table said to be the one at which Christ and his disciples ate the Last Supper; the mouth of the well of the woman of Samaria; and the steps, brought from Jerusalem, said to be the ones Christ ascended when taken before Pilate. Anne wanted to see every cathedral.

William, excited by the gilded, marbled palaces, made notes and sketches about columns and cupolas and arches.

When Anne stayed in to write to Phil, Lit, Aunt Carry and Aunt Eddy, William went out to inquire about hiring artisans. Soon they would be going home. Only one thing remained.

ᘿᘿ

Today must be the day, William thought.

The eleventh of March had dawned with the bountiful beauty of spring. In a carriage with a black-eyed Italian boy as guide, they left the city and drove out to Tivoli to see the ancient resort of the Romans. Their driver had decorated the horses with flowers. The heady perfume made William stammer. He pressed his lips together, silent. But the lad kept bursting into song as the road ascended through thick olive groves, then up the mountain slope. William's hands began to sweat as they passed milky-looking waters that gave off the strong odor of sulphur.

At the Corinthian-columned temple of the Sybil, they stood on the edge of the height, looking down at white froths of waterfalls from the Teverone River spilling into the gorge below.

"This is the most beautiful place we've been," Anne said softly as the youth led them down a winding path, by way of the grotto of Neptune, into the beautiful valley.

"Breathtaking," Anne said as they viewed the multiple cataracts interspersed with bright green foliage. "The music of the cascades is serenading us."

William felt emboldened.

The boy opened a lunch basket. In his melodious, Latin voice, he described each item as he spread a checkered cloth and set out a long slender loaf of bread, a carafe, a hunk of cheese, and a melon.

Munching, savoring, they ate their fill.

Then the young man grinned mischievously and said, "You should find the real joy of vacationing in Italy. It is in *far niente*: doing nothing." This proclaimed, he slid his hat over his eyes for a nap.

William saw a blush rise to Anne's cheekbones at the romantic suggestion in the Italian's voice. Seizing her hand, he led her into the meadow of rich grass, bright with wildflowers. Averting her eyes from his, she wandered this way and that, picking a bouquet of daisies and red and yellow poppies. He could not speak, and she seemed unusually quiet.

Anne sat down in the midst of the flowers and threw aside her bonnet, leaning back, drinking in the sun.

William, standing over her, had ceased to breathe. *No setting could ever be more perfect. Now.* Resolutely, he took a slim volume from his pocket. Softly, he began to read.

> *She walks in beauty, like the night*
> *Of cloudless climes and starry skies;*
> *And all that's best of dark and bright*
> *Meet in her aspect and her eyes:*
> *Thus mellow'd to that tender light*
> *Which heaven to gaudy day denies.*

Incredulous, Anne gazed at him. Brown eyes brimming, face glowing, she had never been so beautiful to him.

"He might have been writing about you."

"About me? Even if I were beautiful, Byron died five years before I was born."

"I know. Now. I've been jealous of a dead poet, but listen . . ."

> *One shade the more, one ray the less,*
> *Had half impair'd the nameless grace*
> *Which waves in every raven tress . . .*

Meaningfully, he loosed the pins and stroked her hair as it fell.

"My terrible hair?"

"Your beautiful hair. Your face, 'Where thoughts serenely sweet express/How pure, how dear their dwelling-place.'"

"My darling husband, how could I not love you?"

"Could you love me? Do you? I love you so very much." His words tumbled out, spontaneous, unbidden.

"Really? You do love me? But you've never said . . . not even when we were courting or when you proposed."

"No. How could I? If I'd told you then how much I loved you—how much I wanted you—it might have frightened you. I'm so much older."

"Are you?"

He smiled. "I'd hoped to arrange a match with your father . . . You became an heiress." He ducked his head. "Your family's so much more prominent and cultured than mine. I was afraid you wouldn't believe that I loved you for your own witty, wonderful self. You were like the poem's conclusion.

> *"The smiles that win, the tints that glow,*
> *But tell of days in goodness spent,*
> *A mind at peace with all below,*
> *A heart whose love is innocent!"*

"You don't know the half of it."

"Innocent, yes, but you shut me out in New York."

"I was frightened, homesick. And you seemed to care only for business. No, I hadn't discovered love then. But I fell in love with you in Paris."

He furrowed his brow. "But everyone falls in love in Paris, I'm told."

"No, I didn't think you were in love with me. Then you gave me Florence and now in wonderful Rome, ecstasy! Knowing you do love me, I even feel beautiful. Thank you for the words. We must never again fail to say I love you."

She held out her arms, and he lay beside her amid the flowers.

⌣∴∾

On the fifteenth of March, the vetturino came at seven in the morning with his carriage. At the gate they showed their passports; then they started on the ancient Apian Way.

Looking back, Anne felt sad at leaving Rome. Besides missing the memorable places, she had hoped for a chance to talk with another woman. Perhaps she should have shared her hopes about the baby while they were in the meadow, but it had been too wonderful a time to spoil. She had questions that needed a motherly woman's answers. A shadow crossed their path, and she shivered. She was not superstitious, but she wished they had waited another day, remembering the warning, "Beware the ides of March."

Chapter VI

William snapped the cover of his gold watch and thrust it in his waistcoat pocket. He leaned against the carriage seat, forcing himself to stop consulting it. *What difference does time make? We have twenty-five miles to go. But I don't like the way Anne's mouth keeps turning down and trembling.*

She was pretending to sleep, but he noticed an occasional lift to her lashes followed by a shudder. A chain of hills rose on one side of the unchanging road; on the other lay the Pontine Marshes, flat, moist, unhealthy, an undulating sea of grass.

Is the strange terrain making her feel seasick? Or could it be? William dared not hope. How he wished she would confide in him! He recalled the glorious day in the meadow when he declared his love and discovered that she loved him. *Since then we've grown closer, but somehow she still holds back.*

He looked at Anne, drawn into a knot in the corner of the seat. She gave him her passion when the lamps were blown out, but in daylight she treated him with deference as strangers did. He had to admit that he craved the respect his money brought. *Everyone calls me "Mr. Johnston." Fine. But I wish I had just one friend who called me William.*

At last the carriage stopped on a promontory overlooking the Bay of Naples.

Anne bounced down, not letting him aid her. Stretching her lovely arms toward the sea, she exclaimed, "Oh, it was worth it! Enduring the ride was worth this reward. How I wish I could paint!" She made large, imaginary brush strokes. "White sails of ships against the deep blue sea. Red roofs of Naples lounging along the curve of the bay. And Mount Vesuvius adding drama with the dark cloud steaming from its crater."

William did not like the looks of the volcano. He shifted uneasily, frowning at the smoke. "Are you sure you want to stay here? I know it's been thirty years since Vesuvius last erupted, but . . ."

"Yes, I do." The tired droop of her face lifted. "Don't change your mind. I must see the dead city of Pompeii."

Anne's perpetual merriment bubbled up. Laughing, she pointed to a group of women spinning in the open air while children ran about and men stretched on their backs soaking up the sun. "Be like the Italian lazzoroui," she said. "Have no fear."

⋘∴∾

The ground was smoking. As the tour group edged toward the fabled entrance to hell, William took Anne's arm. He meant to help her over the rough lava whether she liked it or not. She had consented to only the briefest rest before they began visiting ruins of Roman summer villas and temples. He was worried. Her color was too high. The eerie place made the hair stand on the back of his neck.

"I can see why ancient people believed this is the entrance to hell," William said. "I'd not be much surprised to see flames bursting out. Maybe a devil or two."

The tour director explained the Greek mythology. "Hades was the god of the dead," he said, "and also the name of their abode. Dead were ferried across the river by the boatman, Charon, to where Hades ruled with his wife Persephone. The Greeks so feared Hades that they later renamed him Pluto, 'giver of wealth,' and said he controlled the precious minerals hidden in the earth."

Anne flashed an impish grin at William and whispered, "You should be interested in Pluto, if he was the god of gold."

William felt his ears redden.

I've had enough of this, he thought. But the guide was herding them through the ruins of the villa where he said Persephone spent spring with her mother. Next came the Elysian Fields, the paradise for those deserving reward. William's interest kindled at the richness of the funeral urns in this burial ground, but the tourists were moving to Nero's villa.

Only Nero's vapor baths remained. They followed a flaming torch into a grotto and down a long, close passage in the rock leading to a fountain of boiling water.

Suddenly Anne sank to her knees

"Annie!" William shouted, leaping forward to catch her.

"The heat is suffocating," she gasped.

Supporting her with one arm, he thrust his hand into his pocket and pulled out a coin for the guide.

"Get us to the nearest inn. Quickly!"

The innkeeper and his wife stood beside their table clucking concern as William held a wineglass to Anne's lips, making her sip until her color returned. When she waved off the wine, they brought out oysters. Bowing, they declared, "Excellenti!"

Anne ate a few and proclaimed herself fit. "I was just too hot. I'm ready to go on with the group."

Against William's better judgment, they visited the amphitheater at Pozzuri, riding donkeys. Next they toured an establishment where sulphur was being made. William feared Anne would become ill again at an oval crater where a hot, vile-smelling stream oozed.

He was relieved when they reached the last stop, Virgil's tomb. Anne insisted on climbing the toilsome steep.

"And now, young lady, you have done enough," he said. "Tomorrow we will rest."

She nodded. "I'll sit and feast my eyes on lovely Naples. Maybe visit one museum? But Mr. J.," she said with a jaunty air, "the next day I want to climb Vesuvius."

Mounted on ponies, they rode up the winding way over lava

and ashes to the foot of the volcano. The small animals scrambled up the rocky way with ease, sure-footed even beneath William's weight. He realized it was increasing as, daily, he consumed macaroni freshly made at the local factory, but all of this exercise made him hungry. *I wish I had some now. And that wonderful cheese!*

At the base of the cone, they dismounted. William noticed that the plump, red-haired woman, who had introduced herself as Mrs. Boyd, was getting into a chair. He reached for his money.

Anne tugged his sleeve and shook her head. "I prefer walking to being carried over such dangerous ground."

But walking was fatiguing with their feet sinking into ashes or striking rough lava. As the way got steeper, they struggled to hold the strap of the guide who pulled them along. Before they reached the crater, some women had two helpers pulling and two pushing from behind. *But not my Annie*, William thought proudly, grinning at his sprightly wife.

At the top, their feet were in snow. Awed, they stood looking into the immense, smoky opening. There had been no flames seen since two years ago, in 1850, but sulphuric smoke drove them back.

As they sat eating a picnic lunch, Anne made the acquaintance of the Boyds, asking eagerly about their native Scotland. William was curt, fearing they would get involved. He wanted no one. He was making plans for the evening.

He was glad when it was time to leave. They had an easy slide back down on snow.

⋌∶∾

That evening William ordered a special supper served on a balcony overlooking the half-moon bay. Tired yet content, they watched the sunset. Then in the softly falling evening, he suggested a stroll along the water's edge.

Hopefully, William slipped his arm around her waist. Anne nestled her head against his shoulder. Looking up at him, she opened her mouth as if to speak, then merely stoked his beard.

"What?"

"Oh, nothing. It's . . . Isn't the city a lovely sight in the moonlight?"

"Yes."

He thought her face, radiant tonight, as pretty as any painting they had seen. He wanted to tell her, but, lacking Byron's help, he still could not speak the poetic words.

"It's the twenty-fifth of March," he said instead. "After we see Pompeii, let's return to Rome for Easter."

"That would be nice," Anne murmured. "Do you s'pose we might run into the Hardenburgs again?"

"I didn't think you liked her. She was such a gossip."

"Well, sometimes it's nice to have another more knowledgeable woman to talk with."

William waited, hoping for a confidence, but she said no more.

⌣∴∽

Two red spots shone in Anne's pale cheeks. William had heard her retching after breakfast.

"Naples is unbearably hot," he said. "Let's go back to Rome now."

"Oh, no, I must see the museums here. They say there's even food preserved on plates unearthed from the cities buried by the first recorded eruption of Vesuvius in 79 A.D."

But after visiting the museums, Anne was all the more eager to visit the sites. "On to Pompeii."

William heaved a sigh. "My dear Anne, don't tire yourself. Let this be enough."

"No," she cried out. "Time is stopped there as life was a few short years after Jesus walked the earth. It's a perfect link between past and present. Please!"

"Very well," he replied, knowing she would never give up.

⌣∴∽

At Pompeii, William watched Anne with worry because she ran about the excavated streets like an overexcited child, pointing out wheel marks plainly seen in the pavement. Heat was intense, and he followed, wiping perspiration with his handkerchief. As they viewed theatres, temples, and public buildings, Anne exclaimed over mosaic paving and the brightness of painted walls.

Then they stepped into a private home, and William felt pleasantly cool. His interest quickened. Taking out paper and pencil, he made notes of the architecture and the ways these ancient people had controlled the heat. Suddenly Macon was calling him.

William's plans formed quickly. *I'll ship our paintings home. Probably be best to store the furniture we've bought.*

He made notes about arrangements for workmen. He was ready to build his house. Anne was examining every detail. William smiled at her, thinking her zest for life would never flag. But he had thought of a bribe. *I'll buy tickets for the San Carlo Opera House, and then we'll backtrack toward home.*

⚜

Anne's happiness overshadowed her apprehension, but she wished she could have spoken with that sweet, motherly Mrs. Boyd they met in Naples. She needed to ask about her symptoms, especially the pain.

But when the diligence neared St. Peter's, Anne forgot her worry, seeing Rome abloom with spring.

On April fourth, Palm Sunday, they rose early to attend the ceremonies. Anne wanted to see the pope blessing the palms.

I can't understand why Mr. J. keeps fussing about the press of the crowd and watching me, she thought. *I haven't told him about my suspicions.*

On Wednesday, Mr. J. insisted that she sleep late, and when they reached the Sistine Chapel, there were no seats left. Standing near a red curtain, which made the room still warmer, Anne swooned. She left the Chapel, seeking air.

Nevertheless, saying she would never pass this way again, Anne ignored the pains. She felt driven to return on Thursday, hoping to witness the washing of feet. She was caught in a frightful rush of women squeezed into a small space.

On Easter Sunday they breakfasted early, but even though they reached the cathedral at eight, all seats were taken; they stood for the ceremony. At noon, they walked to the Piazza for the benediction and pealing of the bells.

That evening they returned for the grand illumination. Dizzily, Anne looked ever higher at lamps being lit, defining rows of windows. "I can see the men climbing the cupola," she said. "They look tiny as ants."

"I heard that the man lighting the ball is in such danger that he receives absolution from the pope," Mr. J. replied.

The mighty cathedral seemed to burst into flame.

"Ahhh! What a splendid sight," Anne gasped.

And then she fainted.

Chapter VII

Anne's eyelids refused to open. Struggling against the heaviness, she stirred, felt soft beard, smelt bay rum. Her dear husband's arms tightened around her, and she relaxed into the blessedness of his commanding presence.

When her darkness gradually lightened, she felt a bed beneath her, heard voices speaking in strange accents. Pondering hazily, she wondered. Could that Scottish burr be Mrs. Boyd? A smile twitched her lips. She opened her eyes.

"Aye, now, and if it isn't time you were joining us," said Mrs. Boyd, whose freckled face was as bright as her red hair.

The doctor stepped up and put the wooden rod of his stethoscope against Anne's chest, listening, smiling. He was so handsome that it embarrassed her as he poked, prodded, and questioned half in English, half in Italian. But all was forgotten with the joyous diagnosis. She would have a baby by summer's end.

The doctor left to consult with Mr. Johnston, and Mrs. Boyd spoke softly, "Did not you know about the wee bairn?"

Anne shook her head. "I suspected. Hoped. I tried to get a private word with you in Naples. You see my mother . . ."

Her voice trailed off as Mr. J. bounded into the room. Mrs. Boyd slipped away.

"Annie, Annie," he exclaimed, gathering her in his arms. "Are you all right? I would've been taking better care of you if only you'd told me."

"It was too good to risk spoiling. What if I'd guessed wrong? I had to be sure before I told you such wonderful news."

Folding her hands in his, he kissed each finger. He did not say he was happy, but he was beaming so foolishly that she knew.

"You must stay in bed until you feel fit. Then we'll begin our journey home."

◈

As they rode through the streets of Rome on the morning of April 15, 1852, glorious sunshine beamed warmly on their shoulders, inspiring their carriage driver to begin singing an aria at the top of his voice. Anne looked back, thinking that she might have felt sad at seeing the ancient city for the last time if she had not been basking in bliss.

Their Scottish friends were accompanying them on the trip north, and the good-natured Mr. Boyd kept them laughing as they rode over hills and down into meadows alight with poppies.

They made a leisurely journey. Comforting Mrs. Boyd mothered her, insisting they stop frequently to walk or rest, to eat or spend a night.

"I'm fine," Anne protested. "I'm delaying you."

"Nonsense. The cool lake country is the part of Italy I love the best. Cities are alike, world over. Aye, but each village is unique. The real Italy."

They all agreed. Relaxing, Anne savored every moment, sniffing pine-scented air, gathering wild flowers as she strolled along the rough but romantic road where brilliant colors beckoned her further with each step. At the falls of Serni, she reveled in the cascading water and the unspoiled wilderness, thinking in silent joy, *my baby is forming in beauty*.

Assisi enchanted Anne. The town and cathedral, high on a mountain slope, built of pink stones and tile rooftops in soft beige colors, made her exclaim, "It's like a pink cloud in the summer evening sky!"

She insisted that they visit the crypt of St. Francis, only recently discovered in 1818.

"Just wait until you see Florence from this road," Mr. Boyd

said with heavily burred R's. "It's one of the prettiest views in all of Italy because yon mountain ascends directly. Florence is seen close at hand."

Anne leaned from the window, watching as they approached at four in the afternoon of April twentieth. The cypress trees grew so tall and lovely as the road wound and twisted up the steep slopes that the landscape seemed almost as if it had been planted as a park.

Suddenly Anne exclaimed with delight, "Oh, everyone, look, look down in the plain!" She pointed at the gleaming domes and spires rising on both sides of the blue Arno River. "Florence has never impressed me so pleasantly as now gilt 'round by the hills in the brightness of spring flowers. How lovely the villas are, mantled green with grape vines and olive groves!"

Smiling at her enthusiasm, the driver stopped and they all got out while he plucked some of the roses that hedged the white-pebbled road.

Accepting the bouquet with a gracious curtsy, Anne breathed the heady fragrance. She broke off with a gasp. Laughing, she placed a loving hand on her side at the now unmistakable kick of a tiny foot.

"My dear Annie, you must rest tomorrow. I'm assured the Hotel de York is quite comfortable . . ."

"But, Mr. J., I want to see my old friends all again, the Duomo, the Uffizi, and especially the Baptistery. I want to spend time looking at the Old Testament stories in those beautiful bronze doors. There are so many wonderful things in Florence that to hurry my last look seems a sacrilege . . . Very well," she agreed when he frowned. "Tomorrow I shall rest and sun myself in the Boboli Garden."

On April 22, without warning, Anne collapsed.

Screaming, fearing she was sinking into the waters at the edge of Hades, Anne flailed her arms, struggling to swim to shore. But the ground was smoking.

"Hush, hush," Mr. J. whispered with his lips against her hair. "Wake up, my little Annie. It's all right."

"The baby?"

"Fine. You were having labor-like pains. The doctor gave you laudanum."

She groaned, pressing her temples. "No more. I hate the opium dreams."

"You must take it, Signora Johnston."

She tried to focus her eyes on the doctor. He was not smiling.

"You must take it," he repeated, "to stop the progression of the pains. We will keep you in bed with your feet elevated above your head."

"For how long?"

"As long as it takes."

"I'll rent one of those villas you were admiring," Mr. J. consoled her. "You'll find it pleasant up among the cypress and pines."

Pressing her lips together, she nodded, knowing she could endure if only the baby would wait.

The little villa was perched on a terraced hillside covered with olive trees. When Anne saw the tall house, built of enormous apricot-colored stones, she told her husband, "We have a home sooner than we expected."

She walked though the rooms, liking the bare whitewashed walls and cool terra-cotta floors. The Tuscan sunlight sent golden shafts through every window, but she needed the soothing warmth upon her. She found it on the wrought-iron balcony.

"Sit yourself here, dearie," said Mrs. Boyd. "The Italian sun is 'specially healing. Aye, now. Put your feet up. I'll attend to everything."

Throughout lovely spring days, Anne sat looking down upon

the orchard of fruit and nut trees, reading, resting, and talking with Mrs. Boyd of her longing for children. The men discussed business. Evenings, Mr. Boyd entertained with stories of kilts and clans and brawny heroes.

At night Anne lay in her husband's arms, feeling a warmth of touch and completeness as the passion that had fired them in Paris and in Rome settled into a closer, more binding love. Anne whispered plans for the baby. She listened, smiling as her beloved talked on about the house—the palazzo—he would build for her.

They hired an Italian cook whose food had mouth-watering aromas from the sun-warmed herbs in the garden. They sipped soup made with borage, mallow, dill, fennel, citronella, and leeks, and exclaimed over boned quail stuffed with summer truffles. But when the woman tried to cook an American dish, they had to be careful not to let her hear them laugh as they figured out the pieces of her wildly chopped fried chicken.

Sometimes Anne's pains went away. Strolling in the garden rampant with roses, she kept one hand holding up the baby. On other days, the heaviness threatened that it would surely come now, too soon. She stayed in bed with pillows beneath her feet, head reeling from the laudanum.

Then, with the advent of June, the Boyds returned to Scotland. For the first time, Anne cried. Mr. J. turned away and hurried out of the house. *He's disgusted with me,* she thought.

He came back carrying a large painting. "To remember Florence," he said gruffly. He hung a harbor scene beside her. It was signed Geo. Signiorini F. Firenze, 1852. "Now at least you can get out of bed in your imagination."

"You're so thoughtful," Anne said. "I can walk off into it. It's peaceful yet filled with activity."

ᴗ:ᴖ

By July Anne's premature pains had subsided. William felt he must chance moving her.

"I want you to have the best doctors money can buy," he said. "Do you think you can make a careful journey to Paris?"

"Look at me," Anne joked. "How can I go to Paris when I'm too fat to wear the fashions?"

William's indigestion burned so hotly he feared he might have a heart attack before he could get Anne safely back in the Hotel Meurice. He requested a room where she could see the gardens of the Tuileries. They settled down to wait.

Nervously he watched Anne, busy making tiny garments. He felt hurt that she kept wishing for her stepmother and the other Aunts to sit and sew. *I need no one but her.*

On their wedding anniversary, August 2, 1852, wanting to fill her heart as she filled his, he went to the flower market. He returned, followed by a line of twelve servants, each bringing a bouquet brighter and more fragrant than the last. Only when Anne was surrounded by blossoms did he present a huge beribboned box.

"Oh! I couldn't get out to buy you a gift," she lamented as she drew out a pair of huge Sèvres porcelain vases. She smiled up at him, thanking him profusely.

But he could tell she preferred the flowers.

As days passed, he watched her with increasing concern. She was hot, uncomfortable, yet uncomplaining. On August twenty-first, her twenty-third birthday, he brought her a Worth ball gown of her favorite bright rose pink.

"Soon you'll be slender again, and I'll take you dancing."

Two days later she went into labor.

Frantically, he paced. Hours passed. Nurses bustled in and out carrying bloody bundles they tried not to let him see.

At last they opened the door. Anne's face was all he beheld, stark white with dark sunken holes for eyes. But she smiled.

He rushed to her side, and she turned back a bit of lace from a tiny, puckered face.

"Your daughter," she whispered hoarsely. "Frances Campbell Johnston."

Filled with wonder, he lifted the fragile creature in trembling arms. Even lacking experience, he recognized a frightening rattle as she tried to breathe.

William silently sought the doctor's eyes, not wanting to alarm Anne, but she had fainted.

"Your wife has lost much blood," the doctor told him. "The child, oui, she has the difficulty breathing. We will do our best."

The heat of the August day kept sweat trickling through his beard. Dirty, disheveled, he waited, pounding his fist, pacing, brushing back tears.

Anne wavered in and out of consciousness. Knowing nothing of childbirth, she did not realize anything was wrong. They brought the baby to nurse, then took her away.

Before midnight, their little girl had died.

A week later, Anne hemorrhaged again. Milk fever raged.

Two months passed. Still, she was too infirm to rise from the bed unaided. Plunged in despair, she refused food even though he ordered it from the best restaurants in Paris.

"I want to go home," she wept.

"Eat. Get strong. We'll go as soon as the doctor says you can stand the voyage. Get well, and I'll build you a fairy palace."

Hollow-faced, she stared through glassy eyes.

Heart wrenching, William knew that all of the money by which he set such store could not buy the one thing she wanted most.

"Get well," he repeated huskily, "and we'll try to have another child."

Turning lest he shame himself by crying, he went out to wander through the falling leaves.

Daily, Anne sent him to Greene Company Bankers who received their mail. None came for her, and William hated to return empty handed. She wept bitterly, storming that her family had forgotten her—that they did not care about her grief. It hurt him most to hear her crying for her mother.

William sought diverting books. She dutifully read *Childe Harold* but told him that Byron's mood of disillusionment and melancholy only deepened her depression.

Thinking to stir her to life by firing her temper, he brought *Uncle Tom's Cabin,* which was inflaming the North against slavery.

Anne only sighed. "With Daniel Webster's recent death, Mrs. Stowe's novel might very well bring on war between the North and South. We should be at home, but I'll never be able to cross that hateful ocean."

She buried her face in the pillows, shutting him out.

William stood by the window, snapping and unsnapping his watchcase. He stared unseeingly at the palace garden. Had he lost his wife as well as his daughter? Was his vivacious Annie gone? Could he ever find her again?

Chapter VIII

Laughter rattled in Anne's tight throat, an unaccustomed sound. Reclining on a chaise lounge, she wrapped the satin comforter tightly around her against the November cold and dumped the contents of the packet onto her lap. For months she had lain in the hotel room with milk fever in her breasts making her too weak to walk, feeling utterly alone in her grief, forsaken by her family. She had received no word of consolation from them, and she could not understand why they had not written; then, today, the longed-for letters had arrived all at once.

Mr. Johnston had handed her the thick package and slammed the door behind him. They were strangers again, shutting out all emotion.

Anne stood the letters in the folds of the coverlet, greeting each as if they were family members come to visit. Flourishing handwriting caught her eye. That would be Phil's sassy humor. She read his first, giggling at Phil's irreverent description of the costumes worn to a masquerade ball held at the Lanier House. *I wish I could have been there with my friends! Home. Dear, ordinary, comfortable things.*

In the next one, Phil wrote of preparations for the State Fair always held in Macon. She glanced at the postmark. This letter had been mailed the very day her baby had been born. *Darling brother Phil was thinking of me.*

How she missed him! She loved him as if he were her child.

She remembered how Aunt Carry had laughed at her when Phil began growing up, saying, "Anne has more trouble cutting the apron strings than I do."

Before tears could overtake her, she picked up another, more recent letter from Phil. He had won the office of Judge of the Court of Probate, beating his opponent, Robert Lanier. *I wish I could have voted for him, but I feel sorry for little Sidney's father.*

Phil scolded her for accusing them of forgetting her. "If you haven't received our epistles," he wrote, "ascribe it to the Postmaster General or Louis Napoleon."

A fat envelope contained separate correspondence from two of her mother's sisters. Aunt Eddy consoled her continuing illness after losing the baby and advised taking Port wine and crackers to regain her health.

Aunt Carry insisted upon four ounces of red carbonate of iron mixed with a quart of wine and taken by tablespoonful. "If only I had the wealth to come to you and nurse you, I could make you well."

Hot tears splotched the page. *I want my family. It's awful being sick among strangers. I need to talk about the baby.* But Mr. Johnston would not let her. She knew he was disgusted with her depression. She had never seen him cry. Knuckling her eyes, she opened Aunt Berry's letter, which directed her to First Peter 1:7-8—

> *That the trial of your faith, being much more precious than gold that perisheth, though it be tried with fire might be found unto praise and honor and glory . . . with joy unspeakable and full of glory.*

Anne flung the puzzling words away. *Is she saying I'm being tried by fire? I don't believe it was God's will for my little girl to die. It was my fault riding those donkeys and climbing Vesuvius and . . . Does she mean I'm not building my life on God? Does He care?*

She threw back the comforter, scattering pages of advice on the floor. She had to get up, move, but when she tried to stand, the bottoms of her feet prickled, and her head felt as if her blood was reaching no farther than the bottom of her eyes. Wavering for a moment, she took a faltering step to a gilded chest. With difficulty, she tugged at a drawer.

The tiny clothes lay pressed, still waiting. One by one she held the lacy garments to her cheek. *I won't be satisfied until I have another baby. Then it will be as if little Frances were wearing her clothes.*

Anne closed the drawer lest Mr. Johnston catch her. She stumbled back to gather up the precious papers. Sinking to the floor, she stacked them; then her knees were too weak to lift her. Shivering on the cold floor, she read the words from each family member. Most of them recommended Scripture to strengthen her. All conveyed sympathy to Mr. Johnston in his sorrow and thanked him for his tender care of her.

Humph! All he cares about is that I've interrupted his itinerary.

Aunt Queeny's message was clear, and it went straight to her soul:

> We love you, but remember God cares. You wrote of "The Madonna della Pieta," but Jesus Christ died—not just for the world's sins—but personally for your sin and mine. He arose to comfort and commission his followers in person. When he ascended, he sent the Holy Spirit to dwell within us always near. The hairs of your head are numbered. We need only to repent and accept him as Saviour. Claim James 4:8. "Draw nigh to God, and he will draw nigh to you."

Anne held her breath, waiting to absorb this until she read the last, Caroline Matilda's, note. Her half-sister had written a silly thing to make her laugh. She found another from the child, apologizing, rendering Romans 8:28. "And we know that all things work together for good to them that love God, to them who are called according to his purpose."

Oh, but how? God, how can this be good?

Anne bowed her head against the chaise, opening her hurting heart. *Dear Lord, I've worshiped you as creator without realizing you care personally about me. I have shut you out just when I needed you most.*

Anne poured out her misery. Claiming all of the promises of the Bible, she no longer felt alone. Her prayers brought peace.

She was still on the floor when the door opened. Mr. Johnston ran, heavy-footed, to kneel beside her.

Anne smiled at him with vision washed clear. Tears glistened in his eyes, welled up, held back. *How could I have thought he didn't want a child? Now I can see his heartbreak.*

"Oh, my darling husband," she said, stroking his beard with soothing hands. "My family made me see that God cares about us personally and wants us to call upon Him for comfort in our sorrow. He will give us rest. All of them . . ." she waved her hand over the letters, ". . . said to thank Mr. Johnston for his tender care of me."

He murmured a choked protest. She kissed him. "Darling, I do thank you. You've been wonderful. I know now. It's not my grief. It's your grief, too. But God will see us through. My little sister's wisdom recalled that 'all things work together for good to them that love God.'"

"How could it be good for our child to die?" he retorted bitterly.

"Not for us maybe. But for the child. Not to live and suffer the struggle to breathe. Nobody is to be blamed. Not me. Not you. Not God." Suddenly she felt calm and very wise. "I don't know how it can be good. Our approach must be to search for the good that might come out of it. Together, we can search."

He buried his face in her neck, wetting it with his tears. "Oh, Annie, Annie."

Feeling the older now, she whispered, "Our blessings far outnumber our disappointments. It takes both to build a lasting work. We can stand firm if we're fortified by faith in God."

Mr. J. lifted her and sat in a big chair, holding her on his lap. For a long time they clung to each other. Then he agreed hoarsely, "I'll try to have your faith. We'll do the best we can."

Physical weakness remained, but Anne's spirits rose, and her interest in life returned. Often, she sat by the window looking out upon the comings and goings at the Tuileries. One rainy afternoon when she threatened to sink in despair, she imagined the beautiful hangings of Gobelin tapestry in the palace. *Right now I'm seeing knots and twisted threads and dark colors of sorrow, but Aunt Berry's right. God knows the design He'll make of my life if I'll let Him.* Even though she had not sought Him, He had reached down to her through her family. She took time again to be thankful.

Excitement seized Paris. Daily Anne sat upon the balcony, swathed in shawls and quilts. With lightening spirits, she watched fancifully plumed horses carrying notables to the palace. The streets rang with shouts of "Vive l'Empereur!" She wished she could go out because the city was alive with activity, but Mr. J. kept her abreast of the news as first the Senate and then the people voted to establish the Second Empire.

Louis Napoleon chose the second of December, the anniversary of his coup d'état and also of Napoleon I's coronation, to sign the decree and become Emperor Napoleon III. On January 12, 1853, he was to entertain with a ball.

Anne reflected upon all that had happened to her since last year's ball. *I arrived in Europe an innocent, frightened girl longing to see Paris. I fell in love, found passion, suffering, despair. Now I am a woman, and I have found God.*

But I must keep a young heart. I shall wear my new pink dress and attend this party, she thought, *even if it's only for a moment.*

When she broached the subject, the doctor went into a Gallic tirade. Anne held firm.

Anne sat surrounded by poufs of rose pink silk, having second thoughts. The exertion of putting on the ball gown had drenched her in perspiration. The French maid was long dressing her hair, and she was already tired.

But I must prove to myself that I can, that I may be down, but I'm not defeated.

Mr. J. engaged a carriage even though the short distance could have been walked more easily in the immense crowd.

As they stood among the partygoers, Anne tried to decipher the buzz of French around them. She translated for Mr. J. "They say that despite all opposition, Napoleon intends to make Spanish Countess Eugénie de Montijo his Empress."

The music began, and Mr. J. looked at her with concern. "Do you really think you have the strength to dance?"

"One waltz," she said. "Then I'll leave satisfied."

But Anne longed to know what happened after they left, and the next morning, she broke her reserve and gossiped shamelessly with the maids. They told her the Emperor had led the countess and her mother to a table reserved for the imperial family—thus confirming his intentions.

The French girls considered the bride an immoral woman because she allowed male acquaintances to call her by her Christian name, Eugénie, without prefixing a title.

In her faulty French, Anne could not convince them that, while not acceptable in France or England, first names were perfectly proper in Spain. Anne admired the great beauty. The tedium of her confinement was enlivened by the vicarious excitement.

William was worried about being in a foreign country and losing money. He had spent anxious hours at Greene Company Bankers where he had been investing. The Emperor's impending marriage had panicked the Stock Exchange, and railway shares fell by fifteen percent. But William consoled himself his losses were worth it because Anne's enjoyment of the festivities had revived her.

He was pleased at her improved strength as they sat on a balcony looking down upon the press of people waiting for the grand procession to Notre-Dame Cathedral. It was noon on Sunday, January 30, 1853.

Around them floated banners with Napoleonic eagles, Napoleonic bees, and Napoleonic violets with intertwined letters N and E. Anne leaned forward as cavalrymen appeared, mounted on horses adorned with feathers, causing a cheering that soon drowned in a cacophony of bands.

"Look," Anne exclaimed, clapping when she saw the glass and gilt carriage drawn by eight white-plumed bays. "The Emperor is wearing a General's uniform. And, oh, I love the Empress's gown," she said, sighing. "White silk, satin, and velvet. I think that's Alencon lace. Oooh, that diamond crown glittering upon her red hair. Isn't she beautiful?"

William's heart leaped as Anne flushed with color. Then the roaring of a thousand cannon began, followed by chiming.

Anne pressed her hands over hers ears. "The tintinnabulation of every church bell in Paris is splitting my head," she screamed. William carried her to bed.

~:~

Anne longed to go home. She tried to eat the delicacies Mr. J. brought her. She walked amid the flowers as springtime turned to summer, but still the doctors shook their heads over her. She lacked the strength to survive the inevitable seasickness that would accompany the voyage.

It was fall again before she was able to cross the English Channel. With her husband half-carrying her, she stepped out on English soil.

"Sir, you are required to take a smallpox vaccination," the agent greeted them.

"No," Mr. Johnston protested, "My wife is not well enough to risk it."

"Sorry, sir. She must take it or go back to France. A law has just been passed making the vaccination compulsory in Britain."

"I can stand it," Anne said staunchly.

Then they were again in fog-bound Liverpool. Anne watched the threatening waves of the cold gray Atlantic. *What is to become of my life? Can I live to see the sunshine of home?*

Chapter IX

"Home! How wonderful to start 1854 at home," Anne exclaimed. "Oh, Mr. J., in spite of all the marvels we've seen, can anything be more beautiful than springtime in the wooded hills of Georgia?" She felt her excitement mounting by the minute as the train chugged through pine-scented forests with a sparkling white understory of dogwood.

Anne was already standing, and Mr. J. put a steadying arm around her as the locomotive slowed for the Macon depot with a great hissing of steam and shrieking of brakes.

He flipped a jaunty brush of his beard against her cheek. "I have a surprise."

"What?" She cut her eyes at him questioningly, but he was not ready to tell. She was bursting with joy as the train stopped with a jerk.

"Annie! Annie! Annie!" The shout came from three dozen voices.

Anne jumped down into uplifted arms, kissed her brothers and cousins, and moved into the circle of Aunts, who clucked over her.

"Tch-tch-tch," said Aunt Berry. "How thin she is."

"We have our work cut out for us," agreed Aunt Carry.

"Ohh, your Paris hat," exclaimed Aunt Eddy.

Anne grinned, glad Mr. J. had made her buy the frivolous, flower-trimmed bonnet. She wanted him to be proud of the way she looked for her appraisal by her many relatives. Eleven-year old Harriet was peeping at her crinoline, but bright-eyed brunette Caroline Matilda stood back, waiting.

Anne reached for the older girl. "My dear sister, you're not quite fourteen, and yet you've blossomed into a belle!" She kissed her cheek. "You already possess wisdom beyond your years. Your letter helped pull me back into the land of the living."

Edward Dorr Tracy, Jr. lounged by the baggage wagon, watching his sisters with fondness, eager for his turn with Anne. He hoped she would realize he had become his own man while she was gone. He had graduated from the University of Georgia and been admitted to the Georgia Bar. He also thought he'd grown taller than Phil since she left nearly three years ago. His childhood nickname, Lit, still clung to him, but that was all right, too.

It's Annie who's changed, Lit noted. Her gaunt face and black-smudged eyes betrayed her illness and the stain of grief; yet, she showed peace, happiness. She was no longer the gauche young girl, stooping to hide her height. Lit thought she looked stately, elegant in her long velvet traveling coat.

Perhaps, Phil need not have worried about her marriage after all.

Lit looked up to the car's platform where Mr. Johnston still stood. Hand-in-coat, he had tucked his chin into his beard. With a rush of empathy, Lit sensed his new in-law was overwhelmed by the family and feeling alone.

"Uh-oh. Come on, brother," Lit said hooking his arm through Phil's for fortification. As they approached Mr. Johnston, he swung down the train steps.

"Philemon," the rotund gentleman said. "Congratulations on becoming a judge."

Phil, his face grave for once, pumped his hand. "Thanks. And we appreciate your taking such good care of our Annie."

Mr. Johnston frowned and turned to Lit. "You've been admitted to the bar. Congratulations to you, as well, Edward."

"Thank you," Lit said, "Glad to have you back, sir."

"It's a good time for you to get home," said Phil, pushing his glasses up on his nose. "Business is prospering in spite of the political pot boiling. There's been lots of hurrah about consolidating the *Macon and Western* and the *Central Railroad*."

Lit, eager to show his manhood, asserted himself. "Mr. Johnston, you'll be pleased that the *Macon and Western* freight has increased wonderfully since you left," he said. "The track's completed all the way to Nashville, Tennessee. You remember that little railroad junction at Terminus that they started calling Atlanta a few years back? Well, it's growing. Becoming a city to rival Macon."

"You don't say. Well, boys," Mr. Johnston smiled reservedly. "You need not tell Miss Anne, but I can hardly wait to get back to business."

⌣∴∾

William felt better as the group moved to the Tracy home on Georgia Avenue. All of Anne's relatives were friendly, although they treated him with deference; nevertheless, he renewed his vow that he would not let Anne's family take her love from him. Right now he was hungry, ready for the feast the Aunts spread on a long table set down the dogtrot dividing the two wings of the house.

"It won't seem much to you, Mr. Johnston," said Anne's step-mother. "Not after Paris cuisine."

"On the contrary, Miss Carry," William replied sincerely. "Turnip greens, cornbread and salt-cured country ham are a welcome taste of home." *Even more than the fancy cakes and pies,* he thought.

Mealtime was long, but when everyone was satiated to the point of sitting back telling funny childhood stories, William took Anne by the hand.

"Let's walk off the dessert a bit and look at the view," he said, feeling eager to share his surprise.

"Fine," she said brightly. "I haven't had time to greet the ginkgo."

They strolled toward her favorite tree, arrayed in the yellow-green of spring, and gazed across the Ocmulgee. The sky was clear, affording a good view of the old battlement and ruins of Fort Hawkins.

"Remember standing here as strangers a lifetime ago?" William said. "I was so bashful that speaking was painful."

"I was shy, too," she agreed, "but you've given me confidence."

William's heart filled, but he must not falter now, and he hurried to speak. "Your love has changed my life. I can never do enough for you, but I promised if you'd get well, I'd build you a fairy palace." He watched her face, lifted to him, eyes shining, lips parted. His self-assurance strengthened. "I've been making arrangements with your father's heirs. You've been wanting *home*. I've bought this estate. We'll build right here!"

"How wonderful!" Anne touched the fan-shaped leaves. "Then, Papa's tree is mine," she said, sighing with pleasure. "But, oh, what about Aunt Carry?"

"She's satisfied. Quite content with my plans to move the old house back to a quieter street. It belonged to the area's frontier days. Today, Macon's face should reflect sophisticated times. I've bought the entire block to Cherry Street on the back and up to the spring on the northwest corner. It will furnish water for the house, and . . . ." He took her hands to make sure he had her attention.

"I thought we'd hire an expert Landscape Gardener. I envision an open stream flowing diagonally through the gardens. Maybe with an Italian bridge crossing it?"

Anne sparkled. "Beautiful! With that much room, we can have formal parterres to rival those we saw in Italy."

They looked down the slope toward their soon-to-be neighbors on Mulberry Street. Comfortable houses with inviting porches nestled below their site. It was when William looked up, that his brow furrowed. Above them, steeply rising to a lofty plateau, the highest hill in Macon afforded a view of everything. Atop it was a shining white mansion with eighteen towering columns marching across the front and sides of the portico. Its magnificence made William remember temples they had seen in Rome.

I wish I could've bought that land, William thought, *but in 1836 when Jerry Cowles built that house, I didn't have any money.*

Anne was watching him, puzzled. "What's wrong?"

"That's quite a place for a man not yet forty to have acquired," he said with crossness betraying his jealousy.

Anne laughed. "Yes, but Joseph Bond owns cotton plantations all across southwest Georgia. He should live in a classical masterpiece."

"Landed gentry," William muttered. "Well, people will expect me to build a Greek Revival house as well. But I have a few surprises up my sleeve. I'll impress in a different way. Let's keep our plans a secret."

⌣:∾

William was pleased at seeing Anne thrive in the heat and humidity of Macon's summer, but he wiped perspiration, wishing for a moment in Italy's mountains. Anne suggested he relinquish his white shirt, cravat, and black coat, but he felt it undignified and only changed from wool to broadcloth.

The political scene steamed even hotter than the weather. Every time two or more men met, arguments erupted over the threat to Southern Rights roiling in Kansas and Nebraska. William worried because Philemon Tracy's voice was always the loudest. Anne begged him to intervene when Phil talked of going West and joining the fray. They both felt relieved after Georgia's Congressman, Alexander Stephens, became a national hero by affecting a compromise.

William kept his own views to himself, intent upon preparing the site for their home. First came the task of moving the old Tracy homestead. He found workmen who put the dogtrot house onto logs of virgin timber and rolled it back to a new location on Cherry Street at the foot of Nisbet Place.

By then it was August, and the town was filled with refugees. Every train from Savannah brought people fleeing a terrible scourge of yellow fever.

There was fear the epidemic might spread, but Macon remained healthy, and William was able to secure carpenters to make renovations on a cabin at the back of their block of property. As fall crisped the air, he paid men extra to work long hours. He had endured the summer surrounded by Anne's family. They had visited from one Aunt to the other. Each was eager to outdo her sister in pampering him and feeding him corn and butterbeans and peach cobbler from her garden, but he was thankful that soon they could move into their own little home, alone at last.

~:~

Anne's cheeks reddened as she bent over the hearth, poking up the fire. The little, one-story house was drafty, full of cracks; it was hard to keep warm since November's rain had set in. Usually she needed several flannel petticoats and a woolen corset cover, but tonight she had laid them aside. A petticoat of rustling moiré and a fitted corset cover of long cloth and Valenciennes lace slid beneath the velvet robe she had worn long ago in Liverpool.

Roast beef simmered in its juices in a big iron pot hanging from an arm over the open fire. A black iron Dutch oven squatted in coals on the hearth. Inside it, big fluffy biscuits rose, filling the small room with aroma. As Anne shoveled hot coals on top to make the biscuits brown, hands spanned her waist from behind. She turned into her husband's arms.

"I didn't hear you come in."

"Left my boots on the porch. Didn't want to bring in half the house site." Laughing, he waggled his toes in mud-stained socks. "Supper smells good!"

"What about me?" she asked, pouting her lips because she had lavished on her treasured French perfume.

He nuzzled her neck. "You, too. But attar of roses has a hard time competing with hot biscuits."

Relenting, she served supper on a small table pulled close to the fireplace.

After they had eaten, he pushed aside his plate and reached for her hand. "You look mighty happy tonight."

"I am. It's nice to stop visiting about and have our own place. But haven't you noticed how healthy I am?"

His eyes had a glint as they roamed over her. "Yes, you do look rather healthy." He turned her hands and kissed her palms.

She laughed. "I'm serious. The doctor said I could try again. It's time."

Getting up, he threw a log on the fire. She could see the tenseness of his shoulders as he kept his back to her. For a long while he stirred the embers, making her fear his reply. He turned, his eyes full of tears.

"Annie, I know you want a baby. I love children. I do. But I love you more. I-I couldn't risk living without you." He sat down heavily.

"But I'm older now. Wiser. I'll take care of myself. And my Aunts are around to help with nursing me."

"You know I didn't mind that."

"No. But . . . oh, please. A family is what I want more than anything in the world."

"Well, I did read that Queen Victoria let them give her chloroform last year when she had her seventh child. Perhaps if the birthing were eased . . ."

"Anything." She sat in his lap, twining her arms about his neck. "I'll try it. I'll be careful. I'll be good." She smiled winningly. "Please!"

His arms closed tightly.

Christmas Eve! It was family time, and Anne, content in the chrysalis of her Montgomery and Macon Aunts and cousins and their grandchildren sat aboard a train climbing the rolling hills of the Georgia Piedmont, heading for the old Campbell plantation. Anne knew that not one child, pressing his nose against the smutty window, wondering if Santa Claus could find him in a strange place called Wilkes County, was more excited than she.

Anne felt more secure now that she had been married three years, but she stole a worried glance at her husband. He turned, and she smiled encouragingly. She relished her family's traditions, but this many bubbling, outgoing kinfolk might overwhelm his reserve. Patting his hand, she began describing in mouth-watering detail the recipes each Aunt always made for the occasion. She knew he would enjoy the food.

Before they reached Wilkes County, Anne's eyes were feeling sandy, and her head was nodding, but when the locomotive whistled for the depot, she revived. The family piled into waiting carriages and rode past homes that had been old when Macon was still Indian Territory.

At last they turned into the plantation drive through a grove of ancient oaks and approached the two-story house.

⌣∶∾

The door opened, then banged as Caroline Matilda ran out to meet them. They had not seen her since August when she had been sent to school in New York City, but she greeted them by waggling a warning finger at her brothers.

"Now, you boys behave. I've brought a friend from Madame Canda's School. Don't you be teasing her like you do me."

"We-ell, Car-o-line Matilda," Phil said in an exaggerated drawl, "I ain't gone say a mumbling word to no Yankee girl and have her a-making fun a-the way I talk."

His half-sister grimaced. "I go by Caroline now. They don't understand double names at the North."

"Carolina," chanted fourteen-year-old Campbell Tracy, pulling her hair and chasing her to the house.

Anne laughed at her siblings as they entered the central hallway, filling it with noisy laughter. She noticed Lit, standing as if struck dumb. She followed his gaze to the top of the stairs where a girl in a blue satin gown with a spreading hoop skirt stood poised. Lit's eyes were so soft with wonder that Anne knew he was instantly smitten.

⌣∶∾

Lit, awed by a face of purity, of innocence, could not swallow. For an instant her wide blue eyes met his. He was glad she did not bat her lashes or simper. Her smooth oval face bore no line of guile, and Lit knew he would give his life to protect her from the world.

The tiny-waisted girl descended as gently as if she could float.

She paused at the curve of the stairs, smiled. Her sunny face, framed by clusters of long curls, was the sweetest Lit had ever seen.

Caroline introduced her to the group. "May I present Miss Ellen Elizabeth Steele..." She paused to make a wicked leer at Phil. "...of Huntsville, Alabama. Ellen, this is Anne and Mr. Johnston, Philemon, *Little* Edward, Harriet and Campbell."

Ellen curtsied prettily.

Lit realized he had been standing like a fool. He scrambled to put down his parcels, but Campbell, his round face lovesick, blocked his path. Phil reached Ellen first, bowing gallantly, kissing her hand.

Lit shouldered him aside, bowed less gracefully. Kissing her fingertips, he murmured sincerely, "Your obedient servant, Miss Ellen."

The dimpled smile she bestowed upon him made him stammer, and he feared his adoration was as ill concealed as that of adolescent Campbell. Ellen showed no hint that she realized the brothers were jousting for attention.

Tongue-tied, Lit was brushed aside as suave Phil stepped in with talk of acquaintances in Huntsville. On a flow of clever conversation, Phil led Ellen outside to stroll in the boxwood parterres. Lit stood back in misery as Anne began introducing Mr. Johnston to a new set of kinfolks.

Lit's stomach knotted in agony. Phil was Ellen's supper partner. Barely eating, Lit plotted how to station himself in readiness. When the music room doors were opened for the ceremony of lighting the candles on the Christmas tree, he was beside her.

A thoughtless matriarch foiled him. "Lit, Phil, you boys mind the buckets of water in case the tree catches fire."

Campbell held Ellen's hymnbook while everyone gathered around the piano to sing carols. Too soon, the children were placing their stockings about the parlor, spreading them on the formal chairs and elegant Federal settees. Then, all of the ladies were moving up the stairs.

"Good night, Mr. Tracy."

It was Ellen's sweet voice. Probably she was addressing Phil, but Lit looked up hopefully. Again, she stood at the curve of the stairs. Her gaze was directed at him.

"I'll look forward to seeing you tomorrow, Miss Ellen," he said, thankful that his voice stayed deep. "Sweet dreams."

He lay awake far into the night, thinking of her. He knew that she was to share a trundle bed with Caroline, but he hoped she did not know he was relegated to a pallet in the traveler's room off the back porch amid a floor full of kicking little boys.

⌣∴∾

"Christmas gift!"

"Christmas gift!"

The cry arose in one room, then another, spreading over the house.

Lit jumped up, dressed quickly, and stepped over sleeping children onto the porch to enjoy the first light of dawn. Instantly he was accosted.

A lanky black boy leaped out, shouting, "Christmas give! I seed you first."

"You caught me!" Lit laughed. Prepared, he tossed him the expected silver coin.

Lit's ambition was to catch Phil. He never did.

I wish I had a present for Ellen. Why didn't Caroline Matilda warn me?

With sudden inspiration he snapped his fingers and loped down a pine-straw-covered path. Musket fire startled him. He halted, but a second shot, then another echoed in the cold gray dawn. Relief smoothed his face. In lieu of city church bells, relayed shots carried the message from plantation to plantation: "Christ is born."

With a swelling heart, he hurried on his quest.

By the time Lit reached the music room, everyone had gathered. Hands behind him, he stepped carefully over the spilled contents of the stockings—fire crackers, rockets, marbles, tops, oranges, Brazil nuts—and knelt beside Ellen. In her fuzzy flannel wrapper with the flush of sleep still on her cheeks, she made him want to hug and kiss her as the little girls were embracing their dolls.

Ellen greeted him with a twinkle in her eye. "Christmas give."

With a mock bow, Lit presented his treasure, the most perfect pink camellia he could find.

Ellen drew in her breath. "I was teasing. But, oh, it's lovely! Edward Tracy, how thoughtful you are! I shall pin it to my dress for dinner." She cocked her head to one side and fanned her lashes at him "You'll sit beside me?"

"I'll beat the others off with a stick."

～:～

"Annie, you do like Ellen, don't you?" Lit whispered to her as he waited at the foot of the stairs.

"Very much," Anne replied. "She has intelligence and good humor. I could love her like a sister."

Lit hugged her. Then he saw Ellen with his camellia nestled in the white lace at the bosom of her blue velvet gown. He knew that he loved her.

Offering his arm, Lit led her to the table that stretched the length of the dining room.

"How pretty!" Ellen said. "With that lovely Spode and the coin silver shining and all the candles and flowers and fruit, why, the table doesn't need any food."

"But I do," Lit laughed. "Suddenly, I'm famished."

When everyone was seated, Mr. Johnston was called upon to grace the table.

Under the flurry of serving, Ellen whispered, "Why does everyone call him 'Mr.' Johnston?"

"Dunno. Except folks don't call a rich man by his first name."

Then began a parade. From the little log kitchen in the back yard, white-gloved butlers brought heaped platters of turkey, Virginia-baked ham, and fresh pork. Next came cornbread dressing, sweet potato soufflé, dried butter beans, candied apples, and pears. On and on they presented specialties, and Lit, appetite raging with the rising hope that Ellen returned his love, ate some of all.

Afterwards in the parlor, Lit lounged at Ellen's feet while Phil recounted an endless anecdote. She gave Phil polite attention, but her eyes met Lit's often enough to make him content.

⌒∴⌒

At sunset young and old poured into the yard on a wave of happy chatter. Two long hay-filled wagons waited.

"This has been such a lovely day. I hate for it to end," Ellen told Lit.

"Yes. But this last tradition is a Christmas memory that lingers with me," Lit said as he lifted her onto the hay.

Singing filled the warm night air as the wagons, pulled by perfectly matched brown mules, rolled through gathering darkness. A bonfire blazed beside a pond, its golden glow reflecting on fog rising from the water.

As Lit helped Ellen from the wagon, Campbell threw a string of firecrackers at her feet. Shrieking, she leaped into Lit's arms.

"Thank you, baby brother," he said to Campbell, who slunk off, defeated.

Ellen blushed and turned away, pretending interest in the little girls, who were twirling sparklers to make the fire fly upward.

Darkness had fallen all too quickly. Lit wondered if he dared to tell her that he loved her. *Will she believe me? No. You dolt. She wouldn't think you could fall in love so fast.*

Rockets fired, lighting the sky. Everyone joined in caroling, "Hark The Herald Angels Sing." Close beside Lit, Ellen sang in a sweet, clear voice. He knew he sounded husky, broken.

Time had come for the last display: Roman Candles, whooshing, booming, throwing balls of red, green, gold over the misty water, filling the Christmas sky.

If I were clever like Phil, I'd tell her that's my heart shooting flames, Lit thought. Mute, he reached for her hand. She did not take it away.

"You were right," she whispered. "This memory will cling to me always. Edward Tracy, I'll never forget you or this day. I'll press your camellia in my prayer book tonight and take it with me."

Panic struck. "You sound as if you're saying good-bye."

"I am. I'm to catch the morning train to continue my journey to Huntsville."

"You can't! Not just when we've found each other."

"I must. I just stopped with Caroline to break my tedious trip. The railroad has been completed toward Huntsville in bits and pieces. I take the cars awhile, then get off and ride the stage, then . . ." She threw up her hands "I haven't a moment more to stay. My family gathers on the Sunday after Christmas."

Lit grasped for time to get his wits together. "Tell me about your family."

"I have four brothers and two sisters. Home is Oak Place Plantation. My father, George Steele, designed and built it." She ducked her head shyly. "He's a rather distinguished architect."

"In all that crowd, would they miss you?"

Ellen laughed. "I hope they would. And I've been pretty homesick."

"Could I visit?"

"My holiday's short. I have to return for six more months at Madame Canda's."

"Then you'll be traveling back north with Caroline Matilda?" Lit asked with pulses pounding.

"Yes."

He took both her hands and bent close to her, pleading, "Stop in Macon for New Year's Eve. Our neighbor, Joseph Bond, hosts the grandest ball. Say you'll go with me. Please! We must begin 1855 together."

"I'll try."

William sat rigid in white tie and tails as the carriage ascended the hilltop he coveted. The astonishing mansion gleamed, stuccoed by the same formula as the nation's White House. Cross, William blew air through surly lips, but then he looked at Anne, and his face relaxed.

He consoled himself that Anne would be happier in the spot

halfway down the slope. Above all she valued home. She glowed tonight in the bright pink ball gown. Jealousy that Bond's house was situated above his gave way to a puff of pride in his wife.

"Your gown will be the most expensive at the ball," he said. "I'm sure it's the only one from Charles Frederick Worth's salon in Paris."

Anne laughed. "The biggest hoop certainly. It's a challenge to dance in. I feel like Empress Eugénie in it, but please don't brag. Remember. Mr. Bond is the largest cotton planter in the State. Don't try to impress him."

They alighted from the carriage and strolled up the walkway and across the wide portico.

Joseph Bond, tall, suntanned, stood greeting guests at the massive door. "Good evening, Miss Anne." He bowed low, kissing her hand. "Glad we're going to be neighbors, William B.," he said exuberantly. "Say, I've a new hobby. Are you interested in growing peaches?"

William colored with pleasure. *A friend to call me by name!* "I'd like to learn, neighbor."

The ballroom was a covered porch that stretched across the entire rear of the house. The orchestra was already playing. Later he would request Anne's favorite waltz. Now he performed a bow worthy of Emperor Napoleon and asked his elegant wife to dance.

ᴗːᴖ

Anne's happiness bubbled up, making her giddier than the dancing. She needed a quiet moment, and relief came when Mr. Bond invited her eager husband into the library. She rested amid the potted palms, rehearsing what she intended to say. She would wait until midnight.

She watched Lit and Ellen Steele as they came into the room. Walking in step, they seemed already to be dancing before the music began. Lit's sensitive face exposed his emotions.

The poor boy's love sick, Anne thought. *I hope he doesn't scare her to death. I'll warn Phil to leave her alone.*

But when she found Phil, he was gazing into a pair of dark,

almond eyes. Anne was struck by the girl's beauty. She had a fair complexion, but her flashing eyes and black hair gave her the look of a Spanish lady. Phil's ardor made Anne steal away, humming softly at the delights the New Year might bring.

The moment was nearing, and she could hardly wait to share her news. She moved to the library door, and as her husband emerged, she grasped his arm.

"Let's get some air and look at the view. I want to tell you something."

⌒∴⌒

Anne led Mr. J. to a private spot at the edge of the Bond's lawn, which spread to the sheer drop overlooking Macon, twinkling below.

"I feel that we are among the stars," Anne whispered. She could hear the strains of Auld Lang Syne drifting on the crisp air. The moment had come. "Darling, I . . ."

"Annie, Annie. We've got to tell you."

She turned. It was Lit, fairly dragging Ellen across the grass.

"We have an understanding!" Lit proclaimed. "For just as soon as she finishes Madame Canda's.''

"If Father gives consent," Ellen added in a small voice.

Anne caught Ellen's tinge of apprehension, but she ignored it and kissed them both. "I'm delighted."

Behind them Caroline was beaming at John Baxter, who was on holiday from Jefferson Medical College at Philadelphia.

"Hey, is this a family gathering?" Phil bellowed. He had the stunning brunette by the hand. "I'd like to introduce y'all to Miz Matilda Rawls Walker."

Anne sensed her husband's frustration. A look of foreboding marred his face, and she patted him, leaning close so that her words would be for him alone. "We're . . ." But he could not hear because Macon's church bells began pealing. It was 1855.

Anne's only thought was a Psalm: "Joy cometh in the morning."

Chapter X

Susan Mary Johnston lay in the curve of Anne's arm. Anne could not stop looking at her. The newborn's puckered red face twitched.

"Look, she's smiling!"

"Of course, with a mother such as you."

"And you for a father." She touched his tousled beard as he bent over the bed. *You are strange yet wonderful, William Johnston,* she thought, and love for him flowed through her, giving strength. She was tired, but the delivery had been easier this time, and the precious infant had a loud, strong cry.

The August sun streamed across the counterpane, and she knew her husband was hot. His cravat swung loose like a panting tongue. She laughed, glad of the warmth and the help it gave the baby's breathing. She fingered the day gown she had embroidered in Paris. *The little clothes are filled now, and I'm satisfied. And at last I feel connected with my mother.*

"Thank you for letting me call her Susan."

Trembling with emotion, he spoke brusquely. "Now I have extra reason to hurry with the house. Next month—when I'm sure you and the baby are fine—I must go to New York to meet with the architects. Did I tell you I've hired Thomas and Son, the leading practitioners of new styles? They . . ."

At that moment Adeline entered, her boiled, starched apron and cap emphasizing her shining black face.

"Miss Anne need sleep," the nurse said softly as she scooped Susan up and into the waiting cradle.

"You need rest, too, dear," Anne said. Feeling secure with family all around her, she let her eyes close.

◡∴◡

The August temperature was cooler in the mountains of northern Alabama, but Lit felt sweaty and so tense that his back ached as the stagecoach lumbered through the beautiful valley of the Tennessee River. He spit dust and groaned when the wheel struck a rock.

Lit looked down at his pretty little sister and asked, "Are you all right?"

"I'm having fun," Caroline replied. "And won't we have a surprise for Ellen since she's only expecting me?"

Lit grimaced. Uneasiness at meeting Ellen's family was all the worse because he had not asked her permission to visit. During her last six months at Madame Canda's School, they had written, pledging their love, planning their marriage; but from the moment she had returned home he had struggled to contact her father to no avail. He had written George Steele, politely asking for Ellen's hand in marriage. He received no reply.

Ellen had finally answered that her father, ill, had refused to open a letter from a stranger. At long last, at her urging, he had turned the matter over to his oldest son, Matthew. Again there was a delay because Matt was somewhere on a steamboat between Memphis and New Orleans on his job as a cotton factor. Eventually, Matt had asked Lawson Clay of Huntsville, who had married into Macon's Comer family, to investigate Lit.

Lit heard of the inquires, and he felt certain of a recommendation, but no consent arrived.

Now, with the stage descending through cedar-covered points of the Cumberland Mountains, Lit looked out of the window and sighed. He had done the only thing he could think of by asking Caroline to write Ellen that she was coming for a visit.

For better or worse, it's done, he thought as the road led into an amphitheater carved amid the hills. Commodious houses and green gardens passed in a blur.

"Huntsville!" shouted the driver.

Lit saw Ellen waiting to meet the stage, but when he jumped down in anticipation, her face turned pale.

"Mr. Tracy!" she gasped. "I-I only expected Caroline."

"I couldn't stand it any longer," Lit said, catching her fluttering hand and kissing her fingertips. He was glad that Caroline stepped away on the pretense of seeing to the baggage because Ellen drew back, dismayed.

"Father's gone. He went to Bailey's Springs, hoping the waters will restore his health."

"Is there no chance of seeing him?"

Ellen shook her head, unable to speak.

"Have I upset you so by coming? I felt I couldn't stand it unless I saw you."

"I've been longing to see you, too." Her voice was barely above a whisper. "It's just that the impropriety of your coming might keep him from granting consent."

"Then I'll go to a hotel," Lit said, aching with the need to be near enough to breath the same air that his beloved walked in.

Ellen gave a half-laugh. "That wouldn't make enough difference to count with Papa. Come on to Oak Place. Kate, Matt's wife, is there as chaperone. And my aunt. And Papa has taken care of such anyway," she added cryptically. "You can visit, but, oh, dear, my parents probably won't return."

Lit's desire to take Ellen in his arms and kiss the worry from her face drove all thoughts from his mind, and he could think of little to say as they loaded their trunks onto the Steele's carriage and headed east of town.

Caroline chattered, trying to lessen the strain between them.

When they approached Oak Place, Lit's tongue loosened. "I'm quite impressed with Mr. Steele's architecture." The house was columned Greek Revival, built out of white-stuccoed brick, but he could see a back portico that told him the design was unconventional.

They stepped into an unusual L-shaped hallway that was on

split-levels with two separate staircases. There, Kate Steele greeted them. She was tall, slim-faced, but quite beautiful. Lit noticed that her eyes held such a haze of discontent that she did not even register surprise at seeing him.

"Welcome, Mr. Tracy," Kate said. "The men's dormitory is that way." She motioned to an elliptical stairway rising from the entrance hall.

So! George Steele insured no breath of scandal among overnight guests by creating entirely separate quarters, Lit realized. There would be no chance of even meeting Ellen in a hallway.

His frustration mounted daily. The pleasure of seeing Ellen in the bosom of her family was overshadowed by his inability to announce their engagement and set a wedding date. When the time came to leave, he was still without hope of speaking with her father. Chaperones and staircases had even dashed his dreams of stealing a kiss.

༄

On a late September morning, Anne welcomed Lit into the nursery with a hug.

"How wonderful to see you smiling," Anne exclaimed. "Do you finally have good news about your wedding?"

"Yes! I wrote Mr. Steele at Bailey's Springs, and Ellen did too, imploring him to let us be married in December. I received a letter from her brother, Matt, that their father finally decided his health is so precarious that it would be best for Ellen to be provided for."

Anne kissed him. "Congratulations. I know Ellen's busy getting ready."

"Yes. Everyone's giving teas and her trousseau isn't finished. Time is hanging for me."

Anne lifted Susan from her cradle and placed her in Lit's arms. Flushing with pleasure, he sat in the rosewood rocker, nestling the infant against the nape of his neck.

"You look right holding a baby."

Lit blushed. "I can hardly wait for us to have a child . . . How are you feeling? You *will* be able to travel to Huntsville by

December? The *Memphis and Charleston Railroad* is supposed to be completed into town by then, so the trip won't be as hard. Our wedding wouldn't be the same without you."

"Of course. I wouldn't miss it for anything. I love you both. Now Ellen and I will officially be sisters."

꒳:꒳

But a month later, Lit felt as if his world were crashing about his ears. His hands shook as he read Ellen's note telling him that on October 21, George Steele had died. Ellen felt that she must postpone their wedding and stay with her mother. He beat his fist, wondering how he could continue to live without her. Then he thought about how close she had been to her father and sat down to write to console her.

Macon, Georgia
31 October 1855

My Darling Ellen,

How shall I express to you my dearest, my heartfelt sympathy for you in your day of sorrow?

Would that I could alleviate your misery by sharing the burden of grief, which oppresses you. You have lost your earliest and best friend—one whose place can never be supplied. You can never feel the same reverence, confidence, and love which so beautifully distinguish the affection of a child for a father.

At fifteen (Phil being at the North) I was left the head of the family. How frequently have I sighed for the assistance and sympathy of my father. Sorrow then, my precious Ellen. It is both proper and right.

Religion would teach us that grief is natural and right-that despair wicked and infidel. Grieve then, but not as one without hope—Remember! "Whom the Lord loveth, he chasteneth." While you weep for him departed, there are those in life who look to you for happiness.

Yours devotedly,
Edward D. Tracy

⌣∶⌣

A few weeks later, Anne dropped the dish she been drying with a stunned shriek, "Murder?"

"I'm glad you weren't holding Susan," Mr. J. said with a grin.

"Me too," Anne conceded, "but you shocked me so. Lit and Phil accused of *murder?* What does the newspaper say?"

"The headline screams, 'Diabolical Outrage and Attempt to Murder.' The story says, 'On Tuesday the Editor of the *Georgia Citizen*, L.F.W. Andrews, was assaulted with a club in the hands of Phil Tracy, Editor of the *Macon Telegraph*, along with his brother Edward Tracy and a fellow named William King,' Andrews goes on with words like 'dastardly, cold-blooded attempt to murder.'"

Anne wiped her hands and reached for the *Citizen*. She scanned the article. "Andrews says he was bruised at the hands of Judge Tracy and Deacon Tracy, but has no bones broken. He mentions a band of Irish Catholics backing them. Do you think my brothers really beat him?"

"Probably." He laughed. "I thought when Phil and Greene and Barnes bought the *Telegraph*, it would give Phil a vent in words. Apparently, he enjoys fisticuffs."

"It's not funny. Go downtown and find out what really happened from the old cronies sitting around the livery stable."

"They'll tell a dozen stories."

"Just see if my brothers are in serious trouble. Meanwhile, I'm going to write Ellen. Phil can charm his way out of a hornet's nest, but Lit's so lovesick that he can't think. He can't endure a whole year of mourning. I'll suggest waiting a few months to satisfy convention. Then they can have a quiet family ceremony."

⌣∶⌣

Meanwhile, Phil sat at his desk, reading his own version of the brawl in the *Macon Telegraph*. His editorial attacked Andrews for backing the new secret political party, the Know Nothings, who were against all foreign immigrants and were plotting to prevent Catholics from voting.

Phil smirked at his cleverness in quoting Georgia's revered Congressman Alexander Stephens: "Our Uncle Sam guarantees religious freedom. The Know Nothing crusade against Catholics violates religious freedom."

Perhaps, I was a bit hasty in taking that paddle to Andrews, Phil thought. *Guess I'd better find out how folks feel about it.*

Hitching up his pants, he sauntered down Third Street, trying to conceal his limp. He wondered if his lameness and poor vision made him too feisty. He was relieved when several men slapped him on the back, repeating his quote while others shouted, "Hey Phil, we'll help you carry your bludgeon."

Phil saw Mr. Johnston, knew Anne had sent him, and gave him a broad wink.

Anne was comforted that Andrews was afraid to press charges and quiet settled. She forgot it entirely when Ellen and Lit set a new date for February 19, thinking winter's worse would be passed before Lit brought his bride to Macon.

But 1856 blew in with torrential rains, driving across the entire Southland. It turned into a freak snowstorm. Sleet fell, then hail, breaking down many of Macon's prized trees, shearing branches on others.

Anne and Adeline worked frantically to keep the nursery warm, but Susan caught cold. With her tiny nose clogged, she was unable to breath unless they walked the floor, holding her upright.

Anne felt a sense of unreality, heightened by the strange spectacle of snow blanketing their building site. Hastily assembled sleighs, piled with hilarious Maconites, slid down Georgia Avenue. The jingling bells and squeals of laughter grated on Anne's nerves as the child's fever rose.

Susan croaked a cough.

"Mr. J., you must fetch Dr. Green."

"Immediately, my dear, though I may have difficulty getting him up the hill."

When at last the doctor arrived, he pronounced the dreaded

word, "Croup! Boil kettles and set them close to her crib so she can breathe steam." He patted Anne. "She'll be all right."

Susan did improve for a time, but when February 19 approached, her nose was running. Anne kissed Lit, begging forgiveness. "You do understand I can't risk traveling to Huntsville?"

"Yes, but it won't be the same without you," Lit replied.

"I know Oak Place will be splendid even in mourning, and Ellen will be a doll-like bride."

She saw Lit, Phil, and Caroline off on the train, and then she wept.

༄

As Lit waited by an altar of magnolia leaves banked in the end of the immense drawing room at Oak Place, he decided he liked the quiet reverence of only family members. He beamed at Phil, as always, beside him.

Music heralded the bride, and Lit looked up as Ellen floated down the central stairs. He recaptured the moment he had first seen her.

Now, Ellen Elizabeth Steele, you are mine to cherish and protect, to love. No more of slow mails and separate staircases.

༄

William wakened with a start. At first he thought the March wind had roused him. Then he heard it again, a croupy cough.

His hand closed around the tiny head. Fever! A frightening rattle.

"Anne," he called softly, "boil the kettles. I have an idea to give her more steam to breathe."

Ripping a sheet from their bed, he draped it over the crib, fashioning a tent. When Anne brought a tea kettle, he put the spout inside. They worked, adding, changing kettles until the rasping eased.

"Dare we take a nap?" Anne asked, exhausted.

"You sleep. I'll try to stay awake."

They lay in each others arms, and he, too, dozed.

118

He awakened to find the tent dripping water. He snatched it off. The child's skin and clothing were wet.

Oh, dear God, have I killed her?

But she was breathing.

༄

For a week they all breathed easily. Then on a cold blustery night, the terror returned. Adeline was summoned; her husband, George, was sent for Dr. Green.

Nothing would stop the croupy coughing. Then the room became quiet.

Susan was gone.

William put his arms around Anne to comfort her. And then he burrowed his face in her neck, sobbing.

༄

After his paroxysm of weeping had passed, Anne drew away, feeling she could not look at her grieving husband. She bustled about the cottage, tidying, keeping her hands occupied.

When daylight broke, she stumbled through their unkempt grounds to the spring. Huddling in the grotto, she let her tears flow at last. She wept herself into such lethargy that she could barely walk down the slope toward home.

The funeral was a thing to be endured. Anne sat, stoic, swathed in crepe. The Aunts surrounded her, some sniffing, others sobbing. She tried to stop sound, even Father Shanklin's words.

But through the dimness of the sanctuary, the rector's voice penetrated. He was reading of King David's grief at the loss of his and Bathsheba's infant son. "'And the servants of David feared to tell him that the child was dead; . . . Then David arose from the earth, and washed and anointed himself . . . and came into the house of Jehovah and worshiped.'"

David could worship? Forgive me, Lord, for my grief, Anne prayed. *Thank you for the joy of Susan's brief life.*

Father Shanklin's ringing tones read David's declaration, "'But now he is dead, wherefore should I fast? Can I bring him back again? I shall go to him, but he shall not return to me.'"

The rector lowered his voice. "And you dear parents shall likewise one day go to your child."

Sidney Lanier, tall now but with a child-like face, rose, lifted his flute, and played trembling notes. Anne felt the music within her as soft memories lifting her soul toward heaven.

She paused to kiss Sidney before she went out. She had been too busy of late to listen to his songs and poems. She must change that. She straightened her shoulders, sustained by her Church, upheld by family and friends, and went out into the sunlight

I will sorrow, but I won't be overwhelmed as I was alone in Paris. There is no blame. I must seek all the good I can find.

"Mr. J.?" She reached back for his hand. Tear-cleansed, she saw him now instead of herself. She stopped, shocked. His eyes were as blank as if his spirit had left his body. His beard, untrimmed, had grizzled. The gray frightened her. For the first time since Liverpool, their age difference caused concern.

I'm young enough to recover. What if he is not?

⌣∴⌣

William worked on the house, but he no longer whistled. When he looked at his hands, he could imagine Susan's tiny fingers gripping his thumb. His heart ached all the more because Anne was pouring so much tenderness upon him.

Annie turns her hurt to sympathy for others, he realized. If a sickness or bereavement came to her notice, she was there. She had even begun going to the Georgia Academy for the Blind to read. *And I can scarcely speak. I see her faith, but mine is failing. I can't stop asking why. Why?*

Mud sloshed on him from a puddle left by May's rains, but he did not mind. Eager as he had been to exchange dirty farm work for dressed-up city life, he enjoyed this construction.

"William B. How's the house coming?"

Startled, he turned and was pleased to see Joseph Bond.

"Slowly but surely, Joseph. Let me show you my ventilation system. I got the idea when we were sweltering in the sun of Pompeii, and I stepped into a ruined house and felt cool."

He led the way down into a gash in the red earth that formed his wind tunnel. He explained. "This will stretch across the front. Above it a marble-floored portico will keep air down here cool. That part will be the root cellar. The trench continues around the sides of the house, forming an air moat."

"Effective! I feel the difference."

"Pompeii is a remarkable place. In the portion of the city that is just being dug, we saw the skeletons of Roman sentries still at the gates. Even the convulsions of nature did not terrify them from their posts."

"Amazing! I should take Henrietta to see it."

They explored the foundations of the house, and then they sat on a stack of two-by-fours.

Joseph tamped his pipe. "I was downtown. Bad news is in from Kansas. There's been a massacre that's set the territory aflame with burning, pillaging, killing. It's an all-out civil war."

"I've been worried ever since the ox trains carrying Georgia and Alabama settlers reached Kansas. Bloodshed was inevitable when they clashed with the abolitionist group of squatters there from Massachusetts."

"Yes. Adding that mix to the Missouri Border Ruffians and the Kansas Jayhawkers could only spell trouble. Now it seems an abolitionist named John Brown led a self-proclaimed 'Northern Army' of eight men to Pottawatomie Creek and hacked to death five proslavery men."

William tugged on his beard. "A massacre like that can't go without satisfaction of Southern chivalry. Sparks will fly from young hotheads across the South, and I fear my brothers-in-law will light the firebrands."

Lit sat in his law office, worrying. He liked being a married man, but his practice was far from flourishing. Macon was full of lawyers. And now men had no time for lawsuits. They shouted on street corners about the Kansas war. He read in the paper that fighting had erupted in the nation's Congress when South Carolina's Representative Preston Brooks beat Massachusetts's

Senator Charles Sumner on the head with a gutta percha cane. The incident made Lit feel a little better about letting Phil get him, a church deacon, involved with Andrews. But Macon reflected the hot tempers across the nation, and even the most prominent men were flaring over the slightest insult, not suing, challenging each other to duels.

Better watch your step, man, Lit told himself. *You've got a wife.*

The thought eased his tension. He reared back in his chair, thinking how happy he was in the enjoyment of Ellen's love—even though they were living with his mother.

What joy it is to go home certain of an affectionate welcome! After tea, he would go into his own sanctum with his little wife so tidy and dear. He would light his cigar and read aloud to her as she snuggled close.

Every day that I live convinces me that up to my marriage I but poorly fulfilled my destiny.

Ellen had sweetly taken all of his family into her heart. She especially loved Anne.

Lit closed the brief on which he was supposed to be working. He would drop by to see how the remodeling was coming on the house they planned to move into, and then he would go home to Ellen.

⌣∴∾

By the time summer's heat cooled into October and they were preparing to move into their own house, Ellen's dainty figure was growing round. One moment Lit rode on clouds of bliss, the next he withdrew into fear. When he put his arm around Ellen's shoulder she seemed so little.

What if Ellen isn't strong enough to be a mother? She's so fragile. What if she can't bear a child and survive? I could not live without her.

Chapter XI

Anne's steps were light, and she hummed as she walked from the cottage toward her rapidly rising villa. The bright December day added to her cheeriness now that the rain, which had kept her housebound, seemed past. She wore a black cloak to conceal her burgeoning figure from the workmen merely because of convention; she wanted to proclaim her joy. Come spring, she would have a baby, and Ellen would, too.

I've never seen two people as much in love as Lit and Ellen, Anne thought as she skirted the carriage house and stopped by her kitchen garden to check the cold frames. *I knew Lit was besotted. Thank goodness, Ellen is, as well.*

Ellen was not even homesick. She had confided to Anne that she had married such a good Christian she must endeavor to become a better one herself. She had been impressed when Lit took her to the "colored church" on Sunday afternoon where he performed services and delivered a sermon.

Anne smiled as she came up the driveway and waved to her own dear husband who waited in the doorway of the first floor. He had constructed this utility area to be ground level but hidden behind the marble staircase on the front.

Mr. J. reached out for her. "Let me help you over the threshold." He beamed as she entered the central hallway, wider than the rooms in their cottage, and turned about, arms outstretched in delight.

"It's looking like a house at last," Anne exclaimed. "Oh, Mr. J., only you would make a service floor so beautiful."

His face reddened with pleasure. "I mean to make everything in your sight a thing of beauty."

"'A joy forever,'" she quoted, kissing him. "What did I do to deserve you?"

"You let me love you." He cleared his throat, embarrassed. "What would you say to moving into this part when we can? It'll take another year to finish the remaining floors."

"Yes. We'll be needing more room than the cottage," Anne replied. *The third story is merely framing. The house might take several years to reach my precious husband's planned pinnacle.*

She looked into a long room where carpenters were building two tremendous bay windows. They opened onto the air moat. On the southeast side of the house, the air conducting trench was but four feet across and waist high, but here on the northwest side, a twenty or thirty foot area was encompassed by a curving brick wall that Anne guessed to be twelve to fifteen feet high.

What a safe place for children to play, she thought. *I could watch them from these big windows while I worked.*

She turned to her eager husband and smiled. "This will make a lovely living and dining space," she said. "And with the bedroom on that east corner, why, this floor has everything we need, what with the kitchen . . ."

Anne took a deep breath, reminding herself that she wasn't going to worry about the innovation of the kitchen being inside the house. Hadn't Mr. J. promised that the slate tile floor would make it safe from fire?

"The pantry's finished. Come see." He tugged at her hand, looking like a little boy.

She patted his cheek. Stepping into the cavernous room, she smiled appreciatively as he showed her the wooden platforms swinging from the ceiling.

"You see, this will hold all the provisions, and rats can't get at the food. Hams can hang from these hooks."

"Your attention to detail amazes me."

"Wait 'til you see the root cellar." He opened massive grilled doors and beckoned.

She followed, smiling at his enthusiasm. *I haven't seen him this happy since Susan Mary left us,* she thought. *I must stop worrying and be happy, too. It's the home I've always wanted.* She placed a protective hand on her stomach. *But what if this child doesn't live? Can I bear all of this space if it isn't filled with childish laughter and little running feet?*

⌣∴∾

With the New Year, 1857, and only the finishing work remaining on the ground floor, the house began to rise, swiftly at times, at others with infuriating slowness. Anne's eagerness grew as she looked forward to taking possession of her home.

On a February day that was so warm and lovely she had to be outdoors, she stood in the back yard contemplating the work the Landscape Gardener had accomplished in a sea of mud. The bones of the garden were in place. The spring had been channeled into a lovely little lake and stream that reflected the large trees at the back of the grounds. Anne perched on the banister of the little arched bridge and thought of Phil.

His courtship of wealthy John Rawls' daughter had settled him down. Anne sympathized with the girl, who had been married briefly to Governor Johnson's son and then widowed.

Matilda's as gentle and amiable as she is beautiful, Anne thought. *I wish my house were complete so I could give a grand party. What can I do?*

As she pondered, she noticed a carriage stop on Spring Street. A group of townsfolk gaped at the enormous size of the house. They exclaimed over the suddenly appearing fourth floor.

What will they say when the villa towers with a cupola that makes it seven stories? Anne chuckled to herself.

At that moment she saw Adeline running toward her, flapping her apron, calling, "Come quick. Miss Ellen's baby done been born."

Anne hurried to Lit's house where she found both mother and infant weak.

Two weeks later Anne opened the cottage door at an alarming knock. Lit's manservant, wearing black armbands, wordlessly handed her a note.

Anne's hand trembled so that she could barely read the fearful words. The child had died.

Without a wrap, Anne ran down Mulberry with agony plain on her face. As she passed their first neighbor, Mrs. Judge Holt hailed her from the porch.

"What's wrong, dear?"

"Oh, Miss Mary," Anne cried, turning up the walkway. "Lit's baby died. I've been through it. I should know what to say. But I don't. How can I console them?"

The older woman swayed and clutched the white column. Then she came down the steps, opening her arms. Anne fell against her soft shoulder, weeping.

"You're being tried, but you'll come through," Mary Holt said. "You might not be strong enough to help them, but you can lead them to the One who can."

"Yes." Anne wiped her tears. "Pray for me."

Strengthened, Anne hurried on. When she entered the house, it was hushed, dim. She tiptoed, feeling a sense of angels hovering. She found the young couple huddled on a settee. She kissed both blank faces and knelt before them.

"What sort of curse is making us the last of the Tracy line?" Lit flung out with a bitterness he had never before spoken.

"No, no, dear little brother. It's not a curse. We can't understand it, but death is part of life. Many infants don't survive. Whatever the storm, Jesus can give you peace." She paused, adding softly. "Go to Him, remembering his promise to Paul, 'My grace is sufficient for thee: for my strength is made perfect in weakness.'"

They wept together, and at last as shadows lengthened, Anne persuaded them to take a little food.

After the funeral, Anne was dealt another blow when Ellen

told her, "We've decided to move back to Oak Place."

"We hate to leave you, Annie," Lit explained, "but Ellen wants to go home to her mother. And I need a new start. Huntsville is an affluent county seat. Why, most of northern Alabama's United States Senators have been from there. With so many legal and political lights residing in the town, I should have a good law practice."

Anne swallowed her grief at losing them. "I'll miss you. Please write often."

꒦꒷꒦

Joy reigned on March 20, 1857, when Anne gave birth to a chubby boy. Awestruck, they named him William Butler Johnston, Jr.

Summer laid a warm blessing upon them. Anne moved in a halo of happiness as they watched their child grow. She liked to push his perambulator along the avenue among the mulberry trees herself, but Adeline was adamant. She insisted it was proper for her to do it. Dressed in her finest uniform, Adeline promenaded down the street among the other nannies as if she were the queen.

Anne knew the devoted woman loved the child as her own, but she could hardly tear herself from blue-eyed Willie B.'s side even to attend all of the social events surrounding Phil's wedding.

Caroline Matilda Walker made a stunning bride. Anne found her new sister-in-law to be as calm as a windless evening. She settled Phil's restlessness. Anne had never seen him so happy.

Anne's correspondence with Ellen and Lit satisfied her that they were content at Oak Place. The year seemed to float by on a cloud of bliss. Anne smiled every time she heard Mr. J. whistling.

꒦꒷꒦

Then came 1858. Phil's wife, Matilda, died during childbirth March third. Phil told his sad story in one line on her tombstone in Rose Hill cemetery: "Her infant sleeps beside her."

Phil stood at the grave, reading the poem he'd had inscribed: "Weep not for her! Her memory is the shrine of pleasant thoughts, soft as the scent of flowers . . . Weep not for her."

The words caught in his throat, but he could not shed his tears. It hurt too much.

I can't bear the sympathy of my garrulous friends who keep telling me to cry. Even Lit's letters are too painful to read. But he keeps telling me to travel. He's right. I've got to get away.

Phil walked out of the garden of graves, packed a valise, and boarded a train. Forgetting his enmity with the North, he headed for New York State. He wanted to be with no one except taciturn old Uncle Phineas.

Papa's big brother was my mainstay when he died, he thought numbly as the train jolted along. He tried to recall the summers he had spent in Batavia with his uncle. A respected judge, Phineas Tracy had helped Phil prepare for Yale.

College days. Marvin Waite, he thought. Anne had suggested looking up his old chum. *No. Not just now. Help me, Uncle Phineas.*

On the fifth day of June, suddenly, Anne's beautiful boy, William Butler Johnston, Jr. died. Croup. On a summer's day, two months after his first birthday, he was gone. Anne moved in such lethargy that she felt her whole world was swathed in black crepe.

When barrels of china arrived from Paris, Anne could barely summon strength to unpack them to check for breakage. Listlessly lifting the glowing, pink-banded pieces, she sat in the dining room examining the different fruit or flower that adorned each plate. She re-lived her tour of Sèvres.

I often thought a piece was finished. Then it was put back into the fire for refining, she recalled. *Is the master's hand placing me into the fire, trying my faith? But I'm not becoming more lustrous. I'm perishing.*

She felt small and alone in the forty-foot dining room with the mauve ceiling arching high above. She sank against the barrel, giving way, needing to weep but too drained for tears.

"Could I help, Miss Anne?" A soft voice broke into her misery.

She gazed up into long-lashed, compassionate eyes. Sidney Lanier stood before her, tall and slender.

He's sixteen now, she realized. *A young man. He must surely break the girls' hearts with that handsome face.*

⌣⦂⌣

Sidney looked down at his mentor, shocked, wondering what he might say to ease the deep lines of hurt in her face.

Miss Anne held out her hand to him. "Why, Sidney, dear. I heard you were ill and had to come home from Oglethorpe College."

"Yes. I'm better now and working at the Post Office temporarily, but I plan to re-enter Oglethorpe."

"The dishes can wait. Come tell me about yourself. Have you decided what you want to do?"

"No. I'm trying to seek God's will for my life. What am I fit for?"

"Music certainly. You have great talent."

Sidney nodded agreement, then, embarrassed, he blushed. "Not boasting, for God gave it to me. But I cannot believe I was intended for a musician. It seems so small a business in comparison with other things I might do. What is the province of music in the economy of the world?"

Miss Anne shook her head, sighing. "I'm not any help, I'm afraid. My life is not worth much."

"Oh, but you're so gracious. I've never known anyone so self-giving. You've always stopped to listen to my songs and poems. You don't know how much you've encouraged me, especially since my father doesn't think music and poetry fit work for a man."

"What about King David? He was a warrior, but he was also a poet and musician."

Sidney smiled. "Thank you for caring. I know you'll pray for me. Miss Anne, you're feeling dark shadows just now, but I'm sure God has a special place for you. Sometimes we have to search."

129

"Umm. Yes. How often I forget."

"God who watches the sparrow has a plan for your life."

"It's certain He has one for you. You're wise beyond your years. You have the soul of a poet."

Sidney looked deeply into her eyes. *Even in her sorrow, she's helped me ascertain my capacities.* He had felt fervor of the divine birth. Her approval made him know. He brushed the lock of hair that had fallen over his forehead and sat back on his heels, drinking a deep consciousness of his power.

I am a poet. I know it and she confirms it. He reached out and clasped her hand, wishing he could impart this great peace that filled him.

Instead, he laughed, and they fell to discussing Byron and Keats as they unpacked the rest of the china.

In July, a telegram arrived from Huntsville. Anne looked at her husband pleadingly. Ellen had miscarried in her last attempt at childbearing, and now with another due . . .

"Mr. J . . ."

He opened the envelope, smiled. "'Come see our beautiful baby born July first. Love, Lit and Ellen.'"

"Oh, can we? Can we?"

"If I left, these workmen would stop. But you can go, of course."

Anne enjoyed the fresh greenness as the train rolled through the Alabama mountains. It was good to get away from the problems and endless delays of house building. Entering Huntsville, she was impressed with the town. A carriage took her down Maysville Road to Oak Place.

It's tremendous! Anne thought when she saw the mansion. They are well established.

Lit came striding out to meet her. She could see a change in him. Ellen's letters were chatty, almost like a visit, but she had not exaggerated about his thriving law practice and prominence in local affairs and politics. Anne confirmed it by his confidence.

Anne reached up to hug him. "How's Ellen?" *I must know before I see her.*

"Frail but fine," Lit assured her. "And the baby is strong."

༺༃༄

Ellen, all dimples and lace, greeted her happily. "Dear Sister. Would you like to hold our little girl?"

Anne reached out hungry arms. "What a beautiful baby!" she exclaimed as she cupped her fat round face and kissed thick, dark hair that Ellen had parted and combed to the side. She nestled the child to her breast, and tenderness flooded through her. When at last she looked up, she saw the couple, arms entwined, watching her as one with gleaming anticipation. *They are wanting something of me.*

"What . . ." She stammered. "What's her name?"

"Susan Campbell Tracy," they chorused.

"For Mama? And my baby, too? Oh, how sweet of you!" She kissed the tiny fist. "I love your Susan as if she were my own."

༺༃༄

Anne's family sustained her. She rejoiced over Lit's little Susan, and when John Baxter, declaring his medical practice well established, proposed to her half-sister Caroline, she welcomed him into the clan. The two had been childhood sweethearts, and he had attended every Tracy gathering as long as anyone could remember, anyway.

After Caroline's November tenth wedding, Anne decided to have a surprise birthday party for Mr. J. at the Lanier House. He remained so distant, so morose. It worried her to realize he was forty-nine.

She would invite their neighbors: Colonel and Henrietta Bond, Judge and Mary Holt, and Robert and Mary Jane Lanier.

Oh, and William and Rebecca Wadley, she thought. He had recently resigned as Superintendent of the *Central Railroad,* and Mr. J. liked to talk railroads.

She knew that her husband's heart remained hollow since the loss of Willie B., and she must do something to elicit a smile.

William sat on the balustrade surrounding the porch. It was warm for New Year's Day of 1859, and the sun felt good on his tense neck as he watched the carpenters installing double front doors. Painted to look like aged bronze, each was carved with a lion's head. William had planned them to proclaim power, but the pride he had expected in this entrance was a dull throb. It was six months since his son's death, and he must stop withdrawing from Annie. He had shut himself away from everyone, letting his beard become a great gray bush that he hid behind.

What good is the fortune I've amassed if I'm to have no heir? Money can be cold comfort. Will I be remembered for anything?

I started Macon Manufacturing Company ten years ago as an outlet for cotton and jobs for many textile workers. But no one remembers my part in the beginning. I recognized the potential of the spring on College Hill and started the City Waterworks. No one credits me for civic mindedness since every project I touch makes me richer. And the gas works. Didn't I provide safety to the streets for this little village when only a handful of cities in the North have gaslights?

"Good morning neighbor," called a jovial voice.

William felt a lift when he saw the pleasant face of Joseph Bond who had been on a lengthy trip supervising the cotton harvest on his many scattered plantations.

"Come up, friend. I'll give you the two-cent tour."

Joseph Bond bounded up the tall white marble steps two at a time, not pausing to be impressed. He shook hands warmly.

But William noted Joseph's jaw drop when the massive doors swung effortlessly on silver hinges, revealing the marble hall.

"Well, I'll be swabbed for a boll worm. I've never seen the like." His eyes lifted slowly from the black and white marble floor, and he gaped at the Italian artisans perched on scaffolding. He expelled a long breath. "You've put more work in that pink and yellow ceiling than I did in my whole house. Has my wife seen it?"

William nodded, bursting with pleasure.

"What do you call this style?"

"Italian Renaissance."

"Guess I'd better tack some of this new stuff onto the summer house I'm building. Are you trying to put us poor simple farmers to shame?"

William exploded in laughter that warmed him to his fingertips. "Poor farmer? All the talk downtown is how you made the largest cotton crop in one season by one planter in the State."

Bond beamed. "Yep. Made 2,200 bales."

"They're saying Mr. Bloom bought it for over $100,000.00."

"Yep. But cotton's good one year, bad next. Might not make a decent boll next year, but right now the South's enjoying a golden era." He laughed. "And the North can hardly stand it."

As they moved into the room that was to be his study, William thought how nice it was to have a friend he could discuss business with. "I'm not worried about you. It's you cotton-rich planters with no debts that kept the South's banks open during '58's national panic."

"Don't forget to credit our good Governor Brown. But I stayed away from that financial storm in the North and West. I don't understand all that jobbing in stocks on Wall Street like you do."

"Fortunately, I hadn't invested in those Northern and Western railroads that were declared insolvent," William replied. "I put my money in Southern railroads and real estate. I learned about banks in the panic of '37. I wouldn't be surprised if the rumors about skullduggery behind the Northern bank closings were true. I believe a corner was arranged among them to aggravate the panic and speculate by purchasing valuable property while prices were tumbling down."

"Well, you're the financial wizard . . . and the building genius. This house will stand as your monument. Proud to have you for a neighbor. Guess I'd better amble back to my simple little abode."

Grinning, William watched Joseph, tall in the saddle, urge his horse up the hill to his simple little Greek temple. He pulled at his beard and thought, *I'd better go to the barbershop.*

Chapter XII

"My friend Joseph murdered?" William scoffed. "You must be mistaken, my dear. Whatever you heard is foolishness—like that about Philemon. Joseph's a happy-go-lucky fellow. The soul of kindness. No one would . . ." He faltered as he looked at Anne. She stood there, oblivious to the March wind snatching her clothes. The paleness of her face made his knees grow weak.

"It's true! It's true," Anne wailed. "Colonel Bond caught his overseer beating an old and trusted slave. He was outraged, and he . . ."

"Yes, he told me about that. He never allows anyone to be beaten. He fired the man. So you see the rumor . . ."

"But the overseer was hired on the adjoining plantation. For some unknown reason, he kept coming back and mistreating the Bond's servants. The Colonel caught him at it and knocked him off his horse. The man pulled a gun." Anne shook with sobs. "Colonel Bond died a half hour after the shooting."

William collapsed on a pile of lumber. Anne leaned toward him, seeking comfort, but he had none to give. They remained motionless. At long last, it was she who helped him to the cottage to bed.

When he could control his grief, William knew he must help young Henrietta Bond prepare the gravesite. He went to Rose Hill Cemetery and stood on the bluff where Anne's parents and their own dear babies were buried beside a sheer drop to the river below. Next to their lot was an equally large plot.

I'll build a concrete wall with a wrought iron fence around both lots, he thought. *I'd like a red marble obelisk for myself, but Joseph was so good . . . I think a white marble angel . . . One day, we'll be neighbors again, but now—Oh Joseph, you were the only friend I had to call me William.*

⤜∵⤛

Anne's concern grew. As the spring of 1859 passed, she watched her husband remain mired in grief. Losing his friend had intensified the loss of little Willie B.

He has none of the comfort I feel in Church and family or in holding Ellen's baby Susan. If only I can have another child who can survive the terrors of infancy. Oh, Lord, I want children so badly.

But could she endure it again if she lost another? And would she have a chance. They had become estranged. Her husband had lost all passion for making money, for completing the house, for her.

I've got to do something. Sidney called me self-giving, but I'm not except with children. I'm thirty years old. It's time to cast aside my reserve and help others. I must fan a spark in Mr. J. But how?

⤜∵⤛

Anne poured out acts of tenderness upon her husband, forcing them from her own emptiness. He responded vaguely to her love making, but all her cajoling could not push him into working again to finish the house. Nothing moved him.

One afternoon in late June, she peeped into the half-finished study where he sat submerged in cigar smoke. Pushing back wisps of hair, she squared her shoulders and marched in.

"Mr. Johnston! You simply must do something!" she said sharply. "Those Italians are taking 'far niente' to the extreme. They siesta in the sun while I perish in that cottage."

He sat up, looking shocked, and she swallowed, recalling teachers at Montpelier who warned that a lady never spoke in

136

such a tone or enforced her opinions. Nevertheless, she had set her course. She could not falter.

"I cannot spend another winter in that mere servant's cottage. I'm going to have—I think maybe—I hope another baby. I must be in this well-heated house."

"A child?" Emotion awoke in his face at last. He rushed to take her in his arms and usher her to a chair.

Anne sank into it gladly, weak from asserting herself.

"Rest. Cool. The carpenters should be installing the windows around the ceiling in the art gallery. I'll go see to it."

On a sunny August day, Anne sang as she attached tasseled cords to the paintings they had collected in Europe. How emotional they had been that day in Genoa when they bought their first painting. Each thought they were in love alone. Now, Mr. J. had completed an art gallery the size of a small museum. Anne threw back her head, looking at the encircling clerestory, reveling in the light.

In my youth I longed to see a picture gallery, she recalled, *and now I have one of my own.*

Happily she arranged the groupings, pausing at a warm scene depicting Mary with young Jesus joined by Elizabeth with John. She caressed the baby she was carrying and whispered a prayer of thankfulness that she was to be a mother once more.

Anne looked up to see Mr. J. smiling down at her. She laughed at his expression.

"Whatever are you up to?" she asked. "You look like a boy who's been stealing apples."

"A surprise. I've been waiting until everyone had left for the day."

He led her out of the gallery and up the first flight of the grand staircase. As they paused on the landing, rays of setting sun streamed through the stained glass window, illuminating the medallion portrait of George Gordon Lord Byron she had daringly requested.

"Oh, it really shows up this time of day," Anne said. She

laughed. "People won't understand why I display such a scandalous man. They'll never know what he means to us."

The glee on Mr. J.'s face made her lean back, waiting for him to read another poem, but he moved away from her touch, reaching behind him.

Silently, the wall niche swung away, revealing another space.

Anne clapped her hands together. "A secret room! Why, you've fitted the door as closely as a watchcase. It's completely concealed. How clever you are!"

He beamed as she kissed his cheek. "Step inside. See, it has a window. It works into the symmetry outside and goes unnoticed because the nannies' little room is above it."

Anne rubbed her hands together and grinned devilishly. "What shall we hide in here?"

⌣∴∾

With work accelerated, Anne's excitement mounted. In September she wrote Ellen, "My fairy palace is nearly finished, that is it will be completed about Christmas."

Anne was filled with ideas one hot Monday afternoon in October as she sat gazing at the ginkgo, enjoying its blaze of glory. *We must plant several more ginkgos,* she thought.

A horse galloping wildly up Mulberry interrupted her planning. She looked up, surprised to see her brother.

"Sister, sister," shouted Phil, waving his hat. "Have you heard the news about the abolitionist John Brown?"

"That awful man who led that massacre in Kansas? What now?"

Phil jumped down from his horse and gulped for breath, "Last evening Brown, leading a band of five blacks and thirteen whites, seized the Federal arsenal in Harpers Ferry, Virginia."

"Whatever for?" Anne shrugged.

"Procuring arms to lead a slave uprising. They say the fanatic believes himself God's agent sent to hack us Southerners to death in the name of defeating slavery."

Anne's happy mood shattered, turned to fear. "Oh, Phil, it can't be so."

"What's all this?" came from behind them.

Paling, Anne turned. "Oh, Mr. J., the most terrible news."

She told him in a frightened burst, and he caught her agitated hands.

"Calmly. Calmly, now. Nothing will come of it. Brown was stopped wasn't he?" he asked Phil.

"Well, yes," Phil sputtered. "Colonel Robert E. Lee arrived with the U.S. Marines. They crushed the rebellion. But that's not the point. People at the North are making Brown a champion. They want us murdered in our beds, Mr. Johnston. I'm joining the militia. We must train ourselves."

Phil remounted his horse, ready to spread the story. "I wish I hadn't sold the newspaper. If I were still editor, I'd call for secession."

"No, man." Mr. J. put his hand on the bridle. "I strongly oppose Georgia leaving the Union."

Phil was adamant. "John Brown's a product of Black Republicanism. If a Republican—especially Lincoln—wins next year's election, we'll be called on to choose sides."

As Phil snatched his horse around and pounded away, Anne plucked at her husband's sleeve. Anger flamed. She had not heard him speak out against secession before. She thought withdrawing from the United States as logical an idea as the Colonies separating from England. Had not attempts at national government proved impossible? A multitude of issues separated North and South. She stamped her foot. *If only women could vote.*

Suddenly, militancy sloughed from Anne's shoulders as the implications of Mr. J.'s opinion struck. She sagged into his arms, forgetting they were standing in public.

My views are those of local folks, she thought frantically. *How will our neighbors and relations treat us if he opposes secession? I don't fear the rent in the nation, but I do the split in my family.*

Is danger imminent? She knew it could be, given Bibb County's population mix of nine thousand whites and six thousand slaves.

As she clung to her husband's unyielding body, she saw the Macon Volunteers marching up Mulberry. Already they were shouldering muskets.

◡∴◡

Tension mounted. Macon men drilled beneath flags reduced to fifteen stars. Anne tried to forget her fears by concentrating on bringing couches and dining furniture into the bay-windowed room on the ground floor.

As she reached around the now noticeable bulk of her expected child, she looked up into the smiling eyes of a handsome Italian. There were also German carpenters here, to say nothing of two Yankees from the architect's firm.

If I try to move into the basement with them still working upstairs, I'll need the company of another woman. I long for Ellen. And I haven't seen Susan since she started walking. I'll write.

◡∴◡

Macon, Georgia
November 11, 1859

My Dear Sister,

Please come to Macon to be with me over the winter. I need your help and understanding and the joy of Susan. I have not yet my new house in which to welcome you, but hope you will not despise the day of very small things—We propose to move in the basement the first of January—I suppose the whole house will be complete by that time, but as we will not furnish this year we will be obliged to confine ourselves to small quarters.

The yard still looks very much like chaos. If I should live to be 100 and nothing unforeseen occurs, I really think I will be comfortably fixed and quite well educated . . .

Lovingly,
Anne

ᴗː᷉

But it turned out Ellen was expecting a child before Anne.

ᴗː᷉

"A smallpox epidemic? But really Mr. J., I'm not afraid. We can't let the servants be carted off to the horror of the Rest House. I'll nurse them."

Fighting tears, she sat down heavily, tired as only a woman in the eighth month of pregnancy could be. It was bitter irony that it was New Year's Day 1860, the appointed day for a joyous move into the house; instead this terror was sweeping through Macon.

Her husband eyed her worriedly, tugging at his beard. "I can't let you risk being around people with a plague."

"But we're protected. Don't you remember those vaccinations we didn't want to take in England? Our people are frightened enough. We mustn't curse them to the isolation of all those infected."

"But your condition."

"I can't sit and worry about myself." She patted her stomach and stood resolutely. "We can set up beds in the outside kitchen. I'll have to get used to our cooking inside the house sooner or later anyway."

"I assure you it's safe. But I'd planned for you to sit back in the luxury of living in your mansion." He went out muttering.

ᴗː᷉

In the outdoor kitchen, turned into a hospital ward, Anne moved between rows of cots dispersing soothing words along with soup or salve. Trusting eyes peered at her from sunken faces of her black servants. A handful of frightened foreigners, left by their fellows who had packed up and sailed for home, propped up on their beds and questioned her with broken English.

When Anne got a good scab from the arm of the first man taken ill, she vaccinated Adeline and George. She planned to protect the others who remained well as soon as she got another scab.

In spite of quarantines, smallpox continued to spread, and when Lit wrote that Georgia Eliza Tracy had been born on January 26, Anne felt that she could not leave her makeshift hospital to visit Huntsville.

She wrote her regrets to Ellen and Lit, saying, "We're in quite a sea of trouble."

February brought no letup to the epidemic. Anne worked doggedly, but pain felled her at last.

"I is puttin' my mistress to bed," Adeline declared firmly.

✧

Settled in a high, canopy bed in Aunt Flora Campbell's nearby home, Anne relaxed, away from the smell of infection, of death. Soon the pains began in earnest. On February 22, 1860, a boy was born.

His happy father held him proudly. "It wasn't meant for my namesake, Willie B., to live," he said, " but would you like to christen this one for your father and your brother Edward?"

"Mr. J., you're too good to me. That would please Lit, especially since his children are girls."

Anne felt like Queen Victoria as everyone waited upon her and the precious child, Edward Tracy Johnston.

✧

The epidemic abated. Mr. Johnston burned the outbuilding that had housed their infirmary to disinfect the household.

Adeline prepared the sunny east bedroom on the ground floor of the new house and they moved in, a family.

"My fairy palace at last," Anne said, kissing her husband rapturously.

Happily she chattered and planned furnishing and decorating the upper stories. But through the cold, wet spring she was content in the spacious basement doing little but enjoying baby Edward.

⸱⸱⸱

Summer's sunshine drew Anne outside. She strolled with Edward to the springs and sat in the cool grotto built over them. She thought of how her husband had channeled the constant fifty-eight degree water into their home's supply, and along with the springs on College Hill, into the waterworks for the town as well.

He really is an amazing man, she realized. *Here we have an indoor bathroom with hot and cold running water when no one in the South has heard of such. We have gaslights when even the White House does not. That should show those high and mighty Yankees a thing or two.*

The flash of anger energized her, and she walked briskly along paths through the parterres. Mr. J. had spent his evenings studying botany, and the geometric beds were formally planted with imported evergreens of marvelously differing textures.

Anne wished he were here to enjoy the garden, but he spent his days downtown now, even though he was dismayed by the furor of politics. The loungers around the big stable at the corner of Third and Mulberry talked heatedly of organizing Minute Men because the national Democratic Party, in disarray, had split into three separate conventions disagreeing on how to fight the Lincoln Republicans.

There is really no use in my worrying about the presidential election, she thought. But she was delighted to be distracted from anxious thoughts by the sight of Sidney Lanier ambling toward her across the small bridge. At that moment a pair of swans floated beneath it.

Sidney paused to watch the swans. He waved. "Hello, Miss Anne. Your garden is the only peaceful place in town just now. I could write a poem about it."

Anne laughed. "Congratulations," she said. "Your mother told me you graduated from Oglethorpe College with the highest average in your class."

Sidney beamed. "Thank you. And even better than that, they made me an offer to return as tutor. It will be the perfect job to continue my studies with ample time to write. Don't tell anyone, but I must share it with you. I have an idea for a novel."

"Stay with it! I think it's right that you feel led to become a writer."

As they talked, she held Edward up to watch the goldfish play while Sidney told her how he planned to save his salary toward graduate studies at Heidelberg.

Anne watched him as he left, playing his flute while he walked toward home. Frowning, she thought, *I hope all these old men with their war talk don't rob our young men of their dreams.*

⌣∴〜

Anne wakened to the creaking of wagons and oxcarts at daylight on October 31. She stepped outside where she could see the streets, which rang with country folk moving toward the depot to see their beloved former Congressman Little Alex Stephens, who was escorting the presidential candidate, Stephen A. Douglas.

The political frenzy suddenly infected her, and she pleaded, "You must let me go, Mr. J."

"It would be foolhardy in such a crowd, Annie. All factions are going. Anything can happen."

"Oh, pshaw, not in Macon. Mrs. Douglas is making the trip. They say she's a real beauty. I want to see her. Please."

He sighed, defeated.

⌣∴〜

As they made their way into the railroad station, Anne reflected that she had not been in such a press of people since Napoleon's ball. But in Macon the way parted for Mr. Johnston.

Stephens spoke first, advising calmness and cooperation in preserving the Union. Douglas argued for hours against secession.

As they walked home that evening, Anne realized from the clamor of the crowd that for the first time in an American presidential election, the fate of the nation hung in the balance.

✧✦✧

On November sixth grim men went to the polls. There was a hush over the town as they waited, knowing it would be days before official results.

But the next morning, Mr. Johnston came in with a Northern newspaper claiming enough returns for Lincoln to boast that the South must prepare for subordination.

Anne read the article angrily. "I know Southern men won't let their honor be challenged like this."

"No. Six cotton states have already called conventions. Governor Brown is demanding Georgia secede. The Legislature has requested twenty-two of the state's most prominent citizens to come to the capital to offer advice."

"That means you will be wanted in Milledgeville, and I'm going with you!"

✧✦✧

The beautiful old Georgia capital rang with shouts of secessionists led by towering Robert Toombs, tossing his lion's mane of hair. But to Anne's gratification, Mr. J.'s voice was not the only one raised for Union.

After several days' harangues, Alexander Stephens took the speaker's podium. Long and earnestly, he counseled that only the people could decide such a question. Frail, he could barely speak in a room so thick with smoke and yellow gaslight that it was nearly impossible to see. But at last, Little Alex won a two-month delay; a vote would be called in January.

Anne went home much relieved.

✧✦✧

But on December 20, 1860, church bells pealed, cannons boomed. Anne feared war had begun.

She ran down Mulberry, hands over ears until she met Judge Holt. "What's happening?" she asked the old man.

"A one-hundred gun salute," he replied. "South Carolina has seceded."

"Good!" she said. "I hope Georgia does, too. It's time we had our own country. Of all the affronts the people at the North have handed us, the worst is saying we aren't Christian enough to commune with them. I couldn't believe it when they withdrew their churches from ours."

Judge Holt looked shocked at her outburst, but he nodded. "I quite agree, Miss Anne."

Anne walked on, reaching Payne Apothecary before she realized that she had not donned hat and gloves. She stood on the corner anyway, listening to excited plans for illumination night. The entire town would be a blaze of light to show support for South Carolina.

She longed to be part of it. Over supper she begged. "Mr. J., can't we participate?"

He sank dourly into his beard. "No!"

꒳:꒳

Anne puttered about after Mr. J. went to bed. He had squelched all of her arguments. Hearing music, she bounded up the stairs to the third floor and opened the doors onto the balcony.

She leaned over the fretwork banister, waving to the marchers. Many carried banners or transparencies. They could not see her because she was standing in darkness. She looked about, pursing her lips. Not one other house was unlit, except, of course, that of Joseph Bond's young widow. In every window she could see a lighted candle set on a torchier.

What will our neighbors think? Maybe they'll remember we don't live upstairs yet. No. They'll know. Our villa is the height of national fashion. It doesn't even look Southern. They'll believe Mr. J.'s a Northern sympathizer. Is he?

Another band brought up the rear of the long procession. As it rounded onto College Street, Anne ran to the fourth floor and looked out the back of the house.

Atop College Hill, Wesleyan's white-columned facade glowed from basement to tower.

Another hundred-gun salute began firing. With sudden resolve, Anne climbed to the fifth floor attic space beneath the hip roof. Her candle was shaking as she mounted the spiral staircase through the cupola.

Six, Seven, she puffed. She stepped out onto the octagonal widows' walk surrounding the dome. She gulped the night air. Below, Macon was united in light.

Mouth firm, Anne went inside the tower and lit the gaslight.

Chapter XIII

Tension mounted when January 1861 blazed in with political fires so hot even Anne did not notice the wintry weather. First Mississippi, Florida, and Alabama joined South Carolina. Then on January 19, Georgia voted to secede. That night Macon erupted with a torchlight parade of Minute Men.

Anne ran along the boulevard, glad for once of being tall. Proud of Phil, she had to see him marching. He could have stayed out of the service because of his poor vision and his limp, but he had given up his judgeship to become an officer in the Macon Volunteers.

She spotted him with Sidney striding beside him. She hated that he had resigned his teachership at Oglethorpe to enlist as a private, but she understood that the men were heart and soul for the conflict that must be waged to protect home and heritage and the right to independent government.

The youths had no eyes for her. Belles of the town crowded the wrought iron balconies suspended over double doors of houses along Mulberry. They squealed, cheered, and waved handkerchiefs. Anne noticed Phil salute Genie Wiley, who kept her attention following him.

Anne had not asked Mr. Johnston's permission, but she had invited Phil's cronies to the house for hot cider and gingerbread after the parade. Anne tried not to mind that her husband went upstairs to his study, leaving the guests in the ground floor living room. As she served them, she could not help but eavesdrop.

"Then we're all set, Sid?" asked Phil. "You'll serenade under Genie's window for me?"

"Sure," said Sidney. "What shall I play?"

"How should I know? You serenade all the girls."

They left laughing, and Anne smiled after them. Happy to see Phil interested in a girl for the first time since the loss of his wife, she yet worried. Considering how Macon's ladies languished over Sidney's music and sighed into his great gray eyes, she wondered if Phil was taking along too much competition.

⌣∴∾

Excitement continued through January, filling Anne with enthusiasm. But on cold evenings, guilt rode her as she watched her husband growing more despondent, old.

On a false spring day in February, she was working with a man planting a rose garden with China tea roses she had selected while in France. They would be a fragrant array ranging from deep purple to crimson to pink to white. She reserved a special place for her favorite, "Adam," a rose pink.

"This one really smells like tea," she told the gardener.

Even as she worked, her anticipation in the spring blooms was dimmed. *Perhaps, the season's brides won't accept what I have to offer. If Mr. Johnston declares himself a Unionist, we'll be ostracized.*

As if he heard her thoughts, her husband called her to come inside the house.

Silently he handed her a black velvet box. Puzzled, she opened it, gasped. "Exquisite!" she exclaimed, blinking at a tiered necklace of flashing diamonds. Wondering why he had given it, she searched his face. "A lovely Valentine . . ." *Where would I wear such an elaborate piece?*

He smiled warmly. "I set it for you myself. But it's not just for Valentine's Day. Pack your Paris gowns. We've been invited to join the delegates convening in Montgomery to form the Confederate States of America."

This startled her more than the diamonds, and she stammered. "But I thought you disagreed."

He struggled. "It's not that I disagree with the grievances. It was because the North has industry, Wall Street Banking, railroads, an army and navy. Twice as many people. The South has only foodstuffs, immense territory, and cotton."

Anne frowned. *And courage, honor, gallantry.*

"At any rate..." He spread his hands expansively. "I question that we can win, but I've quietly submitted under the pressure. Since all my interests are in the State, it seems the only alternative."

Anne sifted the diamonds though her fingers, trying to comprehend this sudden change in her life.

A brass band was playing a sprightly minstrel tune called "Dixie" when they stepped down from the train in Montgomery, Alabama. Anne's pulses quickened as the carriage took them to their hotel and she glimpsed the flurry of importance. Ladies promenaded in fringe-trimmed hoopskirts, obviously the latest fashions from Paris. She saw no mourning, and she realized this was to be an event.

Anne discovered that Washington's social whirl had been led by the Southern Senators' wives. They simply resumed giving their banquets and balls in Montgomery. Georgia's stately beauty, Julia Toombs seemed the accepted leader. And she was the only one who could control the vociferous Robert.

At a dinner, Anne met South Carolina's Mrs. James Chesnut. At first, Anne thought her sardonic, but soon she was seeking her company. Mary Chesnut was as plain-faced as she, but she offered interesting conversation seasoned with gossip. Anne shared confidences as she seldom did with this fellow-lover of poetry.

One afternoon as she enjoyed high tea, she realized how much she had shut herself away from Macon's society, enjoying Edward. Now that they had their own nation and could travel with their servants, she had brought Adeline. She could trust her to care for him.

I must start getting out and make myself a more interesting per-

son. I can stop this constant worrying now that Edward is a year old—can't I?

"May I join you?"

Anne looked up to see Alexander Stephens standing before her with a plate of petit fours.

"I'd be delighted," she said, moving her reticule and ivory fan off the next chair.

As they chatted, Anne found that she could express herself freely. Here was a man who liked intelligent women. People called him "Little Alex," but he was quite as tall as she. He was thin, hollow-cheeked. His look of pathos made her think of Byron.

"Do you like poetry, Congressman Stephens?" she asked.

"Yes, I read a great deal," he replied. "And I enjoy whist. Do you play?"

"No, but it would be fun to learn." Anne smiled at him. "My husband and I were in France at the beginning of the Empire of Napoleon III. This is a great deal more exciting, seeing the birth of our own new nation."

⌣∴⌣

William felt a surge of pride when Anne came down from their hotel suite dressed for the ball at Judge Bibb's home.

The new necklace goes well with the Worth gown, he thought.

The women here seemed covered with diamonds from breakfast until midnight. *None wear them better than Annie. She has a sparkle in her eyes I haven't seen for a long time.*

It was good that she was taking part in things since he was so busy. He felt better himself, working long hours, helping form a system of financial credits for the new Confederate States of America.

He strode across the lobby to meet her, anticipating the full conclave tonight with the drawing room bulging with Judges, Governors, Senators, Generals, and Congressmen. He could feel a sense of importance, too. His old friend Christopher Memminger was Secretary of the Treasury. He could hardly wait to tell Anne that the distinguished Charleston lawyer was about to appoint him as Loan Commissioner for the Confederacy.

⌣∴⌯

The crowd was singing, "Farewell to the Star Spangled Banner," when they arrived to watch Jefferson Davis' inauguration on February 18, 1861. Anne tiptoed to see the president as he stepped from a coach pulled by four white horses.

She thought Davis distinguished with his slate-gray hair and beard and tall slender frame. She listened in agreement as he asserted that the seceded states merely upheld the rights of all sovereign states under the Declaration of Independence to resume the authority they had delegated.

Oh, dear God, she prayed. *Let them allow us our own nation in peace.*

But as the band played "Dixie," her stomach churned. She looked at Alexander Stephens, now Vice-president. She knew he had been bypassed for the top office because he refused to say he would ever strike the first blow.

⌣∴⌯

When Anne returned to the Macon depot, she noticed the "Stars and Bars," adopted in Montgomery, was already flying in the March breeze. Anne sensed other changes all over town. Activity stirred the agreeable circle of well-born, well-to-do, who had conducted their society in sedate patterns. Courtships and engagements, which had once lasted years, were being replaced with swift weddings.

Some Macon troops had already gone to the defense of Georgia's coast since Governor Brown had seized Savannah's Fort Pulaski. The Rifles and the Volunteers drilled, wondering what might happen. Other states in the Confederacy had similarly assumed possession of former United States garrisons in their territory as their due, but in the mouth of Charleston's harbor, despite demands for evacuation of Fort Sumter, the "Stars and Stripes" still flew.

Anne prayed for Davis' negotiations toward independence, but Lincoln seemed to be ignoring them. Instead he sent a vessel of war to provision Fort Sumter.

But Anne's immediate worry was Phil. She watched his face, hoping for a sign of happiness, but although he laughed and joked, his eyes remained dull. Genie had married Jim Blount.

Perhaps I should have a party to celebrate our new nation, she thought. *With all the young ladies of the town here to see how clever and handsome Phil is, perhaps he would find a new love. Besides, it's time I showed off my fairy palace, even if all of the finishing work isn't complete and the furniture for the entertaining floor is somewhere on the high seas. But what will Mr. J. think?*

As always, her husband surprised her.

"I've been planning along those lines myself," he said heartily. "But not a mere party. A grand ball. We'll ask so many people it won't matter that the chairs haven't come. Our new government is woefully lacking in finances. Would it embarrass you to invite all of Macon and then ask them to buy bonds to raise money for the Confederacy?"

The first carriage to arrive was an elegant Clarence with a top-hatted driver seated high in front. Anne smiled, noting that guests were coming to their ball with style.

She stood in the open doorway, letting in the wisteria-scented April breeze. The house was cool, fresh, thanks to Mr. J.'s ventilation system, and she had arranged fragrant bouquets of roses and lilies in tall baskets standing about.

My home is more than I ever dreamed, she thought, pleased at how it gleamed in the golden gaslight. She knew she glowed as well in her diamond necklace and new gown of pale pink gros de Naples. She wondered how much wider hoops could become.

Where is Phil? I wanted him by the door. I wish Lit and Ellen were here. Caroline is doing all right helping receive, but she still seems like a child.

"I do hope everyone will have a good time," Anne told her uneasily.

"Of course, they will," replied Caroline.

Anne worried as she shook hands with early arrivals. Mr. J. had catalogued every moment of the evening. *Oh, if only he doesn't keep his schedule too stiff and rigid!*

First, he ushered guests to the picture gallery. There in a specially designed alcove, the statue, "Ruth Gleaning," graced a pedestal. A servant rotated the kneeling, barefoot figure to be admired from all sides. Only after the visitors appreciated Ruth would they be allowed to view the paintings.

As the rooms filled with glittering gowns, Anne tried to expel a breath that seemed caught in her corset. Phil had not come, and the people were standing idle. She was eager for the music to begin. At last she saw Mr. J. take out his watch and signal the orchestra.

Then he bowed before her, looking imposing in white tie and tails. She stopped worrying as he led her to the ballroom, the twin parlors on the right of the hall. Even without the French chairs that would one day be placed around the long room, it was beautiful with its tall arched windows and white Carrara mantelpieces.

The musicians, ensconced in the bay, struck up "Winter Flowers," and Anne's heart swelled. *How could I not love him? What difference does it make if the evening is regimented and an army of butlers is at everyone's elbow waiting to whisk away crumbs?*

A swirling sea of silks and satins surrounded them as dancers joined the waltz, and the whole evening took on a golden aura.

At precisely midnight, supper was served in the vaulted dining room. Ham and turkey and all manner of salads and cakes were showcased on the brilliant china and silver.

Vibrant talk filled the room as people, weary, yet at fever pitch, relished their perfect evening.

In the wee hours of morning, Anne looked up to see Phil enter at last. Glasses askew, hair looking as if he'd been running his fingers through it, he raised both hands and signaled for silence.

"The newspaper office has received momentous tidings," he shouted. "Shots have been fired at Fort Sumter. General Beauregard is ringing it with fire. The Federals' surrender is eminent."

A cheer broke out, but Phil waved, indicating more news.

"Lincoln has called up 75,000 troops. He refuses to let us have our own nation. War has begun."

~:~

The glad cries accompanying Phil's announcement that the long tension between regions had reached a climax rang in Anne's ears for days.

Events spiraled rapidly. Virginia, North Carolina, Tennessee, and Arkansas joined the Confederacy.

On April 19, Macon's Rifles and Volunteers received a call from President Davis to come to Virginia. They rushed to leave the next day, eager for the distinction of being the first troops from another state to come to Virginia's aid.

The honor of the South will be avenged, Anne rejoiced.

But as she paid afternoon calls and saw innocent brides packing to move with soldier husbands to Portsmouth, she felt qualms. She thought of Mr. J. and understood a little of his hesitancy in leaving the Union.

At the train station as she kissed Phil good-by, he grinned. "We'll lick 'em in the first dash and soon be home."

Anne's smile felt stiff. "Look after Campbell," she said. She wished their teen-aged half-brother had not insisted upon joining. It was Phil who worried her most. *Will he be foolhardy if called into battle? If only he had a bride to give him reason for staying alive.*

Chapter XIV

Anne sat in the ground floor living room by the big bay window, clutching her lap desk. She dropped her pen, and the sound echoed. The house seemed a hollow shell. She had never felt more alone. She almost wished for the workmen who had so fretted her, but the foreigners had fled at the declaration of war. All of the finishing work had stopped.

As my whole life seems to have done, she thought, pressing her hands against emptiness below her rib cage. Dry-eyed, she stared out the window, which was encircled with a lattice draped with heart shaped leaves of coral vine. A hummingbird drank of the tiny rose-pink flowers. Since early May, the fragile creatures had been coming to the special garden she had created for them and for Edward. Against the high brick wall that encompassed the private area, she had planted hollyhocks, yarrow, and four o'clocks. Now, instead of joy, the very beauty brought pain.

Hummingbirds are no fun without a child to share them with.

She tried not to remember, but the picture stayed before her eyes. She had returned from seeing the soldiers off on the train and met Adeline running to find her. Edward's whole body had been red. The doctor had come quickly, pronounced it scarlet fever. But deep down she had known.

The next day, April 21, 1861, Edward had died, choking with croup.

With a sigh that became a shudder, Anne pulled a shawl

around her and reached for the packet of mail Mr. J. had brought before he left on his travels to secure capital for the Confederacy.

I hate I must keep up with my dear ones through letters again. I feel so useless.

The young soldiers had left, reassuring their families their duty would be merely for the purpose of drill, that after a bloodless campaign, they would return; however, it worried Anne that with the seat of the Confederate government moved in May from Montgomery to Richmond the two nations eyed each others' capitals. All of her brothers were on the Virginia front. She opened Phil's letter first.

> We are now called the Second Georgia Battalion, and we are stationed at the Norfolk fairgrounds opposite Fort Monroe. Our workmen have raised a sunken Yankee vessel, the *Merrimac*, and are rebuilding it as the *Virginia*.
>
> We have plenty of time for socializing forays to the surrounding Tidewater plantations. The belles here treat us like heroic darlings as the first Southerners to aid the Virginians.
>
> Love from your
> "Darling Brother" Phil

Anne felt better about Phil. Spirits lifted; she opened the next letter, one from Sidney.

> Life in Norfolk is great fun! Our only duty is to picket the beach. I have organized a band with C.E. Campbell, C.K. Emmell, C.M. Wiley, Granville Connor, and W.A. Hopson. We play at camp and at parties in town. It's hard to get passes, but we've found a trick. In the cemetery between the camp and Norfolk, there's a receiving vault with the door unlocked. We slip in there, change to civilian clothes, and go our merry way for a grand lark.
>
> I think I'm in love with girl up here, but don't tell Gussie Lamar. I love her, too.
>
> Your friend,
> Sidney C. Lanier

Anne smiled. *No one would ever suspect such a mischievous spirit lurks behind that angelic face.*

But her heart froze with terror after reading Lit's letter written from a camp near Harpers Ferry on June 8, 1861.

> . . . I trust I am ready to die when my hour comes, as becomes a Christian soldier and gentlemen; until that hour, I am proof against the shell and shot. If the enemy attacks us, 'we'll memorize another Golgotha' and achieve a victory or martyrdom . . .

Anne knew Lit had hated to leave Ellen weak and ill from having a new baby, whom they named Ellen. Her heart ached for her dear sister left alone. She had saved Ellen's letter until last. When she opened it, she could no longer hold back tears.

> My own darling husband is gone now. He joined the Fourth Alabama Infantry and was commissioned as a captain. Since his regiment has been sent to Harpers Ferry, I have not been able to stop crying. All of the children have been sick, wee Ellie was so ill we were in despair of her life. Days are weary without my Edward. Truly there is none that can lend a ring to the hours but his own dear self.

Anne wondered if it would help Ellen in caring for the new baby if she invited Susan and Georgia to visit. *Could I bear having children around without my heart aching the more for my Edward?*

As if in her dreams, she heard a baby cry. She did not turn.

"Anne."

Startled, she jumped. It was Caroline, jiggling her eight-month-old son Tracy Baxter on her hip.

"Are we intruding?"

"No, no. Come sit down. I need better company than sad thoughts. I've heard from Phil and Lit. Have you heard from Campbell?"

While Caroline talked, Anne looked at her half-sister's smooth dark hair, parted in the middle and pulled back from a perfect, oval face. *How beautiful and intelligent she has become! I remember how jealous I was at eleven when she was born. I guess that's why we've never been close. I should remedy that.* But she could not bring herself to reach out and take chubby-cheeked Tracy.

∾:∾

Caroline was ill. Deciding to pay a call, Anne, walked down the street with a basket on her arm, absorbing the heat of the July afternoon into her bones.

Anne found her lying weakly in bed. She sat beside her, taking warm, damp Tracy on her lap and feeding him a bite of the cake she had brought.

"I have a presentment of death," Caroline confided. "Anne would you love my baby for me?"

"Don't say such a thing!" Anne exclaimed sharply. "Your life is before you. Why, you just turned twenty-one."

But on July 10, 1861, Caroline Matilda Tracy Baxter died. Anne had never seen a man more distraught than John Baxter.

∾:∾

For several days Anne wrestled with the conflicting feelings Caroline's dying request had inflicted upon her. She walked up and down the stairs of the lonely house. There were suites of sunny bedrooms and the bathroom with its big, copper-lined, rosewood bathtub on the third floor. On the fourth floor were five bedrooms and the cistern for the water supply. True, the ceilings were only nine feet. She looked out the windows. They were small because the architects had expected it to be servants' quarters. She sniffed. Northerners did not understand that Southern servants had their own houses. None slept here except Adeline Williams in the nursery.

But since Edward . . . She could again if . . .

Heart fluttering, she decided. She could hardly wait for Mr. J. to get back.

When at last he returned, she confronted him in his study.

"Dearest, what would you say to inviting John and Tracy to move in with us?" She saw his eyes widen and hurried on, pleading, "As a doctor, he must make house calls at all hours of the night, and besides, a man can't care for a ten-month-old.

Mr. J. ducked his head, beard on chest. "We haven't finished furnishing," he mumbled. "You know that since Lincoln's blockade of our Southern ports the week after the firing on Sumter, little goods have slipped through. We won't be getting our furniture. I hadn't told you, but those French chairs we were expecting were confiscated by blockaders."

Anne shrugged. "The war will be over in a few months. Then we'll finish everything properly. For now, I can use some old family pieces."

"I hate for you to put yourself to so much trouble."

"I don't mind. Tracy Baxter needs a mother."

Coughing, he hunched over his desk, piled high with papers. "Do as you like," he muttered. "You always do."

What's wrong? Anne wondered. *I know how much he likes John Baxter.* She started to ask, but in her eagerness she hurried to get her hat and gloves and call on John.

❦

Tracy Baxter was a happy, healthy baby. He went straight into Anne's arms and into her heart.

Anne was thankful she had him to hold onto when news came that the Federal Army had entered the sacred soil of Virginia on July 21, precipitating the first battle of the war.

A gleeful note came from Phil, chafing that he had missed it, but describing how the Confederates had sent the Yankees retreating from Manassas Junction across a muddy stream called Bull Run:

> People came out from Washington City to watch. They scampered back like scared rabbits. The two sides couldn't even agree what to call the battle. We named it for the town. They called it for the creek.

But Lit had been there, and it was Ellen's letter she read and reread:

> Edward was a hero in the very first battle. He wrote me that "the rascally invaders to our soil will not dare to risk war against an army so equipped. I was not recreant in the dread hour. I stood erect in front rank when men lying down were being shot all around."
>
> Oh, I'm so proud of him. He was promoted to Major just before Manassas. They say he "acted with coolness and courage, his voice constantly heard above the din of musketry and the thunder of artillery, exhorting his men to do or die." He was the star of the regiment!
>
> You see, I'm trying to be a brave wife and not fret about him.

Anne thought of Lit's oft-expressed motto, "My God, my country, and my family." *I hope he doesn't try to be too gallant.* She swung Tracy on her hip and took him out to play in the hummingbird garden while she sat on the cast iron bench and wrote to Ellen:

> If it were not for my absolute fatalism and stern belief that whatever is to be will be, I should most surely rebel . . . So many of my loved ones have crossed the dark valley, that I would choose that those that remain should evermore be encircled with the arms of love . . .
>
> I am not at all fond of keeping house, the truth is I am too old to begin, and it seems a rather aimless existence, keeping such an establishment swept and dusted . . .
>
> Why don't you send Susan and Georgia for a visit? They could play with Tracy. He crawls into everything. What will I do when he can walk?
>
> Poor John Baxter is miserable without Caroline. He has left to join the Macon Volunteers in Virginia.

⌇⁖⌇

William wondered if Anne realized his spending his time traveling provided an excuse to stay away from home, from her. He could hardly bear the house filled with the sounds of an infant who was not his own. Anne cared nothing that his every business venture overflowed with success. All she wanted was a child.

Why can't I give her a healthy baby, he agonized.

He was in Augusta again. The other two Georgia loan commissioners resided there, and he could hardly hide his pride that it was he who had convinced the Augusta banks to cash their bank notes in gold or silver coins as the banks in Savannah, Charleston, New Orleans, and Mobile were doing. This specie was vital to the Confederate Treasury's cash flow because the new treasury had been unable to print notes due to lack of printer, press, and paper.

Next he would go to Atlanta for the convention of Georgia bankers he had organized. He would present a platform for extending funds to the Treasury.

Then, before I go to Savannah, I suppose, I must stop off at home.

⌇⁖⌇

"Going again?" Anne wailed. "Oh, Mr. J., I miss you. Can't you stay awhile?"

Seeing his vagueness as he shook is head, she hardly felt he was here now. All he talked about was the Confederate Treasury and this or that thing Christopher Memminger had asked him to do. When he looked up from his desk, the flintiness of his eyes frightened her.

"You have Tracy. You don't need me."

Stung by his bitterness, she wondered, *Did I do the wrong thing asking for the baby?* Now that John was serving as a surgeon in the infantry, what else could she do?

Anne dropped to her knees beside her husband and laid her head on his tense thigh. "Darling, I'd still need you if the house were filled with babies."

"It's highly unlikely to be full of children," he snorted. "I haven't given you one that . . . lived." He crumpled to the desk, burying his head in his arms.

"Do you think it's your fault? It isn't. It isn't mine. What is to be will be." She hugged her body over his, trying to absorb his pain.

He trembled, and she searched for words.

"There's so little doctors can do for infants. Many families share our heartbreak."

"But not the loss of *every* child." He scrubbed at trickling tears. "I can't bear it as gracefully as you."

"Gracefully?" She laughed. "If I do, it might not be the meaning for the word you have in mind. I bear it well by God's grace. Think of the pure joy God gave us of a year with Edward. We can still rejoice at God's blessings and find purpose in showing His love to others."

"Then you don't blame me?"

"Of course not, my darling!"

She felt fervor in his embrace that had been missing a long time.

After a lingering kiss, he shook his head ruefully. "I still must visit the banks in Savannah." He brightened. "I can take the private car. You can go with me."

Anne drew in her breath, wondering what to do about Tracy. But her husband needed her. The beautiful president's car and a time for renewal swam before her. *Aunt Carry and Adeline can keep Tracy,* she decided.

"I'll pack at once," she said, running for the stairs.

༈

They returned from Savannah happy and relaxed, but a telegram from Memminger was waiting.

"Oh, Mr. J. Do you have to go again?"

"Yes, I must re-negotiate the interest rates the Treasury is to pay Georgia banks. Would you like to go to Atlanta?"

Anne shook her head. She hated the dirty little town. She kissed him goodbye, no longer worrying that he was leaving.

164

We can be parted now without feeling separated. At least his life is not in danger like my brothers.

But she had to endure a lonely fall. She heard only from Ellen, saying Lit was at home on sick leave. She could picture Ellen's joy at having him near.

Nestled in a mountain-rimmed valley, Oak Place Plantation lay as calm and serene as Ellen herself. Lit thought about how he had almost hated the house on his first visit here because George Steele had kept him from his beloved. Now, happily married, he loved it as Ellen did and thought of the mellowed mansion, built by his father-in-law in 1840, as his homeplace. He stepped out into the yard and gazed at the orange and gold and red blazing up the mountainsides and was glad they had chosen this Indian summer day for him to venture out.

He leaned heavily on his butler as he struggled to walk. Ahead of them scurried other servants carrying rocking chairs and cushions, seeking a cool spot in the oak grove. They all acted delighted that he was at home even though this furlough was the result of a debilitating fever.

Ellen followed, bringing a tea tray. He looked back and smiled into her wide blue eyes. There was no trace of guile in them, and her sweet oval face still showed the purity and innocence that had first made him want to protect her. *Ellen looks as young and as lovely as that Christmas when I first saw her coming down the stairs,* Lit thought. *And even more in need of my care.*

Three-year-old Susan resembled her mother, but she had a take-charge attitude. He had to laugh because Susan was practically dragging sixteen-month-old Georgia along behind their mother. The toddler already had flashing dark eyes that set things around her into waves of merriment.

He abhorred the thought of leaving again, but he knew protecting his home and family from the Bluecoat invaders was the reason he must go as soon as he was strong.

I should send them to Anne. But I like thinking of my family here. And if I should get a furlough . . .

He held out both hands.

Ellen took them and kissed his forehead. "Darling, take this laudanum and drink this lemonade," she said. "Maybe it will cool you." She stroked her slender fingers over his face and caressed his new mustache and beard. "I do declare, Edward Tracy, you're far too handsome with those whiskers for me to let you out of my sight."

Lit laughed, unable to resist kissing her in spite of his cracked lips. "You're a good nurse. I'm all better."

"Favwer, kiss me," cried Susan.

"Favwer, Favwer," chirped Georgia, waving her arms.

Laughing, Ellen went back to the house and brought out baby Ellie. "Our poor little creature has struggled hard for her life. It's amusing how badly spoiled she is."

Lit took the infant. "You need me. You'll never know how I hate to leave you."

"When you're away time's whole machinery seems to be moved by a snail. I sigh to be with you, to have one look, one smile, a talk with thee, my love."

Lit squeezed her hands, but Ellen continued talking through her tears. "Each time I endure these unpleasant separations, I make vehement resolutions never, never to let you go again."

"You know honor must be served, but I'll be closer by. I have a surprise. I learned of a vacancy in the Nineteenth Alabama Infantry and applied for it. I'm to receive a promotion to Lieutenant-Colonel."

"I'm proud of you," she said, but she could not help sniffing.

⌣∴⌢

When Lit improved, he and Ellen roamed the fields and streams of Oak Place Plantation in idyllic days that passed like a dream. Too soon, on October 19, 1861, the transfer and commission came.

Lit wanted to say good-bye in the privacy of their room. Ellen sat at her writing desk penning a note she would not let him see. She had procured small paper seals that she placed on every envelope she sent him. They bore the words: "Cease Not To Think of Me." She sealed this one and silently handed it to him. Understanding, he put it in the pocket of his gray uniform and took out a small package.

Ellen unwrapped a velvet box. A diamond sparkled in the fleur-de-lis catch of a gold lapel watch. "Lovely," she whispered. Then she held it close to read the inscription, and her eyes misted. It expressed the same sentiment: "Cease Not To Think of Me." Lit pinned it to her bodice. Unable to speak, they clung to each other.

As Lit rode away, he turned his horse for one last look. Tears streaming, Ellen stood on the porch with wee Ellie in her arms and Susan and Georgia clinging to her legs.

It seemed to Lit that winter began that day as he returned to the battlefront in Virginia. Fury rose in his throat each time he thought of Ellen alone.

In the closing months of 1861, a second front developed in the West along the Mississippi River. The threat of the enemy was moving relentlessly closer to home.

Chapter XV

Spring's pink and white blossoms gave Macon's streets a bright newness; the people hurrying along them stepped with lively anticipation, drawn by the aroma of roasting pork. It was April 2, 1862, and the Second Battalion, having enlisted for a year, was coming home. Townsfolk were congregating around the open pits at the Floyd Rifles' Hall on Mulberry and Third and the Macon Volunteers' Armory at Second and Mulberry. There was enough barbecue cooking to feed one thousand.

At Number Two Georgia Avenue, Anne sang as she dressed.

Mr. J. came in, exultantly telling her how Memminger had commended his diplomacy, influence, and business acumen in leading the bankers. "Memminger has established Macon as a Treasury Department Depository. He's appointed me Premier!"

"That's nice dear." Anne kissed him absently. Her mind was occupied with joy. Phil would soon be here, and she was expecting a baby in July.

Anne patted her stomach, glad Empress Eugénie had gotten Frederick Worth to create hoop skirts to conceal early pregnancy. She did not want to miss a minute of the festivities.

"Are you ready, dear?" Anne called as she pinned on a smart pillbox hat with a jaunty feather tilted over her forehead. "I can hear the band playing. I want to be at the depot when Phil and Campbell and Sidney step down from the train."

They descended the marble front steps hand in hand, but when they passed the Holt's garden, a maid ran out, waving her apron.

"Miss Anne. Oh, Miss Anne. Come quick in the house. Miss Mary, she's a-dyin' and she's callin' for you."

⌣∴∾

Phil sat at a makeshift table in the armory, rubbing his stuffed stomach. "Nothing tastes like Georgia barbeque," he said as he pushed back his plate, unable to eat the last hunks of pork swimming in tomato-rich sauce. He tried not to burp aloud.

Phil stretched, feeling good to be surrounded by Macon folks he had known all his life. But he wondered, where is Anne?

When he noticed Campbell shouldering his haversack and following Aunt Carry, he suddenly realized he had sold his house. *Where am I going to sleep?*

"Phil! Oh, my darling brother Phil," Anne shrieked, grabbing him from behind, poking a feather in his ear.

He jumped up from the sawhorse table and opened his arms. Anne smothered him with hugs and kisses. Her tears wet his neck.

"I'm so sorry I couldn't meet the train," Anne wailed.

"No one did." He laughed. "We caught an earlier one, and . . ."

"Where are your things? You're moving in with us."

"I wouldn't want to bother Mr. Johnston." He looked over her shoulder, eying his brother-in-law, grown portly and gray-headed.

"Nonsense, my boy. Glad to have you." The rotund fellow pumped his hand.

"We've oodles of rooms," Anne squealed. "I'll give you one near the bathtub. And I've already invited guests to a ball in your honor."

"Fine. But I'll probably enjoy soaking in that hot running water more."

⌣∴∾

Phil felt as if he were in a dream as he stood with Anne, receiving. His sister had planted banks of sweet shrubs, topiaries of tea olives, and whole hedges of Cape jasmine, making the grounds smell so sweet that guests arrived smiling. Phil poked his glasses and thought wryly that it was a far cry from a tent crowded with young soldiers.

Lest he forget reality, friends clustered around him, asking about the war.

"We've seen little of it," Phil told them, "except for one bit of excitement on the eighth of March. For that one day the Confederate Navy was master of the navies of the world."

They gave him full attention.

"We stood on shore watching when our *Virginia*, which was their abandoned *Merrimac* refitted with new iron-plated sides, steamed into the harbor at Hampton Roads. She took on five Federal vessels. Stuck her iron beak in the *Cumberland's* wooden side like a knife in hot butter. Next she set fire to the *Congress*. We figured she'd finish them all off next day."

"What happened?" Everyone gathered closer.

Phil grinned ruefully. "Unfortunately, the Union had completed their ironclad, *Monitor*. The two battled four hours." He shrugged. "It was like the rest of the war, a little jousting with nothing decided."

The orchestra squawked, tuning up, and people moved into the ballroom, exclaiming how iron ships made all the old wooden navies useless.

Phil lounged against the wall, watching Anne as Mr. Johnston offered his arm. *She's looking at him with such pride. Yes, and real love. I'm thankful she's happy at last. She was so glad when she told me Lit had been transferred to the Western theatre of war to be nearer Ellen. I hope she doesn't find out that all the while we're dancing in her marble palace, Lit might be in serious combat.*

Lit felt grateful he had been sent West. With his duty protecting the rail center at Corinth, in the northeast corner of Mississippi near the Alabama line, at least he was in the Tennessee River Valley again, and he felt he was guarding Ellen. But as he sat in his bleak office, trying to compose a letter, impressing upon his precious wife the inexpressible tenderness of his love for her, the nearness of Oak Place made his heart ache all the more to be home. Quickly, he brushed a tear from the corner of his eye lest someone see.

I must be content to endure as much for my Country as her enemies submit to in order to do her injury.

Lit laid his head on his arms over the letter, but at that moment, his aid entered.

"Sir, spies informed General Beauregard that General U.S. Grant is camped at Pittsburg Landing on the Tennessee River." He grinned. "Grant's unsuspecting, inviting destruction."

Quickly they marshaled forty thousand men. For twenty-miles they marched, a long, gray line up red clay hill and down.

⌒∴⌒

As they burst out of the woods shooting on Sunday morning the sixth of April, Lit saw Grant eating breakfast near a rude log Methodist meeting-house with a sign: Shiloh Chapel.

All day as the battle surged, Lit looked to the church and prayed in snatches, scarcely hearing the bursting shells and whistling bullets. He was soaked as rain ran down the back of his neck in a cold stream. First it pattered, then it poured, bringing on the night.

Now Beauregard had Shiloh Chapel for his headquarters. Lit dried his hair and beard. It felt good to be inside with the enemy fleeing for the river. Aids sent a wire to Richmond announcing complete victory.

⌒∴⌒

With the dawn they discovered that under cover of darkness and thunderstorm, Federal reinforcements had arrived by steamboat. Fighting intensified. Horrified, Lit saw his men falling, mingling lifeblood with oozing mud. He realized the Confederates were outnumbered two to one.

Toward evening, he felt a shot graze his leg. His horse pitched forward, sank beneath him. Now he was covered with red muck and struggling to extricate himself from the poor, dead, innocent, creature.

For three days the bloodletting continued. Then both sides, exhausted, withdrew. The slaughter had decided nothing.

Back in Corinth Lit was working with his superiors planning a different strategy when a message came that walloped him: Yankees had invaded North Alabama. They were occupying Huntsville.

Asking to be excused for a moment, he went outside and knelt. Agonizing, he prayed for his beloved wife.

Back in Macon the furloughing Volunteers and Rifles had celebrated the first news of victory at Shiloh. Every home in town had tried to host a party as their soldiers two-weeks leave sped by.

Phil felt bleary-eyed and over-stuffed. But now the music must end.

He walked with Anne in her amazing garden, trying to think of how he could soften the blow. "We're to report to Goldsboro, North Carolina, by April 30," he said at last. "Our gala advance into war is over."

Phil tried to hold onto a grin, but the grimness he felt emerged. "You'd better know. New wires have come in. Shiloh wasn't victory after all. This thing's lookin' more serious than we Southerners expected."

He hoped she would be too busy to hear that one out of every four soldiers who had gone into battle at Shiloh had been killed, wounded, or captured. He also knew that his own regiment was about to see real action.

Anne knew him too well. She read the revulsion on his face and cried out, "Oh, Phil, you're careless sometimes. Please look out for yourself."

Phil saw panic in her eyes and soothed, "Now don't you be a' thinkin' bad thoughts. You'll mark that baby."

༺⋆༻

Bad news was becoming commonplace; even so, Anne read Lit's letter in disbelief.

> Yankees captured Huntsville on April 11. I can't get word of Ellen, and I'm frantic.
>
> Pray!
>
> I'm sure they mean to stay because Huntsville is the hub of the *Memphis and Charleston Railroad,* and they're cutting our supply route from the western Confederacy to Virginia.
>
> I don't like what I'm hearing about their general, Ormsby Mitchel. They say he's rough on citizens and loose on his soldiers.
>
> Pray!
>
> My troops have been placed under General Kirby Smith and ordered to Tennessee for reorganization. Don't worry about me as I'm unexposed to battle myself. I'm just worried about my family.
>
> > Love,
> >
> > Lit

༺⋆༻

Anne thought wryly that if there were anything to the old wives' tales about frightening thoughts marking a baby, hers had no chance at beauty. She sought word of Ellen to no avail. Her whole world seemed to be sinking beneath her feet.

As the visage of war hardened, the face of Macon changed. Gay cavaliers dueling had become trained soldiers killing; just so the Ordnance Department had turned the sleepy cotton town into a bustling place of factories making swords, buttons, enameled cloth, soap, matches. The arsenal was moved from Savannah to Macon, and in Findlay's Foundry, five hundred artisans and workman turned out twelve-pounder Napoleon cannon, shot, and shell.

Then Union forces occupied New Orleans, May 1, 1862. There would be no more sugar or western beef, but that seemed of no importance because Macon's regiment was seeing action in the Virginia Peninsula Campaign.

They waited daily for reports. At the Battle of Seven Pines near Richmond, on May 31, 1862, Phil was twice wounded. Stunned by a shot to the head, he was shot through the leg between the knee and hip.

Anne's only consolation was that Phil was sent home for his wounds to heal. Tenderly she nursed him. In her spare moments while he slept, she worked with the women as they organized the "Ladies Soldiers' Relief Society." No longer did anyone question that a woman with a baby due should not be seen in public or that fingers only used to delicate embroidery should not sew rough garments for soldiers in the field.

One warm June morning as Anne went about her daily duty of planning the meals and portioning out the day's supply of food-stuffs from the swinging shelves in the pantry, she took the key from the chatelaine pinned to her waist and unlocked the heavy, grilled door to the wine and root cellar beneath the front porch.

Instead of potatoes and carrots, she confronted eight large trunks.

Locking herself into the cool dark place, Anne lifted a lid. Staring back at her was the portrait of Lucy Pickens, wife of South Carolina's Governor; printed on stack after stack of crisp, Confederate one-hundred-dollar bills. Curious, she opened all eight trunks. Each held newly minted paper money.

Anne sat down and laughed until she was nearly hysterical. *Sometimes I worry so over my brothers and Ellen that I forget my husband's important job.*

William arranged his work to stay at home as June ended. He enlisted neighbors and servants in a conspiracy. He must shield Anne from knowing the Macon battalion was at Chickahominy, experiencing warfare at its worst. Young Campbell and Sidney and Clifford Lanier were fighting in the desperate Seven Days' Battles to save Richmond.

Keeping news from her became easier when the doctor put her to bed because of sporadic labor pains.

William's only concern was his Annie. He was sweating with relief when at last, on July 6, 1862, she delivered a girl.

But Anne's face was pale, and her voice was so husky he had to bend over the bed to hear.

"Could I name her Caroline Tracy Johnston to carry on my sister's name?"

"Of course," he replied with gruffness he had meant to conceal. He did not care about the name. He did not care about the baby. The child's breathing rasped, and his heart had been broken too often.

Anne lifted the corner of the receiving blanket for him to see her.

I'm not going to love her, he determined, teeth clenched. But she was the prettiest baby he had ever seen. *She looks like a little rosebud.*

⌣∶∾

Anne sat at her dressing table combing out her hair. She parted it in the middle and smoothed it down to a knot at the nape of her neck. Surveying herself in her silver hand mirror, she decided it was more becoming than it had ever been. Her eyes stared back, open and ready to give love.

But Mr. J.'s eyes are still closed to everyone . . . now even me.

His hair and beard had grizzled, but it was the furrow between his brows and his down-turned mouth that worried her. He had never taken time with Tracy, but it hurt her that he completely ignored Caroline.

Anne forced herself to consider his responsibilities. Now Richmond had sent him one million five hundred thousand dollars in gold. Some was in the jewelry store safe. But the rest . . .

She grinned mischievously at herself in the mirror, thinking, *I hope no one ever finds the latch in the coffin niche and looks under the linens in the secret room.*

Just when Anne's nerves were calming from cuddling Caroline, a letter came from Ellen.

Oak Place
August, 1862

Dear Anne,

All is well. The enemy has evacuated Huntsville. It's been a terrifying experience. I was awakened at dawn on the morning of April 11 by a muffled sound. Thinking Edward, I ran to the window and saw troops leading horses silently past. It was too dark to see their colors, but I knew by their stealth it was the Yankees.

They took over the McDowell's house and some others and arrested leading citizens. They even arrested our preacher, Frederick Ross, because he prayed, "Lord bless our enemies and remove them from our midst as soon as seemeth good in thy sight." Wasn't that awful of them?

Most officers showed respect for ladies, but they did not control their men, and it wasn't safe to be out. I stayed inside Oak Place, cared for tenderly by our faithful servants.

It is exceedingly painful after so long a silence to send a letter of such sad intelligence. But God has seen fit to remove one of our little household treasures. Our little sunbeam, sweet wee Ellie, the merry light of our house, is no more. She died on July 8 of scarlet fever. Others on the place have succumbed in the epidemic, but Susie and Georgia have thus far escaped.

Your devoted sister Ellen

Anne's grief mingled with guilt as she reveled in her own beautiful Caroline. She wrote urging Ellen to move to Macon. Ellen's reply declined.

Dear Anne,

Guess what? Edward was commissioned a Brigadier General on August 16, 1862. Can you believe it, and he's only 28 years old? General Kirby Smith in promoting him said, "He is upright, intelligent, and accomplished."

But we knew that, didn't we? It's so nice having a spirit-sister with whom I can brag! His brigade consists of four regiments of infantry and a battalion of field artillery.

Thank you, but I'll remain in Huntsville. It's nearer Edward. Maybe we'll stay safe so he won't have to worry about the girls and me.

Lovingly,

Ellen

❦

Baby Caroline was growing stronger, and Anne took her into the hummingbird garden every afternoon so that Tracy could run. She did not mind the heat, and the dry August air helped Caroline's breathing. Enclosed by the brick wall, Anne could retreat from the world amid the blossoms and flying flowers. She constantly added plants, predominantly pinks and reds, to bloom at different seasons. But just now the huge butterfly weed, with its bright orange clusters, was the focal point for swarms of hummingbirds and butterflies.

With the sun relaxing her tense neck and the laughter of her children, she could forget for a moment how the war was tearing her family apart.

Because energetic Tracy soon tired of merely watching birds and butterflies, Anne had George build him a joggling board. Long and flexible, with four finials on each end for safety, the thick board could take a small boy's punishment, and Tracy never tired of jumping up and down.

As fall approached, Anne added a few evergreens, cherry laurel against the wall, clipped into spires, and banana shrub between the windows of the summer living room so the creamy blossoms would send their scent into the house.

Now, war news was becoming so encouraging that Anne brought the *Macon Telegraph* into the garden. Devouring every word, she thought, *my family will soon be together again.* Excitedly, she read that Lee had chased McClellan from the Virginia peninsula and defeated Pope at Manassas a second time. The South had never been so near victory. Europe hovered on the verge of granting recognition, assuring Southern independence.

In September, General Lee took the offensive, marching his troops into Northern territory. Lee's Army of Northern Virginia included Georgia's regiments.

Anne thought about Campbell and Sidney. They seemed to her like mere boys. But Phil had just turned thirty-one. Others had joined her in pleading with him to seek discharge because his leg was physically disqualifying. Pride, courage, and patriotism would not permit him to consider it.

Forward to the front was his word and action, she thought. *I know Phil's relishing this invasion.*

Phil shouted to his men to strip off their trousers and tie gear to their muskets. They splashed into the Potomac, wading across at White's ford. Cool water refreshed legs quivering from too many battles, too much marching.

As they climbed out on the far side, the band struck, "Maryland, My Maryland." They stepped to the music, renewed with hope that the border state would turn to them and that the war would soon be won.

But many Marylanders waved them on with unfriendly gestures. Some shouted epithets.

By nightfall on September 13, Phil was in his tent listening to the hammering of rain when Campbell entered with a young courier whose face seemed drained of blood.

"Major Tracy," he stammered, "Campbell says I kin confide in you. Gen'l Lee divided the force in five parts. He sent five sets of Special Orders 191. The set for Gen'l D.H. Hill was wrapped around three of his favorite cigars."

Phil waited for the lad—he looked fifteen—to continue. At last he said, "Sit down, son."

He began to sob. "I don't know where I dropped Gen'l Hill's."

Phil wiped his hand over his mustache, knowing how Yankees pounced on Southern tobacco. "There's million to one odds against its being found in these fields," he said, sounding more confident then he felt, "but we'd better report it up the chain of command to General Colquitt."

⌒∴⌒

As Phil's Sixth Georgia Volunteers neared the sleepy village of Sharpsburg, Lee positioned them around a ridge behind Antietam Creek. Suddenly there was a ripping sound of muskets and a roar of cannon.

Uh-oh, thought Phil, *chicken-heart McClellan must've found the lost order. He never attacks with such surprise or decisiveness.*

Badly outnumbered, they fought, exhausted, hungry.

On the fifteenth, Stonewall Jackson's troops, having taken Harpers Ferry, arrived amid bloodcurdling rebel yells. Phil grinned at his boys, and they yelled back. Hope renewed, Lee's men fought on.

By Wednesday, September 17, dawn hid behind gray mists that shrouded fields and woodlands, but the crash of musketry began at five o'clock. The Bluecoats poured up the hill.

Phil's two hundred fifty men entered a cornfield. An eight hundred-man-strong Twenty-Eighth Pennsylvania attacked at point-blank range. In the savage hand-to-hand combat among the corn stalks, Phil joined other senior officers, leading out their men to keep up the momentum. One idea burned his brain: *We can't retreat. This invasion must not fail if we're to live as independent men!*

About nine o'clock in the morning when Phil was advancing

under terrific fire, he felt a Minnie ball sever the large artery in his thigh. A fellow soldier tied a handkerchief around the gushing wound; then he fell beside Phil.

No longer seeing the glint of muskets. Phil envisioned the beautiful face of Matilda.

Anne stood in the midst of a silent crowd that waited in front of the newspaper office. The terrible word that September seventeenth had been the bloodiest single day's fighting of the war had them white-lipped, staring with wide, dry eyes.

Two boys came out with casualty lists. Anne grabbed. Names swam. Phil's name was not among the dead. *But there!* She gasped as her finger stopped near the bottom.

Major Philemon Tracy. Missing.

Chapter XVI

Macon remained hushed. Word came that McClellan had not renewed his attack the next day, but Lee had felt it wiser to take his tattered army back to Virginia. Stunned townspeople could scarcely grasp the horror that on one day—September 17, 1862—along Sharpsburg Ridge and Antietam Creek, 11,000 Confederates and 12,000 Federals had fallen wounded. In all, 5,000 were dead, others were dying. North and South, people were wearing black.

Except Anne. Cheeks flushed, eyes glittering with determination that Phil would be found, she deliberately donned pink-striped chambray trimmed with crocheted cherries that bounced as she walked the short distance to Aunt Carry's house.

But her stepmother had no word from her son, Campbell, or from Phil.

Anne hurried along Walnut Street and turned in at a picket fence where she found Mary Jane Lanier humming as she cut roses and laid them in a basket that swung over her arm.

"Oh, my," Mary Jane said, putting her hand over her mouth when she saw Anne.

"What news of Sidney?" Anne bit her tongue. "And Clifford?" She often forgot to mention the younger brother.

"Both safe. Oh, my dear, I feel so guilty about being joyful, but I'm thankful to say they weren't . . . there. They had already been transferred to the Mounted Signal Corps. Both my boys are such good horsemen, don't you know?"

Anne nodded, swallowed. "I'm glad they didn't have to witness the slaughter."

⌣∴⌣

At last Anne received a note from John Baxter:

> Campbell has been brought into the field hospital where I'm surgeon. The boy is suffering from superficial wounds. There is no word of Phil. He is listed as missing. We haven't given up hope.
>
> Sincerely,
>
> John Baxter

Anne fell to the floor with her head on the chair. "My darling brother, Phil. My darling brother, Phil," she wept.

No one could comfort her. Weeks passed. Still she stayed in the darkest lower rooms of the house, given to fits of weeping.

Then news came that hardened her, made her tears congeal. Photographs had been displayed in Matthew Brady's studio in New York City, graphic pictures of twisted dead along the Hagerstown Pike, of swollen corpses in cornfields, and of bodies fallen three deep in a sunken road someone christened Bloody Lane.

Anne again sank to her knees, praying, *Dear God, Don't let Phil's body be left piled in Bloody Lane.*

Rising, she washed her face and went into the garden, knowing she must get control of herself.

But the infamy of the photographs turned her heart cold with hatred for the North.

⌣∴⌣

In November, Campbell came home. He stayed only until his wounds finished healing and his transfer came through. He was eager to become aide-de-camp for Lit, who was now commanding five Alabama brigades. The western campaign had shifted to Mississippi, and Campbell told the family they should be proud that Brigadier General Edward Dorr Tracy had been sent to reinforce Vicksburg.

At Christmas Anne received a letter from Lit:

> The river port of Vicksburg has batteries set on high bluffs. It is like the Rock of Gibraltar, keeping the Yankees from going down the Mississippi. President Davis calls it "the nailhead that keeps the two halves of the South together." But I have little active service at this port, and the very fact incapacitates me for discharge of duties of other kinds. I am ennuied past description.
>
> I wish Ellen was with me, but the food supply here is uncertain, and she is so fragile.

Anne frowned as she read, filled with nagging worries.

Anne shook the newspaper and fumed. "I don't know how you get the *New York Times*, Mr. J., or why I read it." She felt the anger, still welled-up from her grief over Phil, spilling out like bile from her throat.

"Listen to this. 'President Lincoln's Emancipation Proclamation took effect January 1, 1863, freeing all slaves in states in rebellion.' What right does he have to pass a law that concerns us?"

"He's wily," Mr. Johnston replied. "He's been wanting to do this but knew it wouldn't wash, what with the South winning the battles."

"But the Yankees didn't *win* at Sharpsburg. There were no decisive results."

"No. But Lincoln claimed it as victory. You see, their army had been indifferent to preserving union with the South. Now, he's ignited them with a nobler cause—freedom."

"And the South will continue to struggle for the right to govern themselves." Anne slumped in her chair with exhaustion born of sorrow. "And the carnage will continue."

Much as she hated being out in the cold January rain, Anne forced herself to add her service to that of the other ladies of the Relief Society and go daily to the *Wayside Home*. They had converted the old Macon Hotel by the railroad tracks into a hospital and eating house for disabled soldiers who were passing through on trains from the battlegrounds. As she tied on her bonnet, she laughed grimly, thinking how the older women had protested their efforts at nursing as unseemly and reminded them that proper ladies do not view the male body. The need had become so great that all able women had to leave their sheltered lives and join the war effort.

Shivering, Anne climbed into the carriage. It was loaded with baskets of sweet potatoes from her root cellar, collards from her winter kitchen garden, and bundles of bandages she had made by tearing her fine sheets.

I hope some gentle lady is aiding Lit and Campbell. At least I'm glad they're together. Family is so important, she thought as her carriage swung onto Mulberry Street. *If only I knew something about Phil.*

"What's the matter, Moses," she asked her coachman as they stopped immediately.

"Judge Holt's butler's flaggin' us, ma'am."

"The Judge want to see you, Miss Anne," said the white-haired old man.

She huddled under the big umbrella he held over her and hurried up the walk. She was surprised to see a woman waiting in the doorway.

"Come in," said Judge Holt. "I want you to meet my new wife, Nora."

Anne smiled through gritted teeth. *Dearly departed Miss Mary,* she thought, *I can't stand one more change.*

Seated under a canopy of dogwood, Anne surveyed her daffodil bed with pride as her fingers flew over knitting an army sock. She had placed a quilt beside the curving brick wall that broke the

March wind. Propped upon it, eight-month-old Caroline banged a spoon, making her golden ringlets bounce.

Tracy ran with arms outstretched to the breeze and his two-year-old legs kicking out like a colt's.

"Go bridge. See swans!" Tracy squealed.

"Not now, Tracy. Come back with Caroline."

Anne tuned out the din, leaning toward the delightful sound of a mockingbird trilling. She searched for him amid the dogwood blossoms. Then her eyes widened. *That melody sounds like Chopin.*

Jumping up, she dropped the yarn, leaving the ball rolling out as she ran toward the gate and the music floating through the trees.

"Sidney!" She threw her arms around him and then held him back, gazing at his hollow cheeks accented by a new swooping mustache. He looked soldierly in his trim gray uniform, but it was the guardedness of his eyes that made her realize he had seen too much of war and was no longer a boy. *He's become a man.*

～∴～

Sidney smiled at his beloved mentor, but he felt shocked. She had put on weight, and her hair was unkempt. Grief had her looking slumped, old.

I won't mention Phil, now, he decided. *She needs cheering.* He followed her to a cast iron chair, bent on chattering brightly.

"Clifford and I are home on furlough," Sidney said. "We've had duty near a great library at Petersburg, Virginia. I've been studying Carlyle, Goethe, and Schiller. I've set some of Tennyson's lyrics to music for my flute."

"I must hear it," Anne said.

"I want you to. I've been over at Gussie Lamar's house. She learned my piece to accompany me. Her mother came in as we practiced. Clasping her hands in extravagant praise, she said it was so beautiful that we must repeat it at the music club tomorrow night. I know you're a member. You will be there, won't you?"

"I don't go anymore. I'm in mourning. You must know about Phil?"

Sidney nodded. "I'm so sorry. I know it's even harder not having closure . . . . But the whole South is wearing black crepe, and it's acceptable to go out. Come this time for me. Please."

"We'll see."

⌣ː◡

The next evening Sidney approached the Lamar house as hoop-skirted women glided up the steps. He was disappointed that he did not see Anne Johnston. *I might not have had the confidence to play and to write if she hadn't listened and encouraged* me.

When Sidney stepped into the music room, a tiny girl, dressed in blue, was already seated on the piano stool. As her melody spun out softly, reverently, he was amazed that such a dainty pair of shoulders could produce music with great depth. He leaned closer, realizing her size had misled him. She was not a child.

The piece ended. She swiveled around, and Sidney caught his breath. Light brown hair, parted in the middle, was pulled back neatly from a face of infinite sweetness that made him want to clasp it in his hands. Her lips twitched in a tentative smile. But it was her eyes that made him fall instantly in love.

Oversized for her face and child-like form, her thick-lashed eyes drew him across the room. *Oval and large and passion-pure, and gray and wise and honor-sure,* he thought, wishing for a pencil.

Gussie stepped between them. "Mary, may I present Sidney Lanier. Sidney, Miss Day moved to Macon while you were gone."

With a flourish, he bowed over her hand, kissing it, hoping she would be impressed with his new mustache. She was such a delicate wisp of a girl that he must take care not to blow her away.

Before he could swallow his admiration and speak more than a few words of greeting, two ladies swept in, dominating the attention of the entire room.

"Paris gowns," Mary Day whispered.

Mrs. Lamar introduced the guests to the group. "Most of you remember Mrs. Hugh Lawson Clay, who's visiting her father Major Anderson Comer. This is her sister-in-law, Mrs. Senator Clement

Clay. They've just arrived from Huntsville, Alabama."

As Sidney looked around, it delighted him to see that Anne Johnston had come after all. She emerged from a dark corner into the candlelight and offered the visitors her hand.

"I'm Anne Johnston," she said. "My brother, Edward Tracy, has spoken often about your family."

"How lovely to meet you at last," responded Virginia Clay. "General Tracy has told us about you and your marvelous home."

"You both must come to tea. But do tell me of Huntsville. I'm frantic about my sister-in-law Ellen."

"The Union soldiers have been beaten back, I'm thankful to say. General Bragg assured my husband that North Alabama is secure now."

"Then it's safe for her to make the trip here. I'll beg her to come . . . . Just in case."

"Mr. Clay had to proceed to Richmond. It's beset with two deadly enemies, Yankees without and smallpox and scarlet fever within. He wouldn't let me go, but I mean to follow him."

Sidney wondered how he could edge around the ladies and get Mary to the porch to talk. When he took a step, Mrs. Clay eyed his uniform and stopped him.

"Young man, will the war die out soon?"

"I don't know," he replied slowly. The vision of Malvern Hill seemed burned behind his eyes. "This blood-red flower of war is such a hardy plant, spreading like a banyan, inserting new branch roots into the ground, overspreading a whole continent. I wish the seed might perish out of sight and memory and hope of resurrection, forever and ever."

"How poetically expressed!" Mary Day exclaimed spontaneously.

Sidney looked deep in her wonderful eyes. "You like it, Miss Day?"

"I love it."

"I'm so grateful," he murmured, smiling. He held her gaze for a long moment before he realized Mrs. Lamar was calling them to begin the program.

Mary Day played first, and Sidney listened enraptured, feeling oneness with her in their shared talent. *All of the girls I have thought I loved have been mere prelude,* he realized. *With Mary, the real music is about to begin.* He tried to calm his bursting heart because next, he must play his own compositions accompanied by Gussie Lamar.

After a triumphant rendition, he filled his refreshment plate, and carried it through the entertaining rooms, seeking Mary. *It's piled so high. I hope she won't think me greedy.* He would not want her to know how hungry he was. There had been scarcely any food in Richmond.

He found her in a corner, eating. "Ah, Miss Day. I adored the way you played 'Papillons.' No other musician fills me so full of heavenly anguish as Robert Schumann. If I had to give up all the writers of music save one, that one would be he."

"I feel that way, too," Mary answered, glowing. "I like all his music, but especially his collection of 'Papillons.'"

"His music burns my soul. I believe I could make the butterflies flutter in my flute to your accompaniment."

Mary laughed. "I'm sure you could. Bring your flute over tomorrow night and meet my father and brother. We're boarding at Wesleyan College."

"I can't wait 'til then." Touching his flute to his lips, he improvised a melody. "This is what you mean to me as you have come into my life this day," he whispered. "Let's call it 'Number One!'"

With intense satisfaction, he saw her tremble.

Anne watched the young musicians across the room as she chatted with vivacious Virginia Clay. She was glad Sidney had insisted she come. *I'm getting lonely and hard,* she thought. Things will be better when Ellen arrives. I'll write her tomorrow. She and the girls must come here where we're sure to be protected.

When Anne crossed the dining room to congratulate Sidney and Mary, she saw the rapturous look on his face. She bit her lip. She had known Mary's father, Charles Day, in the old days when he carried cotton barges down the Ocmulgee to the Georgia coast. Then he built extensive warehouses in Brunswick and Darien, but enemy ships had captured the ports. The Days had escaped to Macon, but the Yankees had confiscated his home and business. Mr. Day was bitter at being penniless. Anne shivered because she'd heard news that might hurt her young protégé.

I hope Sidney knows Mary Day is engaged.

Sidney whistled as he climbed the steps to Wesleyan College. It had surprised him that the Days were boarding here, but his mother had explained that many refugees had taken rooms of students who had left because of the war. The boarders' fees allowed classes to continue for the few who remained.

Mary introduced him to her family, and then she delighted him by leading him to a piano in one of the basement practice rooms.

Sidney took out his flute. "Do you remember 'Number One' I played last night? What I would speak is in the music more fully than I can express in words. One soul alone like my poor flute can only utter a faint life melody; no grand harmony can come from single notes. Join your life to mine; then we two will enchant the dull ear of the world with so sweet a life tune, even its dullness shall recognize God as the only possible Composer of such thrilling harmony."

Mary clapped her hand to her mouth, eyes wide in surprise. "Mr. Lanier! You must not speak love to me. I'm engaged to Captain Fred Andrews."

Only momentarily taken aback, Sidney said, "You've not heard all God has composed of the music of your life. His mournful introduction has but served to heighten the glorious, satisfying effect of the piece." He bent over her, breathed her fragrance. "You must give *us* a chance."

Calmly Mary replied, "I love your poetic expression of emotion, but I should be true to my betrothed. Let's just enjoy music together."

"Then play a prayer."

⸰⸱⸰

Undaunted, Sidney courted Mary throughout his two weeks at home. The perfume of violets and jasmine helped him woo her with poetry. Still she hesitated, so he left her a letter.

Dear Miss Day,

My furlough has nearly expired; at the stern call of duty, I leave here tomorrow to rejoin my comrades in Virginia. I shall probably not meet you again for years; possibly, never. I am indebted to you for many pleasant hours; and I wish to make you my friend.

Under the circumstances, you will surely acquit me of presumption when I ask you to allow me to write you.

The journey of my life has been a rugged wandering alone in a stormy night; and the few stars that have shown through are the friends God has given me. I have indulged the idea you might become my friend; must I give up so delightful a hope?

State your objections or give your refusal if so please you.

> I am, and shall always be,
> Your friend,
> Sidney C. Lanier

He and Clifford left, escorting the two Mrs. Clays on the train to Richmond. Sidney wondered what would befall them all before they might be together in peaceful Macon again.

⸰⸱⸰

Anne's excitement mounted as time came for Ellen to arrive. She could hardly wait to show her the rose garden sparkling with

April's first blooms. She walked through the house. Each room shone.

When Ellen descended from the train, her thin face worried Anne. *She's so pale. I must try to take her mind off Lit. I must make her know she is not alone. We care. God cares.*

Anne embraced her. Then cooing to Georgia and talking liltingly to Susan, she lifted the burden of the children from Ellen and ushered them all into the carriage.

"Y'all look like you need food. How bad was the trip?"

Ellen's tinkling laughter belied her words. "A horror. We rode from Stevenson to Chattanooga on the freight train. We would have been forced to go to the smallpox hotel or remain in the streets but for the gallantry of an officer acquaintance of Edward's who gave his room to us. The next night we reached Atlanta. The hotel seemed so unsafe I put my money and jewelry in my stocking, but we did have a bed. Mother left us to go to my sister's, and we . . . Oh, I'm so thankful to get to Macon! It's wonderfully quiet and peaceful."

After the children were fed and bathed, Anne and Ellen talked far into the night. But the next day Anne's pleasure was dimmed by disappointment.

"I do so love being with you, Anne, but Edward made me promise to stay with his mother."

"With Aunt Carry?" The memory stabbed of how Carry had taken Little Edward away from her, never letting her touch the baby. She tried to swallow the hurt. *She's the only mother he's ever known.*

In the ensuing days, Anne had to content herself with entertaining them all at meals. One afternoon as they sat in the garden watching the children play, Anne thought what a joy it was seeing Susan and Georgia with her two.

Suddenly she caught herself and sat up straighter. *Tracy's not mine even though I treat him the same as Caroline. How will I bear it when John Baxter returns and takes him away?*

Ellen broke into her thoughts saying, "I've received a letter from Edward written March twenty-third. He says:

> We are stationed in rear of that portion of our
> lines about midway between Vicksburg and Snyders
> Bluff, a fortified position held by us on the Yazoo
> River. At the present stage of water, my line is im-
> pregnable.
>
> My men are all in high spirits and feel renewed
> confidence in our ability to hold this Gibraltar, if we
> can only keep supplied with subsistence. Campbell
> got in yesterday. Ten million thanks for your beauti-
> ful present.

Ellen blushed and looked at Anne through tears. "It's awful
to think he might be hungry."

"I'm sure he didn't mean that. The way he describes his location, he should be safe." Anne's voice was hardy, but her insides
quivered. *It's impossible for us to stop thinking of Lit.*

Lit sat enjoying the presents Campbell had brought. The
blanket Ma had sent felt splendid; the peaches Annie had preserved
were delicious. Unfortunately, the tomatoes Ellen canned had
exploded on the journey. It was the three ambrotypes he feasted
upon. He opened the largest of the leather boxes and fingered the
bright copper scrolls encircling the glass from which the portrait
of Ellen smiled at him.

*She looks plump and healthy. Beautiful in that deep blue dress. I'm
so thankful to have her safely cared for by Ma and Anne.*

Lit lifted the glass on which the photographic negative was
etched and pressed his lips against the watered silk that had shown
through, giving the picture color and substance. He remembered
this gown from Ellen's trousseau. He put the case back together
and kissed Ellen's mouth. Then he laughed. He had the other two
ambrotypes set up before him.

I can just hear Susie and Georgia saying, "Favwer, kiss me, too."

He sat for a long time with his family. It gave him the peace
he needed to turn his attention to the worsening situation.

For two-and-a-half years, Confederates had controlled the Mississippi River from the batteries mounted on Vicksburg's bluffs. Neither land nor naval forces had been able to reduce their defenses; now a new invading force under General U.S. Grant was encamped on the west side of the river.

On the night of April 20, 1863, Lit watched vessels flying the stars and stripes, which to him now meant subjugation, steam into view. Showers of shot rained on the city, but they caused little damage. Bombs burst in air, reminding him of the Roman candles the Christmas he met Ellen.

I must write her about this splendid spectacle.

But on April thirtieth, spies warned that the Federals under Grant had crossed the Mississippi to the south of them. They were marching 25,000 strong to cut Vicksburg off from Jackson and burn Port Gibson.

The Confederate commanding general, John C. Pemberton, dispatched Lit's brigade of 1,500 as part of 6,000 troops to protect Port Gibson.

Lit's men arrived about sundown completely jaded after the forced march. As they passed through the town of beautiful homes and blooming gardens, people came out to cheer them on their way. Lit noticed many of the women and old men were sobbing.

He looked at the towering magnolia trees with huge white blossoms wafting their incense heavenward and prayed, *I praise you, Lord, for the beauties of thy creation. If only man could glorify you like nature.*

With quick commands, Lit positioned his men along the road leading from the river, throwing up light earthworks. They settled down for the night, slapping mosquitoes from Bayou Pierre, hoping their artillery would arrive in time.

⤙∴⤚

The next morning, May 1, 1863, about seven forty-five, zinging bullets showered the ground around them. Soon thick action forced the Confederate line to give ground on left and center. Tracy's Brigade held the right flank with Lit on the front line directing their fire.

The Confederate artillery arrived. The Bluecoats fell back.

By one o'clock the continuous roll of small guns almost drowned out the discharge of the artillery. A Confederate bugle called retreat, but the noise was so incessant the command could not be heard.

Lit saw an opportunity for a counterattack. Motioning to his men, he mounted the earthworks.

"Charge!" he screamed, unheard. But his line surged behind him waving tattered battle flags of stars and bars.

Lit scarcely felt the minnie ball as it struck his left shoulder above the clavicle. It penetrated his right lung. He fell.

Campbell crawled under the fire, and eased his brother out of range.

Lit felt other hands tenderly carrying him to Port Gibson. Vaguely he knew his troops were passing his stretcher, pulling back to Vicksburg.

As they came into town, a lady rushed forward, smothering a shriek, "Is that General Tracy? Bring him to my house. I'm Mrs. Baldwin."

Lit felt a clean bed, knew Campbell sat beside him. Time drained away like his strength, and he could not speak.

⤙∴⤚

Anne ran all the way to Aunt Carry's. The cryptic summons had frightened her.

As she burst in, Aunt Carry thrust a telegram at her.

"We were afraid to open it."

Anne glanced at Ellen, slumped in a dwarfing wingback. She tore the envelope. Voice cracking, she read:

Your gallant husband is dead; fell mortally wounded on May first. I have escaped unhurt. Will try to come home.

Signed,

C. Tracy

Ellen fainted.

Chapter XVII

William was worried. He sat in his study, but he could not keep his mind on the weakening Confederate Depository records he was auditing. Since Campbell had arrived on furlough to tell them details of Edward's death and how they had reverently buried him in Judge L. N. Baldwin's family plot, Annie had exhausted herself. Her grief was, once again, taking the form of anger. Furiously sweeping the house one minute, she would throw down the broom the next and go to the garden to dig.

The war is causing concern on two fronts, also, he thought. Shortly after Campbell left Vicksburg, the Federals had surrounded the town, bent on starving it into surrender. *They had little food when he left. How can they hold out? If they don't, it will break the Confederacy in half.*

William knew that Vicksburg desperately needed reinforcements, but the war was heating in the East. Even while Edward's brigade had been suffering defeat at Port Gibson, General Lee had been accomplishing his most brilliant victory at Chancellorsville, Virginia. Now Lee was planning a second invasion of the North.

William pushed back the papers on his desk. *I almost wish I wasn't privy to that knowledge. I'm sure the Confederacy will never be recognized in Europe without a triumph on Northern soil, but our Treasury is depleted. Lee's men are hungry, ill equipped. Can they do it? And what of the threat at Vicksburg?*

He slumped over his work, pressing aching temples. *I must warn Anne to spend only paper money and hide our gold.*

Anne scarcely realized May's and June's passing, but July exploded, awakening her to nightmare. On July first, second, and third, in the greatest single battle of the war, Lee was defeated at Gettysburg, Pennsylvania, and on Saturday, July fourth, after forty-seven days of siege, Vicksburg, Mississippi, surrendered. Anne glared at Mr. J. She had never known him to appear so weak. He looked all of his fifty-three years, sitting there wiping tears as he read the accounts.

William sighed as he met her gaze and began reading aloud. "'The people of Vicksburg were reduced to living in caves against the daily shelling. They survived by eating mules and rats before they gave in.'" He looked up. "Aren't you glad Edward and Campbell didn't have to endure it? Listen to this. They're repeating what Mississippi's military governor, Colonel J. L. Autry said last year when Vicksburg was first told to surrender. 'Mississippians do not know, and refuse to learn, how to surrender. If Admiral Farragut and General Butler want to come and teach them, let them come and try.'"

Ann's temper flared. "There's no higher moral example than a Christian gentleman willing to lay down his life for the principles he holds dear!" She stamped out, slamming the door.

When her anger exhausted itself, Anne felt as if she had melted and run down into her shoes. Aunt Carry sent word she needed her help to comfort Ellen. Her family's letters of sympathy made her weep the more. Her brother, Angelo, wrote that he could not get her to Edward's grave, as she asked, because the enemy occupied the whole country. Then Virginia Clay, returning from war-torn Richmond, brought news that the enemy was re-occupying Huntsville.

I have no solace to give, Anne thought, dropping her hands at her sides.

Refugees from middle Tennessee were filling Macon because the lull in the east and west wings of the war had centered the battle there.

And we have all those rooms on the fourth floor. I should . . . But . . .

She lolled her head against the chair, limp.

ᘳᗕᘰ

For two years, the war had been a distant, horrible monster, moving relentlessly toward them. Now it was reality, a rumble she could almost hear. Anne shook herself by the scruff of her neck and went to work. She nursed not only Ellen, who grieved that she could not put flowers on her husband's grave, but also a seriously ill Mary Jane Lanier.

Anne was too busy to listen to Mr. J.'s anxiety that only the rocky-faced crags of North Georgia's mountains were keeping the enemy out of their State. During August Rosecrans' Federal Army of the Cumberland and Bragg's Confederate Army of Tennessee strove back and forth through the Appalachian gorges. Then, in September, the unthinkable happened. The invaders penetrated Georgia.

The enemy was repelled at Chickamauga Creek, but after the bloody battle, trains loaded with wounded rolled into Macon. Quickly townspeople converted the City Hall into another hospital.

By November, with Bluecoats sweeping through Tennessee, the Southern army, now in tattered butternut homespun and bare feet, pulled back toward Georgia.

Anne knew the time had come to open her fourth-floor bedrooms. She sunned feather beds and washed her now meager supply of linens as farm wagons rolled into town loaded with frightened people, hugging hastily snatched heirlooms.

With her house full of hungry guests, Anne doubled the planting of her winter garden. As Christmas approached and she struggled to deal with strangers and prepare a semblance of Santa

Claus for her two children, Lit's two, and six refugees in her home, she felt unusually tired. Hot and woozy, she sat down, fanning.

Oh, my! With a giggle tinged with hysteria, she realized, *Well, I said I wanted children. I'm going to have another baby.*

༺∴༻

It was New Year's Eve; Anne needed a moment alone with Mr. J., and she led him out to the balcony. They looked down on a silent city. There was no cacophony of church bells to welcome 1864. All except the Presbyterian's, which was attached to the town clock, had been taken down and molded into cannon.

Below them, weary Macon was sleeping except for vigils in the many hospitals. Even the town's children were exhausted from their job of packing cartridges.

Anne snuggled against her husband's comforting bulk. *The town is teeming with women and babies and wounded,* she thought. *What will happen if the enemy comes?*

She stroked Mr. J.'s beard, white now. There was only the militia to protect them, toddling gentlemen who christened themselves the Silver Grays. They drilled, assisted by canes and ear trumpets. Their servants had thrown up earthworks around the town, but what good was that without soldiers?

"We'll be all right," said Mr. J., reading her thoughts. He kissed her. "General Wheeler's cavalry will protect us."

"The Lord will protect us," she said. "Happy New Year." She hugged him, but a niggling thought plagued her. *What good are Little Joe Wheeler's horsemen in a whole, big state?*

༺∴༻

By spring of 1864, Anne's household had grown as rapidly as her girth. She looked into the mirror, thinking her cheeks were positively plump. She felt as if she could explode from the tension. She paced her bedroom, rigid, needing to do something. The women overflowing the town were fighting hysteria, but with only unprotected, rural areas below Macon, there was nowhere else to run.

"Mr. J., every house in this town has a guest from Tennessee or North Georgia. Something should be done about hospitality."

"Your spunk always rises with the sap," he replied, eyes crinkling. "What do you propose?"

"Laugh if you will. But we're still civilized people. I plan to give a tea."

"A tea? I can't get you any sugar from New Orleans since the fall of Vicksburg. Our blockade runners on the east coast are in too much peril for me to ask them to bring tea from England."

"Humph." She tilted her chin and sniffed. "The Bluecoats can't block the bees from my garden hives. I have honey for baking. And I've saved a tiny bit of Twinings Tea. I'll serve it weak with lots of fresh mint."

Mind made up, she bustled out, eager to instruct the cook. She stuck her head back for a last emphasis.

"We'll wear the best we can muster. No black. And we won't talk about war!"

～:～

High-pitched chatter filled the drawing room. Women with nerves raw from worrying over husbands present only in letters from remote battlefields, forced gaiety, trying to pack pleasure into these moments away from hospitals where each incoming patient might be their loved one.

Anne watched from the doorway. They appeared so nervous that she hoped she had done the right thing. "Ladies, please come into the dining room."

They followed into the vast, paneled room. Gathering around the table, they sighed.

"Exquisite!" Mrs. Thomas Hardeman cried out.

"However did you manage such lovely refreshments, Anne?" asked Mrs. Washington Poe.

Anne beamed. The entire creation was from her herb garden. Silver trays held watercress and cucumber sandwiches. Spoonfuls of potato salad flavored with fresh dill were wrapped in thinly sliced ham. Watermelon rind pickles gleamed. Honey-sweetened scones graced the far end. But in the center the pièce-de-résistance, stuffed nasturtiums, glowed on a white platter. Nestled against green leaves, burnt-yellow blossoms were stuffed with cottage cheese and orange-red blooms were filled with chopped egg. Both colors whetted appetites with their mustardy taste. The ladies stood about munching dainties, chatting like teatime of old.

Anne had prevailed upon Ellen to sit at the silver service and pour, reminding her that she had stayed secluded for a year, and anyway, everyone was in mourning. For a brief interlude, even Ellen smiled.

But as shadows lengthened and duties called, conversations slipped to concerns. It started lightly enough when Rebecca Wadley, whose husband William Wadley was now Superintendent of the Railroads of the Confederacy, asked how Anne got the tea.

"I recognize the pekoe you get from Queen Victoria's favored shop in London, but how did even Mr. Johnston get it through the blockade?" Rebecca queried.

"He didn't. I'd saved it. Mr. Johnston says blockade runners are no longer playing daring games. It's deadly serious with risk of shipwreck or worse—capture." Anne saw Mary Day turn pale, and wished she could bite off her tongue.

Mary gasped. "In my last letter from Sidney, he'd asked to be made a signal officer on a blockade runner."

"I'm sorry to hear the dear boy wants such a dangerous mission," said Virginia Clay. She patted Mary's arm. "He'll be all right." She turned to Rebecca. "What do you hear from Colonel Wadley?"

"His last letter was discouragement itself. He spoke of lo-comotives breathing like consumptives or standing cold upon sidings with wrought-iron tires worn away. He said what rolling stock we have left is screaming for lubricating oil and given only pig grease."

The circle of faces mirrored despair.

"Ladies, Ladies," cried out Virginia Clay, "lighten your gloom. This is secret so don't put it in letters. I shouldn't tell. But I will. President Davis sent my Mr. Clay to Canada to arouse the public mind to our cause. Canada could induce suspension of our hostilities!"

"If only they could," went around the group.

Anne hurried to further bolster morale. "And I've heard Louis Napoleon sympathizes with us. He's ready to give French neutrality in American affairs for American neutrality in his Mexican affairs. Reassure each other. We'll keep the enemy from our door!"

William, watching from behind the curving pocket doors connecting the art gallery and dining room, was glad Anne and her friends were enjoying themselves.

It might be the last time, he thought. He knew that Georgia's borders were in danger of being breached. The First Tennessee was retreating into the state, and Governor Joe Brown had called out the Georgia militia to fortify them. *Surely the fortress at Kennesaw Mountain is impregnable.*

If not, William hated to think further. Little Macon was important. Because of diverging railroads, it had become a point for Quartermaster and Commissary Departments as well as the Depository for Confederate gold.

William sighed. *I'll take a chance and wait 'til tomorrow to tell them. Then they must get prepared and hide their valuables.*

Chapter XVIII

Anne backed from the secret room. "It's full. Won't hold one more thing."

"Then something has to come out. 'Ruth Gleaning' shan't be left for grasping hands. And really, my dear, as much as we want to protect our treasures, we must hide our last barrel of flour."

Anne grimaced at Mr. J. with determination. She refused to leave the Repoussé silver for the enemy to steal. Noticing the deep creases lining his face, she relented. She smoothed his forehead, kissing it, knowing his worry was not for replaceable things but for the house, which could never be duplicated since the economic changes brought by war.

Sighing, Anne turned back to the small room, bent and pulled. She shrieked, doubling in pain.

"Babies don't care if what you're doing is important," she gasped, trying to laugh. She leaned on his supporting arm until she got her breath. "Today is going to be the day."

He eased her to the step.

Anne sat, panting until the contraction subsided. "You'll have to help George bury some of these things in the garden. You'd better send Adelaide to me."

"Where is she?"

"On the fifth floor squirreling foodstuffs in the rafters . . . Don't worry. I'm only thirty-four. This is the sixth time I've borne a child, for heaven's sake. It should be easy."

But it became increasingly difficult. As the hot afternoon waned, she sent Adelaide for her husband.

William looked up from burying a silver pitcher beneath a rose bush. Wiping the perspiration dripping from his eyebrows, he took in Adelaide's concern as she stood with Caroline propped on her hip.

"What is it? How's Miss Anne?"

"That baby turned wrong. Mr. William B., you gone haf' to send for that doctor."

He nodded at George who brushed the red clay from his hands and started off at a long-legged lope.

Adelaide remained.

"Yes?"

"Tracy, he's playing, but you gone haf' to take Caroline." She thrust the baby toward him.

The smile on Caroline's round face turned down, and her long-lashed eyes widened with terror.

Remorse tasted sour when he saw her fear. *She's nearly two, and I've never held her.* "Where's Cloe?" he faltered.

"All them kitchen gals be's gone just when I need 'em."

I've been so afraid to love Caroline. What if she dies, too? She was born smaller than the others . . . . But now she looks healthy. Beautiful! Cautiously he tickled her hand with his beard.

"You're pret-ty. Pretty as a rose." He snapped off a bud and handed it to her. His heart ached with yearning deeper than he had felt since he first longed for Anne's love. "Come to Papa."

Caroline's lips parted as she studied him. Then she stretched out chubby arms.

"My little rosebud!" he cried, burying his face in her golden curls, trying not to frighten her with too many kisses.

William had ample time to get acquainted with Caroline. It was many doll-tea-parties later before Mary Ellen Johnston arrived, born May 4, 1864, on her own timing.

William tried to prepare the Confederate Treasury in his charge. He anxiously sought every report as Bluecoats poured down Georgia's mountainsides. The Army of Tennessee fought for every inch of home soil, but they were losing ground as Hooker's Federal artillery pounded them back. Governor Brown ordered the State Militia to leave the border, fall back, and guard Atlanta because of its important factories, its hub of rail connections to the entire South. Refugees fled before the noise and fire and smoke.

William wondered if he should move his family below Macon. *But in the open there'd be less protection. And I need to see to all that's here.* But the settling factor was wife and infant. *Annie's not able to travel.*

Summer. William read communiqués of each development with rising fear. The war edged ever closer.

At last the advance upon Atlanta was stymied by the perpendicular knobs of Kennesaw Mountain. Even the hundred thousand men under General William Tecumseh Sherman could not take that impregnable fortress. But the Federals had men enough to flank, and the Confederates were attacked at the Chattahoochee River, ten miles north of Atlanta.

By July 22, the incessant booming of cannon battling for Atlanta echoed through surrounding counties. Even though Macon was eighty miles south, it felt the impact. Frightened women, who drove wagons for days, claimed Macon's sanctuary. Casualties by trainloads deluged the hospitals. The little town, already staggered by its load, took in more, more.

William wondered how they could protect so many helpless people. In a week's time, Macon's population had swelled to six thousand women and children and an equal number of wounded.

On July 29, William stood on the third floor balcony clenching the rail as he surveyed the quiet streets. Suddenly he saw a stranger approaching. William met him on the front porch.

Identifying himself as a secret agent sent by General Wheeler, the young man warned that raiding parties were circling around Atlanta, heading toward Macon. "They have orders to cut railroads. Stoneman's Raiders are advancing in three columns, one down the Forsyth Road, two down the Clinton Road," he said. "I've alerted General Cobb."

William thanked him and rushed down Mulberry Street to Howell Cobb's house, thankful that the rotund old fellow had been called from the Virginia front to command the Army of Georgia Reserves. Although they were few in number, at least they were headquartered here.

When William entered, Cobb greeted him with the agent's dispatch and more alarming news.

"Our spies tell us Sherman ordered General Stoneman to cut the *Macon and Western Railroad*, but he means to make a name for himself by releasing the prisoners we have here and the 30,000 at Camp Sumter in Andersonville. Captain Dunlap and a party of scouts have already sighted the enemy approaching. Rapidly. We must prepare for battle."

William felt as if he had been hit in the chest. "Then Wheeler can't get here in time to help us. How many trained men do you have?"

Cobb shrugged. "Roughly a thousand." He began writing.

"Man, how can we protect our city with so small a force?"

Cobb glanced up from his desk with an expression meant to quash William's panic. "Governor Brown is at the Lanier House. I'm asking him to issue a proclamation calling every man—citizen or refugee—to bring any kind of gun he can get and report to the courthouse without delay.

⁓∴⁓

That evening as the group assembled in the courthouse, William watched with a scowl. *We're so few. So untrained. So old!*

Fear was impossible to swallow, but he knew they could not

surrender. *There's too much here of importance. But it would take a miracle for this bunch to hold off an army.*

Cobb was speaking, but William was not listening until a sudden clatter alerted him.

William turned to see men on crutches, swathed in every sort of bandage, struggling into the room. Determination was written on each face.

"All who can hold a gun will fight," shouted their leader, wafting his cane. "If you can help us to the firing line," he added with a rueful laugh.

A cheer went up, and at that moment a smart group of soldiers entered, thinking the welcome was for them. A battalion of 600 Tennesseans, they had left guarding Andersonville Prison and were bound for Atlanta to reinforce the troops.

Cobb waved his arms to stop the whistling and stamping of feet. "Here's our strategy. Counting you Tennesseans, we have trained men enough to delude Stoneman. We'll make him think we're strong and can defend ourselves. We'll post our line between East Macon and Walnut Creek, interspersing fit soldiers with wounded or civilians. If you can't shoot, make your presence known with the rebel yell."

The bloodcurdling sound, beginning deep in throats and ending in a series of yips, reverberated from the ceiling.

When the men quieted, Cobb snapped orders quickly. "Cumming's battery, guard the Clinton Road. Major Taliaferro, your battery *will* hold the hill beyond Fort Hawkins. Lieutenant Colonel Findlay, you Georgia Reserves . . ."

William turned to see a man struggling to stow crutches and sit beside him. "Why, Campbell! We haven't heard a word since you went back to the front."

"Our train just arrived from Virginia."

"Are you seriously wounded?"

"Just bad enough to get home to save your skin."

Day was breaking, and Anne tried to hurry Mary Ellen with her nursing. That independent miss would not be rushed, but, at last, Anne handed her to Adelaide to take to the safety of the ground floor with the other children and the women refugees.

"I must see what's happening," Anne muttered, rummaging for Mr. J.'s old field glasses.

The ginkgo tree, shimmering in the heat mists of July 30, drew Anne to the crest of the hill. Holding onto it for support, she strained to see the enemy cannon trained upon them from across the river. Horrified, she saw a bomb fall behind Ocmulgee Hospital. It exploded, but she saw no fire. Other shells lobbed into the city, but none seemed to do damage.

They're held back by the freshet swelling the river, Anne realized She swept the binoculars across the Old Ocmulgee Fields and focused on Dunlap Hill. Fascinated, she watched, realizing the battery was adjusting range. A shriek escaped her as a shell loomed. *They're aiming at this house! They must know about the gold.*

Smoke erupted from the battery. Anne watched the shell as it arched, veered, struck the sand sidewalk in front of her neighbor's home just as six-year-old William Sims Payne skipped down Mulberry Street. Hitching up her hoop skirt, she ran.

The missile bounced, hurled through a column on the Holt's porch, entered a window. Anne reached the child and scooped him into her arms. His linen shorts and white shirt showed only dust. Running with him held close, she burst through the Holt's front door, screaming, "Miss Nora."

Blank-faced, Nora Holt stood on the second step of the hall staircase. The enemy shell had angled through the parlor and stopped in the hall unexploded. It lay at her feet.

Anne led her outdoors just as their troops moved forward.

First came the Silver Greys. The proud old gentlemen set off toward the Vineville Road, coughing as they hobbled along, struggling for breath in morning air so thick it seemed it could be grasped and wrung out. Anne ached for them, but the next unit aroused tears.

Marching briskly, Company B, Macon Volunteers passed on long, skinny legs. Thirteen-and-fourteen-year-olds, some only twelve, they wore frightened looks on their freckled faces. Anne thought of their fathers in Company A, fighting in Virginia, believing they were keeping the enemy from their own hearthsides.

A rattling sound broke the stillness. Wagons loaded with wounded crossed the bridge to East Macon. Factory workers followed, shouldering an assortment of guns.

How can we hope to hold them off with such a ragtag army?

William slapped a mosquito. By seven o'clock that morning, 2000 men had posted a long enough line to look impressive. *How did I draw a place in the swamp?* He wondered. He glanced at the others in his group. The minister of Mulberry Street Methodist Church, J. E. Evans, and the First Presbyterian's pastor, Dr. David Wills, looked as bewildered as he felt. *Can we possibly master the tasks of working the ramrod and biting off the ends of paper cartridges?*

Only Campbell, propped against a tree between the clergymen, steadily returned the enemies' fire.

Suddenly a minnie ball grazed Campbell's face, striking pine bark into his lip and knocking him off his crutches. Blood flowed. He waved his arms for balance, but he fell flat.

Both preachers dropped their muskets and ran to aid him.

"I ain't hurt," Campbell yelled. "Keep firing or the enemy will know they can break through the line."

William determinedly bit off another cartridge and fired, but the other two struggled to hoist Campbell to his feet. He began cursing.

"Campbell!" Rev. Evans shamed him. "Aren't you afraid to take the Lord's name in vain right here in the presence of death and destruction?"

Campbell erupted another oath as a shell burst beside them, and they let him drop.

"Boys, you like to have broke my leg over," he shouted. "Don't try that again."

William's gun felt hot, and the muscle in his weary right arm quivered like jelly. He despaired of ramming home the ball to fire. But while the other three scrambled, the enemy might rush through.

It's up to me, he thought grimly. *Cobb said if we couldn't do anything else to yell.* He had never let himself go enough to try it, even though he had often heard foxhunters on his father's plantation give the cry when their dogs passed from scent to view. He sighed. *Now is the time.*

He squeaked an ineffective yipping. He tried again high in his throat, letting it soar. Down the line others took it up, swelling through the swamp, "Yip, yip, yip, ya-hoo!"

⌣∴∽

Anne opened the door and stepped back, frightened by the back powder caked on her husband's beard and the dried blood obscuring Campbell. Then she saw that beneath the grime, they wore proud grins.

"We did it," they chorused, but they waited until she had set out supper to explain.

"My dear, we inexperienced—and wounded—warriors . . ." he saluted Campbell. ". . . kept up enough firing to reinforce the charges of Nisbet's battalion and the rapid and continuous firing of Taliaferro's battery . . ."

"We skunked Stoneman," Campbell interrupted. "He thought we had so many soldiers that he couldn't possibly capture Macon. At nightfall, he sounded retreat."

"Then it's over? We're saved?" Anne ran around the table to hug her husband.

He smiled up at her. "Yes. But it's really because of General Cobb's wisdom and judicious placing of the men. Do you think you could manage a dinner party to honor him?"

⌣∴∽

The next evening, July 31, Anne's elegantly served, sparse meal was progressing amid a great deal of congratulations when a messenger arrived with a report for General Cobb.

"Sir, a brigade of Wheeler's Cavalry under General Alfred Iverson engaged Stoneman's retreating force at Sunshine Church near Hillsboro. They captured Stoneman and five hundred men. They're marching them into Macon. What are your orders?"

Howell Cobb reared back and folded his hands across his broad expanse. "They wanted to see Andersonville prison. Conduct them there."

Oh, maybe the war will soon be over, Anne thought as she poured coffee improvised by roasting acorns. *It's been so long! If only Atlanta will hold.*

⌣∴∾

On the same evening, Sidney Lanier rode through the forest, headed for a new assignment in Wilmington, North Carolina. He grinned at Clifford. He was glad he had turned down a promotion so they could stay together. They'd had fun as scouts in Milligan's Corp along the James River.

"Those moonlight dashes on the beach of Burwell's Bay and the little brushes with the enemy were mere larks," said Clifford, mirroring Sidney's thoughts. "But I wonder. What are we in for as signal officers on blockade runners?"

Sidney laughed. "Keen excitement, I dare say. Wilmington is holding out long after other ports have closed."

He didn't want to alarm his young brother, but he breathed a prayer for his protection. *Watch over Clifford, Lord. We'll be on different vessels, so I'm leaving him in your hands. I know we're heading toward constant danger.*

⌣∴∾

Wind blew through Sidney's thin clothing, all white so his figure would not be discernable by the enemy. He stood with his feet planted on the bridge of the *Lucy*, bobbing in the choppy Atlantic south of Wilmington. Teeth chattering, he readied his signals.

He was rain soaked, but it could not be helped. Frustrated, they had waited while October's clear sky and harvest moon had made it impossible to slip by the blockaders. Sidney grinned. November had blown in this dandy storm.

Concealed by rain, they had left their haven up the Cape Fear River and ventured into the lair of the outsized Federal Armada.

215

Five ironclads, disclosing the locations of their guns by constant muzzle flashes, bombarded Fort Fisher as they silently floated by.

"We've got to make it, Sidney," his friend, Bob Jones, whispered.

Sidney nodded, knowing that their planned cargo of meat and medicine and shoes was vital.

They scarcely breathed until the *Lucy* was into the Gulf Stream. But the storm ceased. Suddenly the moon sailed from behind a cloud. The *Santiago-de-Cuba* loomed. The lookout spotted them.

The *Lucy* ran up canvas, fled. The cruiser steamed in pursuit. It was over. Sailors in blue peacoats swarmed the deck.

"Hands up, Reb! Gotcha!"

~:~

November rain drummed the windows of their bedroom, and Anne shrank closer into her beloved's embrace. He was warm; yet, still she shivered.

She stared at the ceiling. When Atlanta had fallen on September 2, she had not given up hope. People had said that, cut off from his supply lines, Sherman would be forced to retreat.

Now word had reached them that instead, on November 16, Sherman had left Atlanta burning, an inferno worse than even Dante had imagined. His army struck into Georgia. Sweeping in two columns, each over 30,000 strong, the Yankees were committing a terrible rapine upon the State that was the Confederacy's granary. Burning, pillaging, they were said to be destroying all they could not steal.

The enemy was marching toward Macon.

Anne buried her face against him. "Oh, Mr. J. what's to become of us?"

Chapter XIX

Even as Anne watched Macon's citizenry bravely limping out to defend their homes again, she knew all hope was gone. Like a horde of insects, the Bluecoats were devouring the land, marching toward the capital of Milledgeville with divergent columns making for Augusta . . . for Macon.

Running to Aunt Carry's, Anne brought her and Ellen and the girls to stay with her own brood in the basement.

The moment she settled everyone and caught her breath, she regretted it.

This house will be their first target.

Even if the enemy had not known about the Confederate Depository, they were torching the finest mansions. Riders had brought stories of homes invaded, jewelry snatched from necks and fingers of defenseless women, carpets and furniture stolen, music smashed from pianos . . .

How can the army of a civilized nation wreak such annihilation on people lately friends—even brothers?

Shaking with fury, Anne looked about the long room. She had complained about how hard this house was to keep. Now she realized how much she loved it. *How could I bear to see it burn?*

Ellen was shivering, and her lips looked blue as she tried to sing with the children. The servants huddled in a frightened group.

I must calm my nerves, Anne thought. *It's going to be up to me.*

She realized she should stoke the fire. The day was unusually cold for the twentieth of November.

At that moment, a knock sounded. She stopped mid-step. Every face, white and black, turned toward her.

Anne tiptoed to the door, waited. Rapping persisted. It stopped.

"Miss Anne?" a small voice called.

Flinging the door open, she saw Mary Day, disheveled, tears flowing.

"Dear child! It's dangerous to be out!"

"I had to tell you. Sidney's been captured!" Mary threw herself into Anne's arms, sobbing.

Anne swept her inside and bolted the door.

Anne paced the corridors, fingers clenching then strutting as she tried not to scream. After two days silence, the house meant nothing. It was not a home without her husband.

Where is he? What if he's taken prisoner? William Butler Johnston is a well-known name. What will they do to him?

What if he's wounded? It's so cold. What if . . . She pressed her fists to her temples, blocking out the unthinkable.

All she knew was that the militia was engaging the enemy three miles east of Macon. A small band. A mighty army.

Oh, William, if only I could do more than stand and wait.

Sidney shivered. He moved with the line of prisoners being searched. The guards were taking everything of value. Quickly, he slipped his flute up his sleeve.

The wind off the Chesapeake Bay whipped his thin clothing. He knew only that he was ninety miles south of Baltimore at the extreme southern tip of Maryland. This walled-in stretch of sand—with no shade, hundreds of shabby tents, thousands of Confederate inmates—was Point Lookout Prison.

They were hustled into rude tents pitched on the bare, wet ground.

"Looks as if they're putting us naughty boys to bed without our supper," Sidney joked, smiling at his weary comrades.

The tattered canvas afforded scant protection against the gale. Sidney's throat and chest burned. He began to cough.

∾⁖∾

"Annie, I'll stay up and watch tonight," Ellen insisted on the third evening.

Anne looked into the sweet face, pale, drawn. "Now, what would I do without you if you got sick?" she replied in as joking a tone as she could muster. "Your bed warmer's ready. Get beneath the covers before you catch cold. I'll . . ."

A muffled knock made them turn from the stove, wide-eyed. It sounded again—in signal.

"It's Mr. J.!" Anne flung over her shoulder as she ran. Unhesitating, she opened the door and embraced him.

He leaned upon her until he reached the entry chair. He could go no further.

Kissing him, she felt his coldness. She fetched a quilt while Ellen brought the brass warming pan prepared for her bed and a cup of the soup they had kept simmering.

"The enemy's pulled back," he said when he had drunk the broth.

"Then Macon's safe?"

"For now."

Ellen slipped away as Anne helped William to bed. Only after he stopped shivering did she ask what happened.

"It was the worst thing I've ever endured. They had new Spencer repeating rifles. Our men kept marching out in the face of that horrible fire, sacrificing their lives for their families and homes. Oh, Annie, we lost six hundred and fourteen killed and injured. When we could retrieve the wounded, many had frozen to death on the field."

"Campbell?" It was a small sound.

"In hospital. But the shot was clean through his arm."

"What made the enemy leave in the face of so few?"

"Our fellows advanced within fifty yards of their fire and held firm. It seems Sherman's bummers are moving on when they're met with resistance. Bound on marching through Georgia to the sea."

"Poor Savannah."

"Poor us. They did what they intended. They wrecked our railroad."

"They've cut it before."

"This time they made a job of it. I could see them lining up along the rails, lifting them shoulder high, dropping them until the spikes and chairs shook loose from the joints. Then they stacked the rails over bonfires of cross ties. When they were red hot, they twisted them into knots around pine trees."

"Then the railroad's beyond repair," Anne gasped.

He nodded. "We have no way of getting supplies or hearing where the enemy is. We're cut off from the world."

~:~

In the cold confines of prison, Sidney was told the news by his gleeful captors.

"Hey, Georgia boy, your capital's been sacked, and those plantations you're s'proud of have all been burned," the guard boasted as he slopped weak barley soup into their tin cups. "General Sherman presented Savannah as a Christmas present to Abraham Lincoln."

Several began cursing the enemy. Sidney said nothing.

He felt as if his heart had stopped. *What of Macon?* Sidney wondered. *My parents? My darling Mary?*

Sidney put his hands inside his shirt to warm them. *Already, I feel like a skeleton.*

Clean water and food were as scarce as bugs were abundant. Sidney watched fellow prisoners hunt rats for dinner, but he could not stomach one, even though he was growing feeble.

Through the freezing days, Sidney had often played his flute to encourage himself and others. The melody had drawn one fever-ridden inmate to him, another poet, John Bannister Tabb. They had strengthened each other. Now, Sidney knew, on this night, they all needed music.

I must play again. It's Christmas. But I feel so weak. He took out his flute. *Can I stand?* But he always stood when he played.

The melody spun out to cheer, to console, "Joy to the World! The Lord is Come." From other tents, men followed the sound of hope.

"Emanuel, God with us," Sidney told them. "He is with us still. He will see us through."

Bob wiped tears. "You prove the truth of Sir Galahad's words, 'My strength is the strength of ten, because my heart is pure.'"

Sidney laughed and it started the coughing. He turned away. He did not want his friends to know he was spitting blood.

⌣⋮∼

Anne surveyed her Christmas table, lined with friends old and new, people who had fled the invading army with nothing left. Only chimneys, lonely against the sky, marked where their stately homes had stood.

With her eyes flashing, Anne turned to Genie Blount, seated on her left. "Well, they didn't kill us. They meant to humble us. But I *won't* be humbled."

Genie's smile was wan. "They surely humiliated me. They dumped the keepsakes from my cedar chest, my wedding veil, the baby's clothes, . . ." she choked. " . . . all of it ground beneath someone's boot heel. My courage is pretty low. But at least my house is standing. And your lovely table, this pink china and silver . . . encourages me."

"I regret we've no oysters from Savannah, no oranges for ambrosia, only what is grown on plantations southwest of here."

"I hear that in Sherman's path people have nothing to eat but sweet potatoes."

"At least Georgia had that one unharvested crop the blue locusts missed." Anne laughed harshly.

Her eyes sought Williams at the far end of the table. *What are our people going to do for food?*

Stretching between them, crystal compotes, lifting globes of red and yellow, formed centerpieces. Anne had filled them with apples, take-home favors for these friends who has so much less then they. This she could do, but how could she tell four-year-old Tracy that this year Santa Claus would not come to Georgia.

Through the tall windows, she could see the trees whipping and bending. She felt cold. And her heart was as bitter as the winter wind.

Chapter XX

Anne gripped the arms of her chair, watching her husband with concern. She often despaired, but not he. Now this dear man who always managed everything, who never lacked for an idea, sat slumped with his head in his hands. She waited.

"Annie, 1865 looks like it's ringing in the end of our world."

She knelt, embracing him. "Mr. J., things can't be that bad," she soothed.

"They are, they are. The Confederate Treasury is bankrupt. With what little gold we have, we've been buying up our own currency at $60 for each dollar in gold. We need $500,000,000 to carry on the war."

At that moment Caroline came into the room, as always, running. She bounced into his lap.

"Papa, Papa, I mashed my pinger."

"Papa kiss it and make it well, my little rosebud."

Anne smiled as the golden head snuggled against his chest, and his eyes took on life again. *I don't know how we'll survive,* she thought. *But we will.*

◈

In February, Virginia Clay returned to Macon. Anne, eager for news, invited her to take tea, now brewed out of rose hips. When she arrived, Anne was alarmed at her state of agitation.

"Mr. Clay placed a personal in the newspaper telling me to leave Richmond," she said, words gushing. "It's under constant fire and in hunger. I wouldn't have left if he'd been there, but he's still in Canada, urging them to negotiate peace between the Union and the Confederacy. President Davis also sent Vice-President Stephens to attempt a treaty with Lincoln."

Virginia's rosy cheeks trembled with emotion. "Lincoln's refusal and rudeness to his old friend Mr. Stephens was so harsh that it revived Richmond's war spirit. But all they have left to fight with is gumption."

Anne opened her mouth to comment as she poured the weak tea from a pink porcelain pot, but she pressed her lips together as Virginia swallowed and kept talking.

"I'd only just gotten through the Carolina's when that firebrand Sherman destroyed the *South Carolina Railroad*. It's even worse than the *Central of Georgia*. Sherman's calling cards are everywhere, chimneys, ashes, and ruined crops. No one has anything to eat!"

Anne passed scones and butter, thinking she must start serving heartier fare to hungry guests. "We still have food in western Georgia and southern Alabama."

"But not northern Alabama . . . Huntsville is overrun with enemy soldiers again," Virginia wailed. "I can't go home!"

Anne patted her arm. "You'll always have friends . . . and speaking of that, do you have any word of Sidney Lanier?"

"Oh my dear, haven't I told you? General Cobb was in Augusta and escorted me here. He'd heard a friend of Sidney's smuggled gold into the prison in his mouth. Sidney bribed a guard, and he and some others escaped."

"Wonderful!"

"Yes, but . . . The prison conditions were so deplorable that Sidney contracted tuberculosis. No one knows where he is or if he can live long enough to make it home."

᮪᳟

Sidney lay in the hold of a ship bound for Fortress Monroe.

Moldy hay in the cattle stall afforded little warmth, and he shook with chills and fever. All these months he had fought to live, but exhaustion overwhelmed him. As consciousness slipped from his grasp, he heard a whisper.

"I'm afraid Sidney's dying."

Father, into thy hands I commend my spirit, he prayed as blackness claimed him.

Then, fiery liquid gurgled in his throat. He dreamed the scent of gardenias, felt a soft hand. He cracked one eye. A face. *Mary? An angel? Am I dead?*

"Brother Sid, don't you know me?"

"Move Lilla, dear."

A woman knelt over him as the child stepped aside. She forced a spoon between his lips and more of the blistering stuff trickled down.

"Swallow Sidney. This brandy will revive you."

She persisted for several doses before he could hold his eyes open.

"Lilla," he whispered, but he could not remember the name of his motherly old friend from Montgomery.

Pain pierced his ribs as his comrades lifted him over their heads and passed him out of the animal's domain.

He awoke in his benefactor's cabin, wrapped in clean blankets. His body tingled, and he could barely endure the pain as the heater warmed his numb limbs.

Hours later, restored somewhat by hot soup, quinine, and brandy, he asked for his flute. A few notes trembled through the dark midnight. From below, cheers arose.

꒰ː꒱

Sidney's Samaritan, who was smuggling medicine from New York into Dixie, lavished her supply upon him until he was strong enough to walk.

Then began his slow and painful journey through the Carolinas. By the time he crossed into Georgia, dogwood blossoms lighted the woodlands with their promise, stimulating his efforts to reach the warmth of home.

On March 15, 1865, when he arrived in Macon, he found his mother as ill as he.

"Do you have word of Clifford?" he asked her.

"No. His ship went out at Wilmington and couldn't get back in again through the blockade. But I believe God will bring both my boys back to me before I die."

⌣∴⌣

A fit of coughing seized Sidney, exhausting his last strength as he pulled himself up the hill toward Wesleyan. He must see Mary before he sought his own bed.

Word had reached her, and Mary flew down the stairs to meet him.

Sidney saw shock in Mary's eyes at his wasted condition, but she threw her arms around him and kissed his parched lips, not caring who saw.

"Beautiful Mary. The thought of you kept me alive."

"Sidney my dearest darling. I've prayed constantly."

"I love you, Mary, but I must release you from your promise to marry me. I'm too ill. I have no prospects if I recover."

"Nonsense! You're just in want of nursing and fattening up. I'll care for you, wait for you. Everything around us has changed, but my love for you will never change!"

⌣∴⌣

Anne concocted strengthening broths for Sidney and Mary Jane Lanier, but they barely ate. She and Mary Day sat, watching them as both hovered near death. Repetitiously the two women deplored the fact that medicine was contraband of the war and the South had none.

⌣∴⌣

With the bursting forth of April, usually her favorite month, Anne felt even more frustration. *What's happening in the war,* she wondered. As quickly as communication lines were repaired, the enemy cut them.

226

In the middle of the month, the *Daily Telegraph and Confederate* got a report from the west that a Federal Calvary Corps under General Wilson was sweeping through Alabama with three divisions of horsemen armed with Spencer repeating firearms.

On April 15, General Cobb marshaled the Georgia Reserves to meet Wilson on the state line at Columbus.

While Macon wondered what was happening, the newspaper printed an item Anne read through tears:

> In view of the near approach of the enemy, and the possibilities that our opportunities for prayer may never hereafter be as they have hither-to been, the praying people in the city of Macon are invited to unite in one more prayer for our country at four o'clock this afternoon in the basement of the Presbyterian Church.

⌣∴⌣

At dawn on April 20, William responded to a summons to Cobb's headquarters. Hurrying down Mulberry, he was surprised to see barrels of corn whiskey being emptied into the gutters.

Cobb merely nodded in greeting. "I'm taking precautions to protect our women from drunken soldiers. We left Columbus in flames. We fought nobly, but we could only retreat. I'm throwing up entrenchments and barricading the streets with cotton bales, trying to do better for Macon."

"I must save the railroad's gold," William replied, already half out the door.

Puffing for breath, William rushed to the livery stable and secured a wagon caravan. Quickly, he loaded the gold reserve of the *Central*, his own gold and silver, and that of friends. He dispatched the precious cargo toward the hills north of Athens.

When he returned to Cobb's office at noon, a telegram had just come through from General Beauregard.

"The war is already closed," said Cobb with a heavy sigh. "General Johnston and the Yankee Sherman agreed upon an armistice on the eighteenth. What we didn't know was that General

Lee had surrendered the Army of Northern Virginia on April 9, so I make our fight at Columbus on the sixteenth the last battle of the war. Wilson must not have heard it's over. I'm to halt him on the spot where the official message can reach him. I've sent riders to every road leading into Macon with flags of truce."

⌣:∾

Arrogant, William thought as he stood facing Federal General James H. Wilson. His cavalry had charged into Tattnall Square at six-thirty that evening, having refused to halt where they were met outside of town.

General Cobb said, "Sir, I insist you read this telegram."

Lean and fit, General Wilson looked down his nose at the portly Cobb, ignoring William altogether. He glanced over the dispatch:

> United States Military Telegraph
> Raleigh, North Carolina
> April 19, 1865

> To Major-General Gilmore:

> I have made an agreement with the Confederate Generals for a suspension of hostilities until certain terms are approved at Washington. These terms embrace the disbandment of all the Confederate armies, and a firm and lasting peace. You will, therefore, cease all further depredations on public or private property, and make dispositions looking to a general peace.

> W. T. Sherman,
> General Commanding

"Humph," grunted Wilson. "I'll recognize no instructions from Sherman through Confederate communications. You have *five* minutes to surrender the city or I will fire upon it!"

Cobb spluttered. "Under the rules of war, when an armistice has taken place, men are instructed not to fire a gun. I consider the war at an end. I've disbanded my forces."

"Five minutes."

"You are within my entrenchments. I'm compelled to surrender, but I do so under protest."

Wilson turned to his aid. "Wire Sherman I've captured Macon."

⌣∴⌣

William hurried to reassure his household of women, hoping Anne would never find out that Wilson had fought with the victors both at Antietam and Vicksburg.

"The war is over," William told them.

Soft shrieks stopped him, but he waved them silent.

"There's more. We're under an army of occupation. You must be careful. General Wilson is a tyrant. He boasted he'd have fifteen thousand men here in three days. His staff has taken possession of the Lanier House and Cobb's headquarters. He's commandeered Joseph Bond's house for his residence."

"Oh, what's to become of poor Henrietta and little Joseph," Anne gasped. She jumped up. "I should go to them."

"No." William was firm. "I don't know where she is, and it's unsafe to go out. Wilson turned his men loose. They're robbing and pillaging and . . . Don't go out of the house."

"Just to the garden." Anne smiled, wheedling.

"No." He looked at Ellen and Aunt Carry, big-eyed, silent. *No worry there, but I fear a hard time keeping my Annie indoors.*

He turned away to set servants guarding every door.

After nightfall, he paced the corridors.

On the third night, soldiers set fire to two blocks of Mulberry Street.

⌣∴⌣

On May 9, Anne looked up from boring needlework as the sitting room door flung open. "Why, Mr. J., you look about to have apoplexy. Sit down."

"Downtown is swarming with Federal troops." He puffed. "General Wilson pursued and captured Jefferson Davis and his entire family south of here. They delivered them here by ambulance.

He's at Federal Headquarters in The Lanier House. Arrested!"

Anne clenched her fingers between her teeth.

"There's a warrant for Senator Clay."

"Why?"

"Conspiring in Lincoln's murder."

"Lincoln's dead? Good!"

"Anne! I can't believe a wife of mine said that. You don't mean it."

"I do. I do. He killed my brothers . . . When did it happen?"

"He was shot April 14 and died the following day. We just hadn't heard it."

Anne swallowed acid in her mouth. "Nor are we likely to hear anything they don't want us to know since they've taken over our newspapers, but that's ridiculous about gentle Mr. Clay. Besides, he was on a peace mission in Canada. Got back into this country by lifeboat after being shipwrecked . . . what? Why are you looking at me like that?"

"They're saying the conspiracy formed in Canada."

"Mercy! Well, the Clays left here bound for Alabama. They can escape to the West."

"No. They could have, but they're back. He surrendered to General Wilson to prove his innocence."

"Virginia will be devastated. I must see her. Don't stop me. Where are they?"

"At Colonel Whittle's house. But you can't go. The streets are full of men and mules, of Federal soldiers and disbanded Confederates . . . and Freedmen are lounging about. Besides, anyone on the sidewalk is made to pass under their flag. And with that fire in your eye . . ."

"I'll take the carriage even though it's only a step. They can't defeat me unless I let them. I *will* go out. And I won't bow under their flag."

⌇∴∿

Mrs. Whittle, tears flowing, admitted them and took Anne to the bedroom where Virginia was packing a valise.

"What can I do to help?" Anne asked, pressing her face against Virginia's wet cheek.

"Oh, I don't know. I've begged General Wilson into letting me accompany my husband. He acceded, but he warned it'd be a rough, disagreeable trip. And I don't have time to get my clothes for the journey."

"What do you need?"

"Well, Mrs. Lamar sent her treasured foulard silk for traveling, but I've no underthings."

Anne clapped her hands. "I do. Several sets of lovely lingerie just arrived from Paris since the blockade lifted. I'll be right back."

Anne returned quickly and remained until late that afternoon when the Clays left for the railway station.

The Johnston carriage followed.

"Oh, Mr. J., look!"

He put his arm protectively across her as a cavalry procession approached. "Wherever did they find that worn-out barouche and those half-dead horses?" he wondered aloud.

"Their idea of forcing humility." Anne spat the words as she saw to what lengths the enemy was subjecting President Davis. The tall man in a full suit of Confederate gray helped his wife, Varina, alight from the pitiful conveyance. A carryall arrived, bearing nurses and four children. All were hustled aboard the train by armed guards. "Those poor women. The children. Oh, baby Winnie!" Anne buried her face against his rough jacket and sobbed.

Early in May, Anne called at the Lanier's cottage and found Clifford newly arrived.

Sidney was sitting up in bed, beaming. "His ship couldn't get back into this country, so they sailed to Cuba."

"Then to Galveston," Clifford took up the story. "From there I walked home."

Mary Jane weakly raised both hands. "I praise God for bringing my boys to me."

❦

A few days later Mary Jane gave up her long struggle to live. Sidney rallied his pitiful strength to console his father and sister and brother.

❦

William wiped sweat trickling into his beard as he trudged down the hill from Joseph's house on a humid July day. *I dread telling Anne,* he thought. *She'll call me a coward.*

Wilson's house, he corrected himself. He had filed a second request with the occupation army's commander for the return of the *Central Railroad's* gold as well as his own and his neighbors. *Surely, they should meet my demands. After all, peace had been signed when I sent the caravan.* He sighed. He could not be sure.

He found Anne sweeping, grumbling as usual about the dirt his ventilating system brought in. He thought it worked rather well.

"Annie," he said, taking the broom. "Sit down. I have to talk with you." He cleared his throat. "While I was with General Wilson, I signed a petition for amnesty."

"What?" She jumped up, leaned a belligerent face over his. "How could you pledge allegiance to a country that's treating us so—so horribly?"

"I have no choice. What was it you said? 'They can't defeat me unless I let them.' I, also, refuse to be conquered. But they will if I can't use my ability to rebuild our wasted State."

"But . . ."

"I merely pledged that I had opposed secession, but when Georgia left the Union I quietly submitted under pressure as all my interests were in the State, and it seemed my only alternative. In addition, I asserted that fully one million dollars will be needed to restore the railroad from here to Savannah. Annie, use your reason. There's no money left in our devastated Southland. Without amnesty I wouldn't be allowed to travel to New York."

Anne's stubborn mouth pursed. "Why not someone else on the Board of Directors?"

"Since R. R. Cuyler died during our terrible April, the *Central* Board is proposing to elect me to replace him as president."

Anne relented with a rueful smile. "They know only you can turn that rubble back into a railroad."

"That's my girl."

⌣⋮∾

As he traveled, William found every facet of Northern economy had prospered from the war. In New York business was brisk, but to his surprise he found that, even among his former associates, hatred and desire to punish the South was overwhelming all reason. Many linked all Southerners to one man's assassination of Lincoln.

Despairing, William questioned his ability to find investors. But he engaged the services of a lawyer named Samuel Tilden to draw up the papers he needed to secure loans to rebuild the road.

Then, calling in old favors, he organized groups of businessmen to hear his presentation.

"Gentlemen," he told them, "the *Central of Georgia* was the dominant railroad traversing the State. It had a capital stock valued at $3,750,000 before the war." He paused at their frowns, and then plunged on. "I assure you this line can again turn a profit and pay its bonds."

Group after group denied him. To cheer himself, he went shopping.

⌣⋮∾

Anne and Ellen, feeling they had to get out, sat in the walled garden. It seemed safe since the gardener, Frank Denham, was planting tulips at the open end. Hummingbirds had migrated, but dozens of butterflies, small common ones and some big monarchs, fluttered over blossoms renewed by cooler autumn weather. Georgia and Caroline leaped about, trying to catch a butterfly, while Tracy and Susan bounced on the joggling board. Mary Ellen played on a pallet.

233

Anne needed this moment to relax and chat with Ellen. "Mr. Johnston wrote that he's bought furniture. More than I want," she said with her mouth turned down.

Ellen laughed. "It will take a lot to fill this house. You'll be moving upstairs now, I'm sure."

"Yes. The war kept us in the basement, but it's cozy, and I like it."

"But your family's enlarged. It was good of you to take Campbell in. I know you've never been close like you were with your whole brothers."

"Um. Campbell is different. Not my mother's child. He has no ambition. All he does is lounge around the house or sit at the livery stable whittling and spinning yarns. I can't put fire under him."

"What about John Baxter. Is he going to stay?"

"I've invited him to live here. I think he will." She paused, resting loving eyes on the sturdy five year old. "Can you imagine having to give up Tracy? However, John needs stability, too. I overheard him telling Mr. J. he couldn't face doctoring again after the terrible conditions in the field hospitals and all the amputations he had to perform."

They sat in silence, trying to quiet sad memories.

Suddenly glum in spite of the sunshine and happy shouts of the children, Anne wondered if Mr. J. would provide John another start. *Maybe in one of his railroads?* She felt almost sinful that her husband was still so rich. She understood that his investments had been in gold and banks and utilities while others had put their entire fortunes to cotton. She sighed. With fields ripe for harvest and stored bales burned by the enemy and no railroads to transport a crop to market if they had one, their friends were penniless.

Anne rubbed the furrows of her forehead. *How can we be of help to people whose only asset is pride?*

Savoring the October day, Sidney hurried along College Street. After two months of warm, sea air, camping with his uncle at Point Clear, Alabama, he felt the congestion in his lungs had cleared. He could hardly wait to see Mary.

When the housemother, Miss Burt, had summoned Mary, she floated down Wesleyan's grand staircase. Sidney tried to memorize the vision of her in blue gray organdy with a bright, royal print. She wore a rapturous smile.

"You're better!" she said, holding out her hands. "My prayers have been answered. Come into the parlor and tell me everything that's happened."

Mary led him into a long room, elegant, serene, furnished with Sheraton sofas and rosewood chairs grouped around fine oil portraits. They hesitated. Every area was occupied by students and their guests except a pair of corset-backed chairs.

Sidney felt gratified that her dear oval eyes grew even larger with disappointment. She, too, wanted to sit closer.

After they had exchanged news, he read her the poem he had just completed, "The Dying Words of Stonewall Jackson." He knew he was putting off telling her what he must.

At last Sidney cleared his throat. "Precious girl, I have bad news. I had to give up my tutoring job at Fulton's plantation."

"Why?"

"I took it for one family, but Mrs. Fulton says now she can't come up with my salary unless her neighbors' children attend as well. I'm still too weak for a large, rowdy crew."

"Darling, of course, you are. Is there no hope of your old position at Oglethorpe College?"

Sidney shook his head, "No. They've had to close their doors like colleges everywhere in the South. I must turn to other work." He tried to make his voice bright. "Grandfather's *Lanier House* seems permanently occupied by the army but not his hotel in Montgomery."

"All the way in Alabama?" Mary wailed.

Sidney nodded. "I'm to join Clifford there. We can clerk and still have time to write." Watching tears well in her eyes, he longed to take her in his arms. He plunged on. "I'll save every penny so we can be married."

"Let's marry now! I can go with you. A tiny room's enough for me. Oh, I can't be separated from you again!"

Mary's sudden rush of tears caused surreptitious glances from the others in the parlor. Sidney leaned forward and dried her cheeks. "Those gray eyes are my springs . . . I gaze in my two springs and see Love in his very verity . . . I still see them when we're apart."

"Don't say no."

"Dearest, I can't marry you with your father refusing consent. You wouldn't be happy without his blessing."

"I would!"

Miss Burt, who was keeping watch on the students in the room lest they try to slip in gentlemen callers she had not approved, looked down her considerable nose at Mary's outburst.

"Let's go out and walk," Mary whispered.

"Without a chaperone? Miss Burt wouldn't allow it. And the streets are unsafe. They're patrolled . . ."

"So we won't be alone," Mary said, giggling and hiccoughing. "I'm a boarder, not a student. I don't need her permission." She tugged at his hand.

⌣∴⌣

Ignoring the soldiers leering at them, they started down the steep hill that was Georgia Avenue.

Mary asked, "Is your father still opposing us, too?"

"I'm afraid so. But we must understand our parents. It's hard to have been wealthy and now have nothing. There's no business in Father's law office. Even Grandfather's Tennessee plantation was destroyed."

They passed the Johnston villa, and Mary caught her breath. "Miss Anne would help us."

Sidney drew himself up proudly. "I wouldn't want to ask. I have nothing to offer in return."

He looked at Miss Anne's ginkgo. The leaves had stripped all at once, leaving the tree standing naked like a skeleton. He touched the ribs of his war-ravaged body, feeling as naked before the world. The golden fans sifted around them as they descended the hill, scuffing leaves, fallen as their hopes; they stayed silent save for the crunching.

Reaching the river, they turned into the woodland, stepping softly over a carpet of pine needles and leaf mold. A fawn leaped, bounding over their path with white tail flagging. The beauty brought only a listless smile to Mary's face. Her sorrow pierced him.

Suddenly sunlight broke through the top of a tall poplar, setting it shimmering. The shaft of light surrounded them with its glow, and they received it with one thought. Turning into each other's arms, they kissed, pouring out their love.

Through a long silence, they sat on a log and watched the dark water. Sidney kissed the soft tendrils curling about her ear. "Time, hurry my love to me," he whispered. "We're already one in heart, but if I'm to call you wife I must prove to Mr. Day that I'm not too much of an invalid to make a little bread."

Mary pulled away. "How could God, who you've served faithfully, let you have this terrible consumption?"

"Remember Job? God didn't explain it to him when he suffered. Job was a good man, but God allowed Satan to test him. He was afflicted with boils and then a cyclone took his houses and children. Still, he fell on his face and worshiped. *Worshiped*, Mary. Job said, 'Though he slay me, yet will I trust in him.' That's what we must do. Turn our faces toward God. He's in control. He will see us through. Trust him."

Mary nodded and smiled even though she could not stop weeping. "And you can trust me. I'll wait for you if it takes forever."

"It won't. My novel, *Tiger Lilies,* is moving well. I'll tell you something I couldn't tell anyone else, but you are my dearer self. I believe God gave me a genius to write poetry and music. That's all I want to do. Can you have faith in my ability?"

His answer was in Mary's kiss.

⌣⋰⋱

"I detest Spooney Wilson," Anne hissed to Ellen as they crossed the street to avoid walking under the flag of their enemy. "It's easy to see why the name followed him through Virginia and Alabama to here."

"Whatever does he do with all the silver he steals?" Ellen wondered.

Anne shook her head. "There wouldn't be any left in Macon if it weren't for some sliding panels and secret rooms."

Ellen gasped and caught her arm as a woman ahead of them spit in a soldier's face.

A group of Freedwoman came around the corner, arms locked so they blocked the sidewalk.

Adeline, who had been behind Anne, stepped in front, glaring belligerently. "Don't y'all gals hear that church bell ringing? Be gone. We's all commanded by the president to attend Thanksgiving services."

The group hesitated, broke.

Anne sighed, thankful their servants had remained loyal.

"I don't think the Lord will hear my prayers. I don't feel close to Him anymore. There's too much hatred in my heart for our captors," Anne said. "Ordered to be thankful for a united prosperous nation, indeed, when ours lies in desolation."

"But you must pray for President Davis and Vice-president Stephens and poor Mr. Clay cast into dungeons," begged Ellen.

Anne growled. They had reached the First Presbyterian Church, and she looked up into the hard face of Wilson himself. Despite the floppy mustache and goatee obscuring his mouth, she could read his eyes. They flashed with glee that the people were submissive to the military orders.

He's glorying in our humiliation, she thought. *His thankfulness is that he's added to its severity. Our cup is full and yet one bitter drop more.*

Anne reached the second step. Heat rose within her at the Wilson's insolence. The enemy's banner draped over the church door. She might have turned had not Ellen and Adelaide held to her arms. Gritting her teeth, she lowered her head and stepped under the flag.

Oppressive silence met them. No one could sing. The pastor, David Wills, sat in a pew shaking his head. At long last Rev. Frank Goulding, whose church in Darien had been burned by Union troops, stood in the pulpit and opened the Bible.

"I'll read Psalm 137," he said in a quivering voice.

> *By the rivers of Babylon, there we sat down,*
> *yea, we wept, when we*
> *remembered Zion.*
> *We hanged our harps upon the willows*
> *in the midst thereof.*
> *For there they that carried us away captive*
> *required of us a song; and they that*
> *wasted us required of us mirth, saying*
> *Sing us one of the songs of Zion.*
> *How shall we sing the Lord's song in a strange*
> *land?*
> *If I forget thee, O Jerusalem, let my right hand*
> *forget her cunning.*
> *If I do not remember thee, let my tongue cleave*
> *to the roof my mouth . . .*

As Rev. Goulding finished the Psalm, they sat for a moment, and then, sensing as one that it was over, the grief-stricken congregation filed out.

Chapter XXI

"Anne, please don't oppose me," Ellen said. "I'm resolved to . . ." she choked, voice breaking.

Anne was sprawled in an unladylike flop in the drawing room after receiving callers for New Year's Day 1866. She looked at her sister-in-law through a mist of fatigue. Ellen leaned against the doorjamb. Face red and crumpled, she looked as if tears were about to win out.

"Um. What? Sit down, you're exhausted."

Ellen perched on the edge of a gilt chair. "I'm going to Mississippi to bring Edward's body back. I want him to rest at home. His family and friends should be able to honor his grave by keeping flowers . . ."

"But honey, you're too frail for such an undertaking." Anne summoned the tone she used to sooth children. "The ladies of Port Gibson are placing bouquets in his memory just as our group is doing for the misplaced soldiers here . . . It's too dangerous for you to travel. With us under the heel of the occupation army, you'd encounter impudent Bluecoats everywhere."

"They won't harm me."

Anne looked into her clear eyes and sweet face, as innocent as that first time they saw her coming down the stairs at Grandma's house.

No one would dare to hurt her, Anne thought. *Blessed are the pure in heart.*

Ellen remained silent, and Anne gritted her teeth. At last she said, "I'll go with you."

"No." Ellen's chin stiffened. "I can do this. I've written to Mrs. Baldwin. She says Campbell and I can stay at her house while . . . it's being done. What I want you to do is take my girls. Susan and Georgia love you." Ellen attempted a laugh. "They mind you better than they do me."

Seeing Ellen's mind was made up, Anne nodded. "Of course, I'll keep them and treat them like they're my own."

⌣∴∾

Ellen's plans included a stop at Huntsville to see how badly Oak Place was damaged by the soldiers who had taken it over, but before she and Campbell could leave, she contracted a chest cold that kept her by the fireside for weeks. Anne worried about her wheezing, but in February, a few days of false spring eased her coughing.

On a warm afternoon, Anne arrived at Aunt Carry's house, bearing boiled custard laced with strengthening eggs, to find Ellen had come outside. She was seated on the dogtrot in a patch of sunshine. Anne greeted Mrs. Isaac Winship and Mrs. Thomas Hardeman who were visiting.

"Anne, how delightful you came," said Ellen, holding out both hands. "Pull up a rocker and hear these ladies' exciting plans!"

"Yes, Anne," agreed Jane Hardeman. "Ellen has started our ideas flying by telling us she's bringing General Tracy's body here."

"We'd been discussing whether to disband the Ladies Soldiers' Relief Society," added Mrs. Winship. "We felt there must be something more our group could do, and Ellen has shown us the way."

Puzzled, Anne saw their excitement was going to be too much for Ellen. She reached over to tuck the quilt more closely around her as Jane continued.

"The soldiers who died in our hospitals around town were hastily buried, too. You know how shallow the graves are since we dug some of them ourselves. Think! Why can't we exhume them and re-inter them in an honored group in Rose Hill Cemetery?"

Anne gulped a sharp breath, looking from one shining face to the other, knowing they weren't realizing what a grisly task it would be. They were waiting for her to speak.

"Well . . ." *There is no dissuading them.* "I-I guess we should do it quickly before all the information is lost. We could erect wooden headboards with the name, company, regiment, and date of death."

Jane clapped her hands. "We knew you'd help. But there's more I hadn't told you-all. My friend, Lizzie Rutherford, wrote me from Columbus about reading a novel on the custom of caring for the graves of dead heroes. While Southern ladies are keeping the cemeteries as spontaneous acts of love, Lizzie suggests reorganizing our soldiers' aid societies as a Ladies' Memorial Association with this as a definite object."

"An excellent idea!" said Mrs. Winship. "I'll send invitations to all our ladies to meet at my house tomorrow. Jane, I mean to propose you as president."

Anne feared for Ellen. Noting the gleam in her feverish eyes, she knew there would be no keeping her from her sad journey.

꒰꓆꒱

By the first of March, Ellen was gone, and Macon's women were organized and working.

Anne was in the yard, playing with her five children, when Jane dropped by.

"I needed a respite from my cataloging," Jane said. "Would you believe I've found more than 600 names?"

"Really?" Anne led her to a chair.

"I wanted to tell you that Lizzie's dream caught fire. Women across the South, who felt their hopes were dead, are stirring to new purpose. I thought you'd like to see this article from the Columbus *Georgia Times.* Lizzie's cousin, Mary Ann Williams, is secretary of their association, and she published Lizzie's idea and wrote all the women's groups."

Mary Ellen was fretting so Anne took the two-year-old on her lap as she began to read:

Columbus, Georgia
March 2, 1866

Messrs. Editors:

The ladies are now, and have been for several days, engaged in the sad but pleasant duty or ornamenting and improving that portion of the city cemetery sacred to the memory of our gallant Confederate dead, but we feel that it is unfinished work unless a day be set apart annually for its special attention. We cannot raise monumental shafts and inscribe thereon their many deeds of heroism, but we can keep alive the memory of debt we owe them by dedicating at least one day in the year, by embellishing their humble graves with flowers; therefore, we beg the assistance of the press and the ladies throughout the South to help us in the effort to set apart a certain day to be observed, from the Potomac to the Rio Grande . . . we propose the twenty-sixth day of April. Let all alike be remembered from the heroes of Manassas to those who expired amid the death throes of our hallowed cause.

Sincerely,

Mrs. Charles J. Williams
Secretary, Ladies
Memorial Association

Tears streaming, Anne thrust Mary Ellen into Jane's arms and buried her face in her hands.

"Why, Anne, whatever is wrong?" Jane stroked the baby's straight brown hair. "I-I'm sure all of the women in the South will respond to Lizzie's marvelous idea . . ."

"But-but Phil. My darling brother Phil lies—Oh, I don't know where, but somewhere in Yankeeland. With no one to spread flowers. Nothing to show he died a hero."

༝

Anne's melancholy remained, and when April 26, 1866, arrived, it was difficult for her to attend this first Memorial Day's ceremonies. Rev. David Wills was already speaking when she arrived in Rose Hill Cemetery.

The cold lump lodged against her breastbone became fire and gall as she descended the steep hillside toward the Ocmulgee and saw that the little group of women gathered around the sad rows of white headboards was under an armed Federal guard.

Anne could feel enemy scrutiny on the back of her neck as she set down her buckets of flowers and joined the others decorating the graves. She noticed a little girl arranging blue and white violets and red verbena in a tiny, but forbidden, Confederate flag.

Sunlight flashed on a bayonet as it thrust to destroy the floral emblem.

Stepping between, Anne stayed the blue-clad arm, hissing, "She's only a child!"

The soldier relented under her commanding gaze. His flicker of recognition told her he knew her standing in the community.

I wish I could throw him in the river, Anne thought as he backed away.

Anne received a letter from Virginia Clay that did nothing to sweeten her disposition.

>Wildwood
>Huntsville, Alabama
>May 1, 1866

Dear Anne,

We have returned to Huntsville, and I have seen precious Ellen. She found Oak Place in sad repair. She has left for Mississippi.

My dear Mr. Clay was released on April 17, completely broken in health because he was kept in a cold, wet, dungeon and never allowed to see the sun. Even though I had known President Johnson well when he was a Senator, he refused my many pleas to at least visit my sick husband and care for him, deflecting them with empty promises.

At last I went to the White House at eight in the evening and told Andrew Johnson I would not leave until he gave me the order for my husband's release. He did not believe me. I waited, waited. He'd come in. Go out. Along about eleven, I got the paper!

But it's too late. We returned to find the Clay home burned. We've bought a mountain plantation with a cottage called Wildwood. I'm nursing the love of my life, but I fear I will not have him for long.

Your Friend,

Virginia Clay

Anne wrote and tore up three letters before she could find words for Virginia. Then she wrote Ellen at Port Gibson, fretting because she had not heard from her.

What sort of peril is Ellen in? Anne wondered. *It's dangerous on the streets of Macon. And Mr. J. says we're peaceful and prosperous compared to the war-ravaged areas.*

She got up from her desk, pacing, thinking of the tumultuous currents of change and struggle surging through Macon with former slaves and Scalawags sitting on the city council, levying taxes that were causing foreclosures on neighbors' homes.

With all of the footloose people roaming the streets, committing crimes, she knew she was safe only because of her husband's commanding presence.

Helpless Ellen has only Campbell.

⌣⠒⌣

It was the second week in May before Ellen and Campbell arrived in Macon. Ellen declared in wide-eyed surprise that, no, she had encountered no problems. Campbell only made jokes. Anne learned nothing.

With Lit's body still at the depot, they turned to the matter of his funeral. William went to the new Federal Commandant, who had replaced Wilson, petitioning him to allow a fitting martial tribute to his fellow general. This official was slightly more lenient than his predecessor; however, he refused for military honors to be paid.

But on May 10, 1866, when Maconites learned that Brigadier General Edward Dorr Tracy, Jr. was lying in state in the large hall of the passenger depot, a deep hush fell over the town. Every store closed.

With an outpouring of grief, people came. Anne stood watching, angry that the oaken box covering the casket could not be draped with the flag well served. But she had adorned it with magnolias, Lit's favorite, and soon the bier was hidden with a profusion of wreaths and bouquets.

Ellen had fashioned a placard of a poem by Caroline Augusta Ball:

> *We laid him to rest in his cold, narrow bed,*
> *And 'graved on the marble we placed at his head,*
> *As the proudest tribute our sad hearts could pay.*
> *"He never disgraced it, the jacket of gray."*

At eleven o'clock the procession formed. The coffin was transferred to a newly built wagon drawn by four fine horses. The pallbearers stepped up. In citizen dress, they were alternating members of the Macon Volunteers, Lit's original unit, and the Fire Department. The rest of the Volunteers formed the escort of honor. Their captors refused to allow them to wear uniforms, but no one could strip them of their military bearing, and everyone knew.

Next came Members of the Bar of Macon, then other prominent men afoot or on horseback.

From the family carriage, Anne saw that the streets were lined with people silently weeping. She bore it proudly until they passed through the gates at Rose Hill; then she saw the Macon Volunteers' Band. With instruments hanging by their sides at rest, they paid silent tribute that pierced her heart more than song.

Rev. Wills, Lit's former pastor, performed a simple Christian burial. He could speak no word of Lit's valor and service to his country because of the armed guard threatening them.

Squirming, Anne watched Ellen standing with calm dignity

befitting a general's wife. Anne fretted that there could be no gun salute or folded flag for her to cherish.

Someday, she vowed, *Lit will be immortalized as a Christian gentleman willing to lay down his life for the principles he held dear.*

William stood apart, watching the mourners. He was worried about Anne, regretting that he must leave her to go back to New York. *What can I do to lift her spirits? She's closing her heart, even to the children . . . and especially to me.*

Chapter XXII

"Annie! Annie, I'm home," William called, hurrying through the garden. It was such a perfect day in June 1866 that he knew he would find her there.

He flexed aching shoulders. Although the steamship voyage from New York to Savannah had been restful, the train trip, skirting all of Georgia—north to Augusta, west to Atlanta, then south to reach Macon—-had been frustrating.

Well, thanks to me that will soon be over, and we can go straight to Savannah again.

"Annie!" He found her on her knees, weeding. He pulled her to her feet and kissed her with gusto.

"Congratulate me. I've done it! Secured the balance of the one million dollars. We can pay the bills for repairing the *Central*. And we have money to begin operating. I'm as excited as a lad with a new hoop to roll!"

"That's nice dear," Anne replied listlessly.

Consternation filled him. Since January when he gave up the presidency of the railroad in favor of his old friend, W. M. Wadley, he had devoted every ounce of his ability to dealing with New York investors. *Few men could have accomplished this feat. She could show me a little appreciation.*

But as he looked into her face, anger melted into tenderness. Her cheeks had rounded into pretty plumpness, but their hopeless sag and the cold hardness of her eyes pained him.

What can I do to restore her grit? She's letting life lick her, he thought as she turned back to snatching weeds from her daylilies as if they were hairs on her enemies' heads.

Suddenly he had an idea to give her an immediate purpose. "Annie, I'd like you to have a dinner party for the Wadleys. Children, too."

"Are you sure? They have seven."

William laughed. "Yes. But this is a celebration."

Just as William knew she would, Anne quickly arranged a grand occasion. He sat at the head of the dining table, for this time filled with little ones of various sizes, and grinned at his friend, the towering, broad-shouldered *Central Railroad* president. He raised his glass.

"A toast to you, Colonel Wadley. In just under a year, you've rebuilt and completely reversed Sherman's destruction of 300 miles of railroad. No one but you could have done it."

Wadley's face gleamed as brightly as his white hair, but he protested; "Only you could have raised $1,000,000 in these trying times. By my reckoning, we'll be ready to run the first train between Savannah and Macon on June twelfth."

"Splendid!" William waved his arm over the group. "Let's take our wives and youngsters and make the initial trip." He looked at Anne, and his heart surged at the excitement lighting her face.

"Oh, let's!" Anne clapped her hands. "Don't you think that would be fun, Rebecca?" she said, turning to Wadley's dark-eyed wife.

William reared back, lips twitching with pleasure as the women planned. He felt hopeful that, with the restoration of the *Central*, Georgia's farmlands could begin recovery from the despair of war.

Can Anne?

The trip did Anne good, and William plotted how he could keep her from sinking back into doldrums. He considered that at fifty-seven he was in his prime. He thought his expanding size only emphasized his importance to all who met him. Every enterprise he touched prospered, and he had money enough to do anything he wanted. What he most desired was to complete the grand design for his house, the finishing touches that had been interrupted by the war.

"But what about our neighbors who lack funds for simple repairs?" Anne questioned when he broached his plans.

"I'm sorry for them, my dear, but we must live our lives. I've already sent to Italy for a group of artisans."

⋖∶⋗

Anne felt as if she had returned to the land of her honeymoon as scaffolding surmounted by handsome young Italians filled her foyer. It rang with laughter and song. She had thought the entrance regal enough with its floor of white marble set off by black diamonds, but under the artists' masterful touch, paint in apricots and grays turned plain walls into marbleized panels that looked as much like the real stone as that beneath her feet.

Anne watched, enchanted, as plaster flowered on ceiling and cornice. Looking up, she sighed with pleasure. "Mr. J., my fairy palace is becoming as exquisite as any villa we saw in Florence."

He beamed at her and kissed her hand. "Only the best for you, my dear. Wait 'til you see what I've planned for the back hall."

By fall, Anne saw plain Georgia pine wainscoting and sliding doors turn into dark walnut and rich rosewood, also by the magic of trompe l'oeil.

Interested, busy, Anne was letting the shadowed corners of her heart glimpse light when Ellen plunged her to melancholy.

⋖∶⋗

Ellen stood over her, sweet face trembling with an empathy that made Anne sob harder.

"Please, Sister. Don't." Ellen, fighting tears, patted and soothed. "Let go peacefully."

"I can't! How can you want to leave us? My brothers . . . and now it's like the last piece of me will be gone."

"It's a feeling that I must. Susan and Georgia should know their birthplace. Oh, I'm seized with the notion I have to put Oak Place in order."

Ellen paced about the room, turned, and flung out, "You should understand. You and Mr. Johnston are ridding your home of make-dos and all traces of warfare."

"But I can't bear the loneliness without you. I'd be sick with worry about your being on the plantation alone."

Ellen's laugh was shaky, but her voice held surety of purpose. "I won't be alone. Mother feels she's been in Atlanta at my sister's house quite long enough . . . Anne, let me go home. I need to touch my memories of Edward."

Anne blew her nose, acknowledging defeat. "Promise to write often."

~:~

Anne haunted every mail train, hurting. When she received no word after Christmas greetings, she wrote, scolding, and received a long, newsy letter that eased her ache.

> Oak Place
> Huntsville, Alabama
> January 8, 1867
>
> My Darling Sister,
>
> You know that I love you too much to neglect you willingly. I need not say that my delay in answering your last letter has been unintentional. I have not been well for some time, and have had the blues dreadfully. Today I am fighting against a sore throat, am taking belladonna.
>
> Wednesday being a bright spring day, I thought I would try the outside world to see what it could do for me in the way of restoring my health and spirits. So I dressed myself and daughters in our best clothes

and made quite a visiting tour. They had on their red dresses, white stockings, and nice garters (which you sent them) so you can well imagine they looked uncommonly well in their finery and were the envy of all eyes . . .

Anne laughed, feeling better. With pleasure, she read the account of all of the neighbors the three had visited and was glad they had remained for "an elegant dinner with Mrs. Garth." Houseguests of her own had interrupted Ellen's letter writing, and it was a month before she finished it, giving details of her sewing and tutoring the children. Anne reread the ending from this kindred spirit who was so dear.

I was much grateful to learn you had been to the cemetery. 'Tis a sacred spot to us both, and I am sure an everlasting bond between us. Would that we could visit it together and keep it as beautiful as it should be.

I was sorry to learn from your letter that dear little Caroline had lost all her pretty curls, but dare say they will come back as beautiful as ever. Kiss my darling namesake in her sweet mouth for Aunt Ellen, and tell her it would give her "God Mother" infinite delight to see her when she is dressed up to go visiting. Give much love to Mr. Johnston, and in kissing Mary Ellen, don't forget dear little Carrie also. Susie and Georgia are asleep or would send kisses. Do write soon.

Your loving sister,
Ellen Tracy

On a bright April day, Anne was seated at her secretary writing Ellen when George announced callers. The two who entered the parlor moved as one in such a glow of happiness that Anne laughed. Sidney's and Mary's love always seemed a tangible thing, but something extra had them fairly dancing.

"I sense momentous news," Anne said, hands outstretched in welcome.

"Sidney's finished his novel," the petite girl blurted without taking time for polite greeting.

"*Tiger Lilies* is a book! I feel as if I'd fathered a child," Sidney exclaimed, then ducked his head, red-faced. "I think it's good. Oh, if only I can sell it."

"I'm sure it's great," Anne said, hugging them both, knowing how much this meant to them. "Sit down. Tell me all about it. Read some." She watched them, thinking she had never seen two so closely attuned.

Sidney summarized his book and finished by reading his favorite passage, the hero describing how it felt to play his flute:

> *"It is like walking in the woods, amongst wild flowers, just before you go into some vast cathedral . . . It speaks the gloss of green leaves or the pathos of bare branches; it calls up the strange mosses that are under dead leaves; it breathes of wild plants that hide and oak fragrances that vanish; it expresses to me the natural magic of music."*

When he was through, Anne clapped. "Yes, yes, you must seek a publisher. But there's none left in the South. You must go to New York. At once."

"Do you really deem it worthy?"

"Of course. And you must let me have a role in helping." Sidney was shaking his head, and she hurried to add, "Haven't I always been your mentor? I would be hurt not to have a part."

"I couldn't impose on friendship. We only came to share our happiness. I've relatives to stay with while I'm making the round of publishers."

Anne turned to Mary, whose eyes had widened fearfully at Sidney's refusal. "Will Mr. Day promise your hand if Sidney sells his book?"

Mary nodded, lips pressed together, unable to speak.

"Then we must take no chances." Quickly, Anne crossed to the rosewood desk and touched a hidden spring. From behind a carved panel she took a bag of gold coins. "Just a bit to help you on your journey," she said, pressing the gift into Sidney's hand.

Aboard the train, Sidney was thankful for the repaired track and a swift, direct journey; however, as he gazed from the sooty window at blackened images of his once beautiful homeland, he grieved.

What hurts most, he thought, *is that the Federals burned our universities and great libraries. I would have a position if Oglethorpe College remained. They tried to destroy our culture, but we must keep our literature and music alive.*

But as the train bounced and jerked northward, his resolve lessened. The bristly seating seemed to pierce his skin to the bone. Weary, he began to doubt that a New York company would accept a Southern poet.

I'm foolish to keep struggling. I should save my strength and money. Papa's probably right. I ought to go into his law office. But he hardly has practice enough for one, and I'd hate the work. I wouldn't be able to write, and I feel God has given me the talent. But I must feed Mary, Lord. He looked to the heavens. *Thank you that Mary understands and upholds me. Please show me the way.*

In New York City, Sidney stuck to the humbling task of making rounds of publishers. As fruitless days passed, he was thankful for his uncle's bed and table and his friend's moneybag. Only his faith that God had meant for him to write kept him going. At last at the office of Hurd and Houghton, he was told to leave the manuscript for consideration.

Funds low, hungry for Mary's face, he returned home to wait.

Sidney faced Clarence Day. Breathing hard, he thought, *I can't live without Mary. The sight of her face is breakfast to me.*

"The possibilities of publishing are too uncertain," Mr. Day said, shaking his head. "I can't trust my daughter and possible future grandchildren to you without the assurance of a regular salary."

Sidney's joy in the new book plummeted. "But Hurd and Houghton not only agreed to print it, they expect good sales." Mind reeling, Sidney thought of taking another job and the impossibility of writing when he was exhausted.

But Mr. Day was adamant.

⌣⁙⌣

With great difficulty, Sidney secured a position as head of an academy in Prattville, Alabama. It meant being parted from Mary again.

At first the job was tortuous, and he wrote his father: "I hate the wide-mouthed, villainous-nosed, tallow-faced drudgeries of my eighty-fold life; however, it cannot squeeze the sentimentality from me."

But in a fit of loneliness, he considered setting Mary free of their engagement, writing the sorrowing poem "Barnacles." Even then he knew they could never go separate ways, and when "Barnacles" was published in *The Round Table*, his flute sang with hope.

Nightly, he poured his longing into letters to Mary, filling them with poetry. He wrote "Thou and I":

> *So one in heart and thought, I trow,*
> *That thou might'st press the strings*
> *and I might draw the bow*
> *and both would meet in music sweet,*
> *Thou and I, I trow.*

Mary wrote back:

> Your letters are so beautiful that I'm in danger of
> dreaming all day over their poetry and prose.

Sidney's health was improving; he was eating well. The cotton crop came in, a bountiful harvest that paid the way for more students to attend the school. With improved finances, he acquired a small house, books, lamps, chairs, tables. Now . . .

In November it came, Mary's joyful news of her father's consent. Jubilant, he asked the school for a short leave.

❧

Anne was among the guests sharing the happiness as Macon gathered at Christ Episcopal Church on December 19, 1867, to join Sidney Lanier and Mary Day in marriage.

Watching the diminutive bride and ever more handsome groom, Anne thought, *They have long been entwined by twin seeds of nature.* Mary's smile was so radiant that Anne would not have noticed her dress, had it not been so beautiful. White silk faille with a train, it was embroidered with pearls in a grape design forming panels down the short jacket and the entire length of the skirt. Sidney could not take his eyes from her.

Anne moved with the crowd to the home of Gussie Lamar Ogden, who was giving the wedding reception. Reminiscing about the night at the Lamar's musicale when the couple had met, Anne was beginning to relax when she heard a scream.

Turning, Anne saw a bridesmaid had passed too close to an open grate. Her filmy dress blazed. Quickly the fire was extinguished, but Anne had to sit down. Chiding herself that she was not usually superstitious, Anne continued to shake. She could feel herself sliding again into deep depression, fearing the fire was a portent.

❧

The little house in Prattville became a warm and bliss-filled home as Sidney and Mary rejoiced in their love. Serenity reigned—for two weeks.

Then, on a cold morning in January 1868, Sidney awakened with his mouth full of blood.

Choking, despairing, he looked up at Mary. She wiped his face, holding fast to her smile even though tears escaped her dear gray eyes, hurting him most of all.

"It's come back." He coughed. "I should not have married you. It wasn't fair of me."

"Nonsense, my darling. This is just our first emergency to be met together. God will sustain us. All you need is rest and my care."

Sidney nodded gratefully. "Don't tell my family."

Fear flitted across Mary's face. She regained control and spoke firmly. "I think we should. Let me send to Montgomery for Clifford."

Then it worsened, and for half an hour Sidney hemorrhaged from his lungs.

ᴗ:ᴖ

William stood in the doorway, watching Anne clipping roses. He had never felt so helpless. She had been unusually upset since Sidney's tuberculosis had reappeared and he had to give up his school and move back to Macon. Now this. *How can I tell her?*

He blinked tears as he stepped into the April brightness. "Anne, dear . . . I've news." He took the tools from her hands and led her to a chair in the coolness of the arched loggia.

Anne looked up at him blankly.

"Ellen has been ill again." He swallowed. "She requested that you take her children."

Anne jumped up. "I must go to her."

"Wait! Her last words were for you and Susan and Georgia. Ellen died unexpectedly on April twenty-third." He handed her a letter. "Her sister-in-law, Ada Fearn Steele wrote in care of me to break the news more gently."

With blurred eyes, Anne skimmed down the letter that gave the details of the last three days of Ellen's life.

> Our darling sister kept such a bright happy face until the attacks, which lasted about two hours each. Ellen asked the doctor was not her heart involved, but he laughingly said it was indigestion. He gave her an enema of morphine just over the heart, which acted like a charm for awhile. He gave her quinine with valerian, bismuth and Dovers powders, mus-

tard plasters all over her body. But only brandy and morphine eased the pain. Then we thought she was resting so sweetly. I never witnessed a calmer death-bed . . .

Anne crumpled. Stunned for a moment, she sobbed, "Her poor, broken heart." Suddenly she began to shriek, "It's the war! It caused Sidney's living death. Now it's taken my darling Ellen."

"But Anne . . ."

"Don't say it's not. Ellen grieved herself to death for Lit."

William reached out to take her in his arms, but she stamped about screaming.

"How can you have anything to do with those people who invaded us?" She wept hysterically. "Don't tell me not to hate my enemies. They've taken all my family."

Chapter XXIII

Anne stood alone in Rose Hill Cemetery, looking down at her brother's grave. Raw, red earth showed where they had so recently laid his beloved wife beside him.

"Lit, you have her with you again," she whispered, "but, oh, how I miss you both!" She shivered, cold in spite of the summer sunshine. As an epitaph, she'd had engraved: "Blessed are the pure in heart, for they shall see God." It was perfect for darling Ellen.

Through a blur of tears, Anne could see women moving down the hillside beyond the trees. They were laden with flowers to decorate the soldiers' graves.

Anne shrank behind a shrub. Feeling she could not bear their further condolences, she slipped up a side road toward home.

Anne found her family by following the sound of laughter. Taking off her mourning veil, she went into the basement living room, relishing the coolness from the air moat on her fevered cheeks.

There sat William, filling his overstuffed chair, singing "Old Dan Tucker" loudly if not melodiously.

"Combed his hair with a wagon wheel, died with a toothache in his heel," he screeched.

The two eight-year-olds, Tracy and Georgia, rolled at his feet in a fit of giggling. Susan, tall now at ten, leaned over the arm of his chair. On his broad knees bounced Caroline, six, and baby Mary Ellen, chubby at four.

How the children have changed him! Anne thought. His once closed and hidden look was now open and giving. He had crinkles around eyes that fairly twinkled. But she sighed, so heavy with her enmity and her grief for this one dearer than a blood sister that she could not join the fun

⁖⁖

It became easier for Anne not to hate blue uniforms when she saw their backs marching away. On July 30, 1868, military authority was withdrawn from Georgia, Florida, Alabama, and the Carolinas, and they were organized under civil control. Federal troops still remained in Atlanta, Savannah, Dahlonega, and along the railroads, but Macon was free at last.

Free, yet anarchy remained. Under the despised Governor Bullock, with Carpetbaggers and former slaves in full control of the government, disorder and unrest worsened.

Anne knew it was dangerous for a woman to be out, but, restless, she could not be confined. She was hurrying along High Street to visit a neighbor when she approached Sidney and Mary. Mary glowed with an inner radiance that made Anne study her. Although a lacy shawl concealed the petite girl, Anne could see she was expecting a child. When Anne looked at Sidney, his appearance pierced her heart. *He's positively ashen,* she thought, suppressing the urge to put her arm around him to help him walk. She tried to make her voice light as she met them with a smile of welcome.

"How nice to have you back living in Macon," Anne said. "I'd heard you were working in your father's law office."

Sidney grinned. "I managed to finish my school term in Prattville, and, since we were homeless as Judas Iscariot's ghost, we're here again." His laughter turned to a fit of coughing.

Anne had been glad for the slight shower last night, but in today's heat there was steam rising from the damp earth. As she watched him struggle, taking short breaths of the thick air, her mind cursed the cruelty of the Union prison that had caused Sidney's consumption.

~∴~

Anne's humor lifted when, in September, Charles Day Lanier was born. She thought wryly that Sidney was generous to honor the father-in-law who had kept him so long from his adored Mary.

But Anne's pleasure in the new baby was short-lived, for on a bright October morning, she found Campbell dead.

She had gone to his room to see why he was sleeping so late. As she looked down at him, regret stung her. *I called him lazy. All the time he had doggedness, going back into service time and time again. Oh, why didn't I understand how serious his wounds were?*

Bitterness for the enemy who had taken this last man of her family consumed her. She even resented that their Bishop over Christ Episcopal Church was a New Yorker.

~∴~

William had pleaded with Anne to go with him to the rectory to meet Bishop John Beckwith, but she feigned an excuse. He went alone.

The Bishop greeted him warmly. "Come in. I want you to meet an old friend visiting from New York City. This is William Henry Appleton, founder of Appleton Publishing,"

The man was small, and his bald pate was fringed with cottony hair, but something about his bearing impressed. William welcomed him to the South.

Appleton spoke briskly, going straight to the point, "I'm touched by the devastation I've seen while traveling here. I've told Bishop Beckwith that I want to do something to aid him. I was thinking of building a church that will belong to John."

William nodded, but the clergyman shook his head.

"My heart is full of sympathy for the destitute orphans of Confederate soldiers," said the saintly man. "I wish to establish a home for them, rather than a church."

"An excellent idea," said William, "and I know just the spot. The *Macon and Western Railroad* owns seven acres right off College Street. A fine location. I'll make a donation to buy the property."

"Splendid!" exclaimed Appleton. "I'll give $10,000 for the erection and another $10,000 to establish an endowment fund. Mr. Johnston, see to securing the land, immediately. We must start to work."

⌣∴∽

Construction of the orphanage began early in 1869. Over the next months as the brick building on what was renamed Appleton Street rose to a second story, William tried to interest Anne. He could not.

⌣∴∽

With Sidney back in town and conditions improved, Macon resounded with music again. Sidney reorganized his old army band. They played for every occasion. In the Masonic Hall, they tried out his new composition, "Blackbirds."

"Now we can build memorials for our heroes more lasting than flowers," he told his friends. "Let's raise money for a monument for John Hill Lamar."

They decided on a concert in Ralston Hall. It seemed like old times with Gussie Lamar Ogden and Mrs. A. O. Bacon singing in memory of their fallen brother and Mary playing the piano.

But the next morning in the law office of Lanier and Anderson, his father called him into question.

"In view of your continuing bad health, you should put all your meager energy into law," said Robert Lanier.

"Playing the flute is the best exercise for my lungs," Sidney replied as gently as he could. He laughed. "I know I must toil at this dry-as-dust tracing of land titles to make a little bread to feed my wife and son, but, Father, through army and sickness and business these two figures of music and of poetry have kept steadily in my heart so that I could not banish them."

Sidney could tell that his father did not understand. *How thankful I am that Mary does!*

That night in their room as they shut out the world and felt only bliss, he told her, "I marvel that God made you mine, for when He frowns 'tis then ye shine."

⌣⋮⌣

Anne heard that Sidney was to address the Decoration Day Service to be held on April 26, 1870. Two years had passed since she lost Ellen and Campbell; still she struggled, ambivalent about attending. At last she told herself, *I should go since Sidney's to speak. At least this time we won't have bayonets sticking in our craw.*

But she went late to Rose Hill Cemetery. Poised for flight, Anne hid behind a sculptured angel, watching the group. Sidney stepped before them.

So thin. So pale and wan. Why did he consent to come? Anne wondered. But she edged closer.

A fit of coughing seized him, but everyone stayed motionless until Sidney regained control and began speaking.

"In the unbroken silence of the dead soldierly forms that lie beneath our feet; in the winding processions of these stately trees; . . . in the quiet ripple of yonder patient river . . ."

Agitated, Anne half-listened as he likened the stateliness of the trees to Lee and Jackson, the patience of the river to the soldiers marching through the very shards of hell to the inevitable death that awaited.

I can't stand it. I must go. But his next words stopped her.

"Who in all the world needs tranquility more than we? How shall we bear our load of wrong and injury with the calmness and tranquil dignity that become men and women who would be great in misfortune?"

Like Ellen, Anne thought. *But I can't.* Her heart felt as if it was bursting, and she turned to escape his pleading words. But Sidney's melodious voice rang out, holding her, as he spoke of drawing strength from these departed heroes.

"Lamar, Smith, generous Tracy, good knights, stainless gentlemen. Unto this calmness we shall come at last."

Gallant Lit, she thought. *You would want me to be brave.*

Sidney's call to rise above bitterness and prejudice continued, "For the contemplation of this tranquility, my friends of this Association, in the name of a land stung half to madness, I thank you."

Anne looked at him, handsome, manly, having suffered all, but smiling benignly. She gave him her full attention, and the poetry of his words touched her soul.

> *Today we are here for love and not for hate.*
> *Today we are here for harmony and not for discord.*
> *Today we are risen immeasurably above all vengeance.*
> *Today, standing upon the serene heights of forgiveness,*
> *Our souls choir together the enchanting music of harmonious*
>   *Christian civilization.*
>
> *Today we will not disturb the peaceful slumbers of these sleepers,*
> *With music less sweet than the serenade*
> *of loving remembrances breathing upon our hearts*
> *as the winds of heaven breathe upon these*
> *swaying leaves above us.*

As Sidney finished speaking, there was stillness. Then Mary stepped up with a supporting shoulder and a clean, white handkerchief. Women, smiling, saying little, gripped his hand and made their way up the hill.

Moved, Anne waited, unmindful that tears were flowing down her cheeks. When others were gone and she was beside Sidney, he stood so much taller than she that she smiled, knowing a great deal more than height had changed their positions.

"How can you not point an accusing finger," she asked wondrously, "when their horrid prison caused your consumption?"

Sidney answered softly. "My health is a daily reminder of the war, 'tis true. But only as we forgive, can we feel the cleansing of God's pardon. If there was guilt in any, there was guilt in nigh all of us from Maryland to Mexico."

As Anne began shaking her head, he took her hand and continued, "The seeds of war must perish in the germ. Dear friend, being unforgiving eats at the soul until it shrinks away instead of growing. Forgiveness is a freeing thing."

Anne kissed him, unable to speak. Hugging Mary, she left them and descended to the Ocmulgee.

Walking alone along the riverbank, she wrestled with her miseries, reminding herself that if bitterness did not tarnish dear Sidney's soul, she must come to terms with it, herself.

For an hour she agonized, and then she prayed, Oh, Lord, forgive my unforgiving spirit. Strengthen me. It's so hard. Help me to forgive."

Then she began the long climb toward home.

Chapter XXIV

The ginkgo beckoned Anne upward. She considered it. No longer gawky, the tree had grown slowly, attaining height and beauty, weathering winter's storms, adjusting to the seasons, becoming stalwart. Anne plucked a leaf of golden green, thinking, *It is time I changed the colors of my life.*

Anne ascended the white marble stair, pausing for a moment before the impressive doors of her home. Carved with lions' heads and bronzed, they suddenly made her remember Ghiberti's bronze portals in Florence. Smiling, she let her thoughts caress the remarkable man who had taken her there.

As she entered into the marble hall, Anne saw it in new light. Gold fruit winked at her amid the plaster acanthus leaves of the cornice. Once-plain walls now glowed in glorious hues.

Anne looked up as scampering footsteps overhead alerted her to the children. *Which ones? No matter. They are all my children. Pardon, Lord, that I have not thanked you for the family you have given me to love.*

Surveying her home, completed, furnished to perfection in every corner, Anne realized, *I haven't shown William my gratitude either.*

The need to find him seized her. *Has he gone away again?*

But she found him, right there in his study, seated at his desk. Pressing herself over him, she hugged his broad shoulders.

He turned, delight on his face at her presence. "There you

are. I was hoping you'd come in. Mr. Appleton is visiting Macon again because Appleton Church Home is open. I wish you'd go with me to see it. I'd like you to meet him."

He looked at her with doubt, but he continued, pleading, "We have a part in the orphans' home, you know. I bought the land, but John Baxter, L. N. Whittle, and Edward Padelford insisted on making donations. Bishop Beckwith did, too."

For answer, Anne hugged and kissed him. "You're too wonderful for words. Here I was about to thank you for my palazzo and you've gone and done more. I can't keep up with my appreciation of all you do. I love you, William Johnston."

His face reddened with pleasure, but he was too moved to speak.

"I'll go with you," she said with a lilt in her voice, "but let me wash my face and change my frock."

⌣∴⌣

In her bedroom, Anne stood before her open armoire, unseeing. Courage failed. *Can I do this? Can I be gracious to a man who was my enemy?*

She shook back her hair, straightened. *Are you testing me, Lord?*

Resolutely, she stepped out of the heavy crepe of mourning and threw it aside. It felt good to be able to pray again and to feel God was near. In the wardrobe hung a smart green-poplin walking suit William had brought from New York. She had not tried it on.

It fit remarkably well. She gazed in the cheval glass. These hoops were not round. They were flattened in front. She arched her neck to see the back, which stood out in cascading poufs and ruffles. Even though she was no longer slim—face it, a bit matronly—she decided she still cut an imposing figure in the latest fashion.

Pinning on the matching hat, Anne felt ready to meet her foe.

⌣∴⌣

Anne entered the two-story brick building of Appleton Church Home, moving close to, and slightly behind, her husband. She murmured her greetings to Mr. Appleton and Bishop Beckwith.

Four little girls emerged shyly and curtsied. They were the first, but there was room for thirty.

Anne knelt, hugging each, asking their names. Touched by their pinched faces, she choked with emotion. Here were more precious children in need of her mothering.

Mr. Appleton cleared his throat. "The deaconesses are wearing gray habits in memory of the Confederate soldiers." His drooping white mustache began to tremble, but he continued, "They're called the Order of St. Katherine as a memorial to my daughter, a missionary to Hong Kong—where she died."

With tears of sympathy, Anne said, "I hope your philanthropy in building this institution will help to ease your loss." She reached out a consoling hand. Suddenly she felt unburdened of the heartache she had clung to. Smiling ruefully, she told him, "You have made me see that North and South can again be bound by spiritual ties."

～∴～

Still a corner of Anne's heart bled for Phil. The uncertainty. The awful ache that his body might be one of those in the sacrilege of that horrible man Brady's photographs.

Anne thought of her father's brother in upstate New York. *Uncle Phineas and Phil loved each other so much. I should let him know about Phil. And Lit, too.*

Dutifully, she wrote a letter and received an answer that stunned her.

Batavia, New York
May 31, 1870

My Dear Niece,

Some eighteen months after the battle of Antietam, I learned that Major Philemon Tracy of the Sixth Georgia had been wounded. The Federal soldiers brought him across the river to Shepherdstown where he died and was buried.

You will understand that feeling was still running high on both sides; consequently, I made quiet arrangements and sent a trusted friend. Under cover of night, he had the body exhumed and identified by a mark. Phil was then wrapped in a Union cloak and brought to Batavia under that guise.

On March 15, 1864, we gave him a Christian burial with services from St. James Episcopal Church. He is interred in my family plot with the simple headstone: "Philemon Tracy, Died September 17, 1862, Age 31 years."

I share your heartache, and I hope this gives you ease. But there is one thing yet.

When General John A. Logan, Commander of the Grand Army of the Republic heard of your Southern Ladies' Organization for Decoration Day, he issued an order, setting May 30, 1869, for decorating graves in the North.

Somehow Philemon's identity slipped out, and Batavia's Grand Army of the Republic members questioned putting flowers on his grave. The matter was hotly debated by veterans with bright memories of the carnage of the battle between brothers; but they voted to include Major Tracy's grave, and it has been every year.

Respectfully,
Judge Phineas L. Tracy

Anne read the letter, and then began again, through tears. She fell on her knees and thanked God for Uncle Phineas.

～:～

Joy seemed to radiate to the seventh story of the house as, for the first time since her honeymoon, fun filled Anne's days. They joined the German Club, and at frequent intervals, friends gathered to dance the intricate figures of the German until late-night suppers were served, elegant repasts of oysters, grated ham tongue, salmon salad, chicken, turkey . . .

Anne discovered that she enjoyed playing cards. William beamed with pleasure at her entertaining even though she continued to grab up a broom and fuss, "There's no choice about this house, nothing but dirt upstairs and down."

Then, in the midst of the pleasure, old pain came rushing back when another letter and package arrived, postmarked New York. Anne unwrapped a daguerreotype and recognized Phil's friend from Yale. Marvin Waite wore a Union uniform. Anne clutched a fistful of her shirtwaist and bowed her head as grief and hatred filled her throat. Finally she read the letter. By some quirk of fate, Marvin had also died on that horrendous day the Confederates called Sharpsburg and the Yankees named Antietam. She sat, struggling. Slowly, Sidney's words in the cemetery poured over her again. "Today we are here for love and not for hate . . ." Anne arose and cleared a place on a table in the main floor drawing room. In this honored spot, always decorated with flowers, Marvin's picture would remain.

Summer at the Lanier home sounded with coughing so intense that Dr. Jones told Sidney he must go to New York for treatment.

In October, Sidney returned, greatly improved; however, he realized life was now to be a struggle against the wasting disease. When friends visited, he shook off their sympathy, saying with a grin, "With us of the younger generation of the South, since the war, pretty much the whole of life has been not dying."

Contentedness in each other sustained Sidney and Mary, and they were thrilled when she bore a second son, Sidney Junior. But by December of 1872, his health was so precarious that he was forced to leave his little family to seek a dryer climate in San Antonio, Texas.

Lonely, Sidney hungered for friends. He found them by playing his flute. He was accustomed to his music being taken for granted at home, and the acclaim he received here exhilarated him.

As he rested, poetry poured into his mind, and he wrote

Mary, "All day my soul hath been driven by wind after wind of heavenly melody."

Sidney knew he was not meant to be a country lawyer, and he had a growing conviction that his life would be short.

◡∴◞

Back in Macon, Sidney held Mary close. "My precious wife, I don't know how we'll manage, and my father won't be pleased, but I sense a holy obligation to these two talents that have been given me. I feel that I am called, and I cannot resist it longer."

"You know I can get by on very little."

He took her face in both his hands, watching her eyes. "I feel the Lord has shown me that I will die young."

Mary's gaze remained steady, unwavering. "Then we must live each day in the joy of our love. I have no worries. I believe in your genius. We simply must pray for God to make us a way."

◡∴◞

Anne hurried down the street with a baby gift under her arm. George followed her with a bucket of ice. She was pleased that William had started Macon's first artificial ice plant, and it need no longer be a rare commodity shipped in from the far north. It was June of 1873, and Henry Wysham Lanier had just been born.

Sidney and Mary were always the most serene pair Anne knew, but when they invited her in, pouncing upon the ice treat, she could tell that something wonderful, in addition of the birth of a third son, had happened.

"Oh, Miss Anne," Mary exclaimed, "our way has opened. Sidney's been offered the position of first flutist in the Peabody Symphony Orchestra. We're to move to Baltimore in December."

"They're to pay me sixty dollars a month!" Sidney exulted. "And I'll have what I always wanted. I'll be in a land of books."

Anne recalled the little lad who could make a flute sing, and she poured congratulations upon them.

❧

In Baltimore, Sidney breathed easier, rhapsodizing in a letter to his father, "In the crystalline air and the champagne breeze, I'm rushing about." He begged his father to understand he could not come back to his law office.

After the concerts, many people congratulated Sidney, flattering him that he was the greatest flute player in the world.

As notes floated from his flute, poems poured from his pen, but illness returned. One night after Mary had coped courageously with his hemorrhage, he told her, "I know in my soul that I'm a great poet, but still my name's unknown."

"One day, dear, your name will be revered," Mary replied. "I promise you."

❧

On a trip home Sidney and Mary visited friends in Sunnyside, Georgia. Sidney was struck by the South's continuing devastation, especially the poverty of its farms. The resulting poem, "Corn," was published in *Lippincott's Magazine* in 1875.

The nation took notice. Sidney was asked to write the words to a cantata by Dudley Buck of New York. It was to be sung at the Nation's Centennial Exposition.

❧

The World's Fair of 1876 seemed to bring on an American Renaissance. Anne was thankful for the change, most of all that the entire nation was at last recognizing Sidney Lanier for his genius in music and poetry.

Anne took keen interest in the presidential election. Mr. J.'s New York lawyer, Democrat Samuel Tilden was running against Republican Rutherford B. Hayes. Feelings ran hot. Louisiana, Florida, and South Carolina each sent in two sets of returns, one for Hayes by the Carpetbag government and the other for Tilden from government by ex-Confederates. Left to the Electoral Commission, the dispute was settled by secret deals and President

Grant calling out troops. Hayes was sworn in at a private ceremony at the White House. Anne breathed a prayer when it was over. Hayes had pledged to end Carpetbag rule, remove the last of the Federal troops from the downtrodden region, and allow the South its own civil government. If Hayes kept his promises, the South could at last begin recovery.

We can travel freely again, Anne thought. *It's time we took our five children to the fashionable watering places where they can begin to meet eligible young suitors.*

⌇⦂⦓

Anne contemplated the letter she had just received, telling her that Judge Phineas Tracy had passed on December 22, 1876. He would have been ninety on Christmas Day. Once, she had thought that when he died, she would bring Phil home. Now, she changed her mind. It seemed fitting that he remain with dear Uncle Phineas.

After all, she thought, *his grave is kept with memorials sent from the South and with tributes from the North. What more could I want?*

⌇⦂⦓

Anne sniffed crisp, pine-scented air and gazed at the evergreen peaks ringing Saratoga, New York. At the resort town's depot, she stood amidst a mountain of bandboxes, hatboxes, and trunks.

It was the summer season of 1877, and with Mary Ellen just turned an independent thirteen, they had four teenage daughters to dress in the latest rage, straight skirts embellished with bustles and street-sweeping trains. At these exclusive locales, outfits were changed for every occasion of the day. Just buying enough kid gloves and cashmere shawls and ruffled parasols had been a momentous task.

But as Anne directed her brood and baggage aboard the omnibus, she reminded herself not to worry. William had just started another insurance company that he called Cotton States. He told her to spend as much as she liked; he could afford it.

She knew William had especially wanted to come here this year because the Wadley family would also be at *Congress Hall*. Colonel Wadley was not well.

I hope drinking the water from the springs will help him, but I don't want any of the stuff, myself, Anne thought, making a wry face.

∿

Anne sat of the porch of *Congress Hall*, prodding herself to remember that here it was called a piazza. She was lying in wait for Mrs. William Vanderbilt. Not caring that they did not allow many Southerners into their snobbish "four hundred," she had only one goal. She held a copy of Sidney's newly published book, the first complete edition of his poems. Last night she had arranged to be introduced to Mrs. Vanderbilt. This morning she intended to interest the influential lady into championing Sidney's work in New York.

As Anne rocked, pretending to read the slim volume, her mind raced. She should not fear her prey. She could hold her head high. Reconstruction had ended, and the new era had touched Georgia. Farms were producing again; Macon businesses were growing; Victorian mansions were a-building.

I can enjoy our money now that our neighbors have recovered, she thought. She grinned. *Still, I can't help but be pleased that people here are whispering behind my back that my house is the palace of the South.*

Anne stretched pleasurably, looking across the green expanse. There was Tracy. Properly white-suited, he was playing a new game called lawn tennis.

I'm so glad he could come. She had missed him since John sent him off to school at Emory in Oxford, Georgia.

Susan emerged. In a simple morning outfit, she stood out because she had Lit's patrician nose and regal carriage. Susan paused, asking Anne's permission to join the people parading to the springs to take the waters.

Anne smiled fondly. *She's nineteen. We must think about making a match. But I won't rush her.*

Georgia scampered by without noticing Anne. The beauty of

the family—so like dear Ellen—had her bright eyes fixed ecstatically upon George Dole Wadley.

No worry about a proper beau there. Those two have been pairing off since childhood. Anne watched the door, waited. Where are Caroline and Mary Ellen? What are they up to?

They had been pestering her about going to tonight's hop. She could ask Mrs. Vanderbilt at what age she allowed her daughter to attend the informal dances, but it seemed the lady was not coming. Anne was getting too nervous to sit still.

"Good morning, Mrs. Johnston. You Southern ladies always look so calm and serene." Mrs. Vanderbilt took her place in a rocking chair.

Anne jumped guiltily as she turned to greet the bustled and tasseled matron. She dropped the book.

Mrs. Vanderbilt picked it up. "Tell me what you're reading. I love to hear you talk."

⁖

Anne had her hair tied up in a bandanna, and dirt smudged her face. She was more than a little perturbed as she directed a retinue of servants in cleaning and polishing the great house. It was 1879, and in only a few days Susan was to marry Dr. Appleton Collins at Christ Church. The reception would be here, of course.

"Mama, you just don't enjoy entertaining like I will when it's my house."

Anne turned and blinked at Mary Ellen. "And who says it will be your house, missy?"

She regarded the girl, a picture of herself at fifteen except that she appeared prettier because she was confident, pert, and her chestnut hair curled in a becoming pile on top of her head.

Mary Ellen, not taken aback, replied, "Well, if it was, I'd give constant parties. All of them would be great successes."

"And how would you manage that?"

Mary Ellen cocked her head to one side. "I'd always have plenty of men for the women, and plenty of wine for the men."

Anne whooped. "Well for now, get back to work."

"But, Mama, you're too perfect."

"That's the way your father likes it. And, besides, you know the *Telegraph* will describe every cherub and ribbon and rose we decorate with, and everything we serve for supper."

～:～

After the beautiful wedding, the *Macon Telegraph* gushed:

... The handsome residence of Colonel William B. Johnston blazed with beauty. Within were assembled the very elite of the city. In the centre of the picture gallery, Dr. and Mrs. Collins received the congratulations of friends ... The elegant parlors were thrown open, and the mansion never witnessed a scene more happy or an occasion more enjoyed ...

～:～

Happiness filled the humble home in Baltimore. Sidney was appointed lecturer in English literature at Johns Hopkins University. Too weak to stand, he sat to teach. No one complained.

Sidney realized that with hemorrhages coming more frequently he must press himself to publish. Books for children and serious works of study were written as he blocked out his pain. He knew he was writing his greatest poems. "Song of the Chattahoochee" poured from his pen with words about the Georgia river as musical as notes falling from his flute.

He was content doing what he had always longed to do. But an increasing awareness in Mary's gray eyes told him she knew he was growing weaker.

Sunrise

Chapter XXV

It began in May. Consuming, unrelenting, the fever gripped him; yet, Sidney struggled on, smiling, retaining his interest in life, pleased that he fooled all but his immediate family.

Summer came, and Mary's father took them to West Chester, Pennsylvania. There, in August 1880, Robert Sampson Lanier was born. Sidney delighted in holding this new life, his fourth son, against his fevered cheek.

By Christmas, back in Baltimore, his temperature soared to 104 degrees. The family tiptoed about the house as Sidney lay too weak to raise a spoon to his mouth. Mary sat beside him, easing ice between his parched lips.

Sidney looked into her eyes, and as always, drew strength. *My springs*, he thought. *Soft as a dying violet-breath, yet calmly unafraid of death.*

Mary bent to kiss him, and he whispered hoarsely.

"Get a pencil. I've a few lines for a new poem, 'Sunrise.' It will complete my 'Hymns of the Marshes.'"

With understanding Mary did as he asked. He could tell she knew his only fear was that he would die with the words unuttered.

When May came round again, Sidney's medical advisor held out one last hope.

"Try tent-life in a pure, high climate," the doctor said.

Sidney realized that his form was emaciated and his tottering steps betrayed him, but when he told his friends in Baltimore good-by, he spoke jauntily, "I'm going to Asheville, North Carolina, to write a railroad guide of the region. The good Lord always takes care of me. Just when the doctors said I must go to the mountains, the publishers gave me a commission for a book."

~:~

Beneath fragrant evergreens, Sidney lay, breathing easier in the cold, crisp air. Rhododendron bloomed all around, making it a place of beauty. He named the site for the baby, Camp Robin.

As he watched Clifford and their father setting up and flooring the tent, Sidney thought, *I'm so blest in their loving attention. And that Father finally understood my need to write.*

Sidney's family was satisfied at his improvement. His father had married a second wife, and they took the older boys, leaving Sidney to complete peace.

Content, Sidney and Mary and baby Robin settled into a quiet life. On his good days, Sidney dictated poetry.

~:~

By August, Sidney seemed better, and they decided to move their camp to the slope of Tyron Mountain because it was said to be in a warm current of air. On the way, they stopped to visit a friend whose house clung to an overhanging cliff that afforded a spectacular view.

Sidney was drawn to a piano placed by a western window. Hardwoods scattered across the hills already showed a hint of coming gold, of crimson. In the distance, he could see Mt. Pisgah's height. *How symbolic!* Sidney thought.

With ascending cords, he poured out his soul into music. Intensely flooding from the instrument, music merged with the sunset. He hated to leave Mary, but he was not afraid to die.

Claiming the promises of the Bible, he had faith that he would simply close his eyes and reopen them in the presence of God. *But I've a little more work to be done.*

⌣∴◡

The tent was quiet except for the smacking of Robin as he nursed. Sidney lay beside Mary. The urge was upon him to complete "Sunrise." He would wait until she could take his dictation. When she was ready, he rasped out the words:

> *But I fear not, nay, and I fear not the thing to be done;*
> *I am strong with the strength of my lord the Sun:*
> *How dark, how dark soever the race that must needs be run,*
> *I am lit with the Sun.*

Sidney's breathing became too ragged for further speech. Mary bathed his forehead, soothed him to rest. But soon he was whispering more, ending:

> *And ever my heart through the night shall with knowledge abide thee,*
> *And ever by day shall my spirit, as one that hath tried thee,*
> *Labor, at leisure, in art, 'til yonder beside thee*
> *My soul shall float, friend Sun,*
> *The day being done.*

"'Tis finished precious wife. I'm filled with peace."

"It's your greatest poem, my darling," Mary said, kissing him.

He squeezed her fingers, breathed, "I see a bright light. I am lit with the sun."

⌣∴◡

Anne's tears splotched the page as she read Mary's letter:

> . . . We are left alone (August 29) with one another. On the last night of summer comes a change. His love and immortal will hold off the destroyer of

283

our summer yet one more week, until the forenoon
of September seventh, and then falls the frost, and
that unfaltering will renders its supreme submission
to the adored will of God.

His body was taken to Baltimore where it rests
in Greenmount Cemetery.

Anne thought, *How much life he put into his brief thirty-nine
years!*

⋰∶∾

Anne felt a stab of guilt when her butler announced that
Mary Lanier was calling. She, wrapped in the love of her family,
had just returned from the luxury of White Sulphur Springs, West
Virginia, while Mary was struggling, alone in grief.

As she hurried to the parlor, Anne at least felt assuaged
that Mary was not in want. Anne had heard that a committee
of Baltimore's citizens had started a fund for the sustenance and
education of the poet's family. She had contributed heavily.

But I dread to see Mary solitary and weeping, Anne thought.
They were so in love. Always such a happy pair. She pressed her
hand over her mouth, overwhelmed with sympathy and with a
sudden fear. My William is beginning to look frail. Oh, what will
I do without him?

Anne's throat was full of emotion as she entered the drawing
room with her arms outstretched to embrace the young widow.

Mary was waiting by the window. As she turned, her smile
seemed to brighten the room. Anne sought the lovely eyes that
dominated Mary's face.

Why they're filled with peace—with purpose!

Unable to speak, Anne kissed her and motioned her to a
settee.

"Tell me how you are. If I'd known you were in Macon, I'd
have called upon you."

"I'm fine. Really I am. Busy."

"Yes, I've noticed you've been submitting Sidney's poems.
I've seen them in several of the best magazines."

"More than that!" Mary's eyes sparkled. "I've been editing a large collection. And *Charles Scribner's Sons* have agreed to publish a book!"

"Splendid!"

"And I'm giving readings. Anything I can do. I'm dedicating my life to making the world aware of Sidney's genius."

Anne stared at her in amazement. Mary was a near invalid herself. She was clad in black mourning, of course; yet, she was alive with enthusiasm for her task.

Mary laughed. "I know what you're thinking. I miss Sidney, but I would not have held him in his suffering. Few knew how great his pain was because he would block it out to write. I must try to live as courageously as he. He faced each day, claiming God's promises. Why his last words were uttered with joy. 'I am lit with the sun.'"

﹏:﹏

Anne stood before the sideboard in the dining room fussing with a tall cake adorned with sugared fruit. Carefully, she checked the ribbons attached to symbolic prizes inside the confection. Georgia's bridesmaids would pull them out after the first slice of the wedding cake was cut. On June 27, 1883, Georgia was at last to marry her beloved George Dole Wadley.

For once, Anne was pleased with the house. It was in its prime. She caught her reflection in the mirror and thought, *in August, I'll be fifty-four, but I'm looking my best, too.* Taking a cue from Mary Ellen, she had piled her hair on her forehead, only hers was in braids. Still she had no curl. Her forbidding brows had thinned over eyes that were now open and direct.

Suddenly her face clouded with worry over Georgia. Her sister, Susan, was already reigning in Macon's society as president of this and that, but Georgia was to move to the Wadley's ancestral plantation at Bolingbroke. Anne hated for her to be isolated at Great Hill Place. Bereaved of Colonel Wadley, who had died on a visit to Saratoga Springs, his wife, Rebecca, had settled into grieving. Making matters worse was Rebecca's near blindness from cataracts. Anne shook her head sadly. The tall white house had become a mausoleum.

Anne endured her worry about the newlyweds as long as she could before boarding the train for the short trip to Bolingbroke. When she reached Great Hill Place and stepped onto the porch, she was rehearsing words of encouragement, but she laughed at herself when she entered the broad central hall. All was shining and bright with flowers.

Georgia was flitting about, caring tenderly for her blind mother-in-law. Watching her, Anne remembered how Ellen had loved country living on Oak Place.

Georgia has all of her mother's sweetness and beauty. She's brought this old home place new life and joy.

Once again, Anne sat in the candle-lit sanctuary of Christ Church. She was breathing hard. *Another wedding in barely six months.* Today, January 23, 1884, Caroline was marrying George Washington Duncan, a South Carolinian. This meant many out-of-town guests. A greater banquet than usual waited back at the house. Anne sighed, exhausted.

The music swelled as the bridesmaids entered, twelve in white silk and satin. Of them, Anne saw only Mary Ellen, stealing the show. She was the belle of Macon, having had debuts both here and in Washington.

Oh, my, what sort of grandeur will she demand when it's her turn as bride?

Anne jumped as the organ crescendoed. People stood, turned toward Caroline, elegant in cut velvet with long, flowing train. Anne's heart went out to William.

Escorting Caroline with a brave smile, he blinked tears. Anne knew that he loved them all and was especially proud that Tracy was becoming a lawyer; nevertheless, this sweet, giving girl was his little "Rosebud." Because of George's business, they would be moving all the way to Danville, Virginia.

Anne dabbed at her own eyes, but when William completed his assignment and sat beside her, she realized his problem went deeper. Thin, he was trembling against her leg. Was he coming down with yet another chronic disease? The pit of her stomach knotted with apprehension.

The family lined up on the white, sandy beach of Cumberland Island, twenty-two of them. It was the summer of 1887. Georgia's Golden Isles had been immortalized by Sidney Lanier's poems, especially "The Marshes of Glynn," but of the seven islands, the Johnston-Tracy clan loved Cumberland best. Remote, it was reached only by boat. Primitive, rustic, it let them be themselves with nothing demanded of them; they could stay all day in bathing dress, as they were now, if they chose.

Anne smoothed her knee-length blue serge bathing skirt over her black stockings and surveyed the group. Aunt Carry, plump and smiling, still seemed well because of the constant care of her daughter, Harriet. Mary Ellen was chattering to Tracy. *No doubt about all the millionaires who squired her about Saratoga.* Her eyes came to rest on Caroline. Always tiny, a bit frail, she leaned close to George, who had become as dear as a son to Anne. Her heart ached for the pair, but they had grown even more devoted in their grief.

How happy William was when she came home to have her first child and named him William Butler Duncan! She looked at her husband, so thin in his tank suit in the center of the picture. He had wandered about the empty house when Caroline and the baby had returned to Danville, taking Adeline along as mammy to the second generation. Only a few weeks later, Anne had rushed to Virginia when the little man had contracted the same terrible croup that had taken their own children. *I'm so glad I could be there to wrap them in my love and strength.*

Anne straightened her shoulders with hope. She was sure that Caroline showed promise of a new life.

The older girls' children were sprawling about, making the

photographer's job difficult. Susan had named her first-born Ellen Tracy Collins, her second Sophia Rossetter Collins. Georgia's baby daughter carried on the name Sara Lois Wadley, and her beloved George had agreed if they had a son, he would be Edward Dorr Tracy Wadley.

All those I have loved so dearly live on around me in this continuing devotion, Anne thought, wondrously. *I have what I always wanted. Family.*

⌣∶∾

The next morning Anne woke at dawn. She decided to climb over the magnificent dunes and walk along the beach. She enjoyed the feel of the packed, wet sand and the smell of the salt-clean air in the cool of morning.

As she picked her way down, she saw that her husband was before her. He sat leaning against the bottom ridge, facing the Atlantic.

"Why, William," she exclaimed in surprise. "Couldn't you sleep?"

He turned, and his rheumy eyes were tender. "You've never called me that before."

"Oh! Sorry. It slipped out because I've been thinking it for quite awhile."

"No, no," he waved his hand, erasing her apology. "I've longed for someone to call me William." He held up his arm, and she settled into it, nestling.

"Have you really?" Anne said ruefully. "We've wasted so much precious time closing our feelings from each other. Remember in Paris? How we were searching? I hate to hear the Communists have burned the Tuileries Palace. It was there I first realized I loved you."

"I always loved you, but I didn't know how to reach out." He took her round cheeks in both hands. "You look happy now." He stroked the laugh lines crinkling her eyes and mouth. "You never hide within yourself anymore. Your sweet face is open, ready to pour out love. It shows your heart."

"You've done that. You've given me home and family. It looks like we'll have plenty of grandchildren to care for us in our old age. And Macon will sustain us. I thought when the bloody boots of war marched through that it was gone, but the important things about Macon will remain forever."

She smiled at William fondly. With his striped, tank bathing suit hanging loosely on his small frame, there was nothing of pomposity left about him. *Even he has learned there are more important things in life than gold.*

Anne's throat tightened, but she hurried on. "I think Mary Ellen has had her fling. She's decided on William Felton, although he may not know it yet." She laughed. "You'll approve. His family has instilled him with dignity and propriety. He's just like you, a stickler for doing everything in the proper order."

"Yes, he should keep our rowdy Mary Ellen well grounded," he replied. "I'm glad that he and Tracy are practicing law together. I expect one day he'll be a judge. With her social ability and his political connections, they will make good use of our house after you're gone. Caroline and George should have the other property so he can develop it in his real estate business . . ."

"Wait," Anne interrupted. "After *we're* gone."

"No, I'm afraid I'll soon leave you." His smile was wan. "That's the trouble with such an age difference."

"Oh, is there a difference in our ages?" she asked jokingly.

She felt a quivering, and she looked beyond him to the vast gray ocean. Endless dark waves churned, but there in the east, a golden ball emerged over the rim. Quickly it moved upward, bringing tears by its brilliance. She must put away her fears. She must learn from the faith of Sidney and Mary.

Shimmering light stretched a pathway across the water. Drawn to it, Anne helped William to his feet. He walked feebly, but she trod the hard sand with sure steps.

"We shall face whatever comes, William, and savor each day. There are no shadowy places in my heart. I am lit with the sun."

Sunrise

Acknowledgments

This novel is written as a work of fiction; however, every character actually lived in Macon, Georgia. Although I visualized emotions and scenes, events are true. Most of the letters are actual excerpts, and much of the dialogue is taken from letters.

I am indebted first and foremost to Ann and George Felton (Anne's great-grandson) and their daughter Lisa Felton, who met with me many times, conducted me on personal tours of the house, and entrusted me with the Johnston Family Letters and Anne Johnston's Journal of her Grand Tour honeymoon. By reading between the lines and studying Anne's and William's portraits taken over the years, I drew their characters.

William Butler Johnston died October 20, 1887, and Anne remained in the house enjoying her grandchildren. Caroline and George Duncan built a home nearby and had three children, one named for Anne.

In 1888, Mary Ellen married William Hamilton Felton, and they moved in with Anne, who died of natural causes in 1896.

That same year, Felton was appointed Judge of the Superior Court of Georgia, and the house became the scene of constant entertainments. Their son, William, Jr. and his wife Luisa preferred a quieter life. After his parents' deaths, he sold the house.

William Jr.'s son, George Felton, told me of the time of the sale, remembering trunks of Confederate money still in the root cellar and his father making a bonfire. George Felton also fondly remembered the hummingbird garden. The formal garden, swans and all, is described from a sketch by historian, Bruce Sherwood.

Insurance Magnate P. L. Hay bought the house in 1926. The Hays enjoyed it until their deaths. The Hay children, wishing to preserve it, and their parents' memories, formed the P. L. Hay Foundation and opened the house to the public. In 1977, it was given to the Georgia Trust for Historic Preservation, which currently operates the exquisite mansion as a museum. I greatly appreciate the help of the Johnston-Felton-Hay House Museum staff, especially Julie C. Groce, Curator; Aubrey Newby, Exhibit Intern; and Tammy Ply, Education Director.

Sidney Lanier remains honored throughout Georgia. In Macon, Susan Tracy Collins was the first president of the Sidney Lanier Chapter of the United Daughters of The Confederacy. Lanier is memorialized in Baltimore and in America's Hall of Fame. I received a great deal of information from Kitty Oliver and the staff of the Middle Georgia Historical Society located at the Sidney Lanier Cottage, which is open as a museum.

I also thank Dorothy Cook and the staff of the Cannonball House and Confederate Museum, which is next door to the Johnston-Felton-Hay House. The cannon ball that struck that fateful day is still in the hall.

I received much help from Anne Rogers and Christopher Stokes of Washington Memorial Library, Macon. Mr. Stokes thesis gave me a starting point on W. B. Johnston. Stokes unearthed many articles that led me to other avenues for instance: Batavia, New York.

Miss Kathleen Facer, Research Historian of Richmond Memorial Library, Batavia, kindly sent me information about the Tracy family in New York. I spoke with Mrs. Donald P. Burkel, whose late husband uncovered the amazing story of Phil Tracy. The Burkel's son, Don Burkel, Curator of the Holland Land Office Museum in Batavia, sent information that the grave is still being honored by both Southern and Northern groups. Would not Anne be pleased?

In Huntsville, Alabama, I thank D. L. Kilbourn of Oak Place, owned by East Huntsville Baptist Church, and open for tours. He put me in touch with Patricia Ryan, whose book, *Cease Not To Think of Me*, is a collection of Steele family letters. Patricia received the beautiful love letters of Ellen and Lit from Susan Tracy Collin's daughter, Rossetter. Patricia and Ann Felton gained a great deal of information from Rossetter Collins, who lived to be 103. Patricia Ryan has the seal from the letters, while Ann Felton has the lapel watch, both bearing the sentiment, "Cease not to think of me."

I cannot close without thanking Jane Hendrix and staff of Lake Blackshear Regional Library, Americus, Georgia; and Bruce L. Bridges for information about Appleton Church Home. Aiding me greatly were Lila Karpf, Richard Marek, John Cook, Lynne Cook, John Hyde, Kelli Munn, Samantha Cook, Jo Creel, Casey Dixon, Betty Anne and Bobby Clay, Bill and Marvlyn Story, and my husband J. N. Cook.

I will think of this family for a long time, and I hope, you, my reader will, too.

Jacquelyn Cook

BIBLIOGRAPHY

Unpublished Sources

The Johnston Family Letters. 1834-1911. Courtesy George and Ann Felton.

Journal of Anne Tracy Johnston. November 8, 1851-April 21, 1852. Courtesy George andAnn Felton.

Journal of Rosalind Lipscomb. June 11, 1970-August 31, 1970. Courtesy of Rosalind Lipscomb Forrest.

Pamphlet Oak Place. Huntsville Pilgrimage Association. Huntsville, Georgia, 1996.

Son of Confederate Veterans, Brigadier General Edward Dorr Tracy, Jr. Camp No. 18, Files. Macon, Georgia.

United Daughters of the Confederacy, Sidney Lanier Chapter, Macon, Georgia, application of Georgia Tracy Wadley, October 22,1896.

Vertical Files in Genealogical and Historical Room Washington Memorial Library, Macon, Georgia.

Interviews and Correspondence

George and Ann Felton. July 1996-2000.

Julie Groce. Johnston-Felton-Hay House. July 1996-2000.

Aubrey Newby. Johnston-Felton-Hay House. June 1998-2000.

Tammy Ply. Johnston-Felton-Hay House. August 2000.

Speeches

Edwards, Harry Stillwell. "Recollections of Sidney Lanier." Macon History Club Memorial Service. Macon, Georgia. February, 1913.

Lanier, Sidney Clopton. "Memorial Day Address." Rose Hill Cemetery, Macon, Georgia, April 26, 1870.

Pamphlets

"Brilliant and Delightful": Macon and the American Renaissance 1876-1917. Macon, Georgia, 1998.

The Cannonball House: Mansion of the Old South. Macon, Georgia.

Hay House. Savannah, Georgia, 1982.

The Johnstons, Feltons, and Hays: 100 Years in the Palace of the South. Macon, Georgia, 1993.

Books

Blum, Stella. *Fashions and Costumes from Godey's Lady's Book.* New York, 1985.

Brodsky, Alyn. *Imperial Charade.* Indianapolis, 1978.

Butler, John C. *History of Macon and Central Georgia.* Macon, Georgia, 1879.

Clay-Clopton, Virginia. *A Belle of the Fifties.* New York, 1904.

Coleman, Elliot. ed. *Poems of Byron, Keats, and Shelley.* New York, 1967.

Comer, Harriet Fincher. *History First Presbyterian Church Macon, Georgia 1826-1990.* Macon, Georgia, 1990.

Cornelius, Kay. *More Than Conquerors.* Urichsville, Ohio, 1993.

Cotton, Gordon A. *Vicksburg: Southern Stories of the Siege.* Vicksburg, 1988.

Irby, Mary Lee. *Ghosts of Macon,* Macon, Georgia, 1998.

Lamar, Dolly Blunt. *When All Is Said And Done.* Athens, Georgia, 1952.

Lanier, Mary Day. ed. *Poems of Sidney Lanier.* New York, 1884.

Lorenz, Lincoln. *The Life of Sidney Lanier.* New York, 1935.

Marchand, Leslie A. ed. *The Selected Poetry of Lord Byron.* New York, 1951.

Mims, Edwin. *Sidney Lanier.* Boston, 1905.

Ryan, Patricia H. *Cease Not To Think of Me.* Huntsville, Alabama, 1979.

Ridley, Jasper. *Napoleon III and Eugenie.* New York, 1980.

Starke, Aubrey Harrison. *Sidney Lanier.* New York, 1964.

Thompson, C. Mildred. *Reconstruction in Georgia.* Savannah, 1972.

Wheeler, Richard. *The Seize of Vicksburg.* New York, 1978.

Williams, Roger Lawrence. *The World of Napoleon III 1851-1870.* New York, 1957.

Wolfe, Gerald R. *The House of Appleton.* Metuchen, New Jersey, 1981.

Woodward, C. Vann. *Mary Chesnut's Civil War.* New Haven, 1981.

Articles

Ayers, Mary Frances. "Sidney Lanier." *Georgia Journal.* Winter, 1987: 39-40.

"Brigadier General Edward Dorr Tracy, Jr." Obituary. *Macon Telegraph.* May 19, 1863: 1.

Cook, Jacquelyn. "Elegy in Flowers." *Georgia Journal.* April/May 1983: 11,17.

"The Funeral Honors to General Tracy." *Macon Telegraph.* May 11, 1866: 3.

Garrison, Webb. "Sidney Lanier: Georgia's Greatest Poet." *The Atlanta Journal\Constitution.* May 19, 1985: 2-H.

Maury, Joan West. "A New Estimate of Sidney Lanier." *Boston Evening Transcript.* December 21, 1935: 4.

McKay, Blythe. "Parks Lee Hay House." *Macon Telegraph.* April 2, 1965.

Winegar, Dan. "Confederate Grave Not Forgotten Here." *Batavia Daily News.* May 29, 1962:1.

Winegar, Dan. "Rebels Sleep in Yankeeland." *Batavia Daily News.* July 31, 1990.

Theses and Dissertations

Stokes, Christopher. "Native Georgian, Self-taught Genius: The Life of William Butler Johnston, 1809-1887." M.A. thesis, Georgia College, 1989.

About

Jacquelyn Cook

Jacquelyn Cook has been a nationally published writer since 1963, selling 500,000 copies of her first ten books, but her first love is writing about the South.

"My goal has been to write timeless stories of lasting values," says Cook. "I want to preserve our culture and history and the beauty of our landscape, but most of all I like to reflect the southerner's love of God, country, family and fellowman."

After gaining experience in journalism, Cook began writing the five-book *River* series of inspirational romance for Zondervan, Guideposts Books, and Barbour Books. After twenty years, these books are still in demand. In 2002, Barbour Books combined four of the popular stories in one volume called *Magnolias*, making it the complete novel Jacquelyn desired.

Cook begins a new phase of her career with *Sunrise*. Set in Macon, Georgia, it is the fictionalized account of the true story of Anne Tracy and William Butler Johnston, who built the fabulous Johnston-Felton-Hay House, which is now a museum. Cook's extensive research is enhanced by family reminiscence of their great-grandson George Felton. This personal material makes the story come alive.

Jacquelyn Cook majored in voice at Wesleyan College in Macon. Chartered in 1836, Wesleyan is the oldest women's college in the world to grant degrees and licenses that were previously given only to men. Cook's memories of her husband-to-be courting her in the parlor of the original building color the scene where Sidney Lanier is courting Mary Day.

The Cook family enjoys life on the ancestral farm in the subtropical region of Southwest Georgia. Jacquelyn's hobby is keeping flowers growing all year long. Three and a half dogs own her, two Shih Tzu lapdogs, a guardian Australian Shepherd, and the half a dog, a huge Labrador retriever who belongs to her son's family. The minute they leave home, the sociable lab visits grandmother.

On holidays, the table swells with her daughter's family from the city. Everyone gathers for Jacquelyn Cook's Old South meals, especially Virginia-baked ham, sweet potato soufflé, and devil's food cake with mocha frosting.

Jacquelyn Cook's next novel, *The Greenwood Legacy*, is also based on the true story of Thomas P. and Lavinia Jones who settled the wilderness area of Southwest Georgia in 1827 and created a culture of elegant plantations, seventy of which still exist on 300,000 acres from Thomasville, Georgia, to Tallahassee, Florida.

Sweeping across the Nineteenth Century, *The Greenwood Legacy* in a multi-generational family saga of rising to great wealth, plunging to poverty after the Civil War, and rising again.

Family Heirloom Recipes

Recipes on the following pages came from the cookbooks of

Anne Tracy / Mrs. William Butler Johnston

Mary Ellen, their daughter
(Mrs. Judge William H. Felton, Sr.)

Upon Anne's death, the house went to them.
Because of his political connections and their socal standing,
the house was constantly the scene of elaborate buffets
with dancing in the double parlors.

These recipes were graciously provided by:
Also by Anne Tracy Johnston's great-great-granddaughters:
Lisa Felton
Anne Tracy Felton / Mrs. Arthur Lee Moore
Polly Pierce Felton / Mrs. James B. Morrison

From Anne Tracy's cookbook dated October 11, 1871

Oyster Bisque

Drain 1 qt. of oysters well. Then put them to simmer in 1 qt. of chicken consomme or boullion. Strain and put the oysters through a potato ricer. Add this to the strained liquor in which the oysters were cooked and 1 pint of cream. Put on to heat, milk, a small onion, a celery stalk & the necessary white pepper & salt. Melt 2 ounces of butter & stir in an equal amount of flour. When this is smooth, add a good deal of the soup to it and then add all the soup. Heat and serve, taking out the onion and celery.

From Anne Tracy's cookbook dated October 11, 1871

Peach Pickles

(Mangoes)

1 Pk. peaches - peel and soak in salt water over night

2 lbs. brown sugar

1 cup mustard seed

1/4 cup celery seed

1 teaspoonful mace

1/2 teaspoonful all spice

2 table spoonsfull tumeric

1/2 gallon vinegar

Put vinegar on with spice & let come to a boil - put in peaches & let boil until peaches get tender.

From Mary Ellen Johnston-Felton's cookbook dated March 6, 1912

Ginger Bread

1 quart flour

1 cup brown sugar

1/4 pound butter, melted

1 cup syrup

1 cup sour milk

4 eggs

Level teaspoon of soda

Heaping tablespoon ginger

Preheat oven to 350°. Sift together the dry ingredients. Stir in melted butter, syrup, eggs, and sour milk (or buttermilk). Pour batter into a generously greased and floured 8-inch square pan. Bake for 45 to 50 minutes, until cake springs back when lightly touched with finger.

From Mary Ellen Johnston-Felton's cookbook dated March 6, 1912

Wine Sauce

(for plum pudding or ice cream)

2 sticks butter

2 cups sugar

6 egg yolks (unbeaten)

1 cup sherry

Melt butter in double boiler. Add sugar, egg yolks, sherry; beating constantly. Stir occasionally until served. May be made ahead and kept in refrigerator.

The recipes on pages 304-306 are those of
Ann Corn Felton, whose husband, George Gibson Felton,
was Anne Tracy Johnston's great-grandson.

Butterbeans

Rinse fresh butterbeans in collander. Place in saucepan and add water or chicken broth almost to cover. Bring to a boil and reduce heat to a simmer. Cover and cook for approximately 20 minutes or until tender. Add butter, salt and pepper to taste.

Popovers

2 eggs

1 cup plain flour

1 cup milk

1/2 teaspoon salt

Beat eggs; add milk beating well; add flour and salt. Pour into cold pyrex custard cups which have been greased well; half full. Turn oven to 450 degrees. Put in oven immediately and leave in oven 1/2 hour from time oven is turned on. Then, prick each popover with a fork and turn oven down to 350 degrees for 10-15 minutes.

DO NOT TURN OVEN ON AHEAD OF TIME!

Sally Lunn

This recipe is also written on a piece of paper stuck in Mary Ellen's cookbook. Lisa, Polly and Tracy Felton remember waking up on Sunday mornings to the aroma of Mother's (Ann Corn Felton) popovers and Sally Lunn before going to church.

1/2 cup butter

1/2 cup sugar

1 cup milk

2 cups flour

3 eggs

4 teaspoons baking powder

3/4 teaspoon salt

Cream butter and sugar well. Add eggs, one at a time and beat well. Add milk, a little at atime alternately with flour which has been sifted with baking powder and salt. Bake in a greased shallow pan so the Sally Lunn is about an inch thick when baked. Bake about 30 minutes at 425 degrees. Break into squares and serve hot. (Mary Ellen's recipe also says this can be baked in greased muffin pans.)

Italian Spaghetti Sauce - The Best

Olive Oil

1 can tomatoes

1 can tomato sauce

1 can tomato paste

1 stalk celery, chopped

2 large onions, chopped

2 large bell peppers chopped

1 pound ground steak

Mushrooms (optional) - canned or fresh sauteed in butter

1-1/2 1lbs. long Italian spaghetti

Freshly grated parmesan cheese

Saute celery, onions and bell pepper in oil for 5 minutes or less. Add tomatoes, sauce and paste. In separate pan, cook meat until brown. Add mixture to this. Season with salt, black pepper, bay leaf and red pepper. Add 1 clove garlic, cover and let simmer for hours. Add mushrooms just before serving. Serve over spaghetti and sprinkle with freshly grated parmesan cheese.

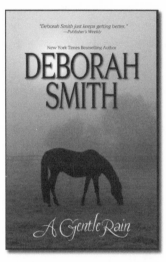
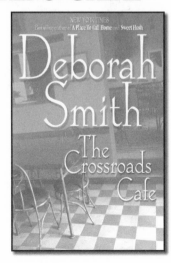

The Mossy Creek

Welcome to Mossy Creek, where you'll find a friendly face at every window and a heartfelt story behind every door.

We've got a mayor who sees breaking the law as her civic duty and a by-the-books police chief trying to live up to his father's legend. We've got a bittersweet feud at the coffee shop and heartwarming battles on the softball field. We've got a world-weary Santa with a poignant dream and a flying Chihuahua with a streak of bad luck. You'll meet Millicent, who believes in stealing joy, and the outrageous patrons of O'Day's Pub, who believe there's no such thing as an honest game of darts. You'll want to tune your radio to the Bereavement Report and prop your feet

Book 1
MOSSY CREEK

Book 2
REUNION AT MOSSY CREEK

Book 3
SUMMER IN MOSSY CREEK

Hometown Series

up at Mama's All You Can Eat Café. While you're there, say hello to our local gossip columnist, Katie Bell. She'll make you feel like one of the family and tell you a story that will make you laugh—or smile through your tears. People are like that in Mossy Creek.

Award-winning authors Deborah Smith, Sandra Chastain, Debra Dixon, Virginia Ellis, Nancy Knight and Donna Ball (*Sweet Tea And Jesus Shoes*) now blend their unique voices in a collective novel about the South, the first in a series set in the fictional mountain town of Mossy Creek, Georgia.

So welcome to Mossy Creek, the town that insists it "Ain't goin' nowhere, and don't want to." Welcome Home.

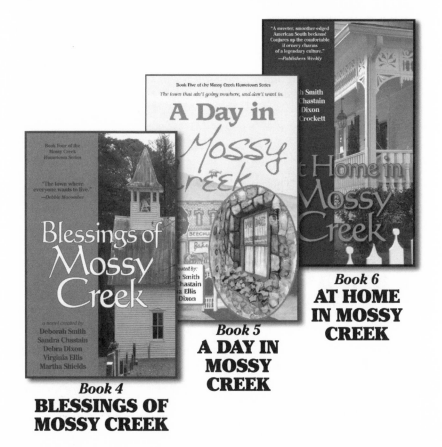

Book 4
BLESSINGS OF MOSSY CREEK

Book 5
A DAY IN MOSSY CREEK

Book 6
AT HOME IN MOSSY CREEK

SWEET TEA & JESUS SHOES

Come sit on the porch a spell. Let's talk about times gone by and folks we remember, about slow summer evenings and lightning bugs in a jar. Listen to the sound of a creaky swing and cicadas chorusing in the background. Let's talk about how things used to be in the South and, for some of us, the way they still are.

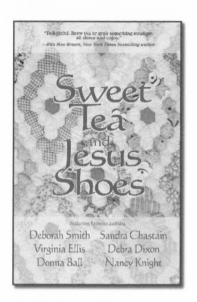

SWEET TEA AND JESUS SHOES
was a selection by VABooks! at the Center for the Book
at the Virginia Foundation for the Humanities,
which suggests books for Virginians to read in common.

MORE SWEET TEA

"Delightful. Brew tea or grab something stronger, sit down and enjoy."

—Rita Mae Brown,
New York Times bestselling author

"A brilliant compilation of Southern women's stories in the tradition of Anne Rivers Siddons."

—Harriet Klausner, *Midwest Book Review*

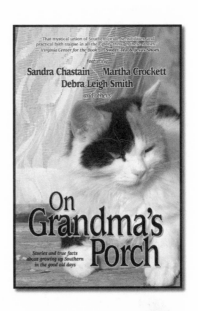

The Mossy Creek Hometown Series

Available in all fine bookstores or direct from BelleBooks

Mossy Creek
Reunion at Mossy Creek
Summer in Mossy Creek
Blessings of Mossy Creek
A Day in Mossy Creek
At Home in Mossy Creek

Other BelleBooks Titles

KaseyBelle: *The Tiniest Fairy in the Kingdom*
by Sandra Chastain

Astronaut Noodle
by Kenlyn Spence

Sweet Tea and Jesus Shoes
More Sweet Tea
On Grandma's Porch

Milam McGraw Propst, author of acclaimed feature film
The Adventures of Oicee Nash

Creoloa's Moonbeam

All God's Creatures
by Carolyn McSparren

Bra Talk
Non-fiction book featured on Oprah - by Susan Nethero

From *NYT* bestselling author **Deborah Smith**

Alice at Heart — *Waterlilies* series
Diary of a Radical Mermaid — *Waterlilies*
The Crossroads Café
A Gentle Rain